Disney Fairies

The Petite Fairy's Diary

By Jun Asuka

TOKYOPOP

HAMBURG // HONG KONG // LOS ANGELES // TOKYO

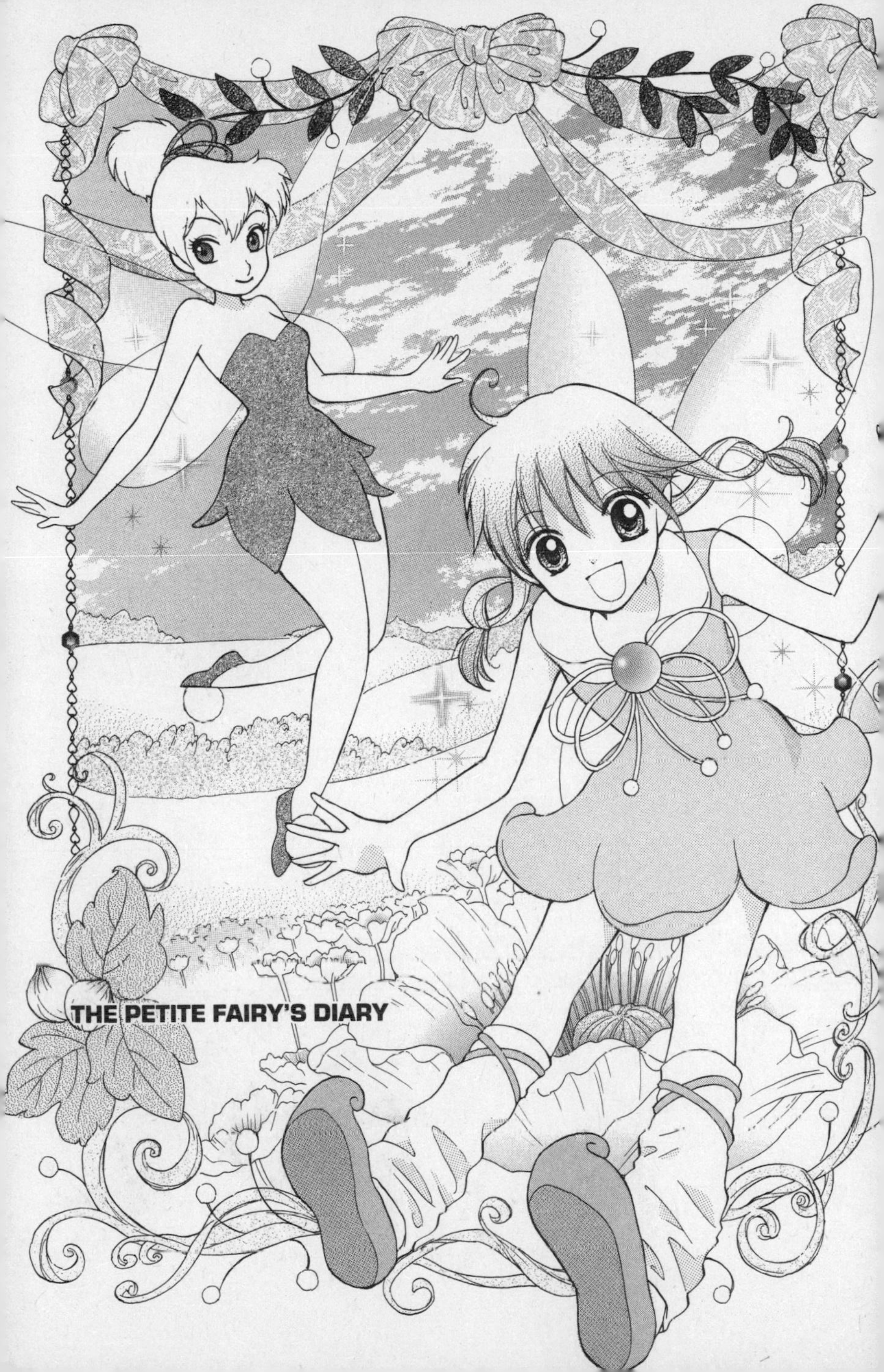
THE PETITE FAIRY'S DIARY

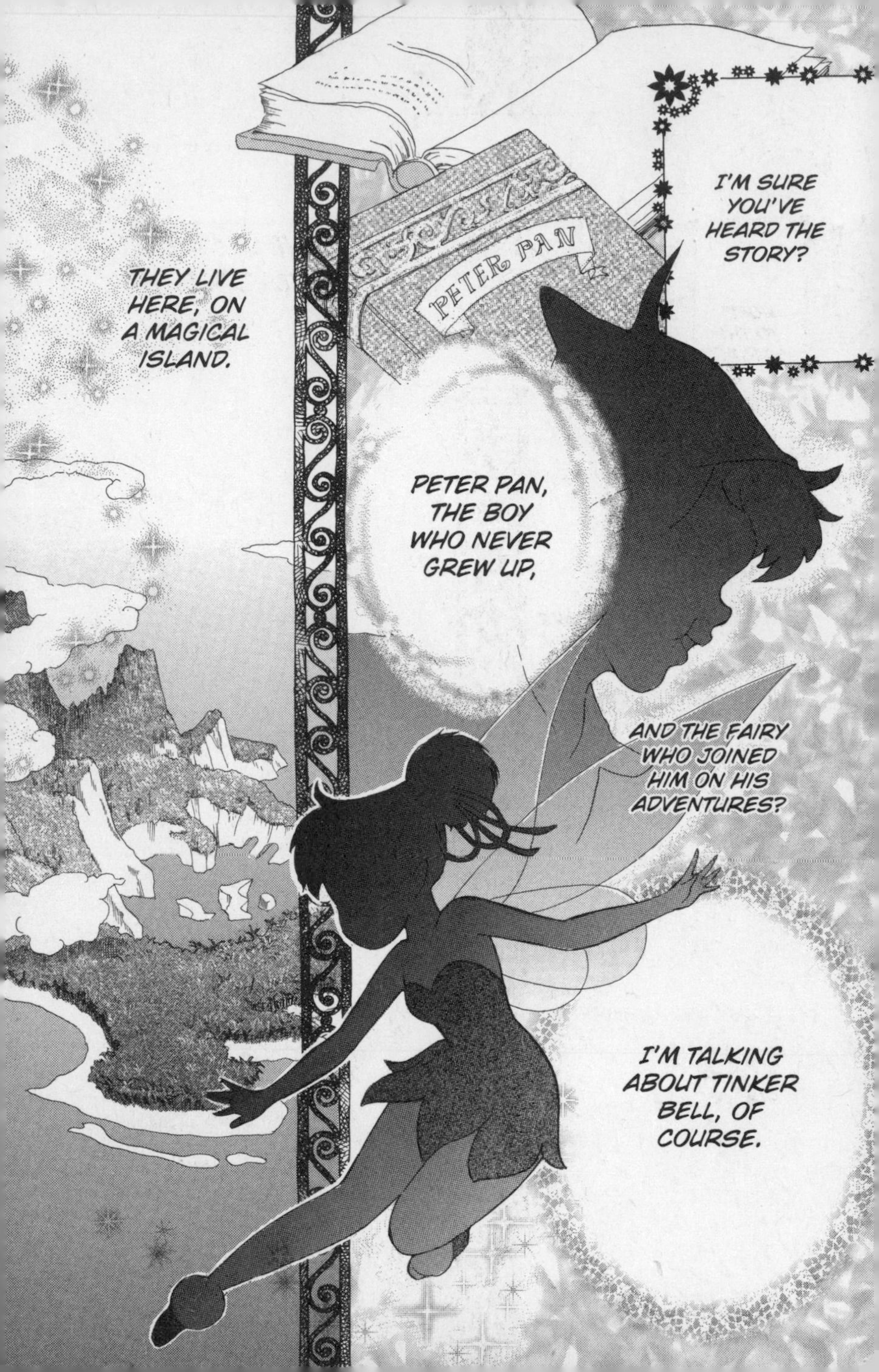
I'M SURE YOU'VE HEARD THE STORY?
PETER PAN
PETER PAN, THE BOY WHO NEVER GREW UP,
AND THE FAIRY WHO JOINED HIM ON HIS ADVENTURES?
I'M TALKING ABOUT TINKER BELL, OF COURSE.
THEY LIVE HERE, ON A MAGICAL ISLAND.

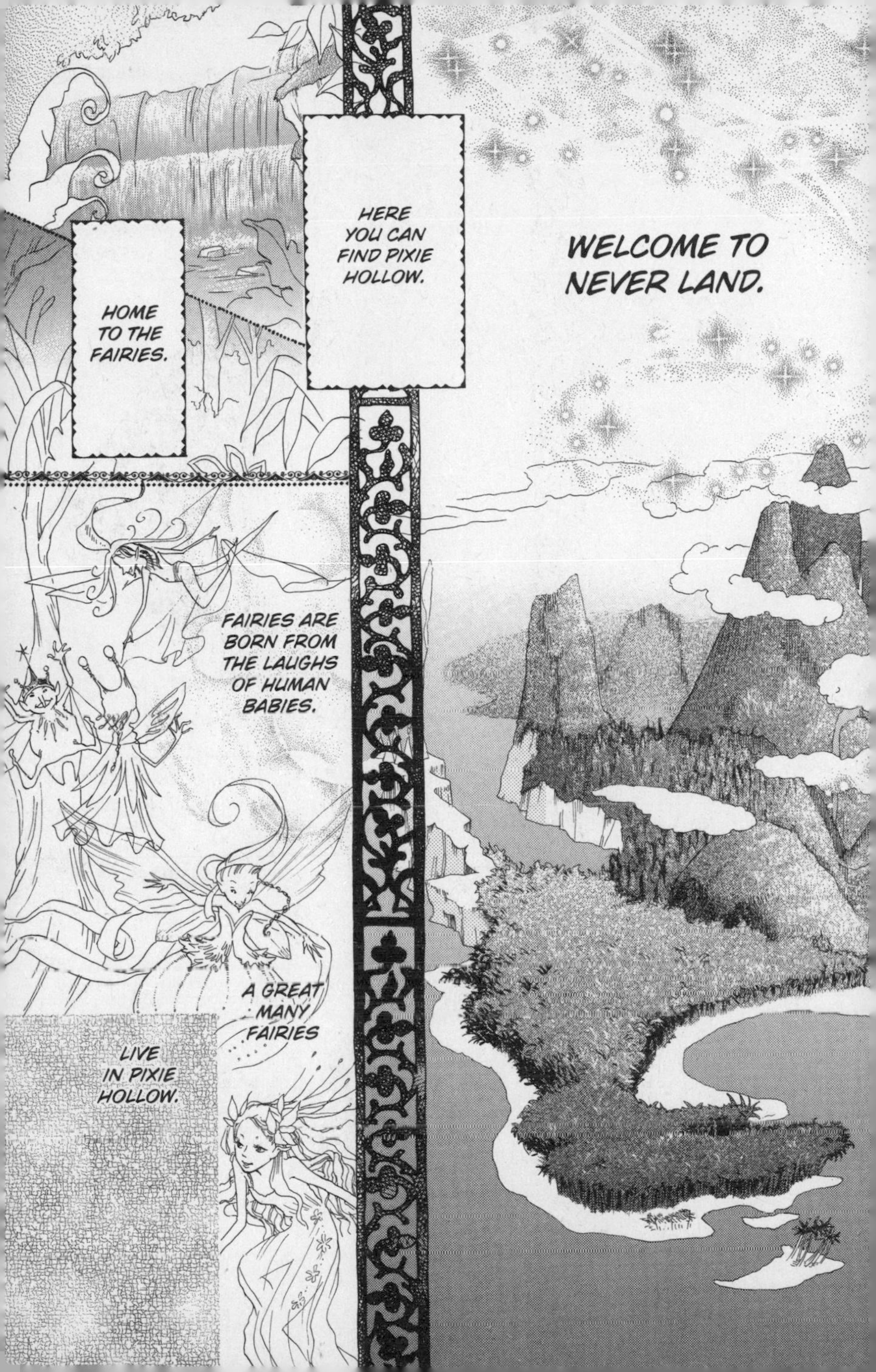
WELCOME TO NEVER LAND.
HERE YOU CAN FIND PIXIE HOLLOW.
HOME TO THE FAIRIES.
FAIRIES ARE BORN FROM THE LAUGHS OF HUMAN BABIES.
A GREAT MANY FAIRIES
LIVE IN PIXIE HOLLOW.

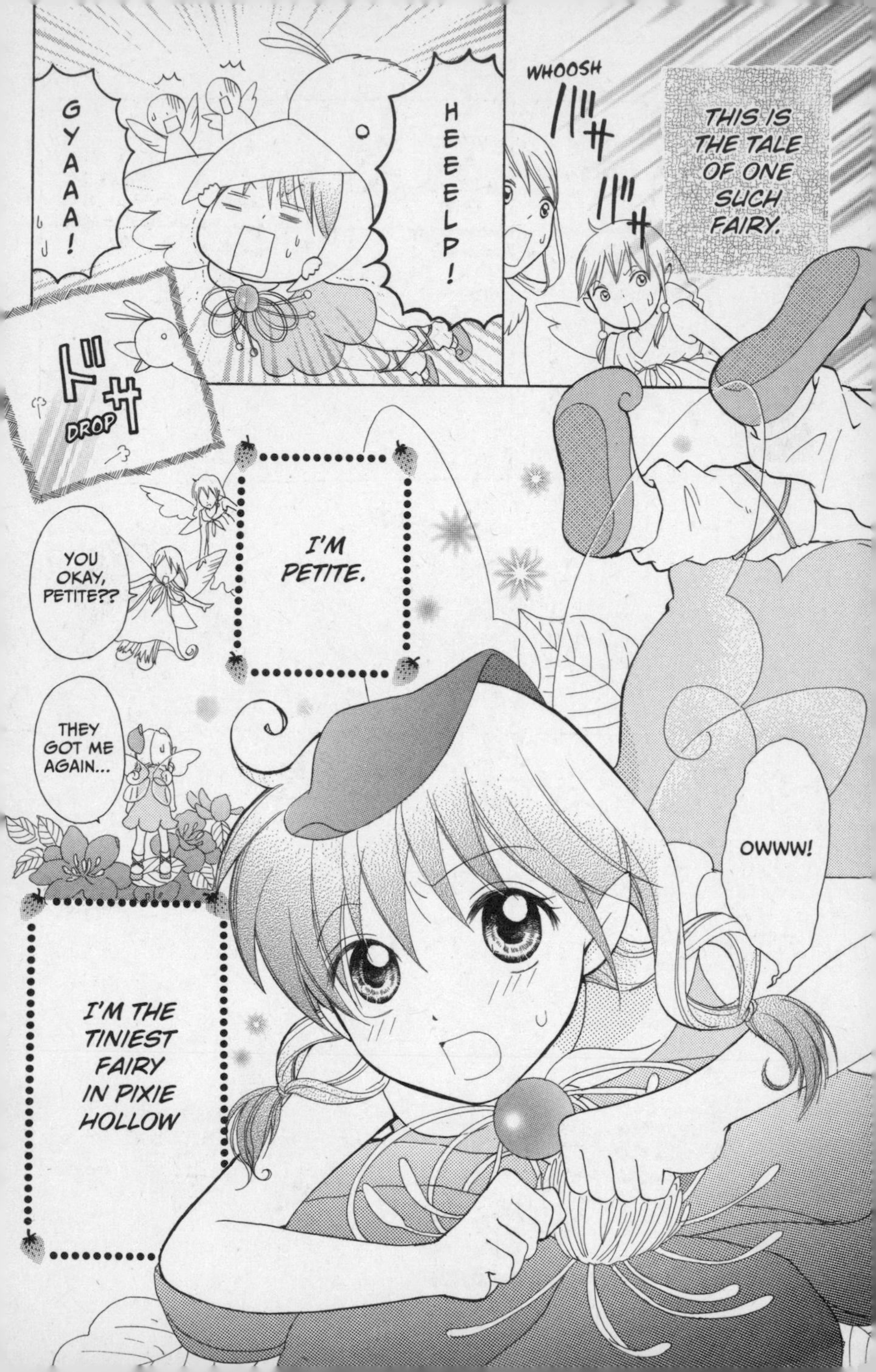

THIS IS THE TALE OF ONE SUCH FAIRY.
WHOOSH
HEEEELP!
GYAAAA!
DROP
OWWW!
I'M PETITE.
YOU OKAY, PETITE??
THEY GOT ME AGAIN...
I'M THE TINIEST FAIRY IN PIXIE HOLLOW

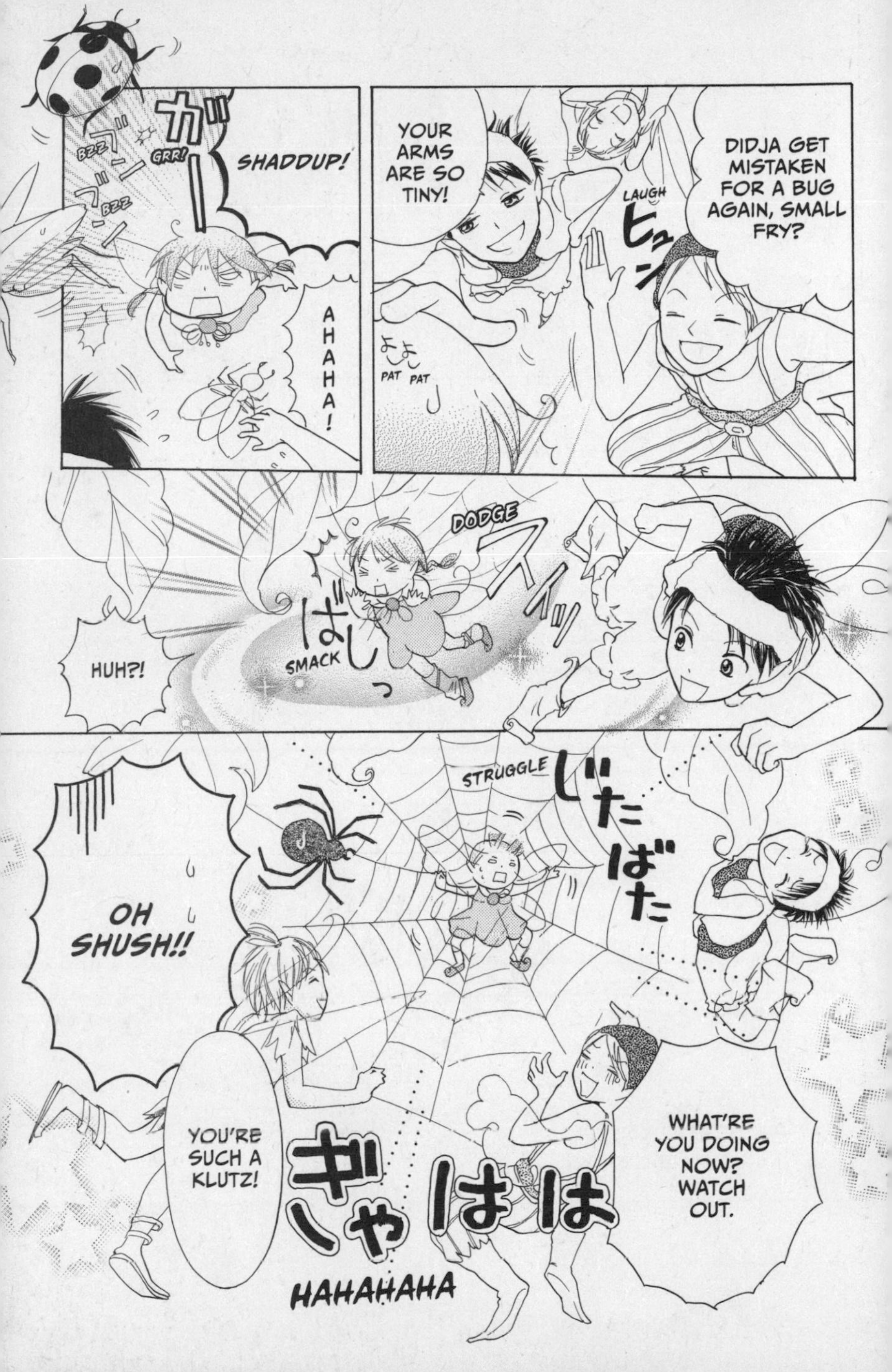
DIDJA GET MISTAKEN FOR A BUG AGAIN, SMALL FRY?
ヒュン
LAUGH
YOUR ARMS ARE SO TINY!
よしよし
PAT PAT
ガー
GRR!
SHADDUP!
ブーン
BZZ
BZZ
AHAHAHA!
スイッ
DODGE
ばしっ
SMACK
HUH?!
じたばた
STRUGGLE
WHAT'RE YOU DOING NOW? WATCH OUT.
ぎゃはは
HAHAHAHA
YOU'RE SUCH A KLUTZ!
OH SHUSH!!

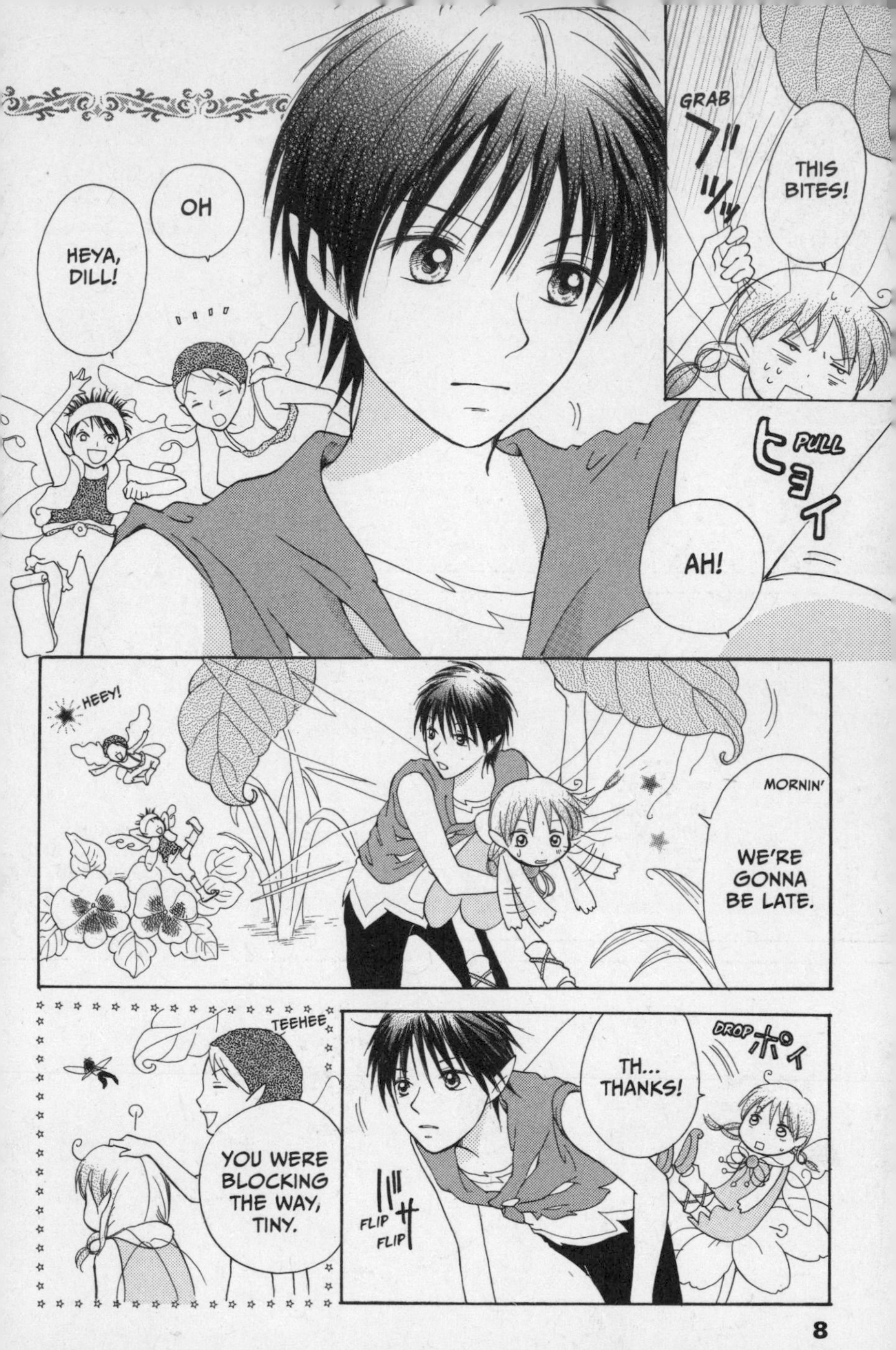
GRAB
ブッ
THIS BITES!
PULL
ヒョイ
AH!
OH
HEYA, DILL!
MORNIN'
WE'RE GONNA BE LATE.
HEEY!
DROP
ポイ
TH... THANKS!
バサ
FLIP FLIP
TEEHEE
YOU WERE BLOCKING THE WAY, TINY.

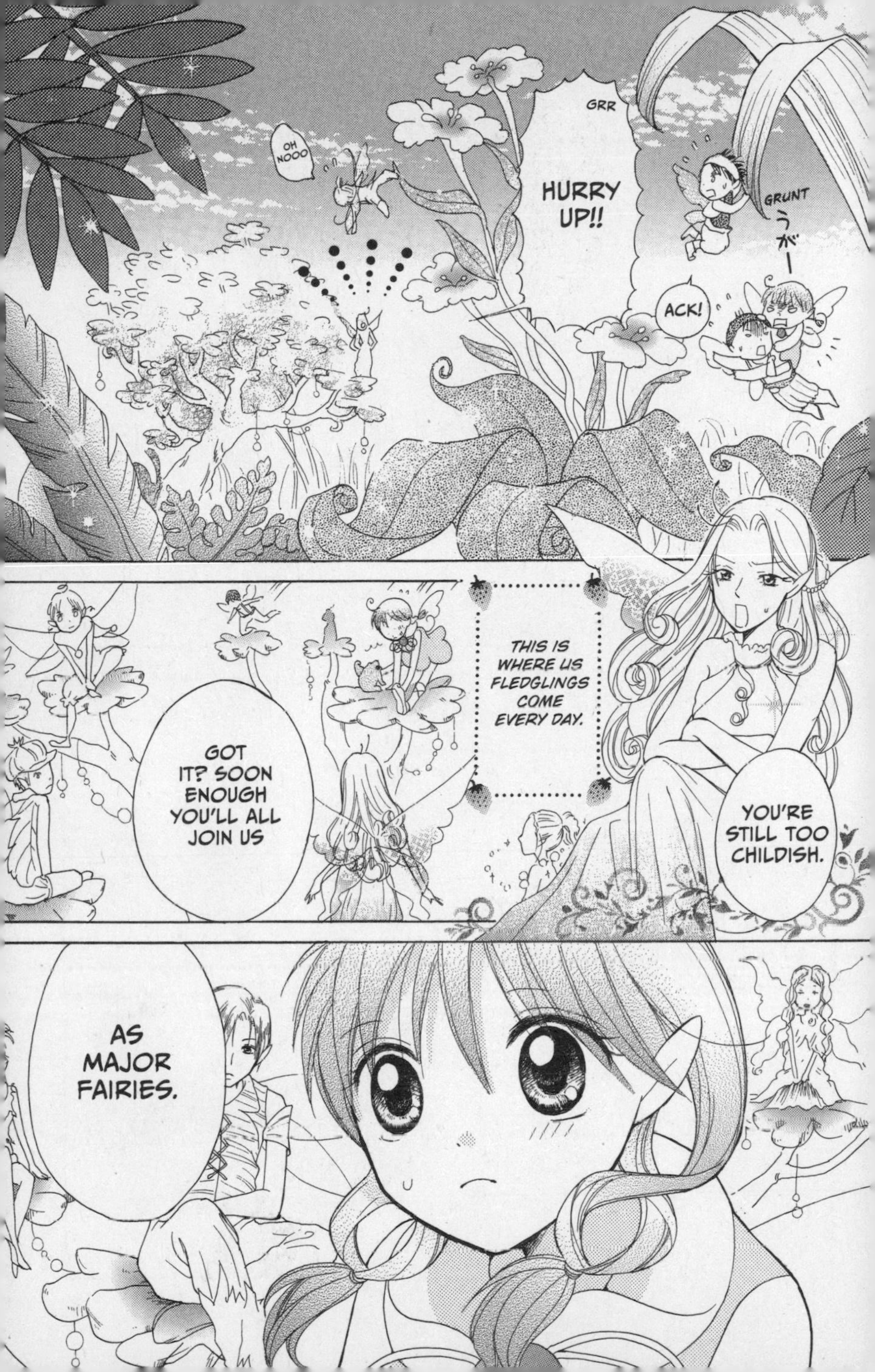
GRR
HURRY UP!!
GRUNT
うがー
ACK!
OH NOOO
THIS IS WHERE US FLEDGLINGS COME EVERY DAY.
YOU'RE STILL TOO CHILDISH.
GOT IT? SOON ENOUGH YOU'LL ALL JOIN US
AS MAJOR FAIRIES.

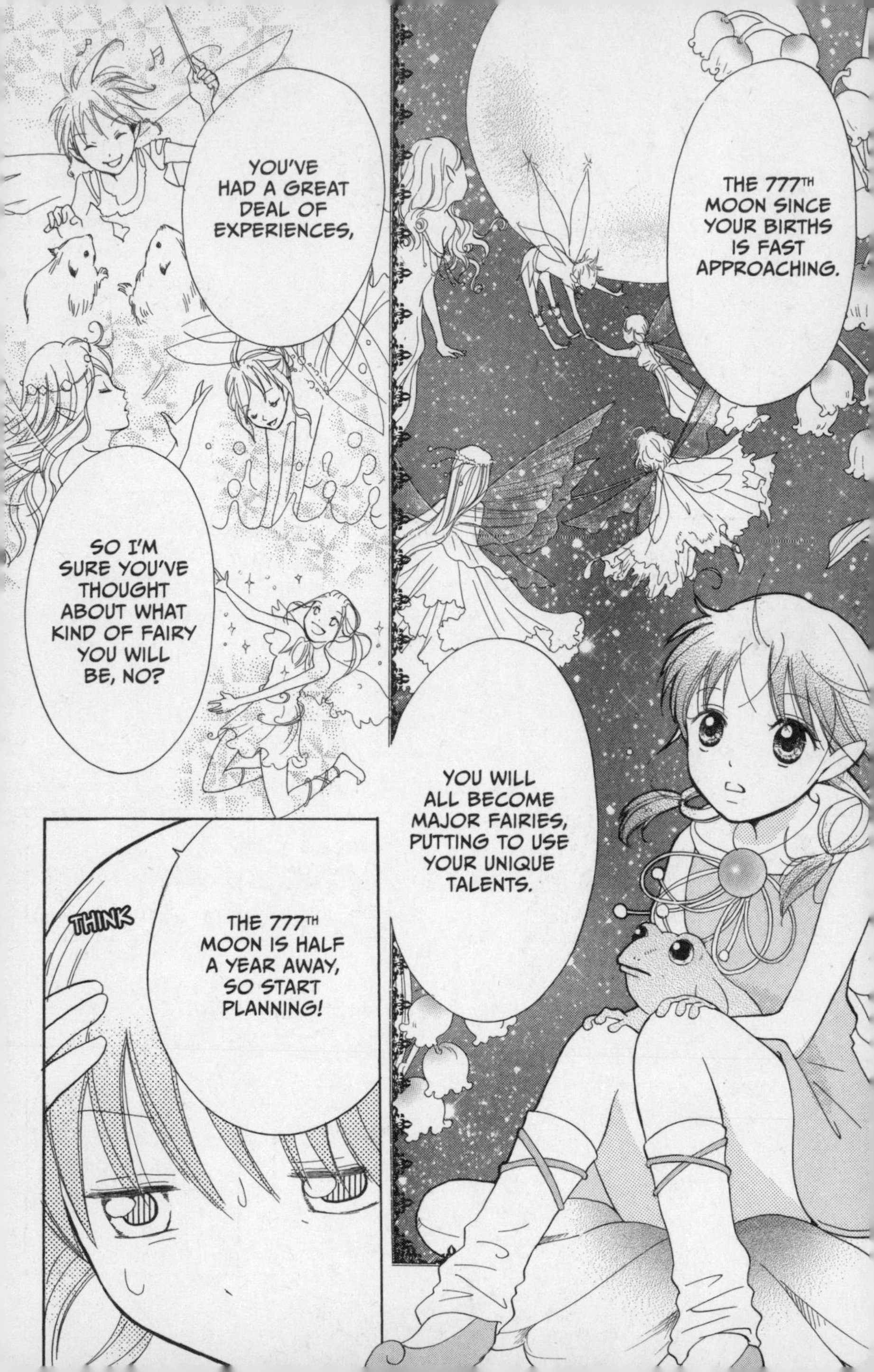
THE 777TH MOON SINCE YOUR BIRTHS IS FAST APPROACHING.
YOU WILL ALL BECOME MAJOR FAIRIES, PUTTING TO USE YOUR UNIQUE TALENTS.
YOU'VE HAD A GREAT DEAL OF EXPERIENCES,
SO I'M SURE YOU'VE THOUGHT ABOUT WHAT KIND OF FAIRY YOU WILL BE, NO?
THINK
THE 777TH MOON IS HALF A YEAR AWAY, SO START PLANNING!

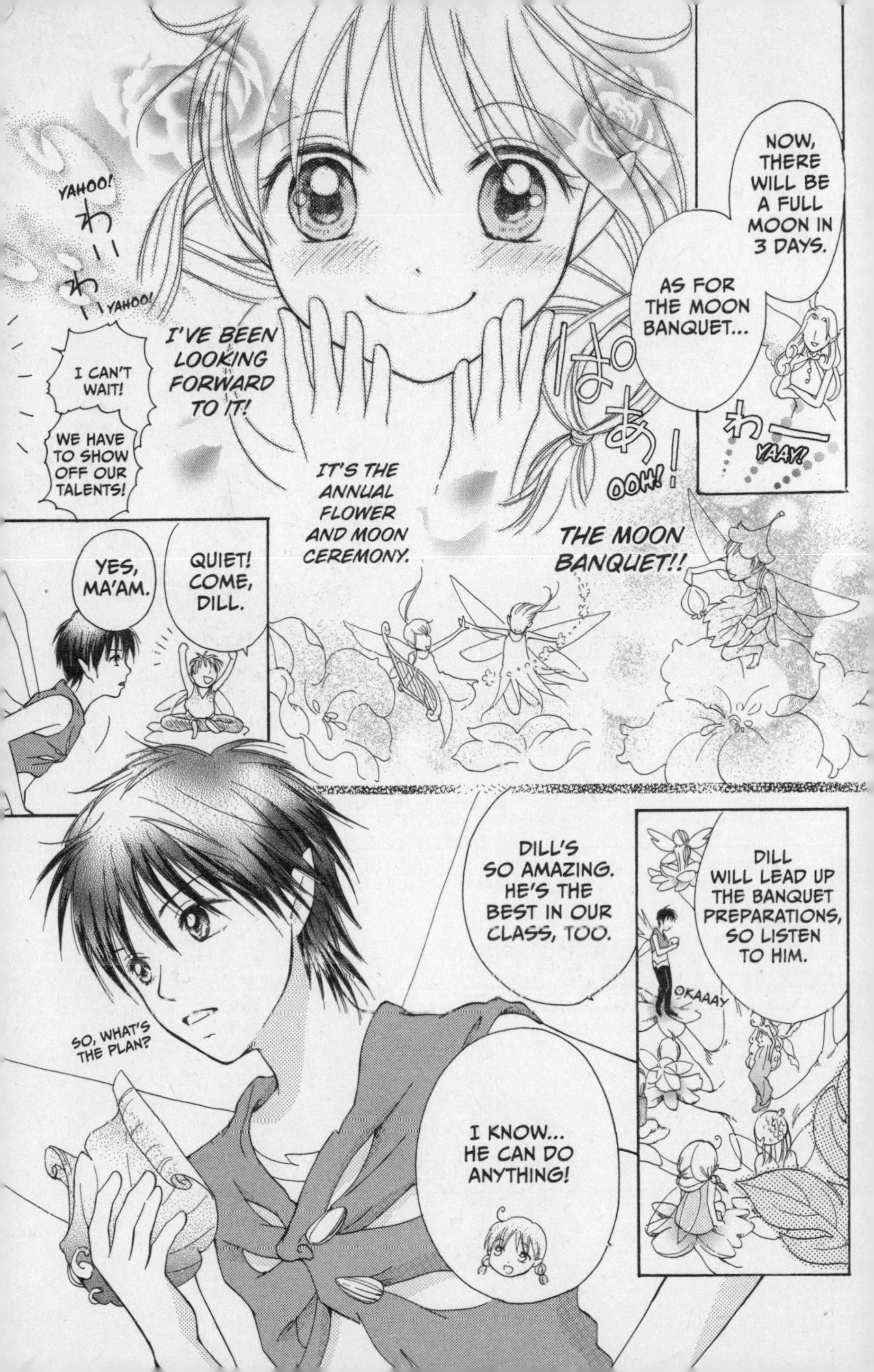
NOW, THERE WILL BE A FULL MOON IN 3 DAYS.
AS FOR THE MOON BANQUET...
わー
YAAY!
はあ!
OOH!
I'VE BEEN LOOKING FORWARD TO IT!
わ
YAHOO!
わ
YAHOO!
I CAN'T WAIT!
WE HAVE TO SHOW OFF OUR TALENTS!
IT'S THE ANNUAL FLOWER AND MOON CEREMONY.
THE MOON BANQUET!!
QUIET! COME, DILL.
YES, MA'AM.
DILL WILL LEAD UP THE BANQUET PREPARATIONS, SO LISTEN TO HIM.
OKAAAY
DILL'S SO AMAZING. HE'S THE BEST IN OUR CLASS, TOO.
I KNOW... HE CAN DO ANYTHING!
SO, WHAT'S THE PLAN?

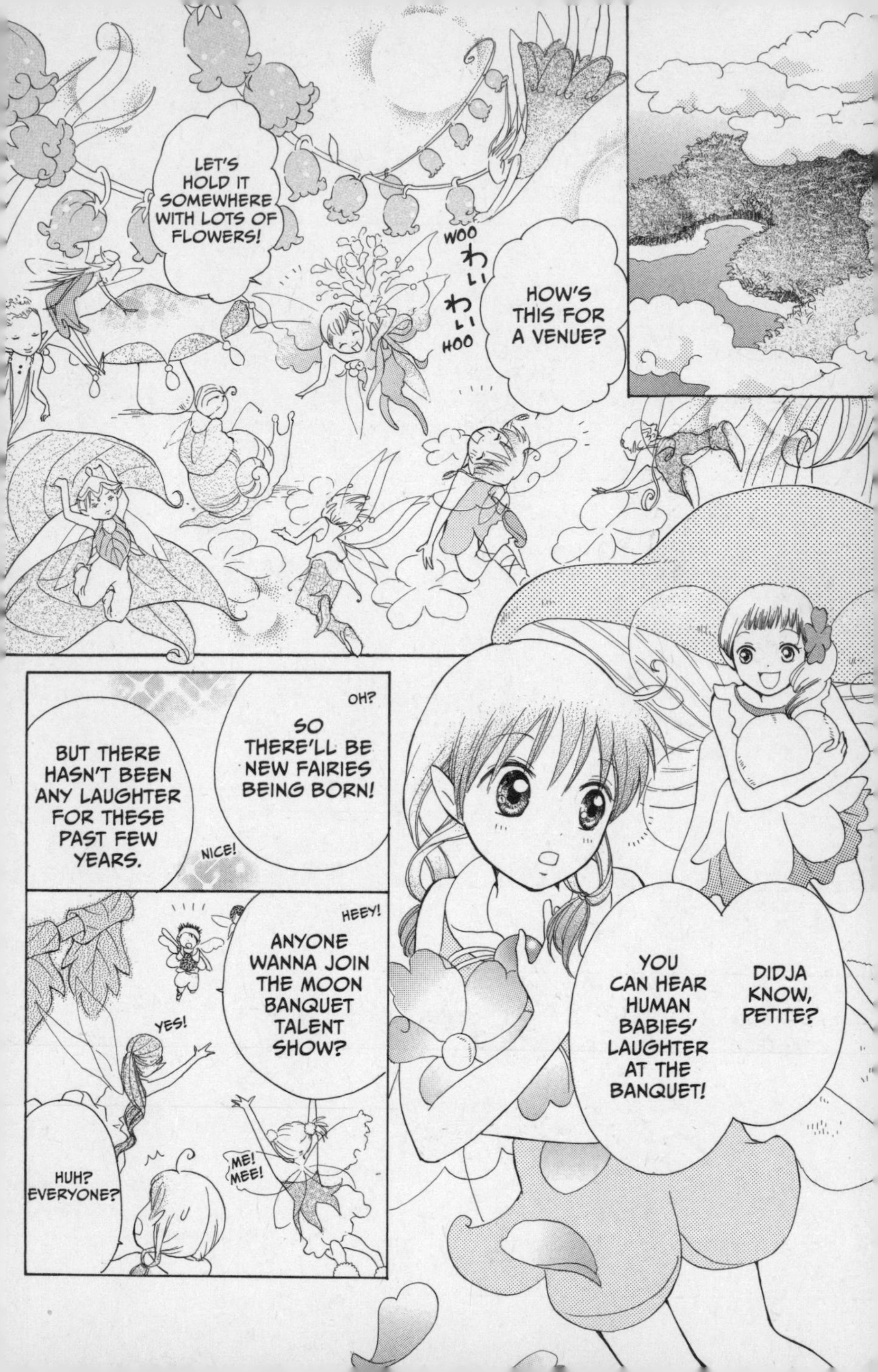
HOW'S THIS FOR A VENUE?
WOO わい わい HOO
LET'S HOLD IT SOMEWHERE WITH LOTS OF FLOWERS!
DIDJA KNOW, PETITE?
YOU CAN HEAR HUMAN BABIES' LAUGHTER AT THE BANQUET!
OH?
SO THERE'LL BE NEW FAIRIES BEING BORN!
NICE!
BUT THERE HASN'T BEEN ANY LAUGHTER FOR THESE PAST FEW YEARS.
HEEY!
ANYONE WANNA JOIN THE MOON BANQUET TALENT SHOW?
YES!
ME! MEE!
HUH? EVERYONE?

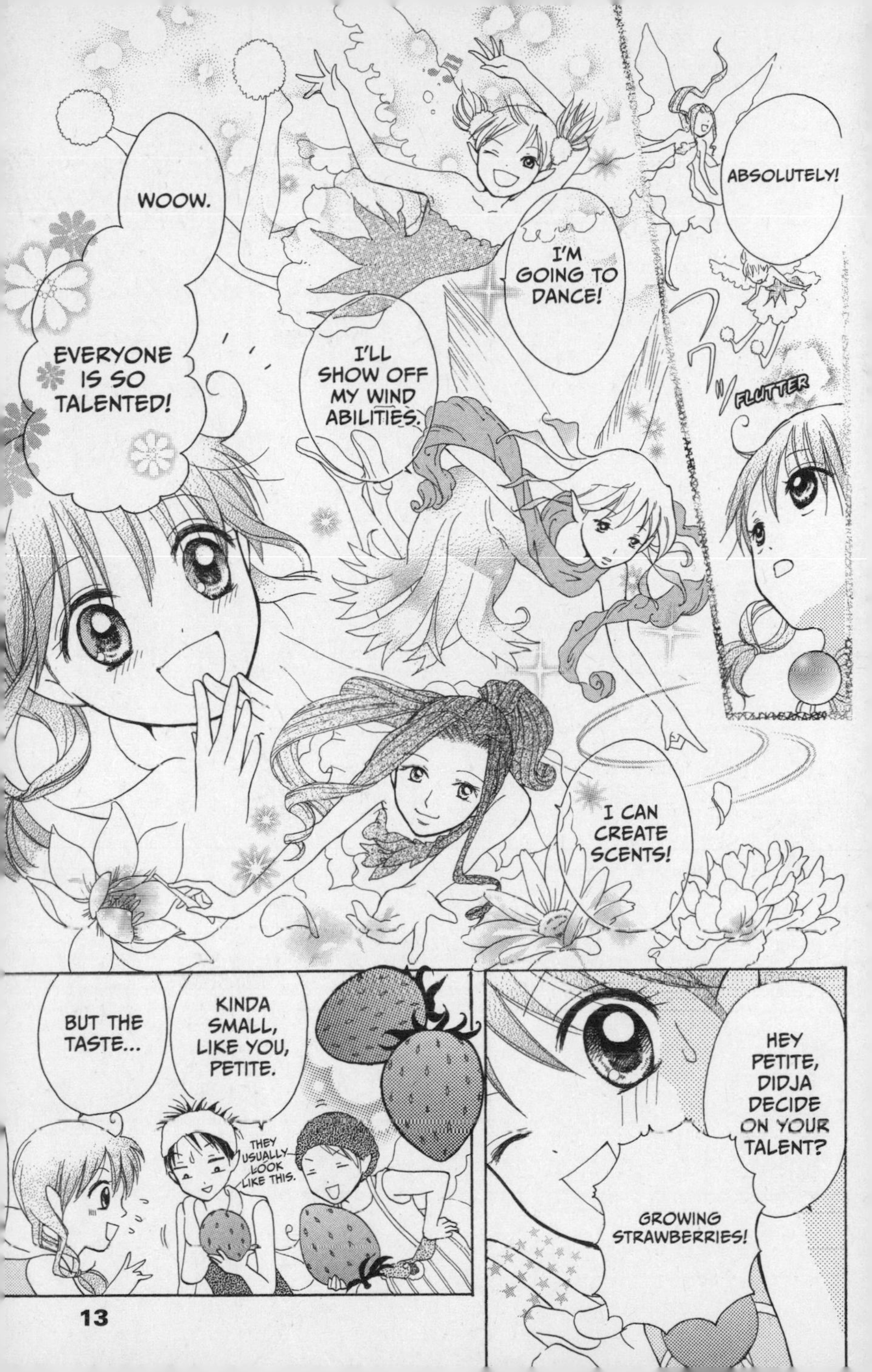
ABSOLUTELY!
FLUTTER
I'M GOING TO DANCE!
I'LL SHOW OFF MY WIND ABILITIES.
WOOW.
EVERYONE IS SO TALENTED!
I CAN CREATE SCENTS!
HEY PETITE, DIDJA DECIDE ON YOUR TALENT?
GROWING STRAWBERRIES!
KINDA SMALL, LIKE YOU, PETITE.
BUT THE TASTE...
THEY USUALLY LOOK LIKE THIS.

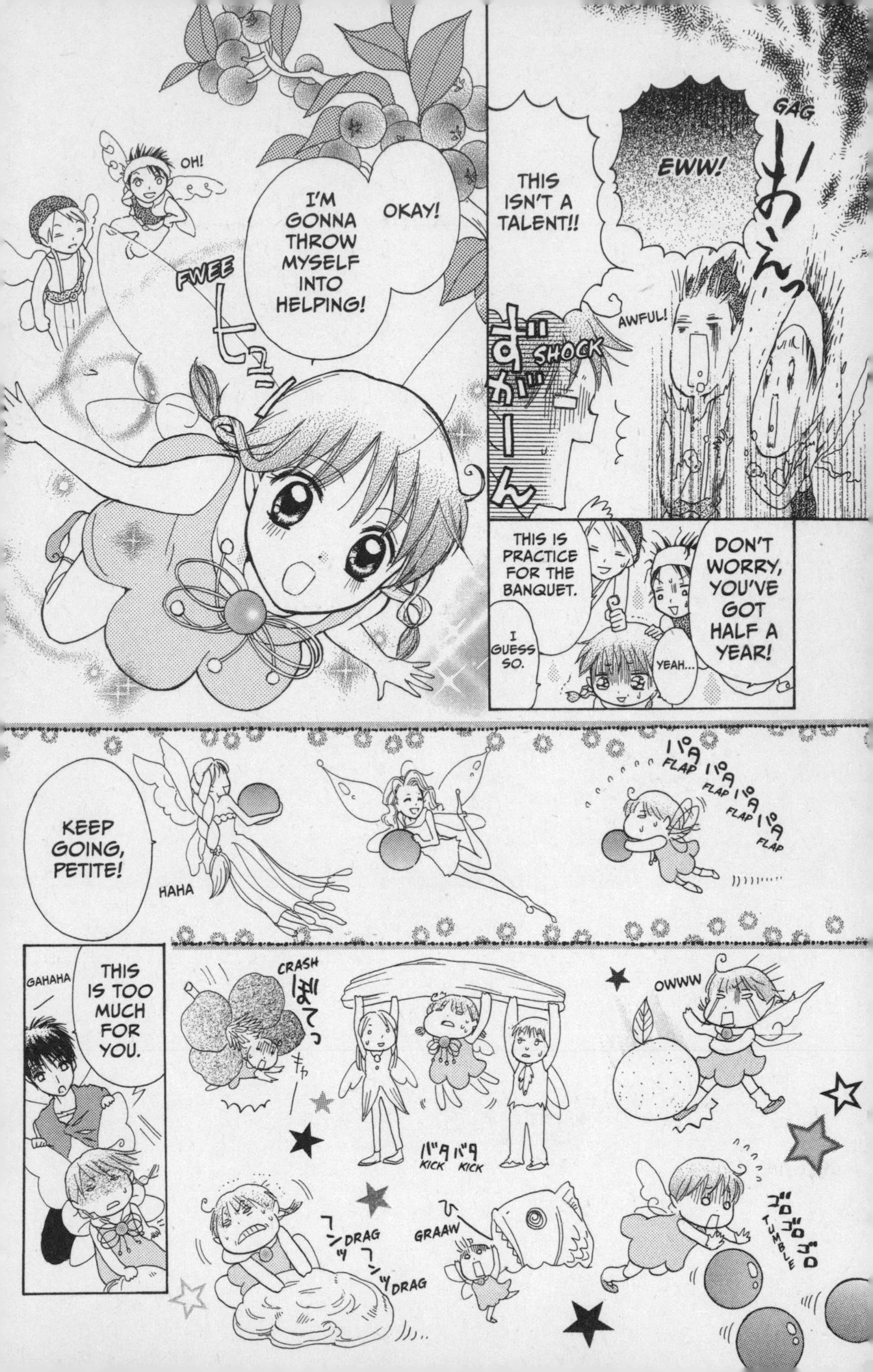
GAG
EWW!
THIS ISN'T A TALENT!!
AWFUL!
SHOCK
ずがーん
DON'T WORRY, YOU'VE GOT HALF A YEAR!
THIS IS PRACTICE FOR THE BANQUET.
YEAH...
I GUESS SO.
OKAY!
I'M GONNA THROW MYSELF INTO HELPING!
OH!
FWEE
パ パ パ パ
FLAP FLAP FLAP FLAP
KEEP GOING, PETITE!
HAHA
OWWW
ゴロゴロ
TUMBLE
GRAAW
バタバタ
KICK KICK
CRASH
ぼてっ
DRAG DRAG
THIS IS TOO MUCH FOR YOU.
GAHAHA

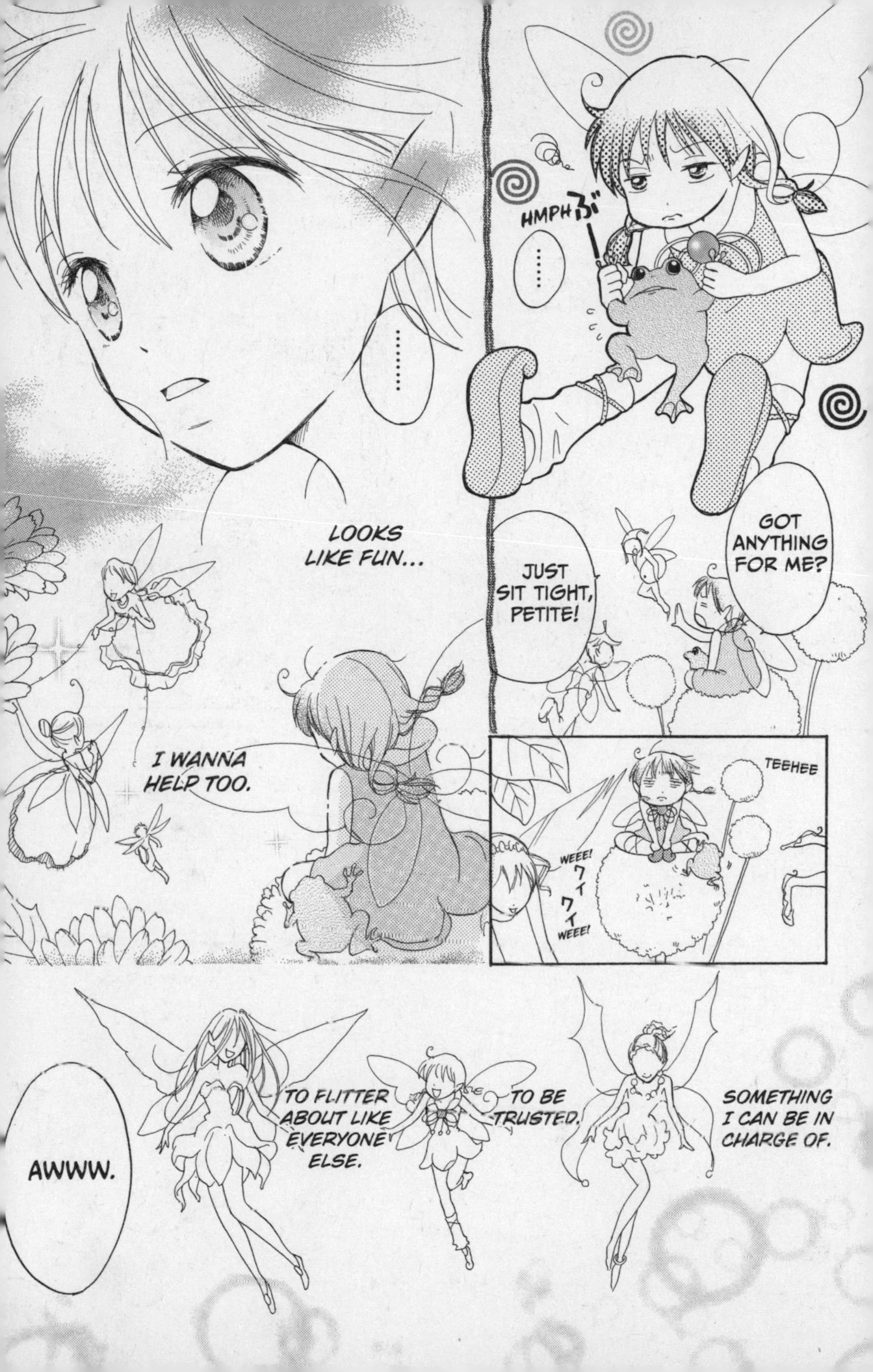
HMPH ぶ
......
GOT ANYTHING FOR ME?
JUST SIT TIGHT, PETITE!
TEEHEE
WEEE! ワイ ワイ WEEE!
......
LOOKS LIKE FUN...
I WANNA HELP TOO.
SOMETHING I CAN BE IN CHARGE OF.
TO BE TRUSTED.
TO FLITTER ABOUT LIKE EVERYONE ELSE.
AWWW.

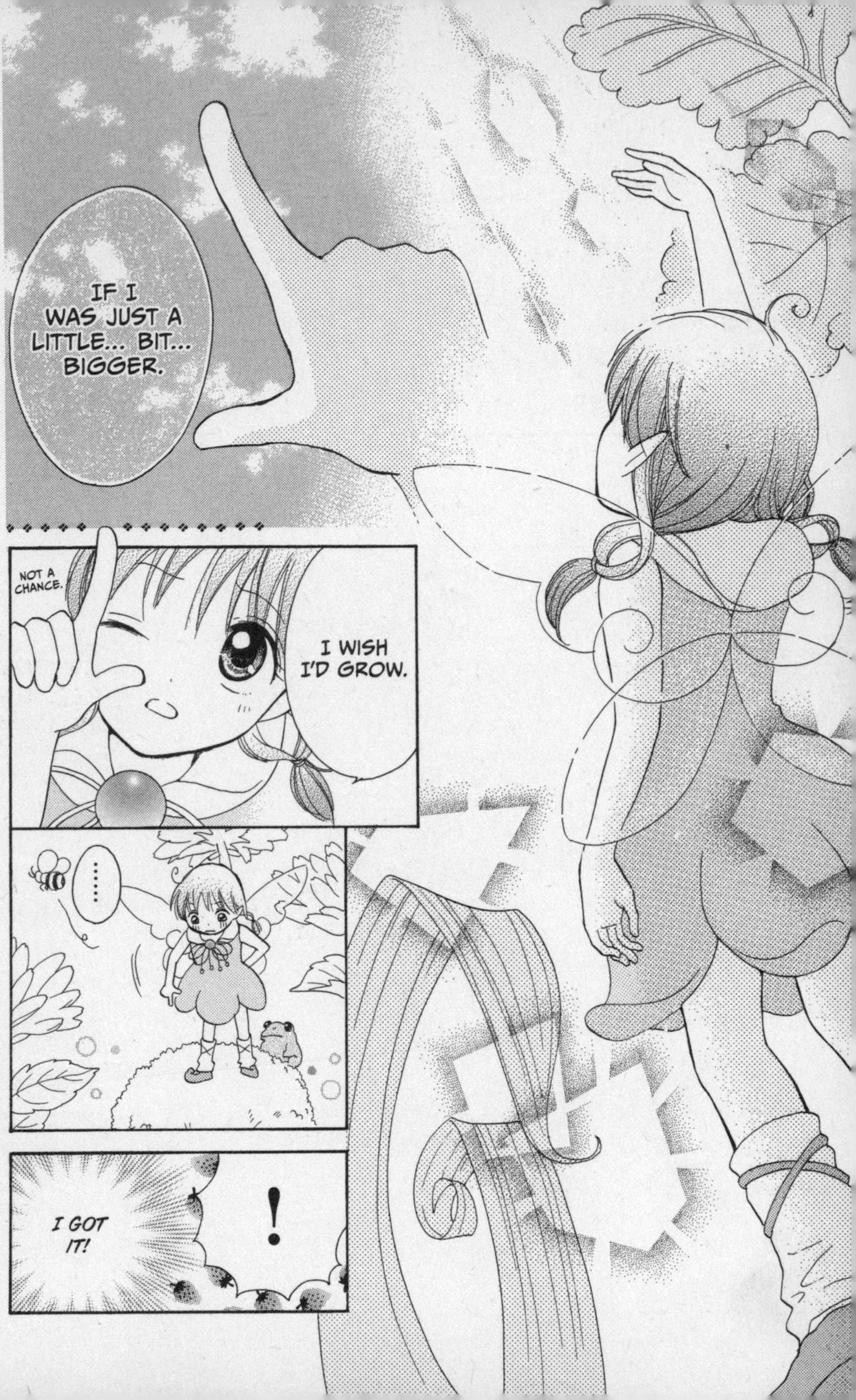
IF I WAS JUST A LITTLE... BIT... BIGGER.
I WISH I'D GROW.
NOT A CHANCE.
......
!
I GOT IT!

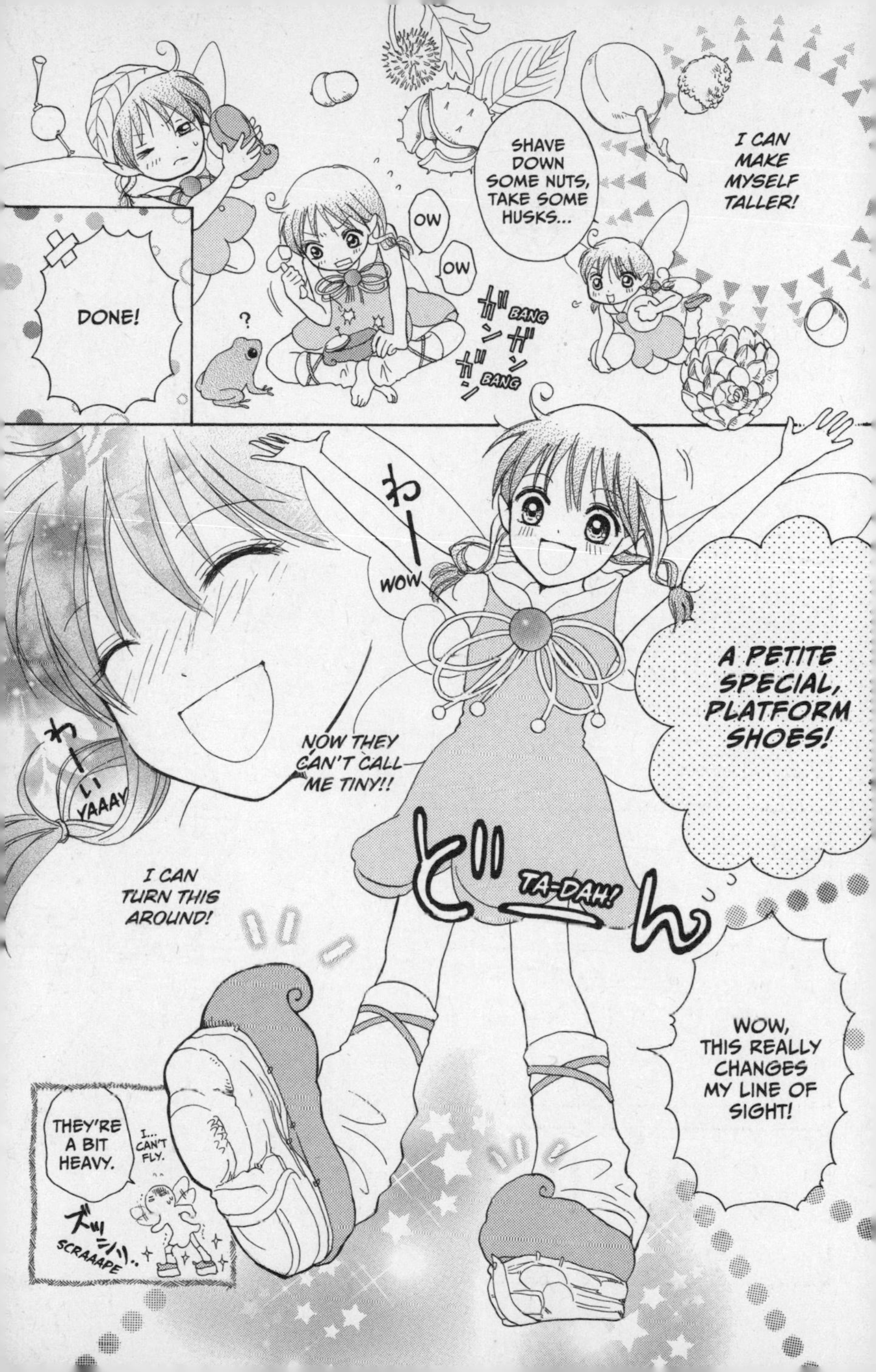
I CAN MAKE MYSELF TALLER!
SHAVE DOWN SOME NUTS, TAKE SOME HUSKS...
BANG BANG
OW
OW
DONE!
A PETITE SPECIAL, PLATFORM SHOES!
WOW
NOW THEY CAN'T CALL ME TINY!!
YAAAY
TA-DAH!
WOW, THIS REALLY CHANGES MY LINE OF SIGHT!
I CAN TURN THIS AROUND!
THEY'RE A BIT HEAVY.
I... CAN'T FLY.
SCRAAAPE

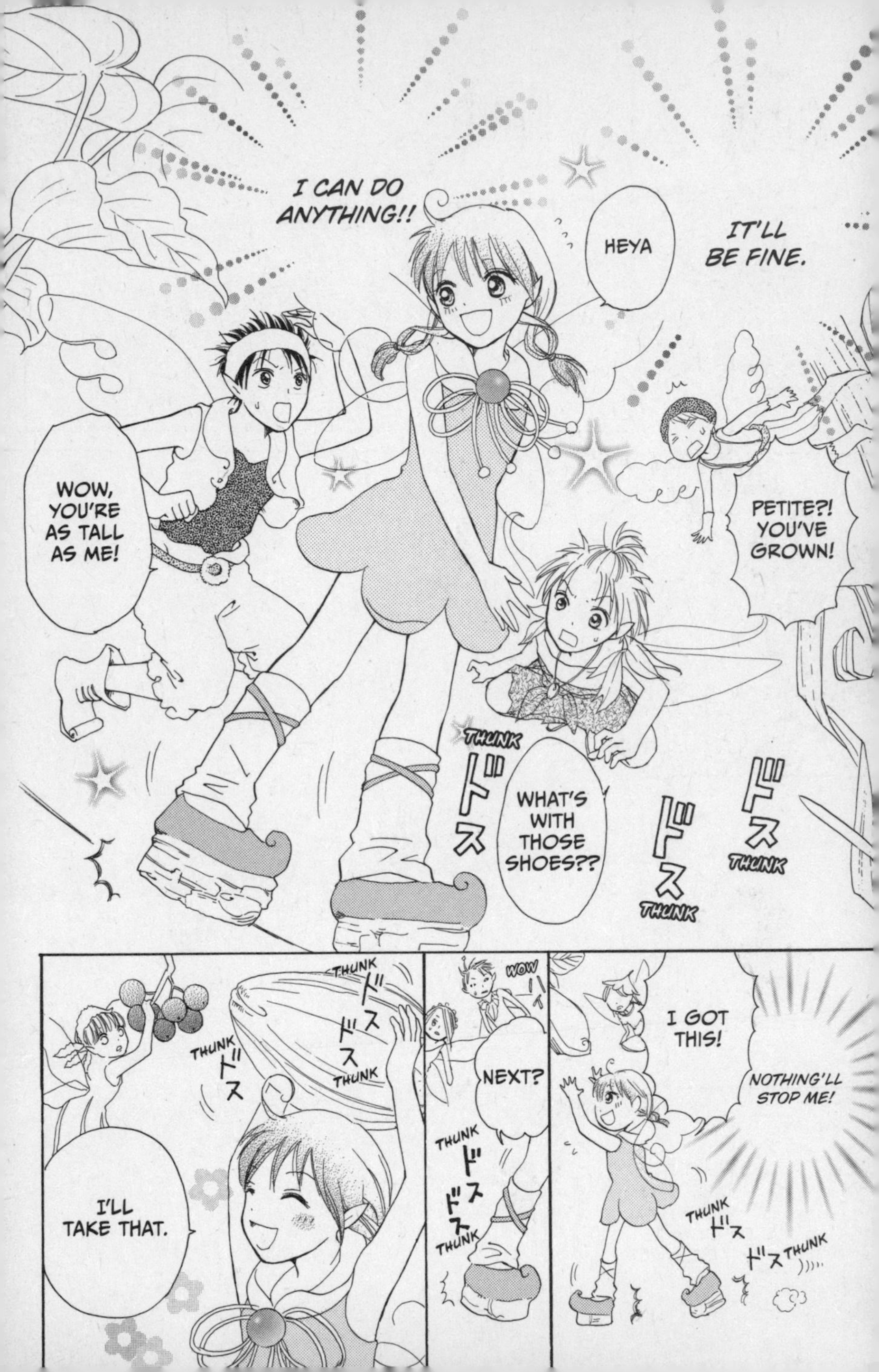
IT'LL BE FINE.
HEYA
I CAN DO ANYTHING!!
PETITE?! YOU'VE GROWN!
WOW, YOU'RE AS TALL AS ME!
ドス THUNK
ドス THUNK
THUNK ドス
WHAT'S WITH THOSE SHOES??
I GOT THIS!
NOTHING'LL STOP ME!
THUNK ドス
ドス THUNK
WOW
NEXT?
THUNK ドス
ドス THUNK
THUNK ドス
ドス THUNK
THUNK ドス
I'LL TAKE THAT.

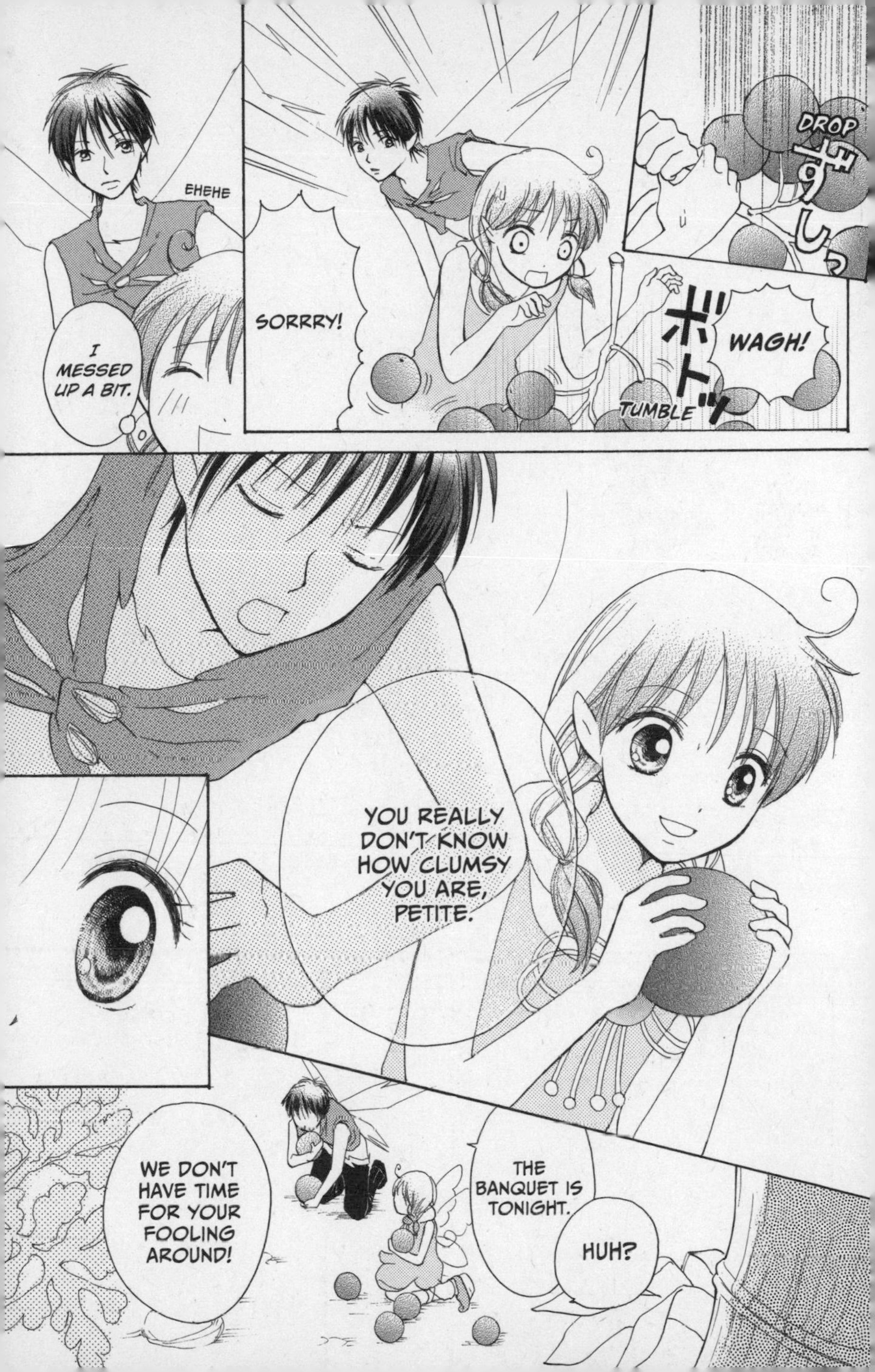
DROP
ずしっ
WAGH!
ボトッ
TUMBLE
SORRRY!
EHEHE
I MESSED UP A BIT.
YOU REALLY DON'T KNOW HOW CLUMSY YOU ARE, PETITE.
THE BANQUET IS TONIGHT.
WE DON'T HAVE TIME FOR YOUR FOOLING AROUND!
HUH?

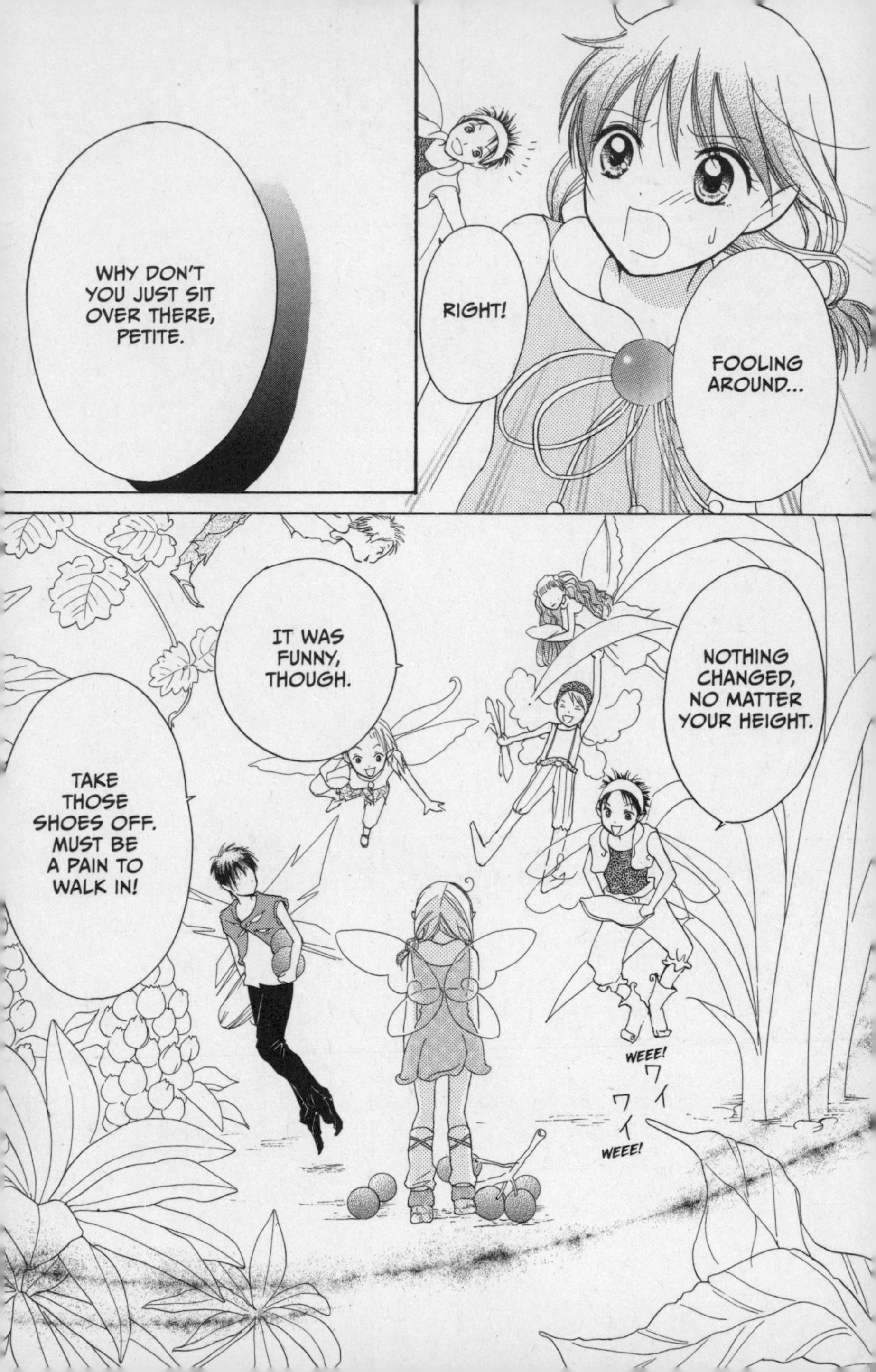
FOOLING AROUND...
RIGHT!
WHY DON'T YOU JUST SIT OVER THERE, PETITE.
NOTHING CHANGED, NO MATTER YOUR HEIGHT.
IT WAS FUNNY, THOUGH.
TAKE THOSE SHOES OFF. MUST BE A PAIN TO WALK IN!
WEEE! ワイ
ワイ WEEE!

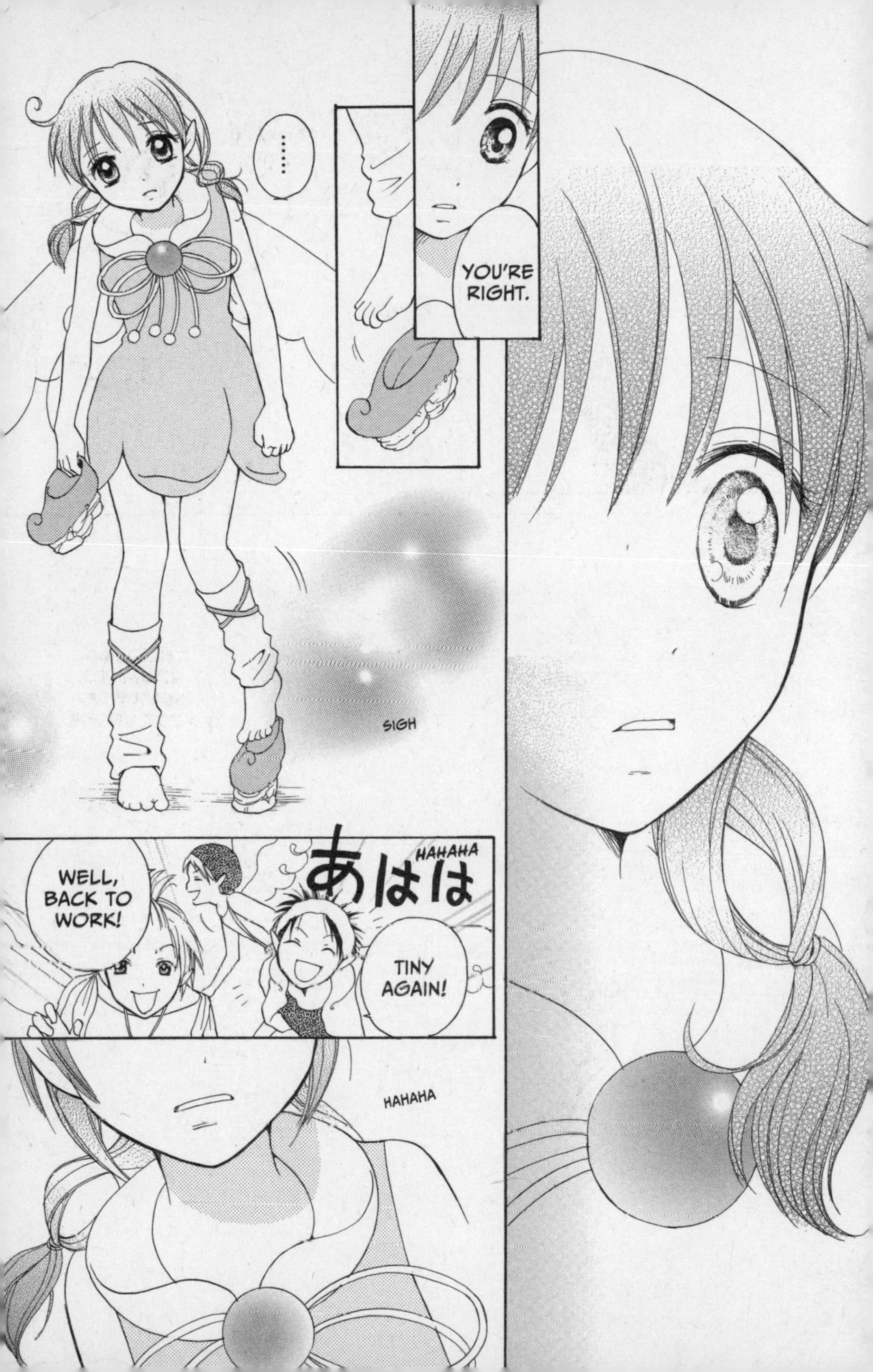

YOU'RE RIGHT.
......
SIGH
あはは
HAHAHA
TINY AGAIN!
WELL, BACK TO WORK!
HAHAHA

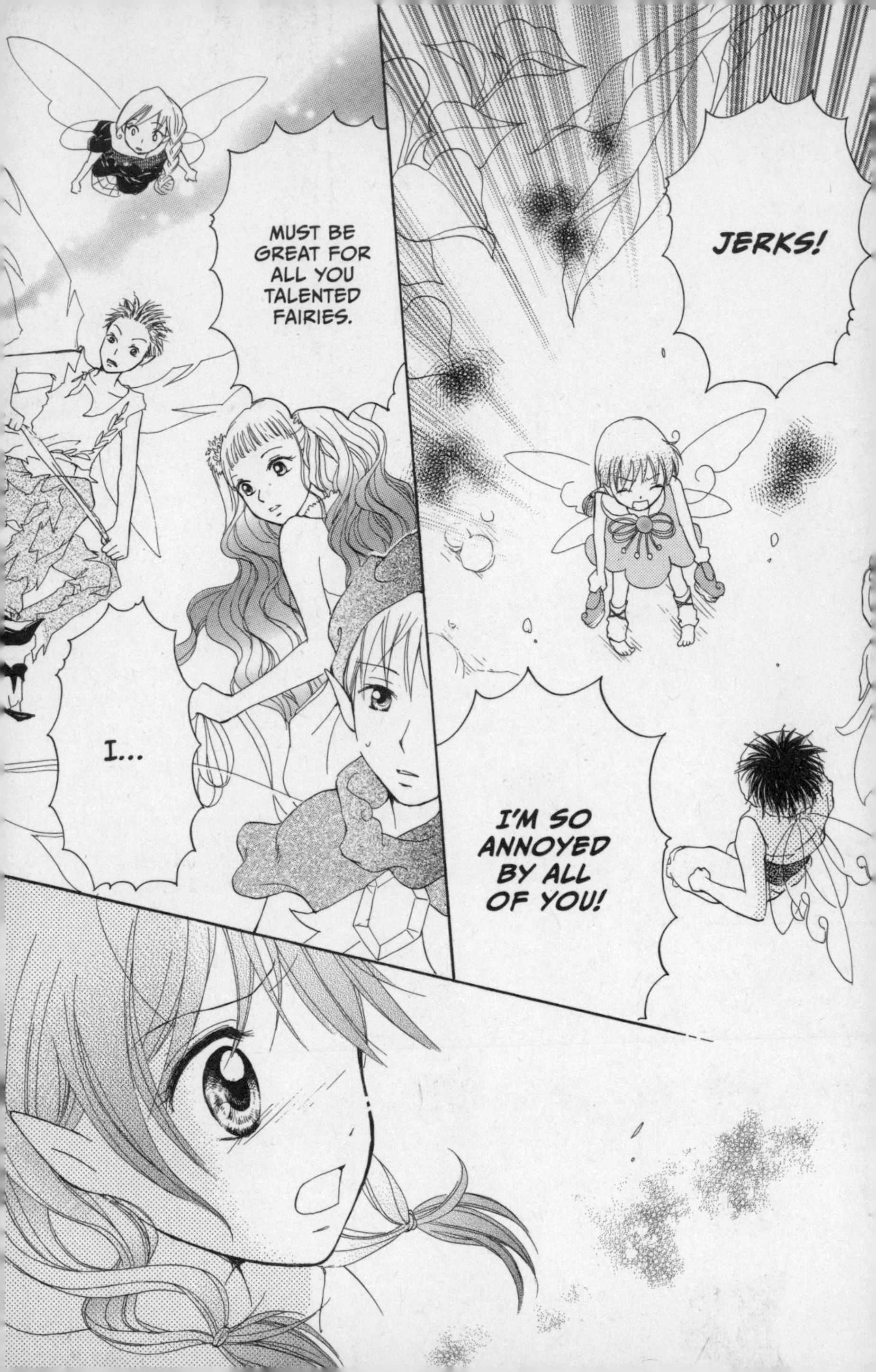
JERKS!
I'M SO ANNOYED BY ALL OF YOU!
MUST BE GREAT FOR ALL YOU TALENTED FAIRIES.
I...

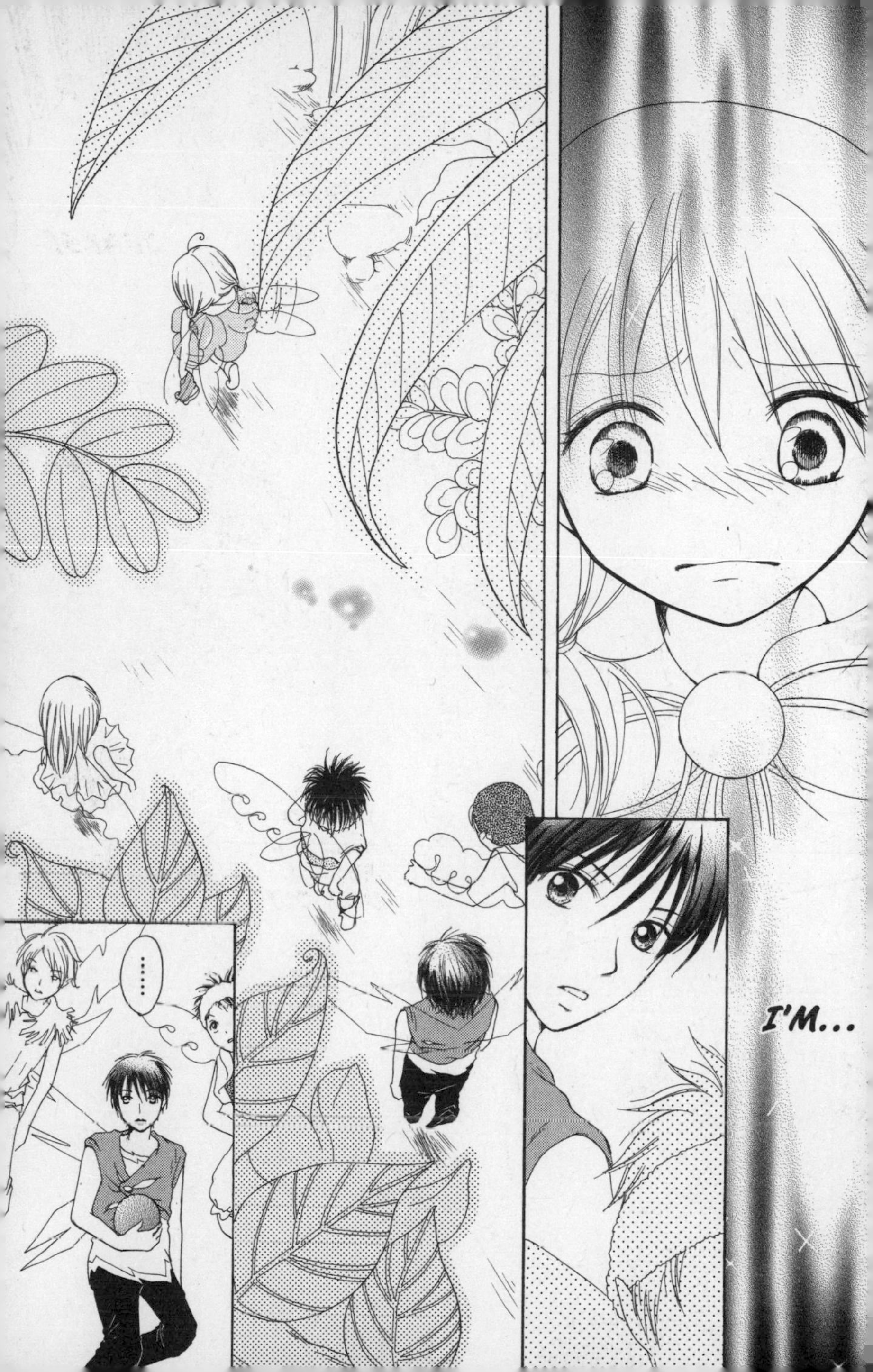
I'M...
......

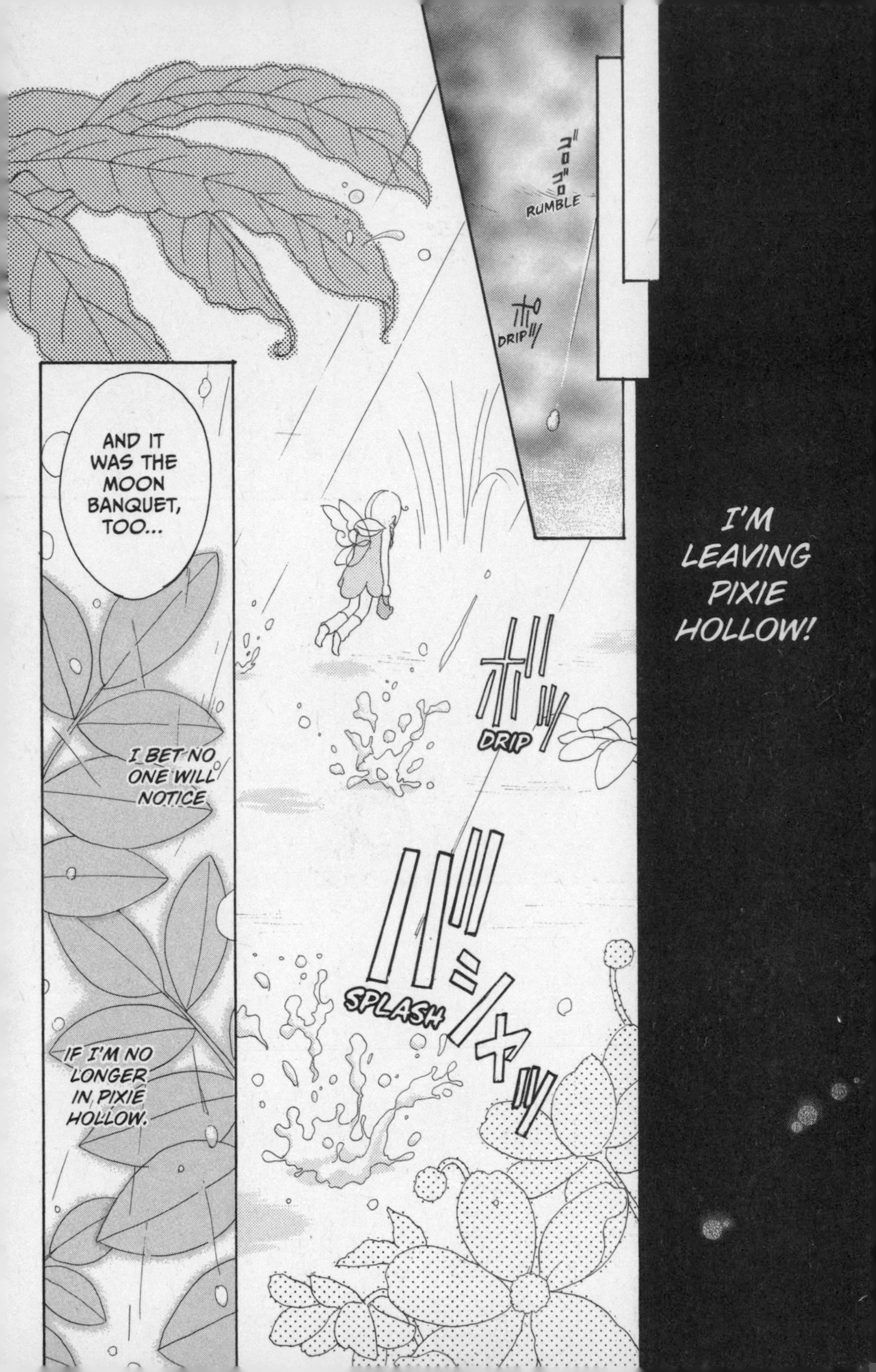

I'M LEAVING PIXIE HOLLOW!
RUMBLE
DRIP
DRIP
SPLASH
AND IT WAS THE MOON BANQUET, TOO...
I BET NO ONE WILL NOTICE
IF I'M NO LONGER IN PIXIE HOLLOW.

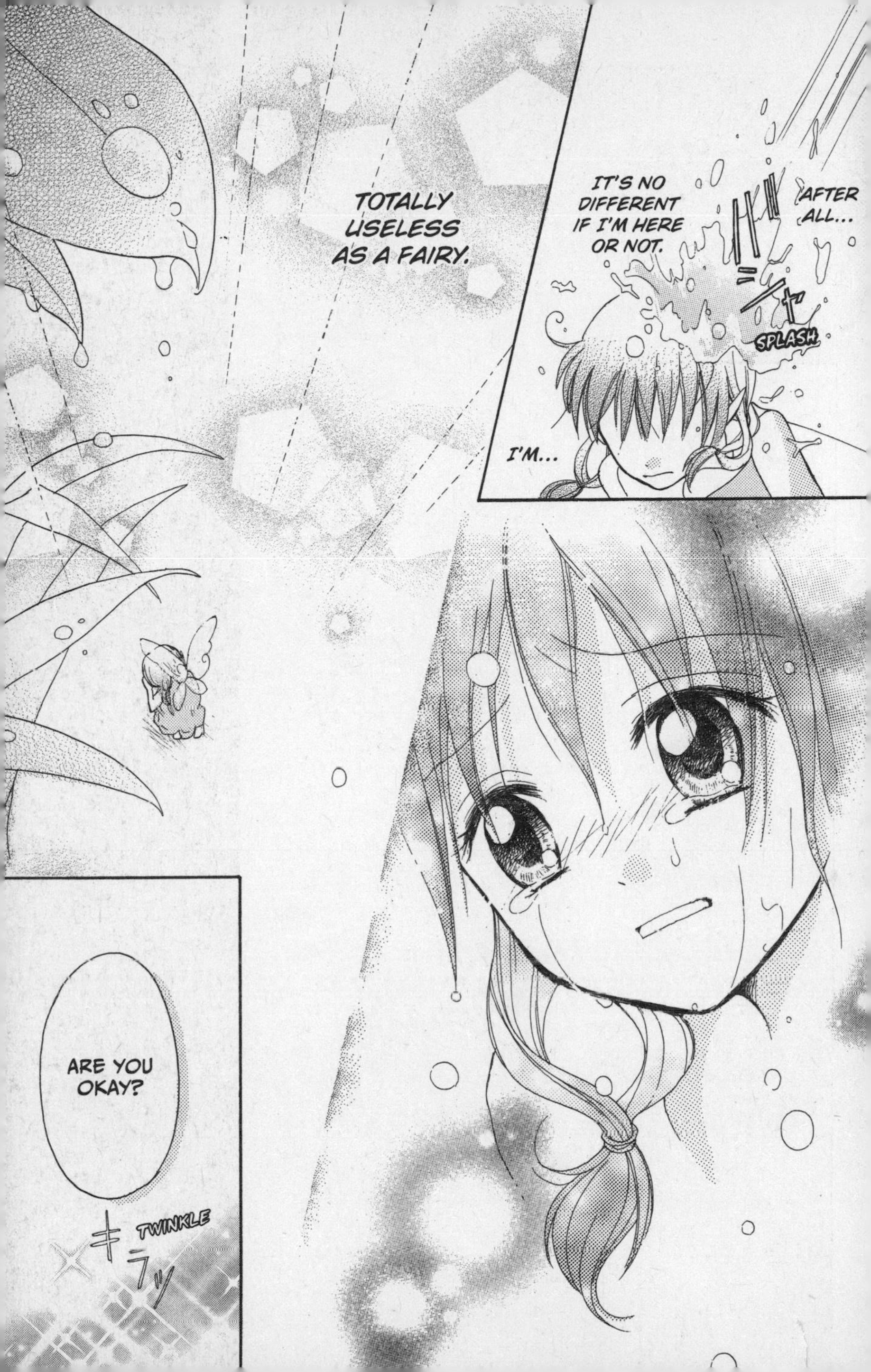
AFTER ALL...
IT'S NO DIFFERENT IF I'M HERE OR NOT.
SPLASH
I'M...
TOTALLY USELESS AS A FAIRY.
ARE YOU OKAY?
TWINKLE
キラッ

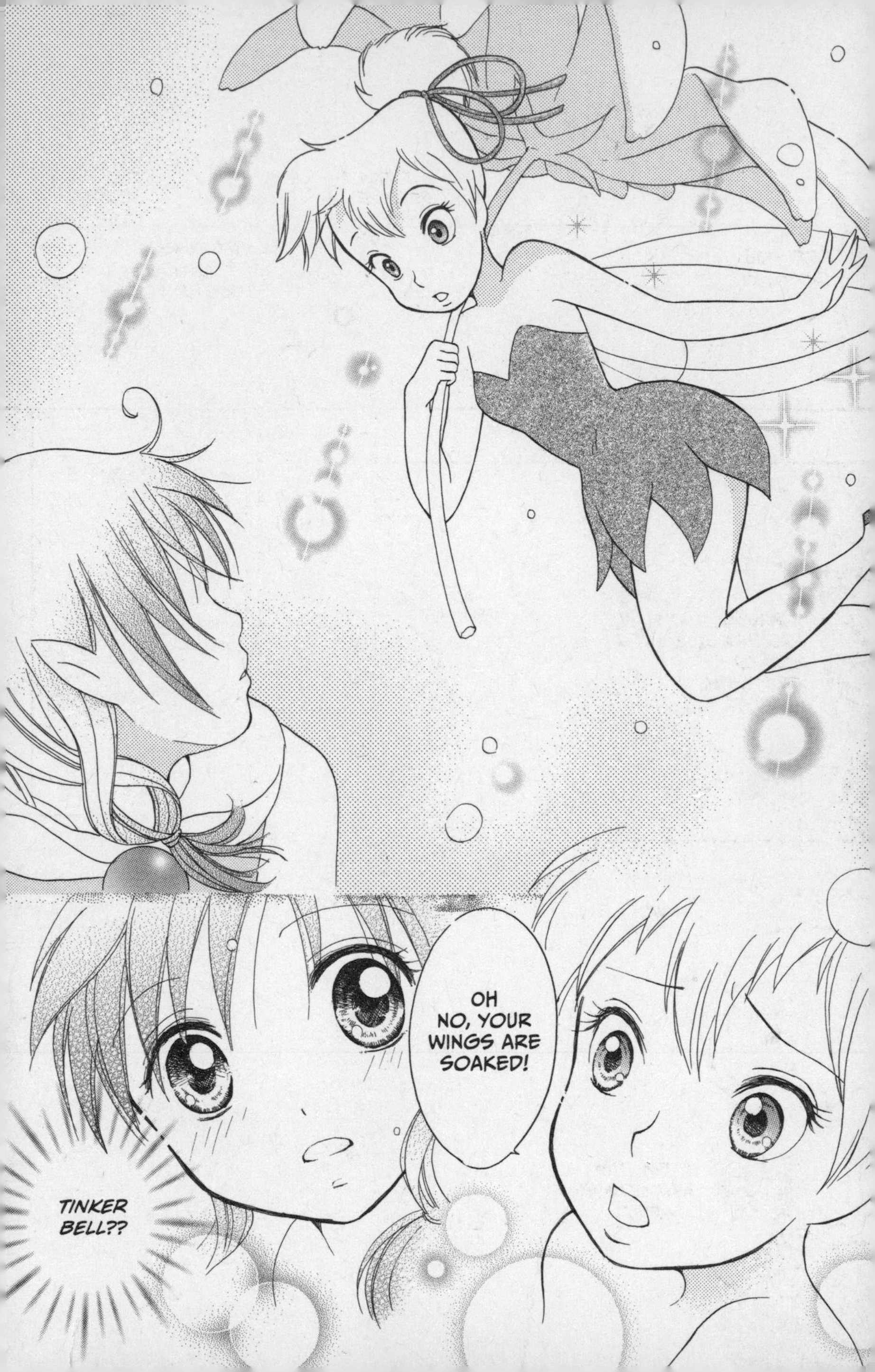
OH NO, YOUR WINGS ARE SOAKED!
TINKER BELL??

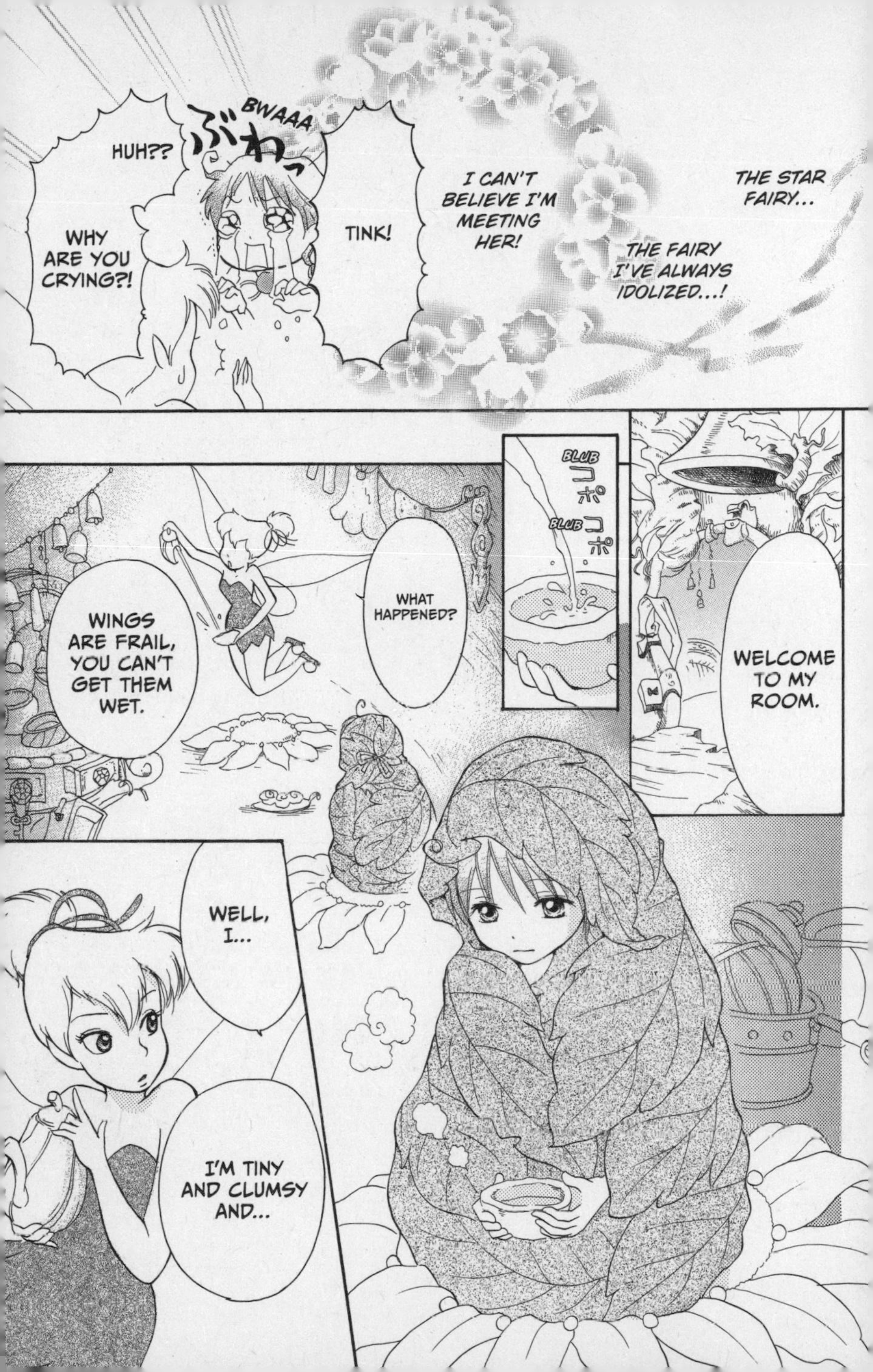
THE STAR FAIRY...
THE FAIRY I'VE ALWAYS IDOLIZED...!
I CAN'T BELIEVE I'M MEETING HER!
TINK!
BWAAA
ぶわっ
HUH??
WHY ARE YOU CRYING?!
WELCOME TO MY ROOM.
BLUB
コポ
BLUB
コポ
WHAT HAPPENED?
WINGS ARE FRAIL, YOU CAN'T GET THEM WET.
WELL, I...
I'M TINY AND CLUMSY AND...

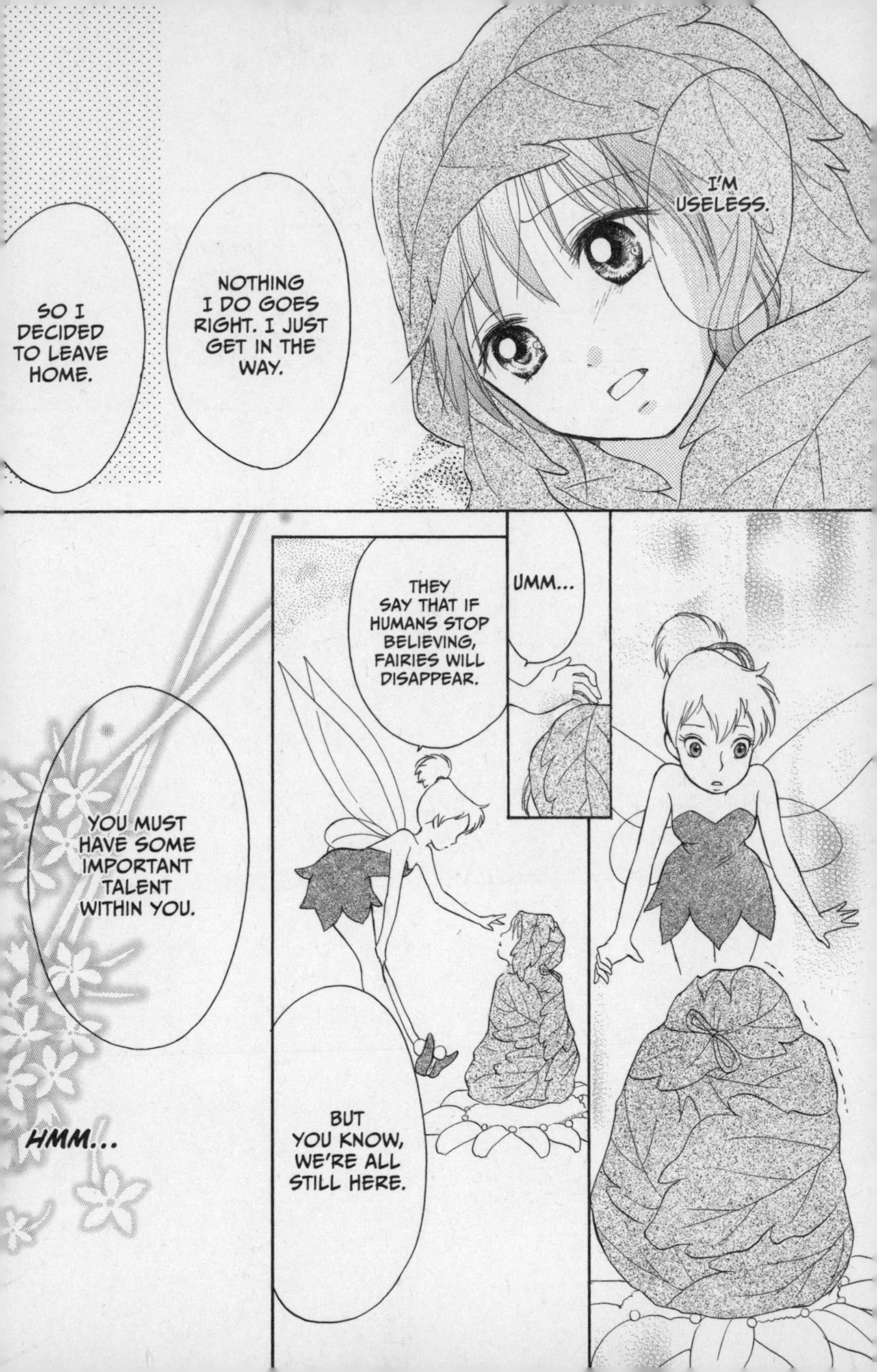
I'M USELESS.
NOTHING I DO GOES RIGHT. I JUST GET IN THE WAY.
SO I DECIDED TO LEAVE HOME.
UMM...
THEY SAY THAT IF HUMANS STOP BELIEVING, FAIRIES WILL DISAPPEAR.
BUT YOU KNOW, WE'RE ALL STILL HERE.
YOU MUST HAVE SOME IMPORTANT TALENT WITHIN YOU.
HMM...

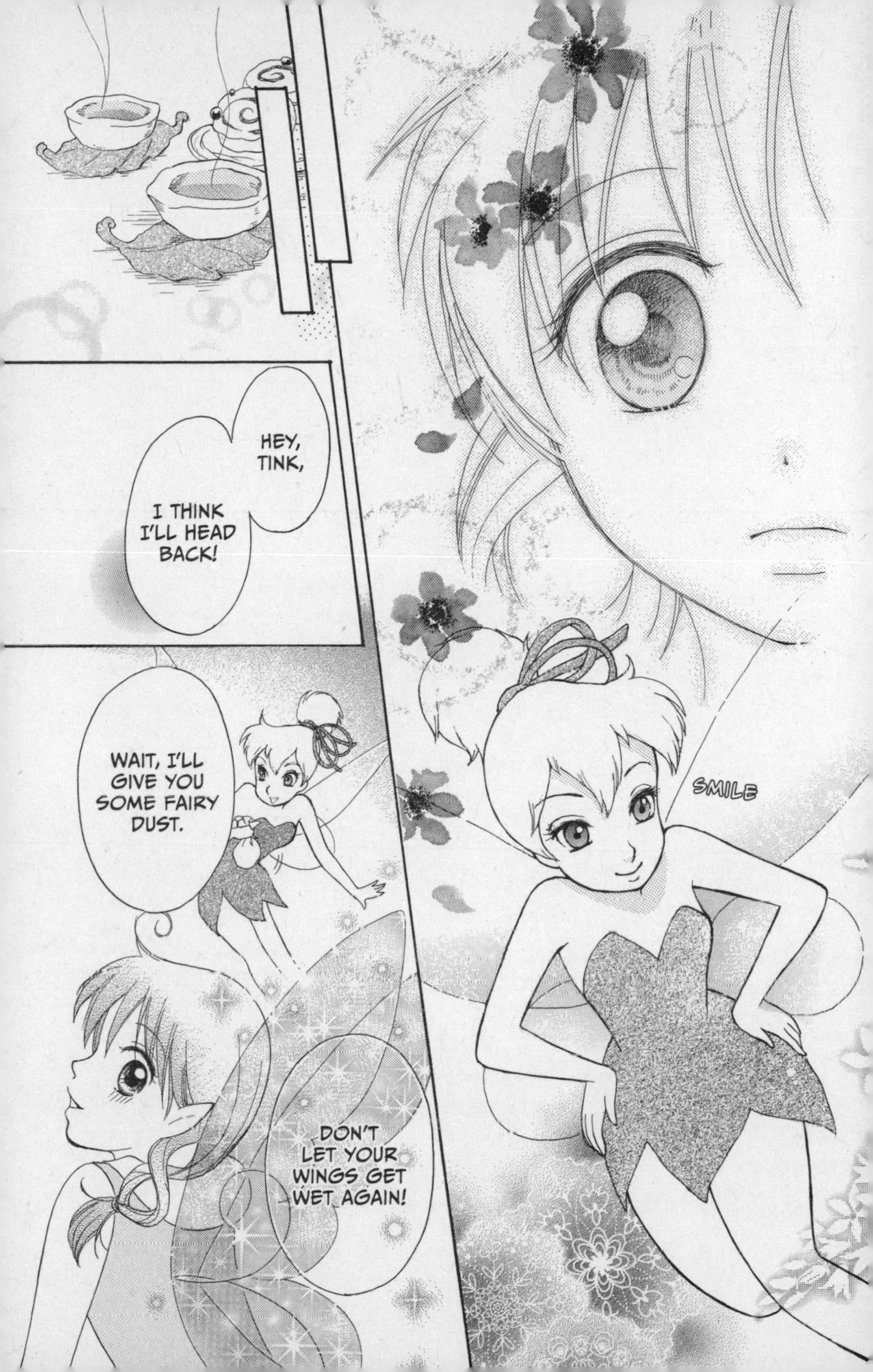
SMILE
HEY, TINK,
I THINK I'LL HEAD BACK!
WAIT, I'LL GIVE YOU SOME FAIRY DUST.
DON'T LET YOUR WINGS GET WET AGAIN!

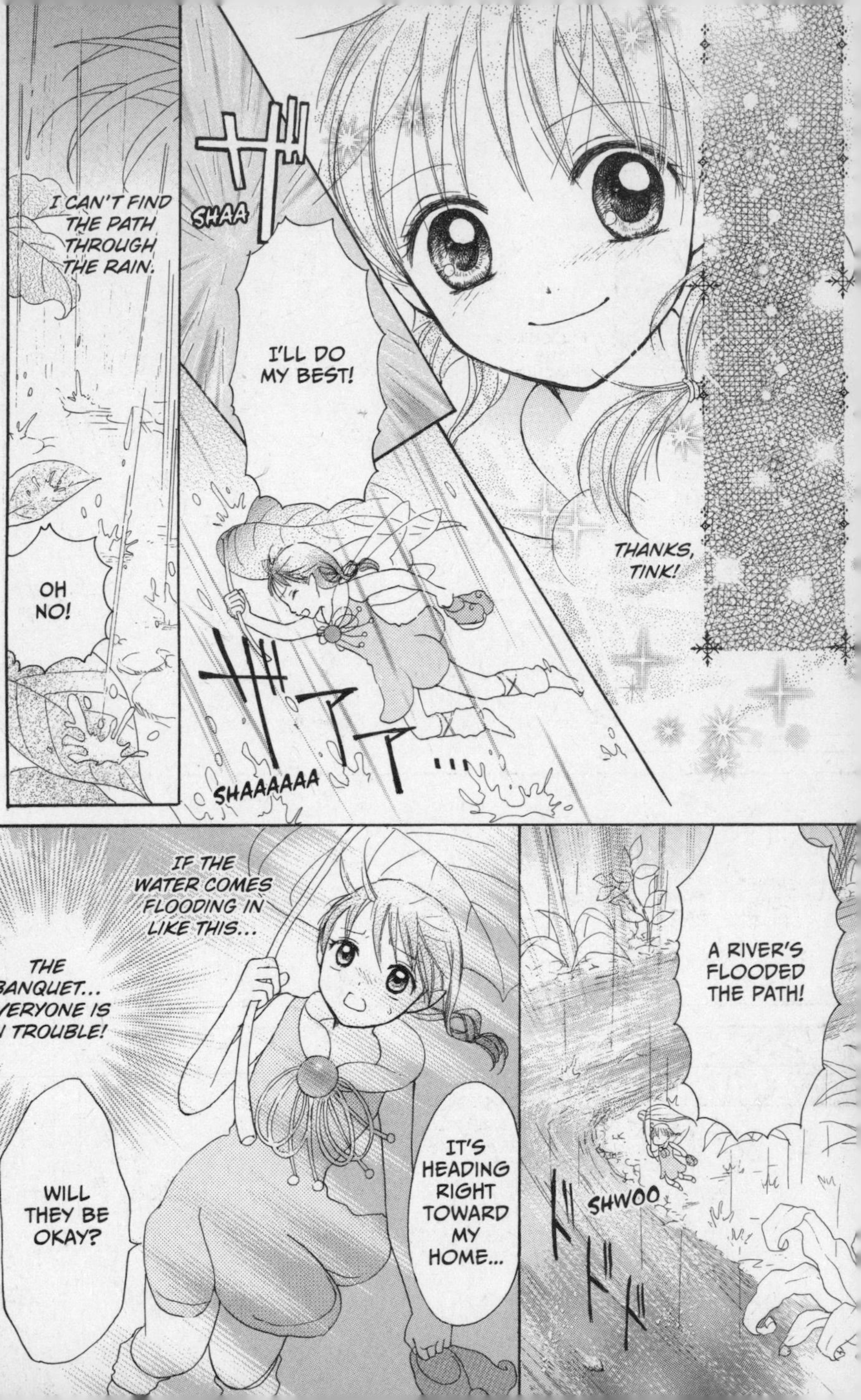
THANKS, TINK!
I'LL DO MY BEST!
SHAA
SHAAAAAA
I CAN'T FIND THE PATH THROUGH THE RAIN.
OH NO!
A RIVER'S FLOODED THE PATH!
SHWOO
IT'S HEADING RIGHT TOWARD MY HOME...
IF THE WATER COMES FLOODING IN LIKE THIS...
THE BANQUET... EVERYONE IS IN TROUBLE!
WILL THEY BE OKAY?

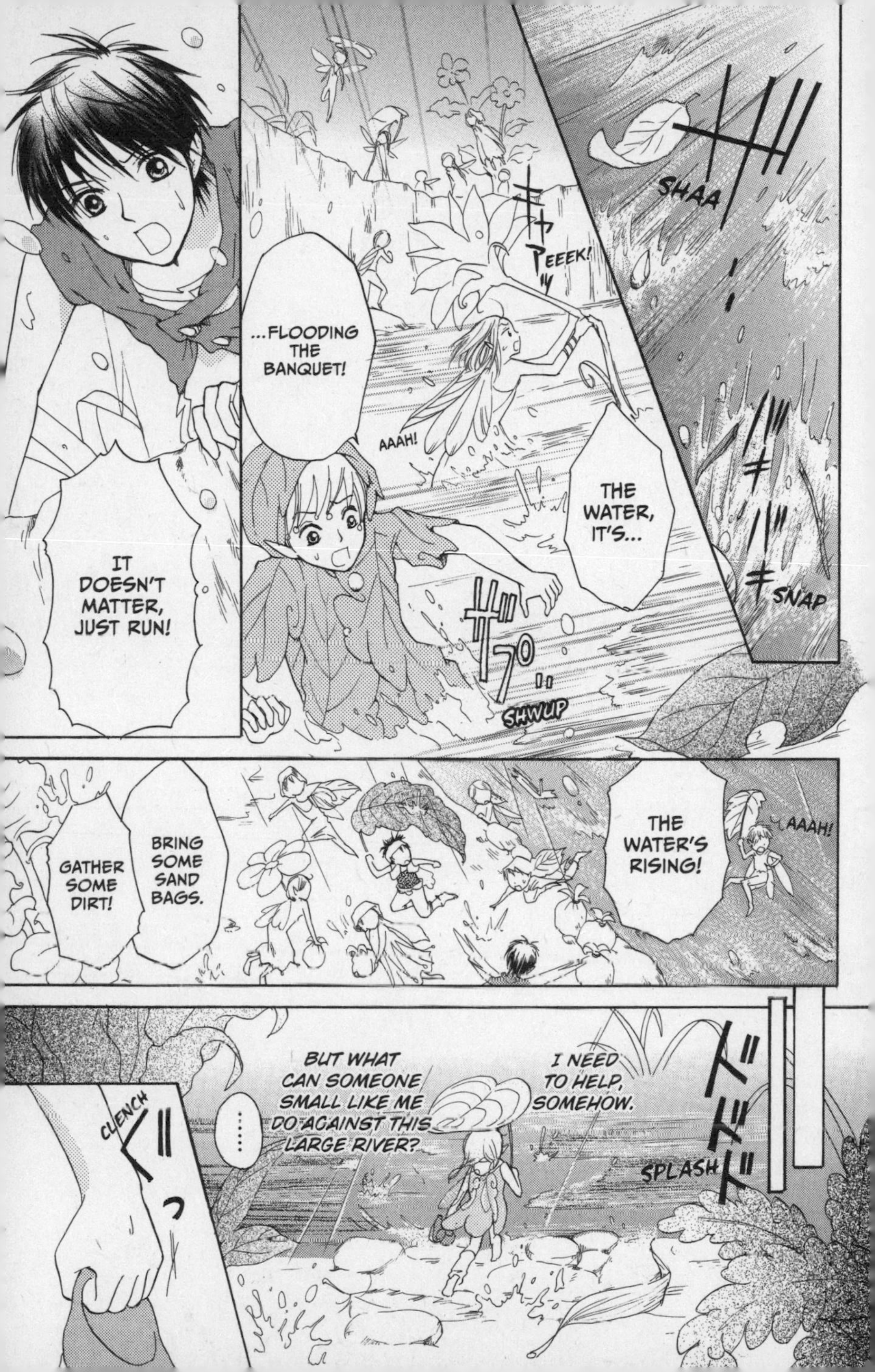
SHAA
SNAP
PEEEK!
THE WATER, IT'S...
...FLOODING THE BANQUET!
AAAH!
SHWUP
IT DOESN'T MATTER, JUST RUN!
AAAH!
THE WATER'S RISING!
BRING SOME SAND BAGS.
GATHER SOME DIRT!
SPLASH
I NEED TO HELP, SOMEHOW.
BUT WHAT CAN SOMEONE SMALL LIKE ME DO AGAINST THIS LARGE RIVER?
......
CLENCH

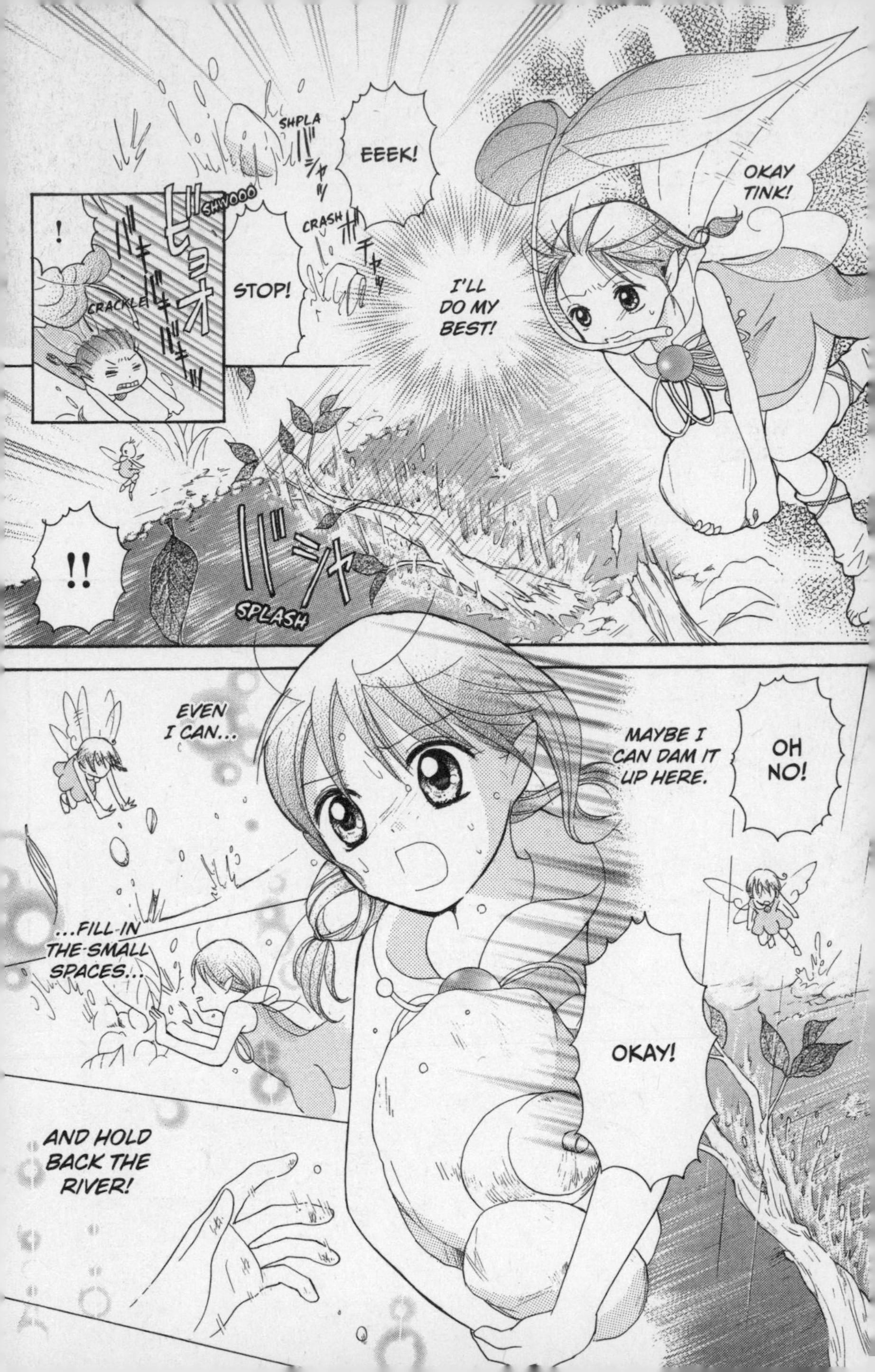

OKAY TINK!
I'LL DO MY BEST!
EEEK!
SHPLA
CRASH
STOP!
SHWOOO
!
CRACKLE!
!!
SPLASH
OH NO!
MAYBE I CAN DAM IT UP HERE.
EVEN I CAN...
OKAY!
...FILL-IN THE-SMALL SPACES...
AND HOLD BACK THE RIVER!

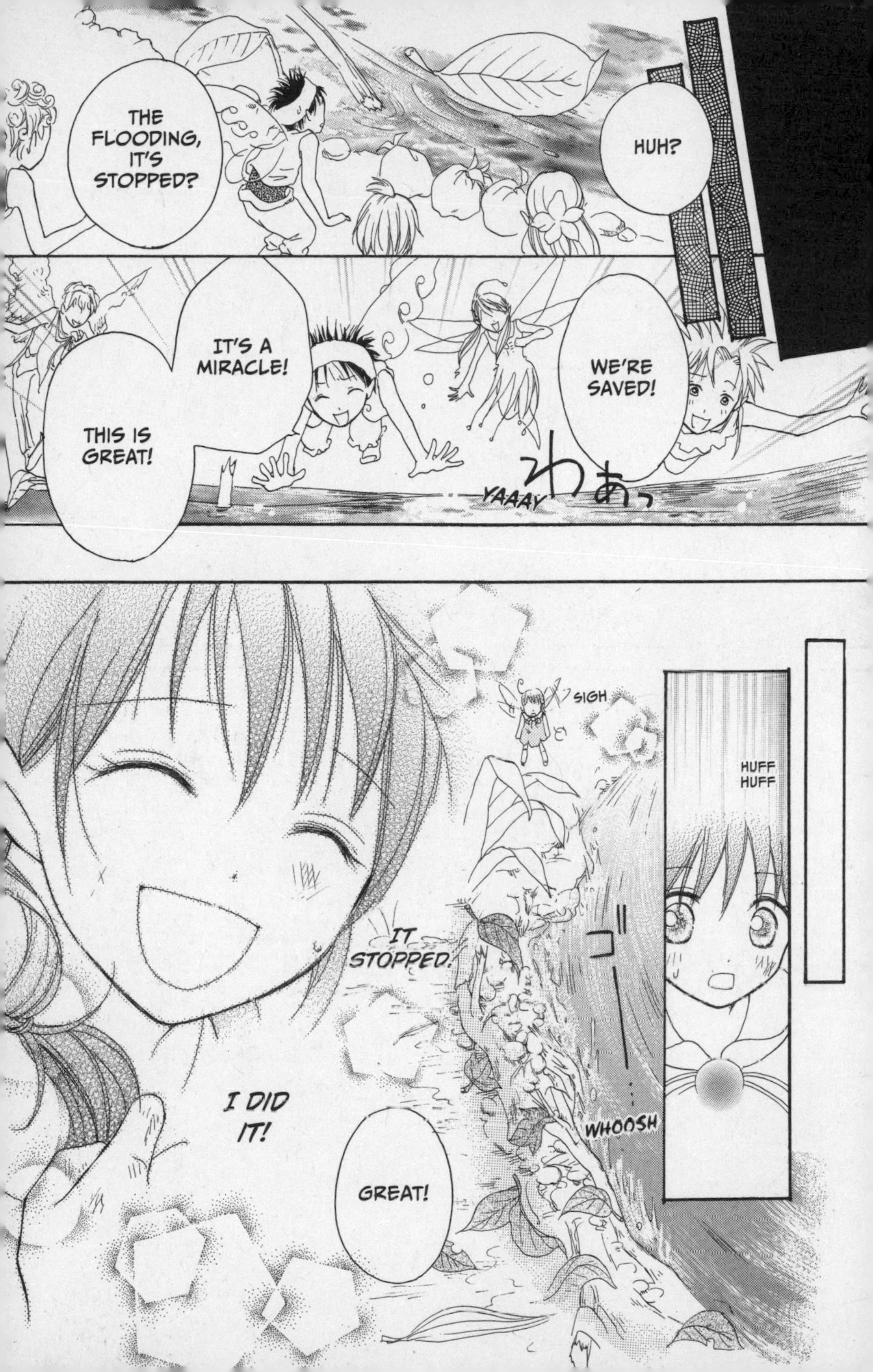
HUH?
THE FLOODING, IT'S STOPPED?
WE'RE SAVED!
IT'S A MIRACLE!
THIS IS GREAT!
YAAAY わあっ
HUFF HUFF
ゴー…
WHOOSH
SIGH
IT STOPPED.
GREAT!
I DID IT!

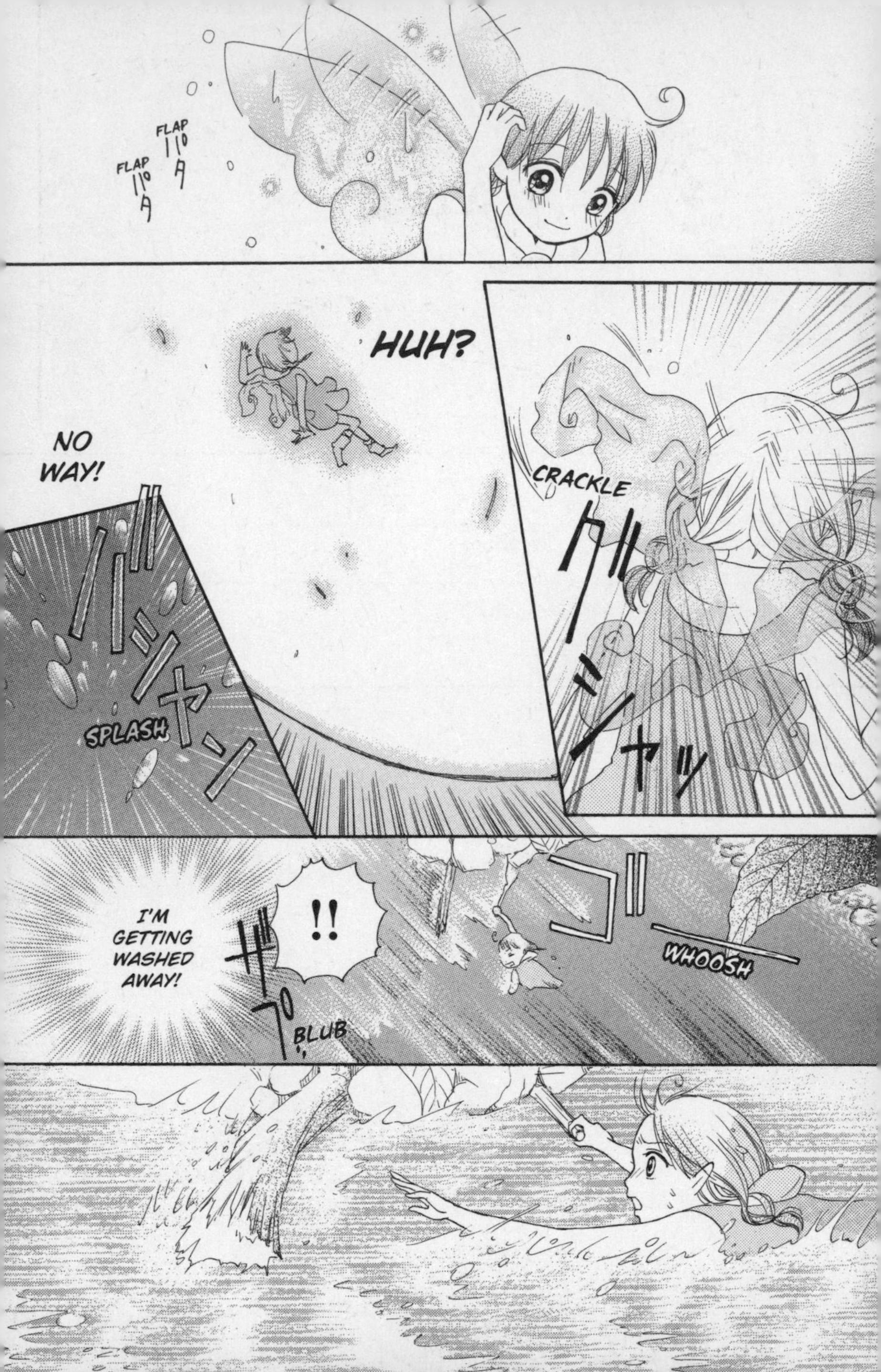
FLAP
FLAP
CRACKLE
HUH?
NO WAY!
SPLASH
WHOOSH
!!
BLUB
I'M GETTING WASHED AWAY!

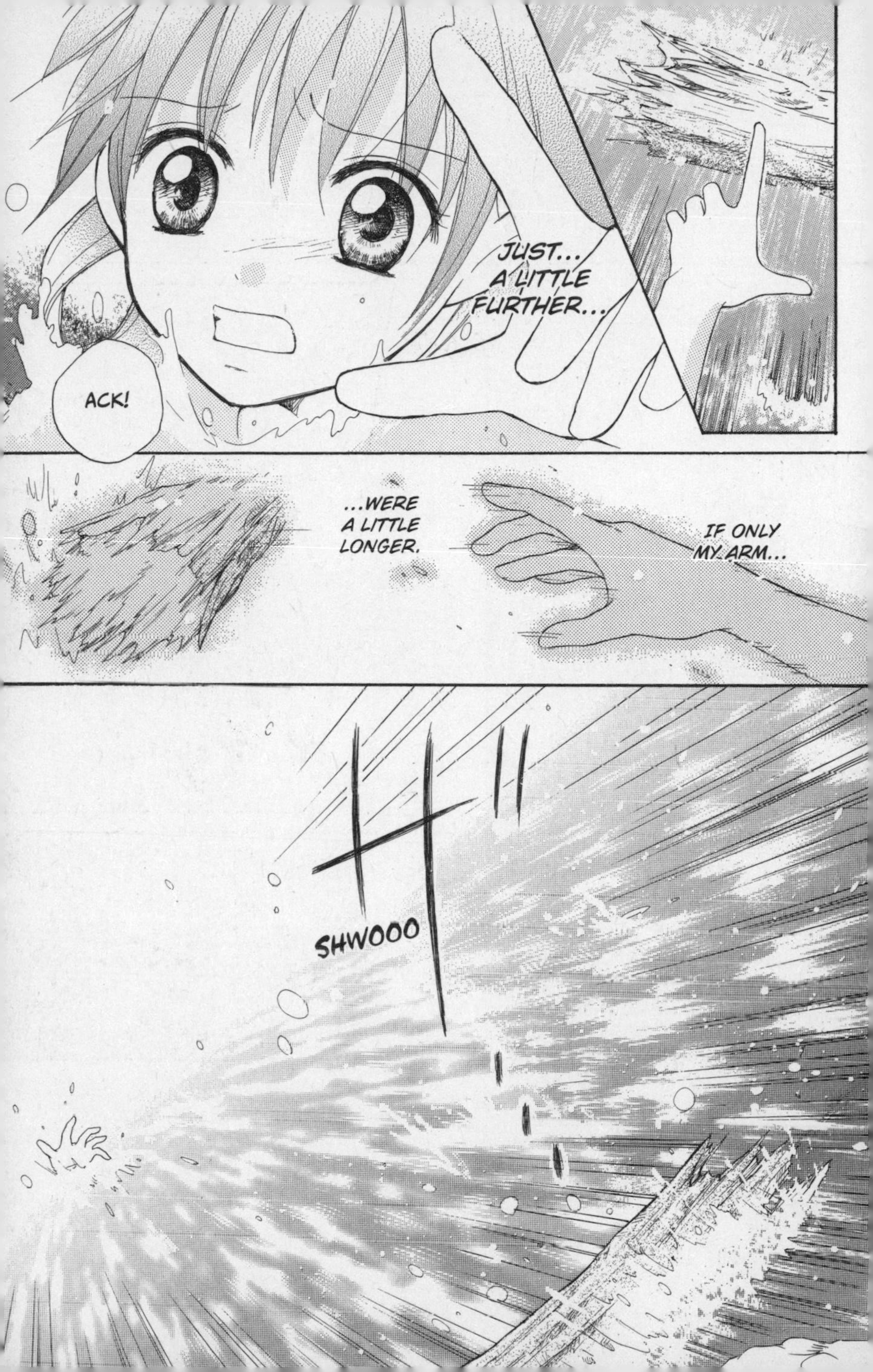
JUST... A LITTLE FURTHER...
ACK!
IF ONLY MY ARM...
...WERE A LITTLE LONGER.
SHWOOO

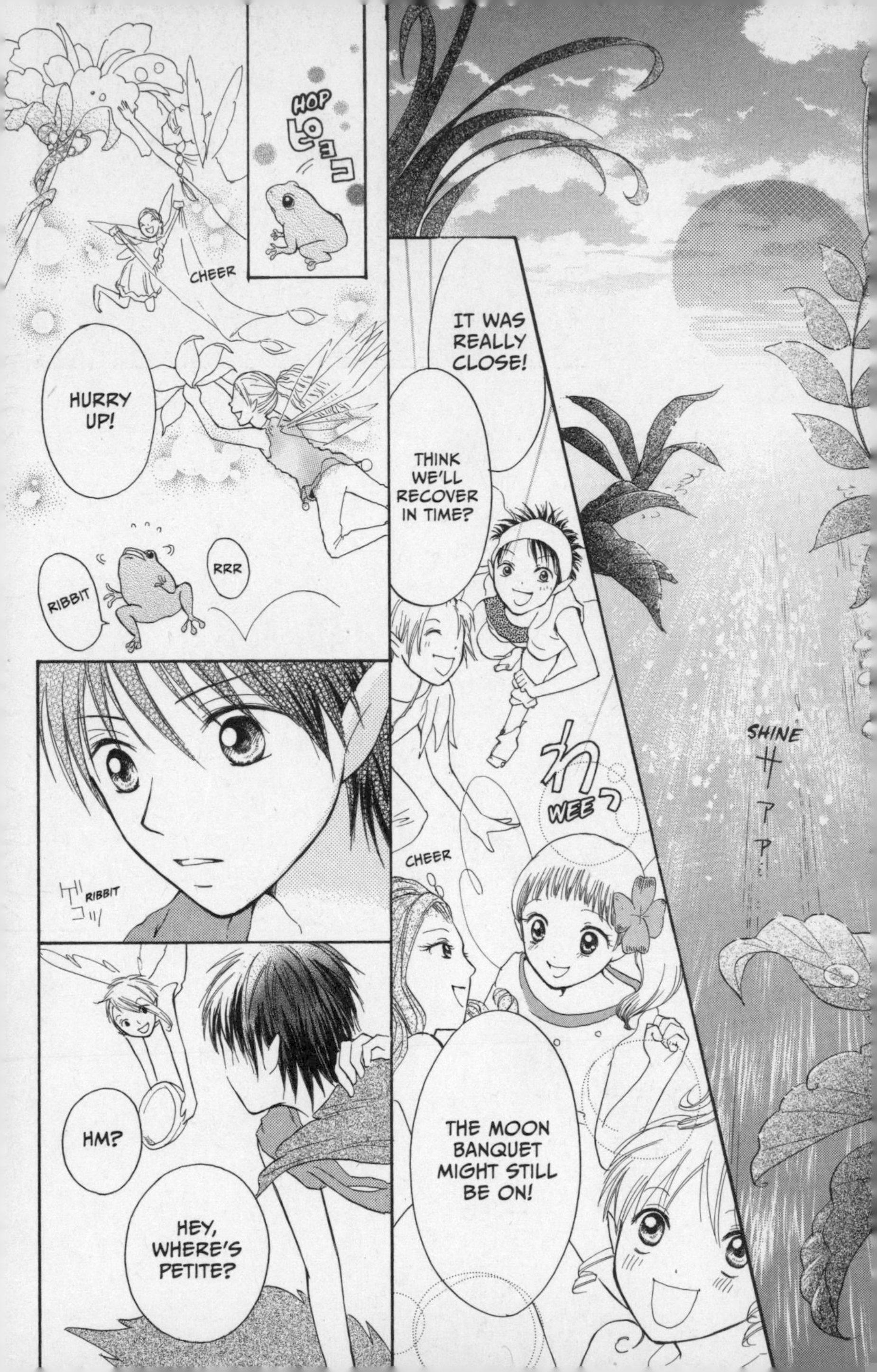
IT WAS REALLY CLOSE!
THINK WE'LL RECOVER IN TIME?
SHINE
WEE
CHEER
THE MOON BANQUET MIGHT STILL BE ON!
HOP
CHEER
HURRY UP!
RRR
RIBBIT
RIBBIT
HM?
HEY, WHERE'S PETITE?

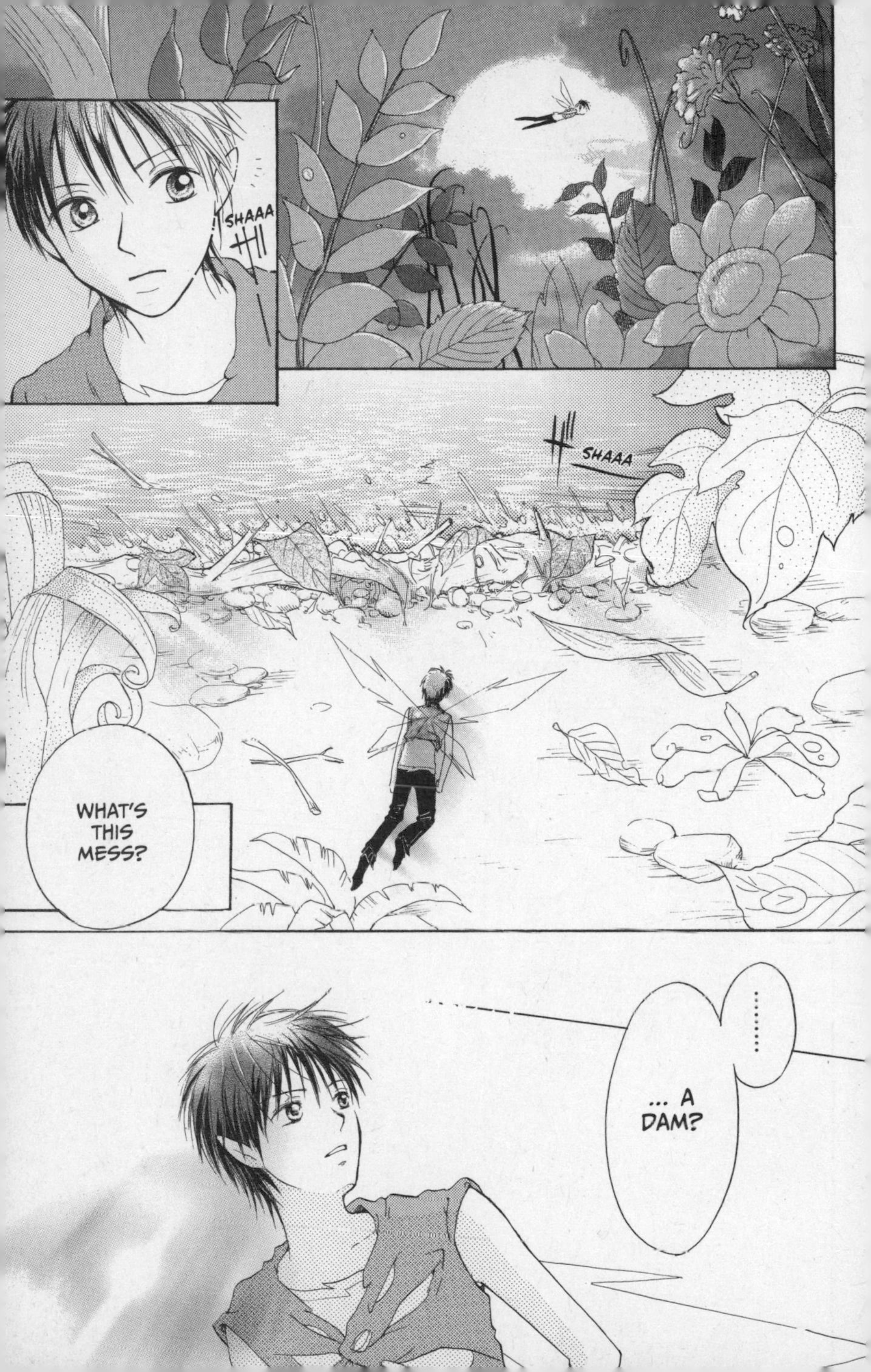
SHAAA
SHAAA
WHAT'S THIS MESS?
......
... A DAM?

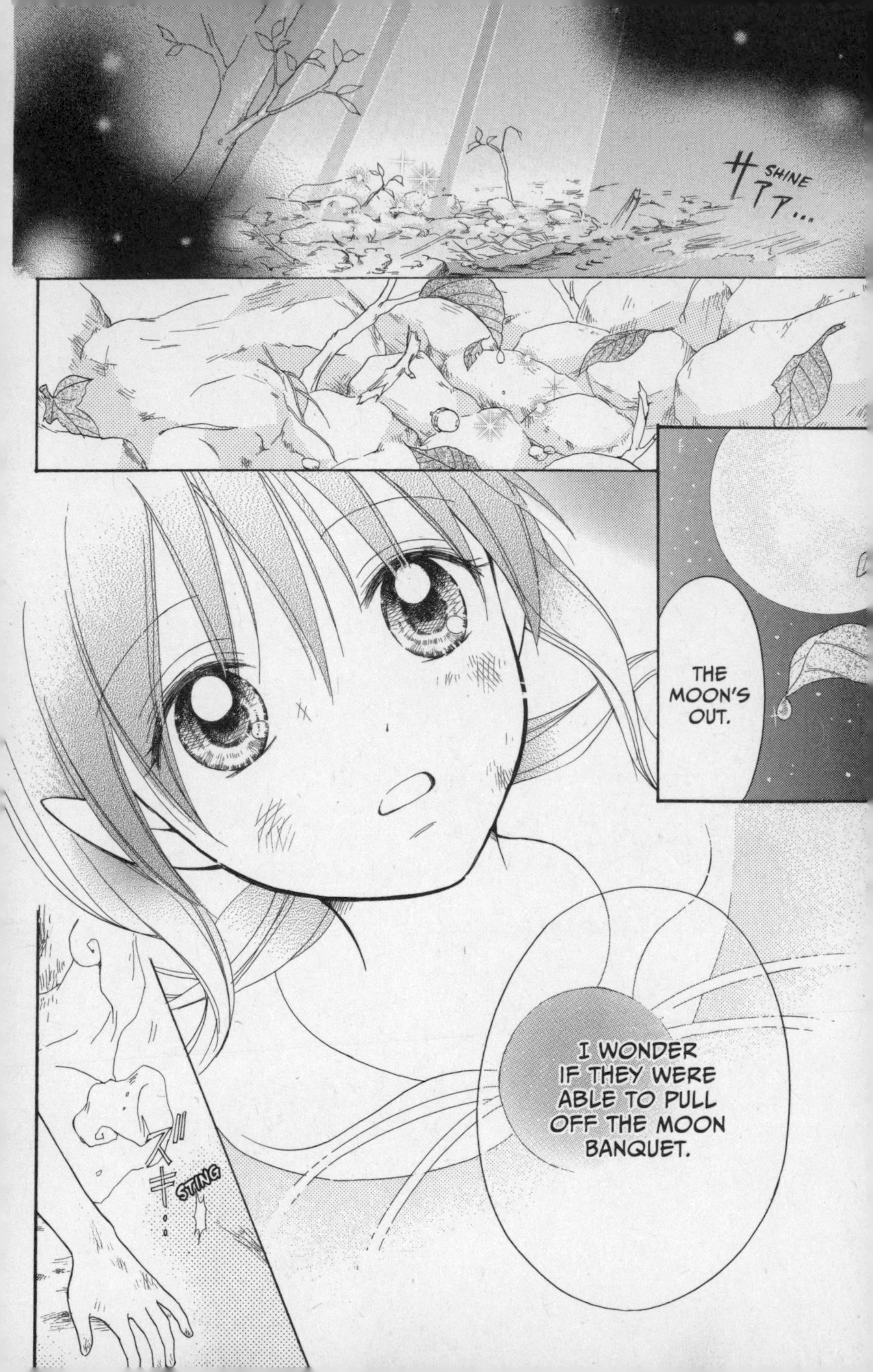

SHINE
サァア…
THE MOON'S OUT.
I WONDER IF THEY WERE ABLE TO PULL OFF THE MOON BANQUET.
ズキ
STING
…

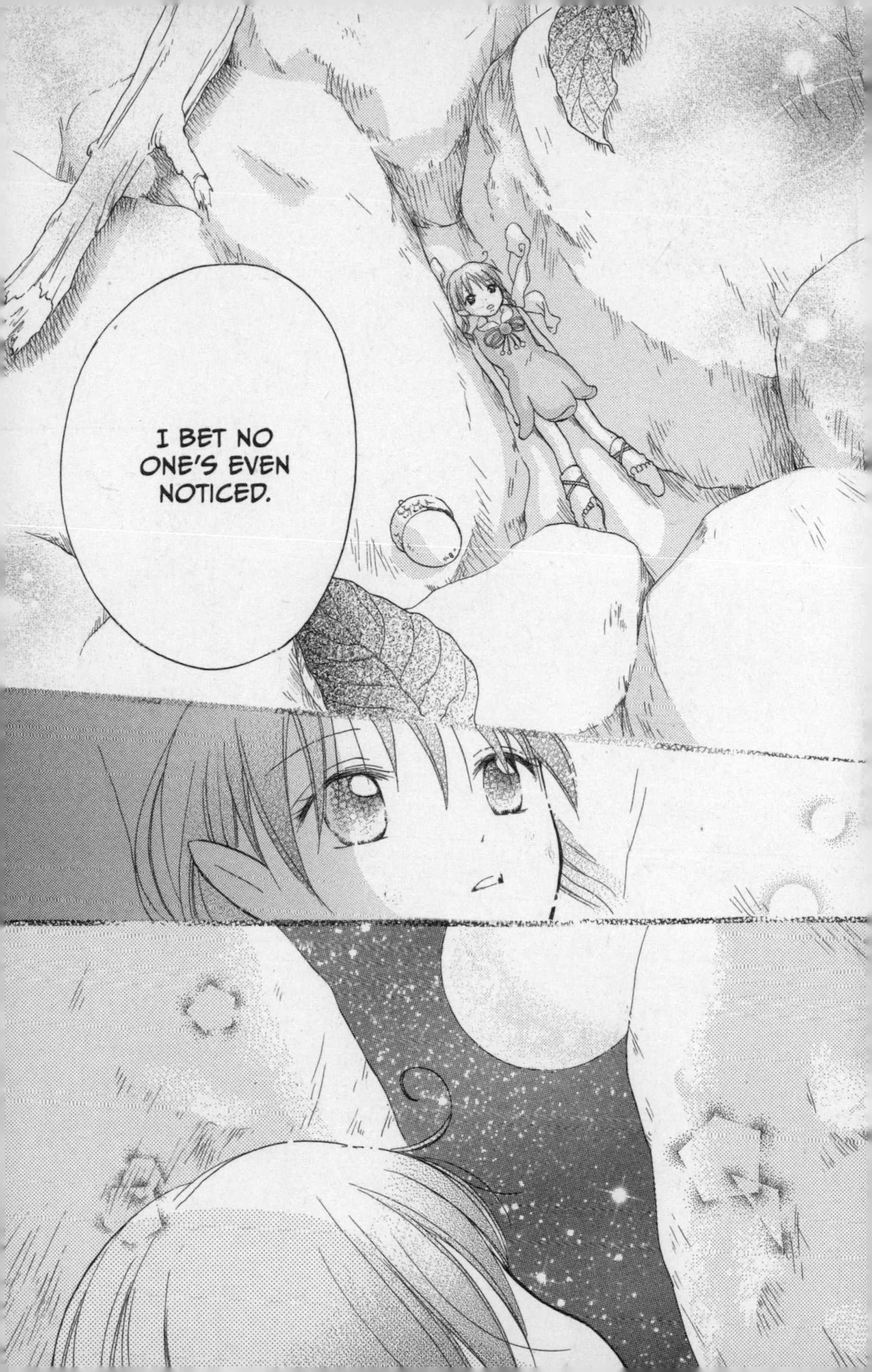
I BET NO ONE'S EVEN NOTICED.

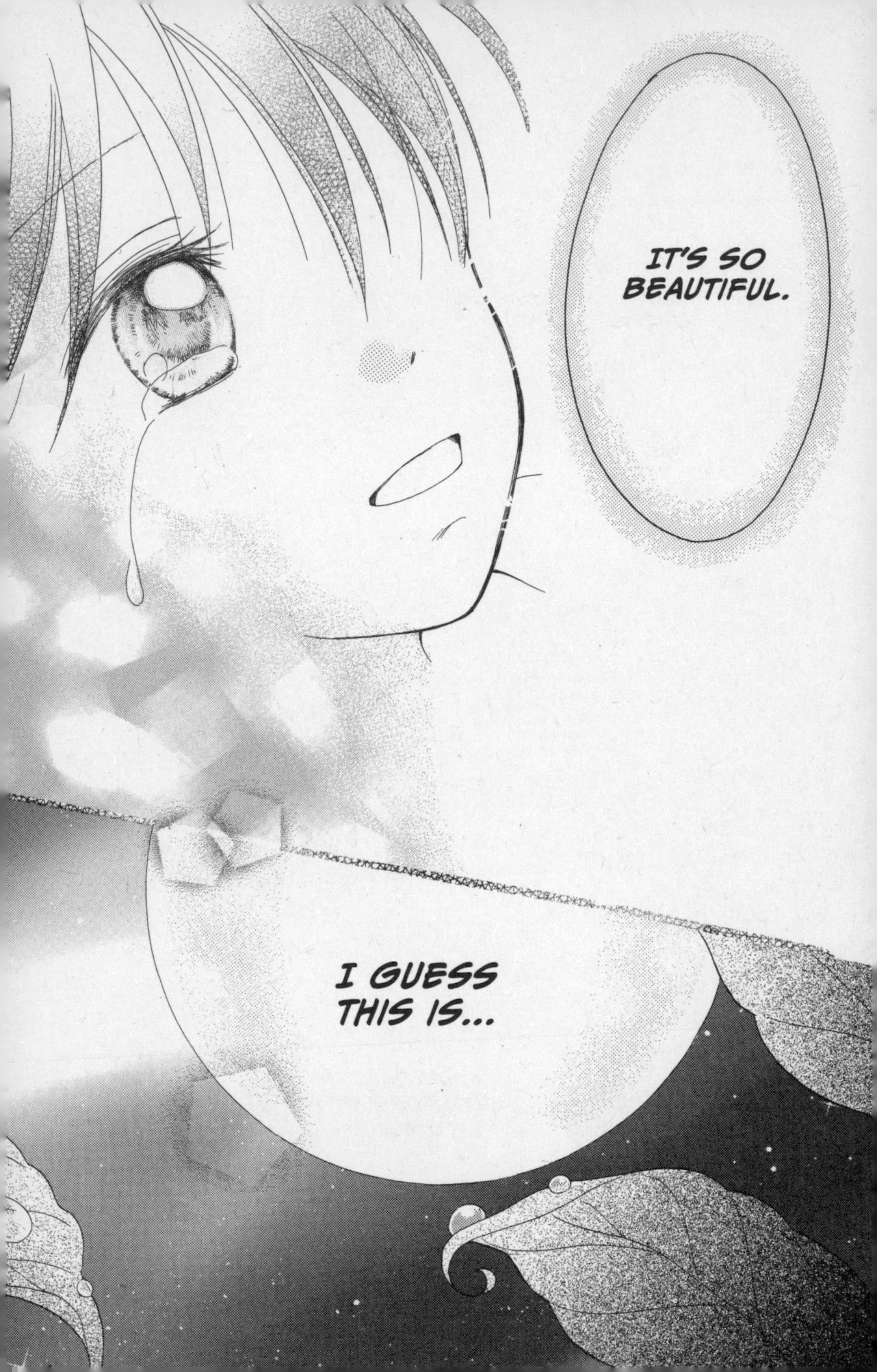
IT'S SO BEAUTIFUL.
I GUESS THIS IS...

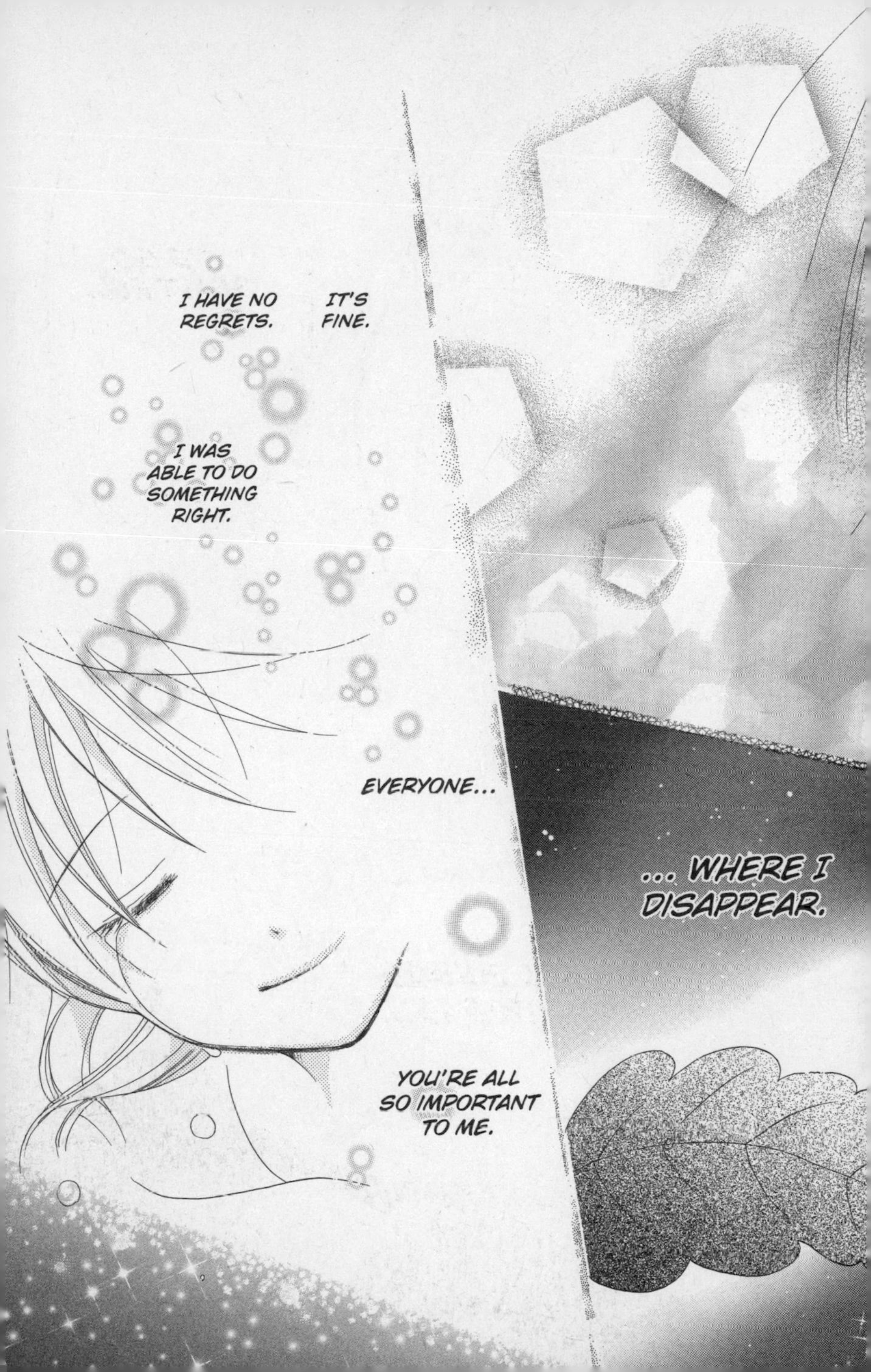
... WHERE I DISAPPEAR.
IT'S FINE.
I HAVE NO REGRETS.
I WAS ABLE TO DO SOMETHING RIGHT.
EVERYONE...
YOU'RE ALL SO IMPORTANT TO ME.

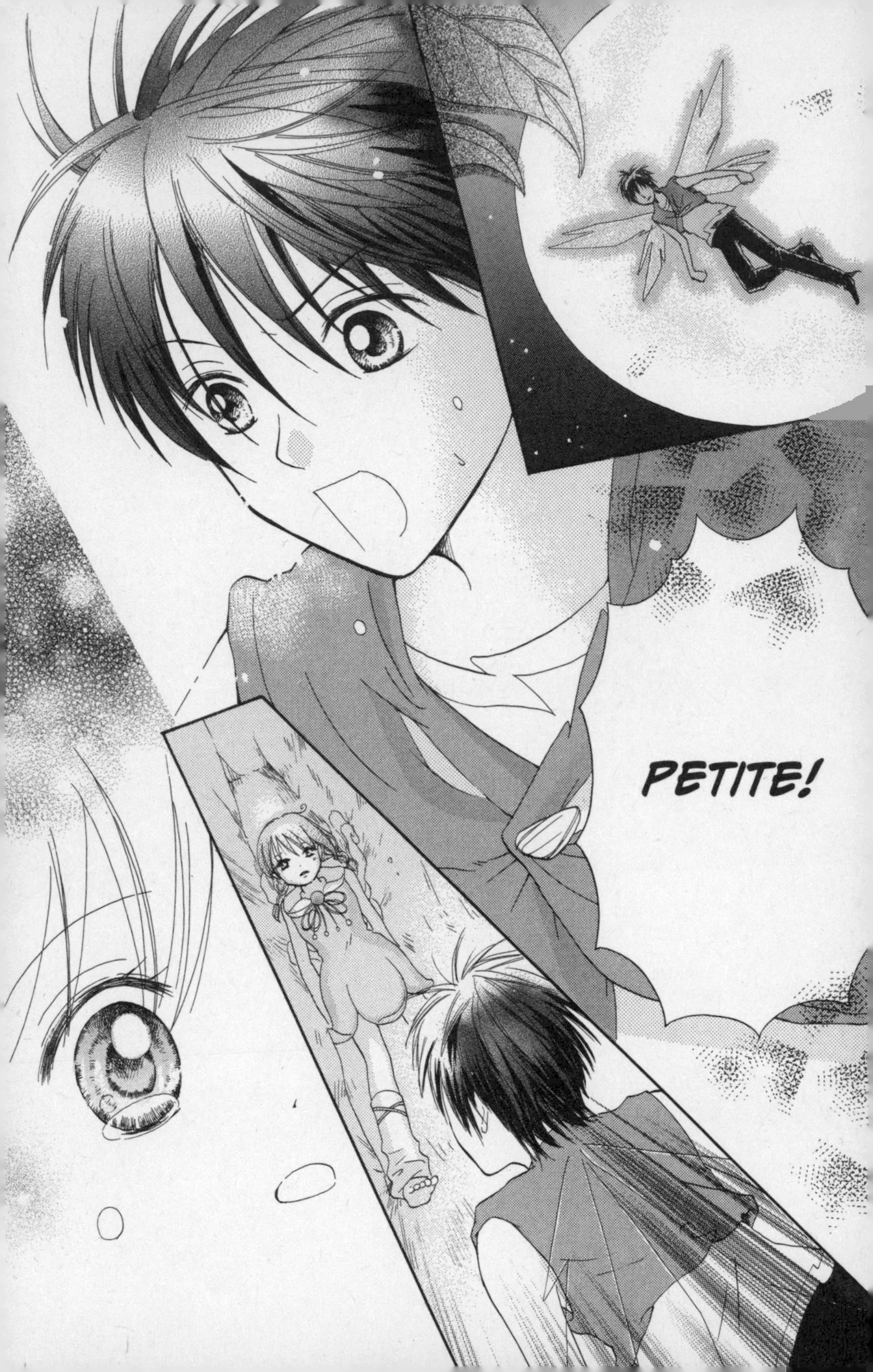
PETITE!

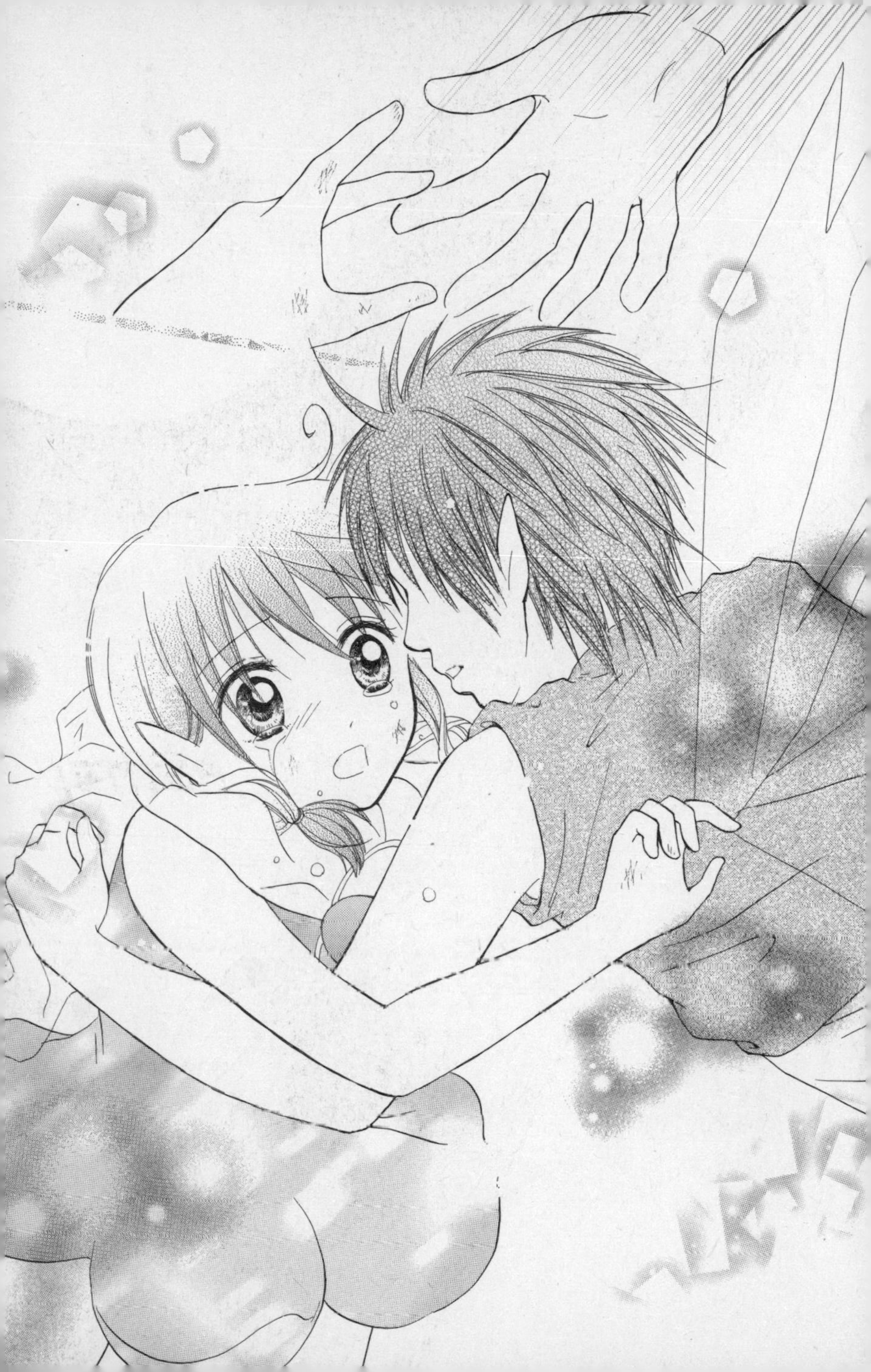

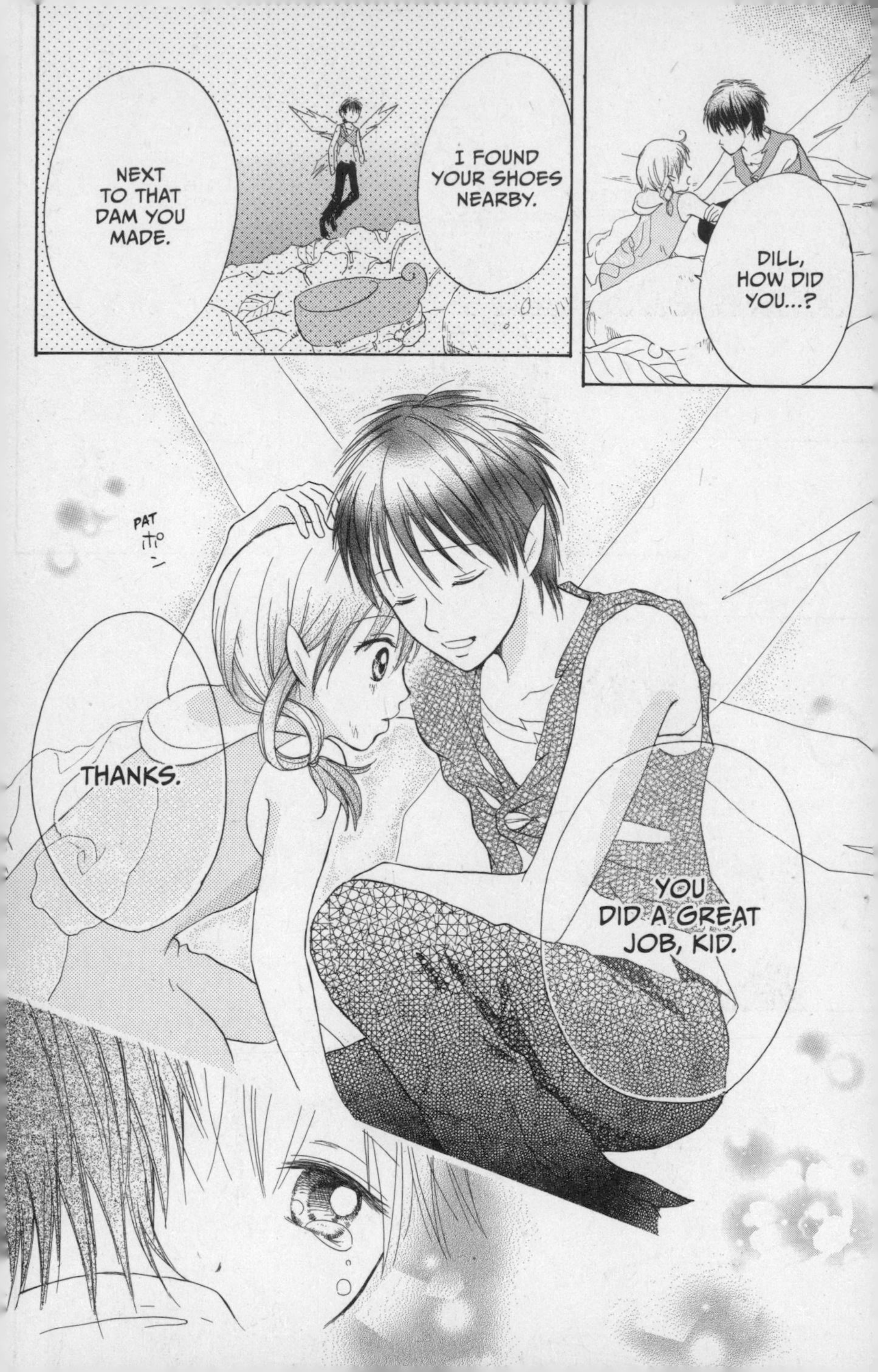
DILL, HOW DID YOU...?
I FOUND YOUR SHOES NEARBY.
NEXT TO THAT DAM YOU MADE.
PAT
YOU DID A GREAT JOB, KID.
THANKS.

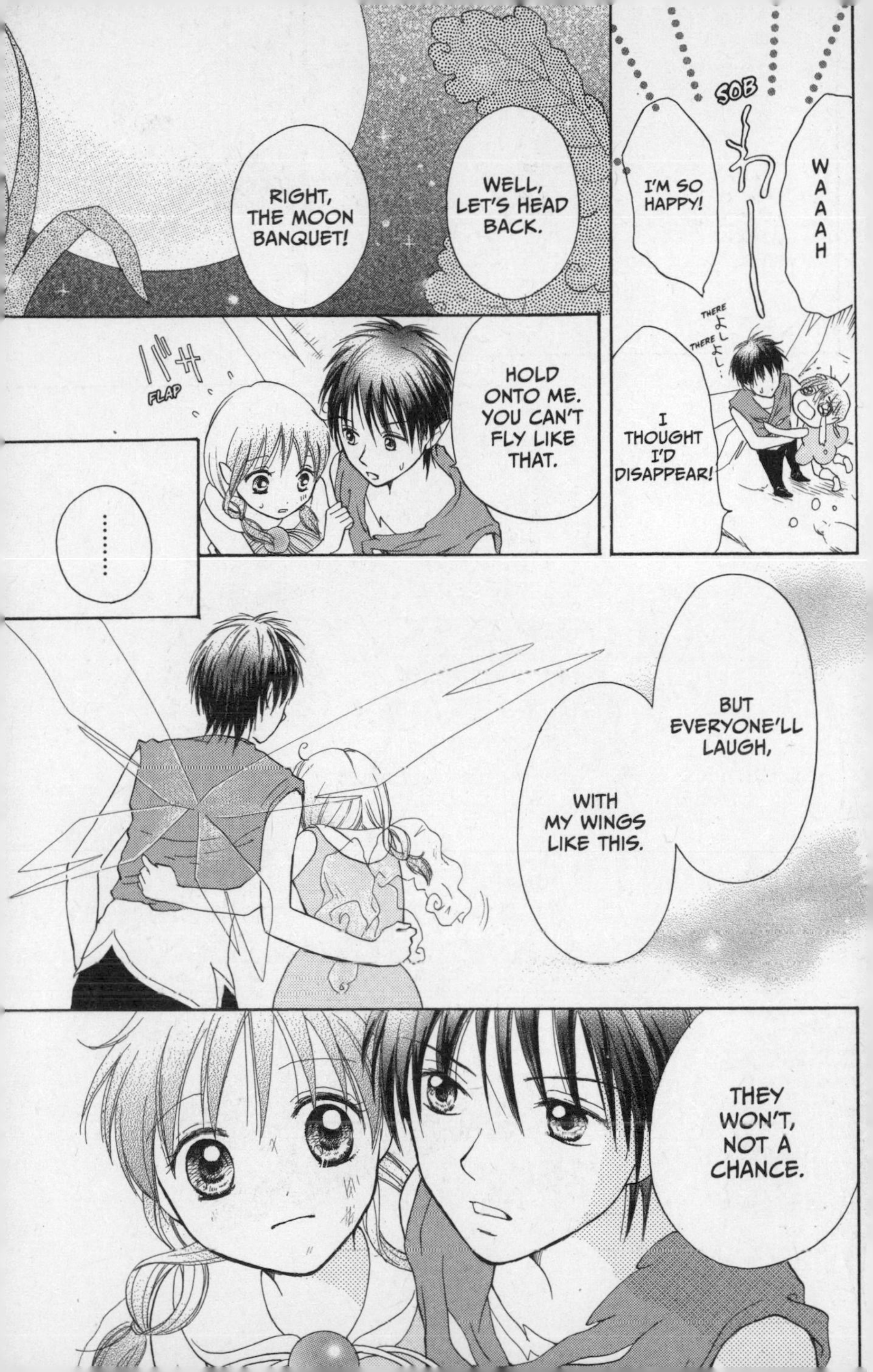
WAAAH
SOB
わー
I'M SO HAPPY!
THERE THERE
よしよし…
I THOUGHT I'D DISAPPEAR!
WELL, LET'S HEAD BACK.
RIGHT, THE MOON BANQUET!
HOLD ONTO ME. YOU CAN'T FLY LIKE THAT.
バサ
FLAP
……
BUT EVERYONE'LL LAUGH,
WITH MY WINGS LIKE THIS.
THEY WON'T, NOT A CHANCE.

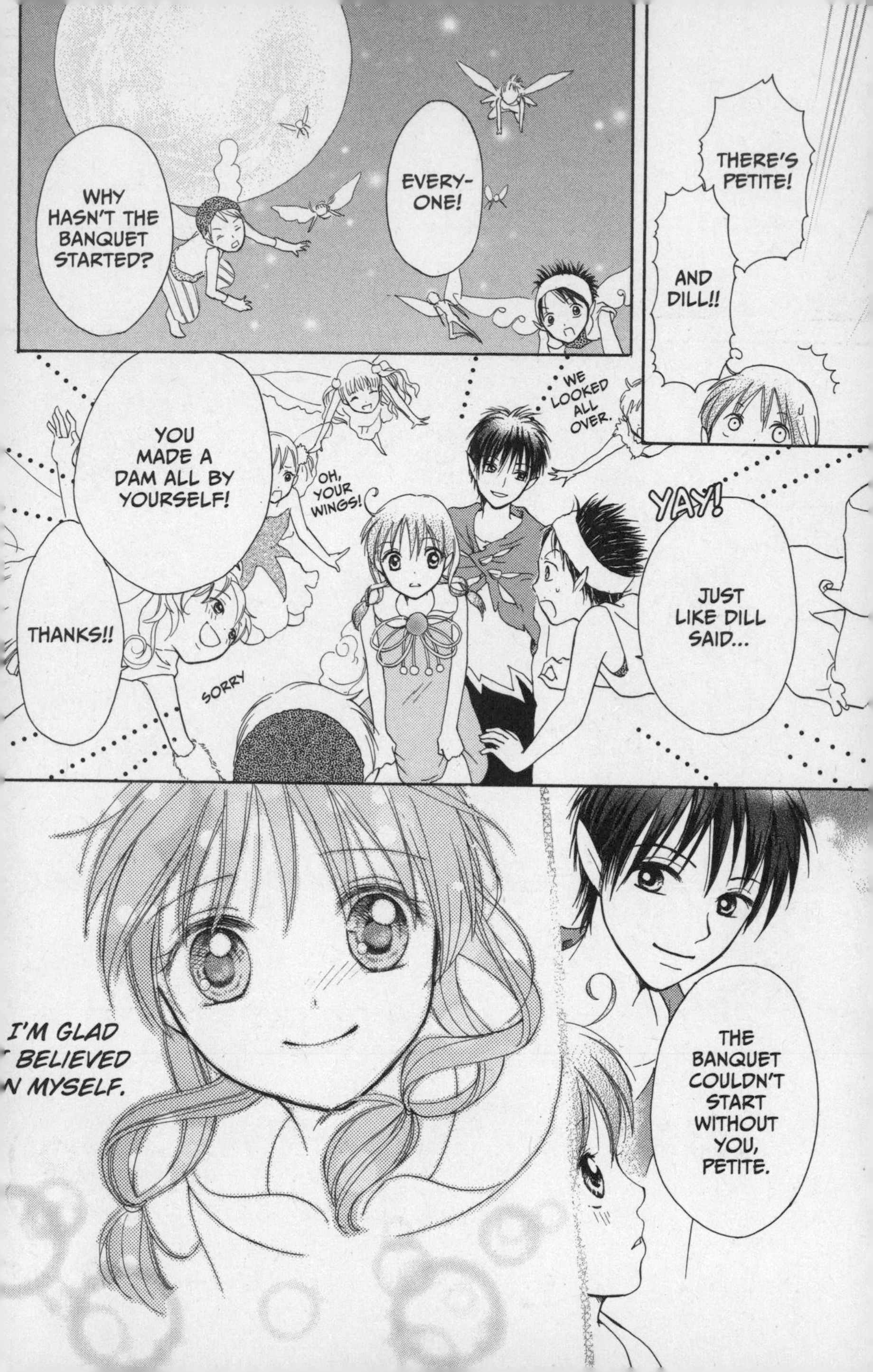
THERE'S PETITE!
AND DILL!!
EVERY-ONE!
WHY HASN'T THE BANQUET STARTED?
YAY!
JUST LIKE DILL SAID...
WE LOOKED ALL OVER.
OH, YOUR WINGS!
YOU MADE A DAM ALL BY YOURSELF!
THANKS!!
SORRY
THE BANQUET COULDN'T START WITHOUT YOU, PETITE.
I'M GLAD
BELIEVED
N MYSELF.

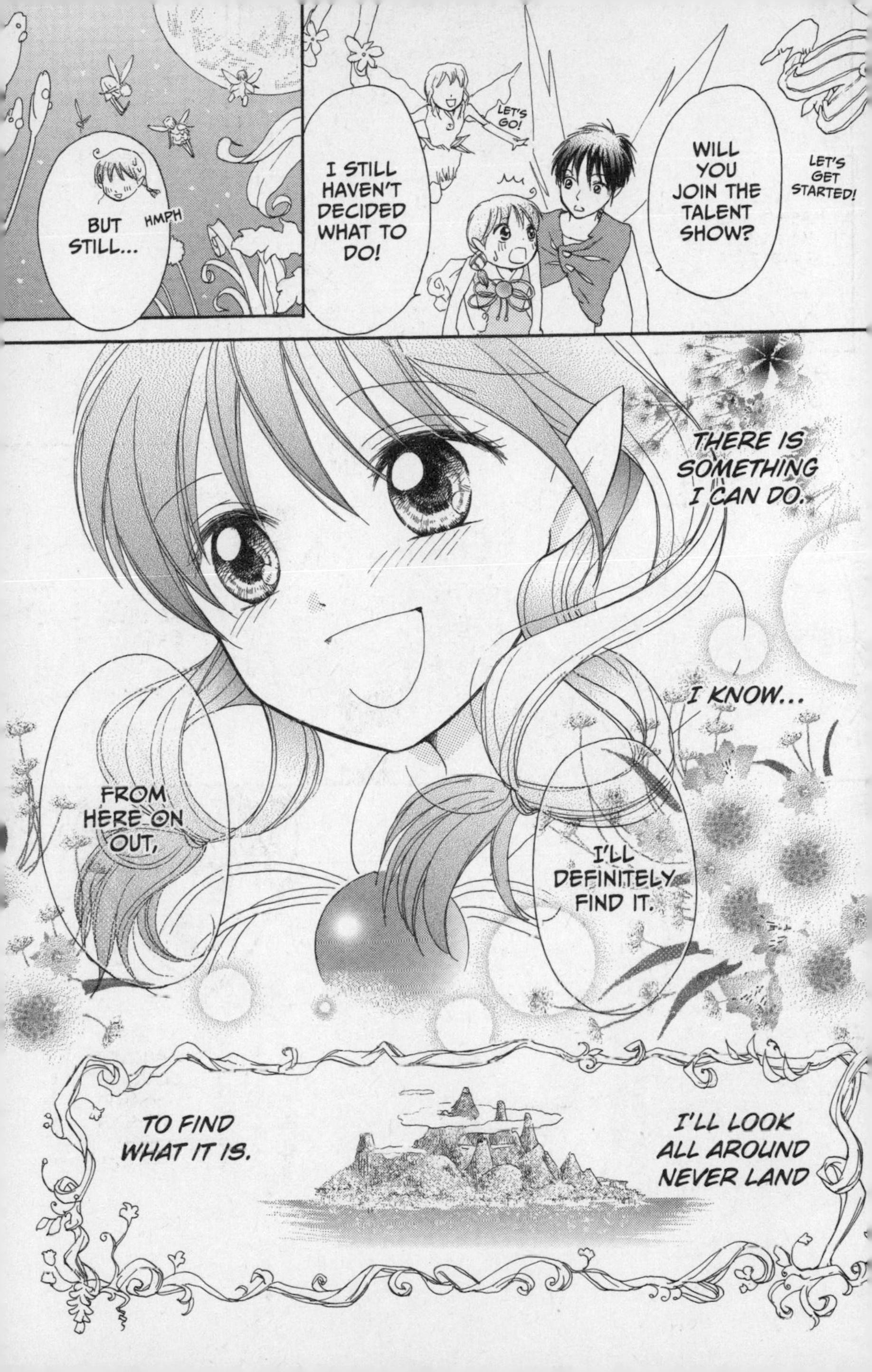
LET'S GET STARTED!
WILL YOU JOIN THE TALENT SHOW?
LET'S GO!
I STILL HAVEN'T DECIDED WHAT TO DO!
HMPH
BUT STILL...
THERE IS SOMETHING I CAN DO.
I KNOW...
I'LL DEFINITELY FIND IT.
FROM HERE ON OUT,
I'LL LOOK ALL AROUND NEVER LAND
TO FIND WHAT IT IS.

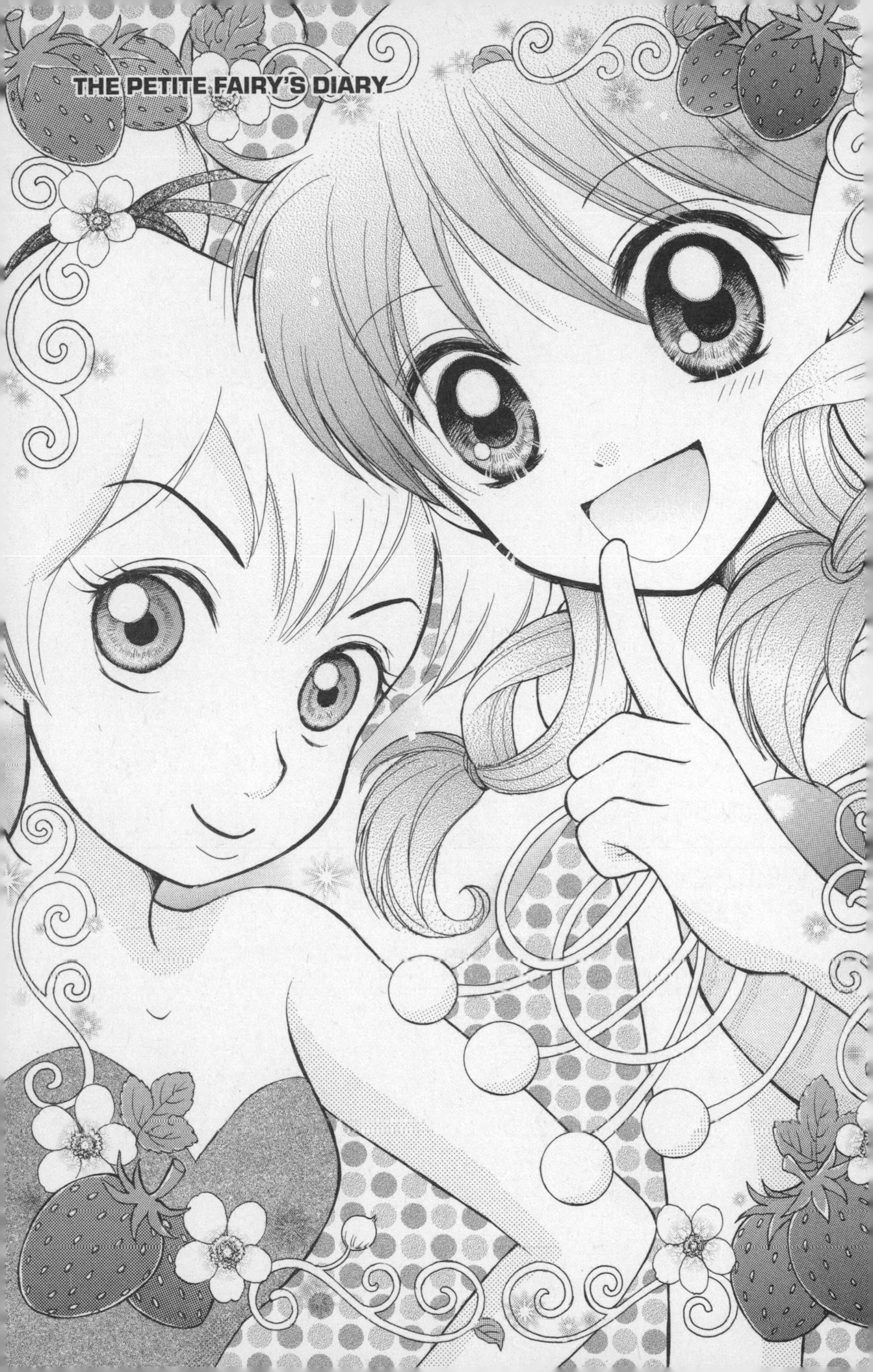
THE PETITE FAIRY'S DIARY

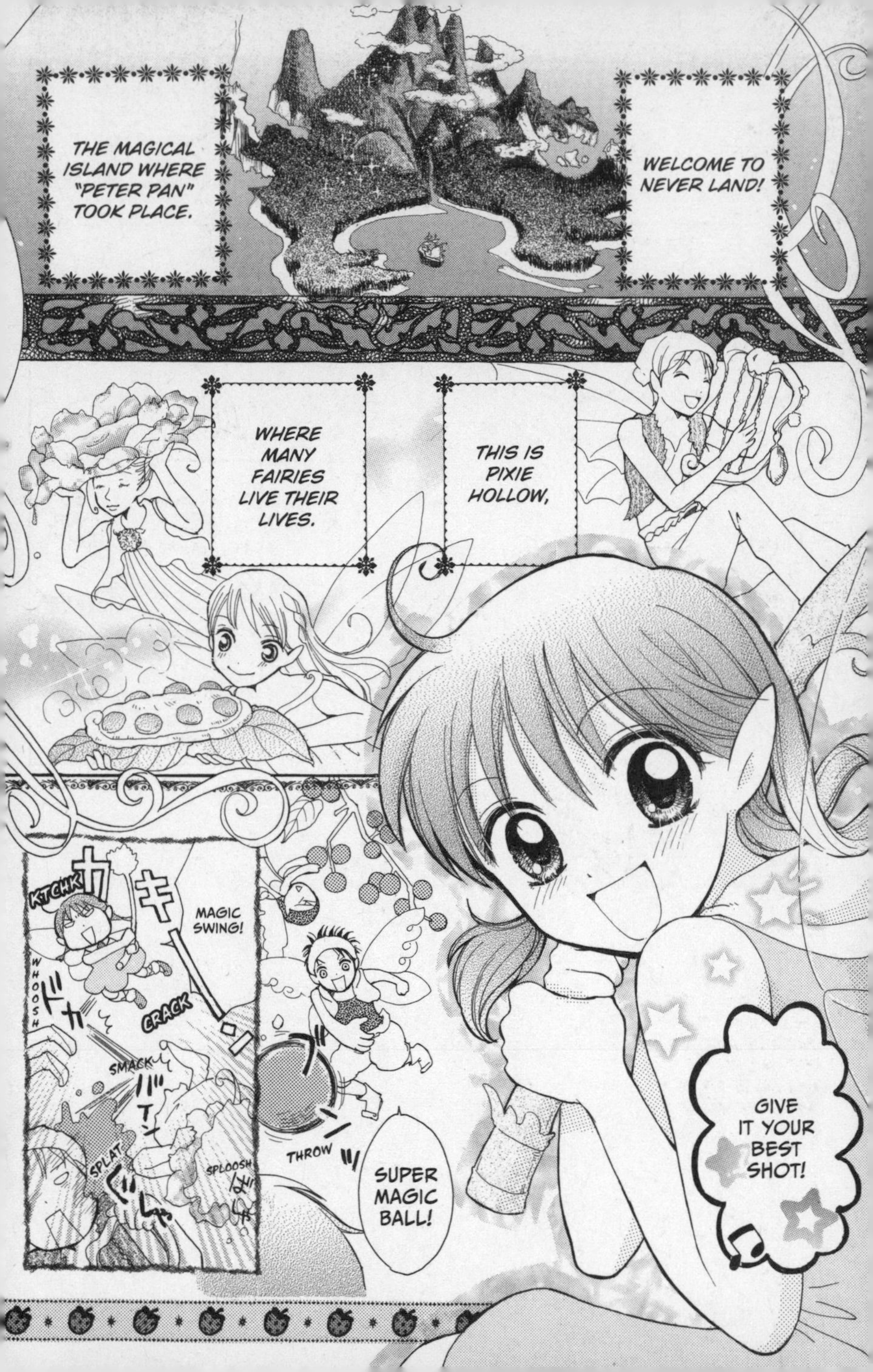
WELCOME TO NEVER LAND!
THE MAGICAL ISLAND WHERE "PETER PAN" TOOK PLACE.
THIS IS PIXIE HOLLOW,
WHERE MANY FAIRIES LIVE THEIR LIVES.
GIVE IT YOUR BEST SHOT!
SUPER MAGIC BALL!
THROW
MAGIC SWING!
KTCHK
WHOOSH
CRACK
SMACK
SPLAT
SPLOOSH

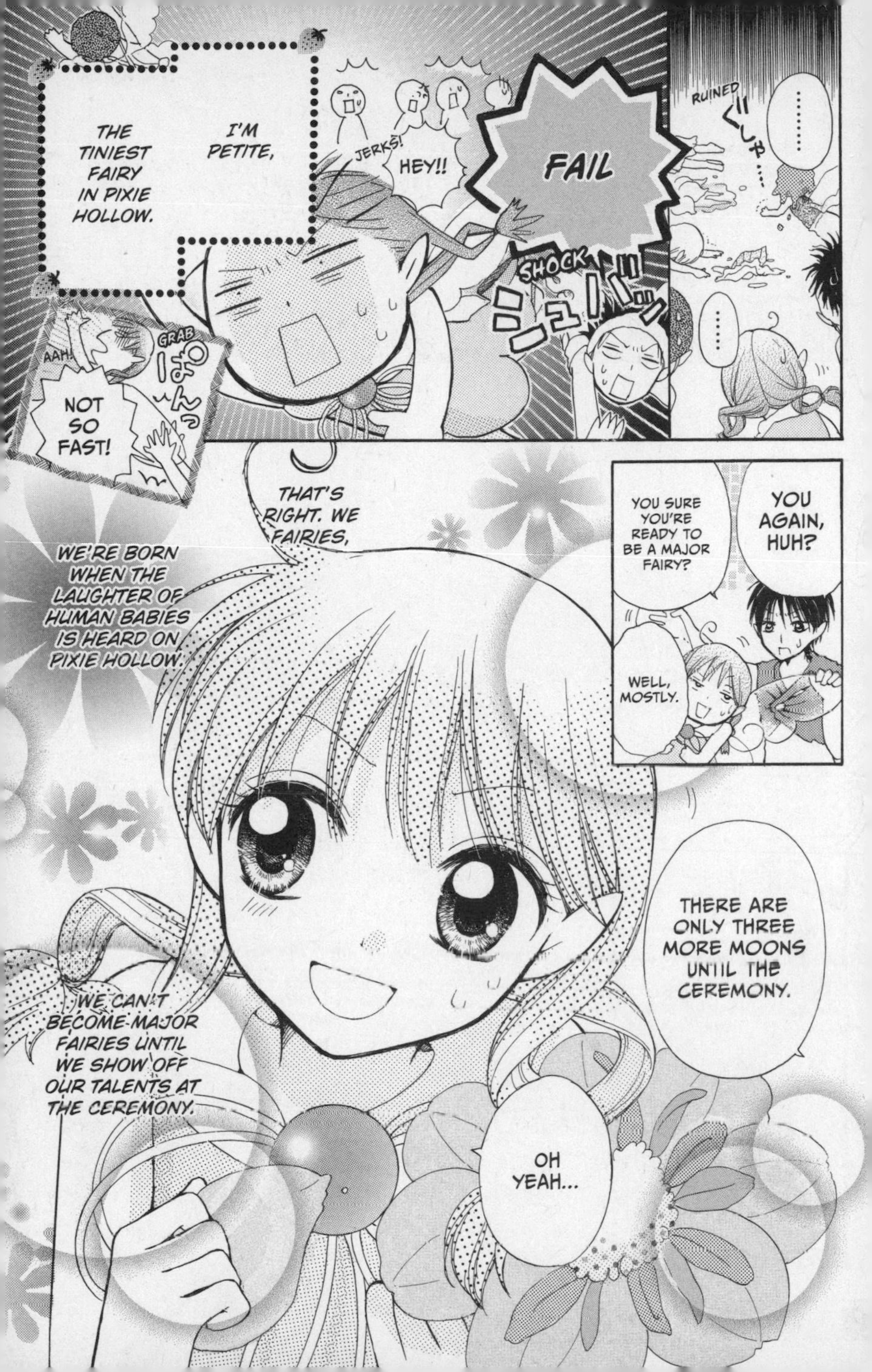

RUINED
......
......
FAIL
SHOCK
HEY!!
JERKS!
I'M PETITE,
THE TINIEST FAIRY IN PIXIE HOLLOW.
GRAB
AAH!
NOT SO FAST!
YOU AGAIN, HUH?
YOU SURE YOU'RE READY TO BE A MAJOR FAIRY?
WELL, MOSTLY.
THAT'S RIGHT. WE FAIRIES,
WE'RE BORN WHEN THE LAUGHTER OF HUMAN BABIES IS HEARD ON PIXIE HOLLOW.
THERE ARE ONLY THREE MORE MOONS UNTIL THE CEREMONY.
OH YEAH...
WE CAN'T BECOME MAJOR FAIRIES UNTIL WE SHOW OFF OUR TALENTS AT THE CEREMONY.

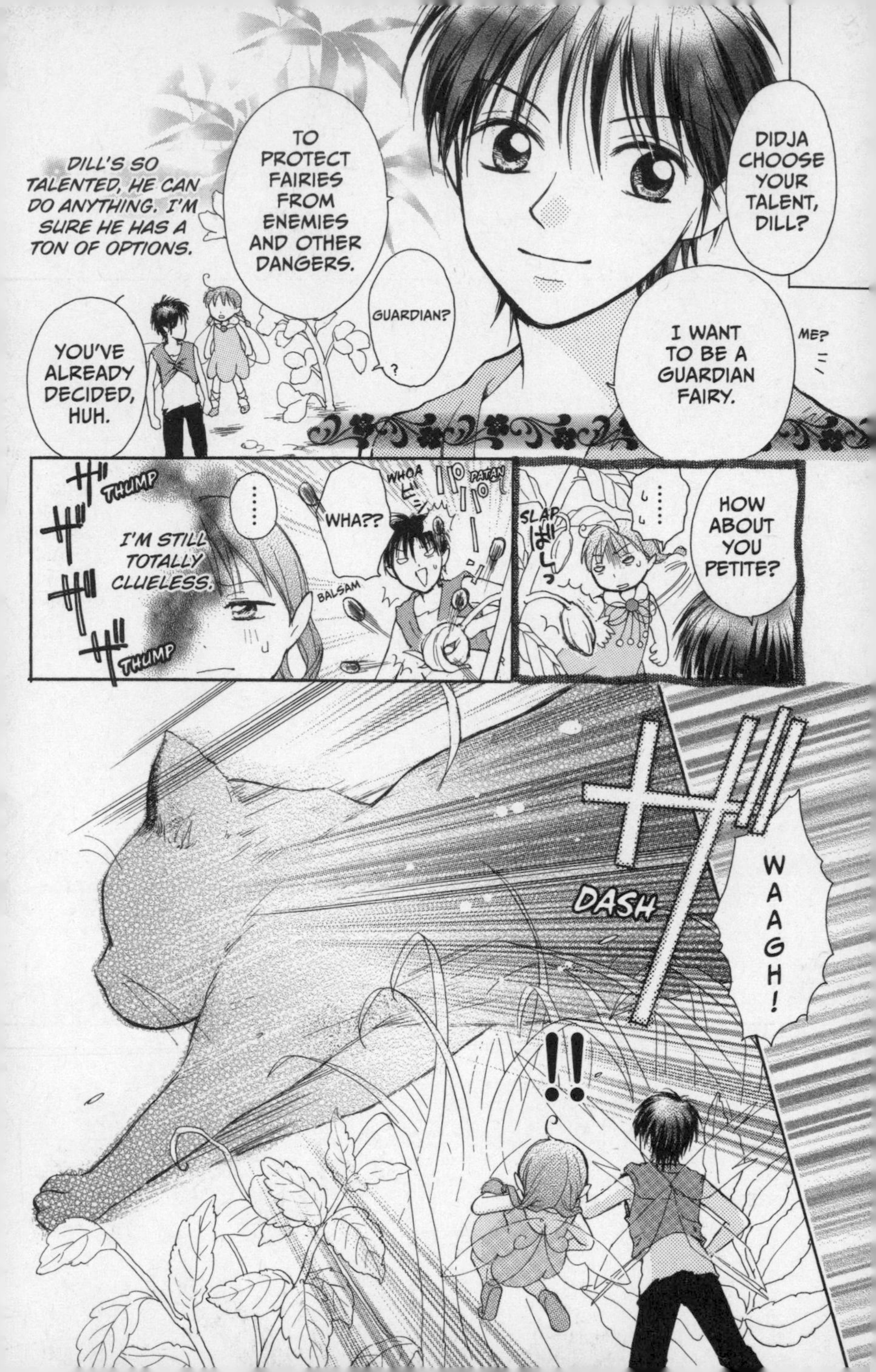
DIDJA CHOOSE YOUR TALENT, DILL?
ME?
I WANT TO BE A GUARDIAN FAIRY.
GUARDIAN?
?
TO PROTECT FAIRIES FROM ENEMIES AND OTHER DANGERS.
DILL'S SO TALENTED, HE CAN DO ANYTHING. I'M SURE HE HAS A TON OF OPTIONS.
YOU'VE ALREADY DECIDED, HUH.
HOW ABOUT YOU PETITE?
......
SLAP
PATAN
WHOA
WHA??
BALSAM
......
I'M STILL TOTALLY CLUELESS.
THUMP
THUMP
WAAGH!
DASH
!!

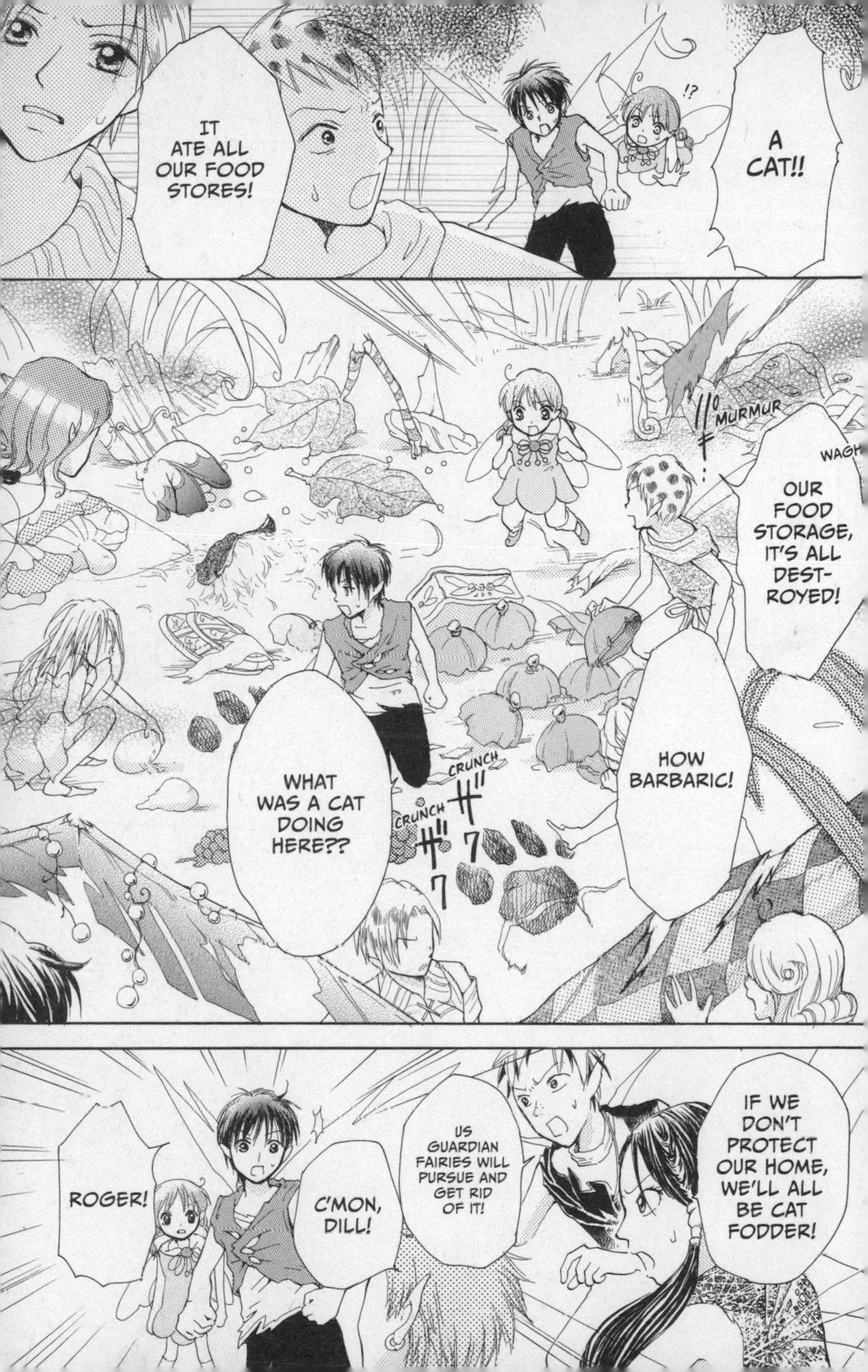
A CAT!!
!?
IT ATE ALL OUR FOOD STORES!
MURMUR
WAGH
OUR FOOD STORAGE, IT'S ALL DEST-ROYED!
HOW BARBARIC!
CRUNCH
CRUNCH
WHAT WAS A CAT DOING HERE??
IF WE DON'T PROTECT OUR HOME, WE'LL ALL BE CAT FODDER!
US GUARDIAN FAIRIES WILL PURSUE AND GET RID OF IT!
C'MON, DILL!
ROGER!

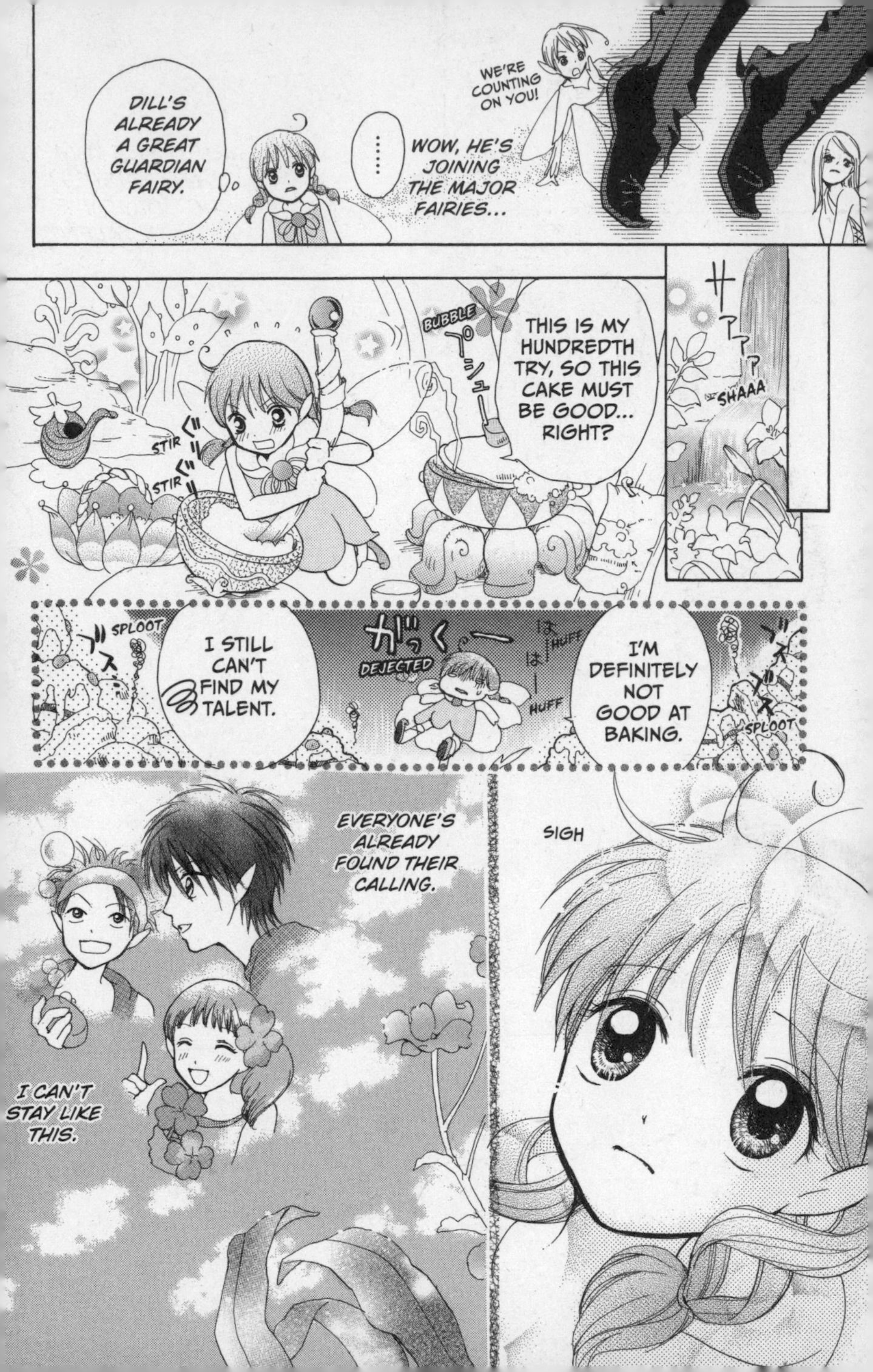
WE'RE COUNTING ON YOU!
WOW, HE'S JOINING THE MAJOR FAIRIES...
......
DILL'S ALREADY A GREAT GUARDIAN FAIRY.
SHAAA
THIS IS MY HUNDREDTH TRY, SO THIS CAKE MUST BE GOOD... RIGHT?
BUBBLE
STIR
STIR
SPLOOT
I'M DEFINITELY NOT GOOD AT BAKING.
HUFF
HUFF
DEJECTED
I STILL CAN'T FIND MY TALENT.
SPLOOT
SIGH
EVERYONE'S ALREADY FOUND THEIR CALLING.
I CAN'T STAY LIKE THIS.

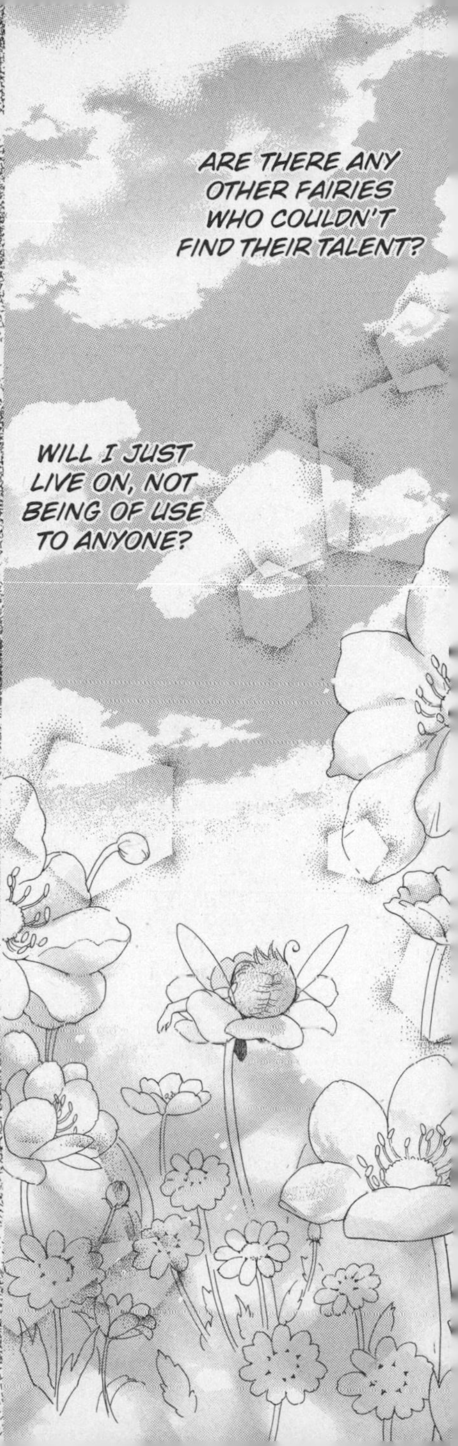
ARE THERE ANY OTHER FAIRIES WHO COULDN'T FIND THEIR TALENT?
WILL I JUST LIVE ON, NOT BEING OF USE TO ANYONE?

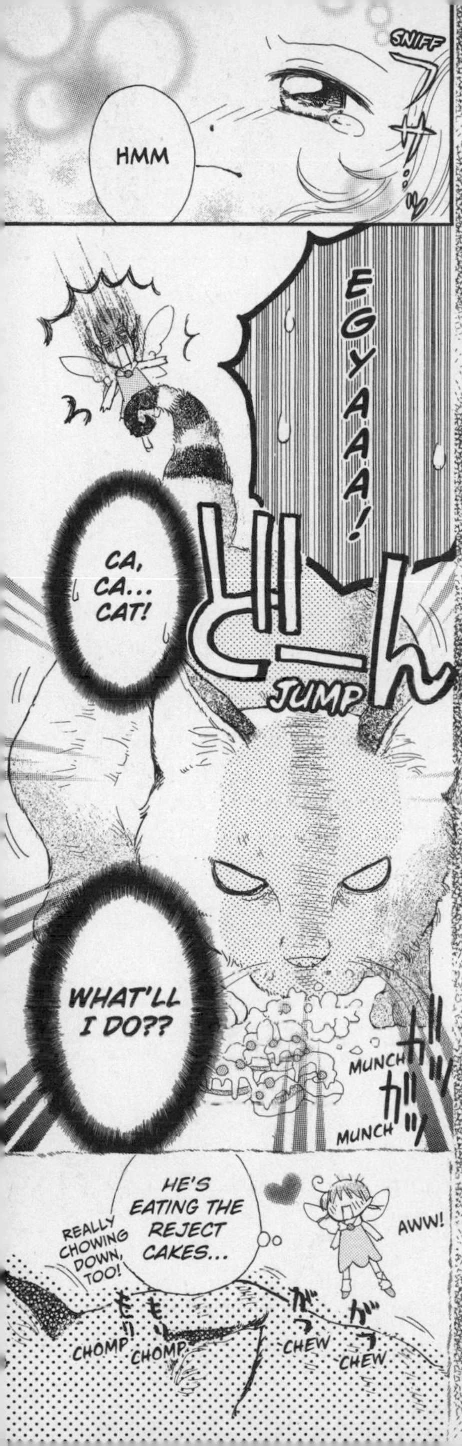
SNIFF
HMM
EGYAAAA!
CA, CA... CAT!
どーん
JUMP
WHAT'LL I DO??
MUNCH
MUNCH
AWW!
HE'S EATING THE REJECT CAKES...
REALLY CHOWING DOWN, TOO!
CHEW
CHEW
CHOMP
CHOMP

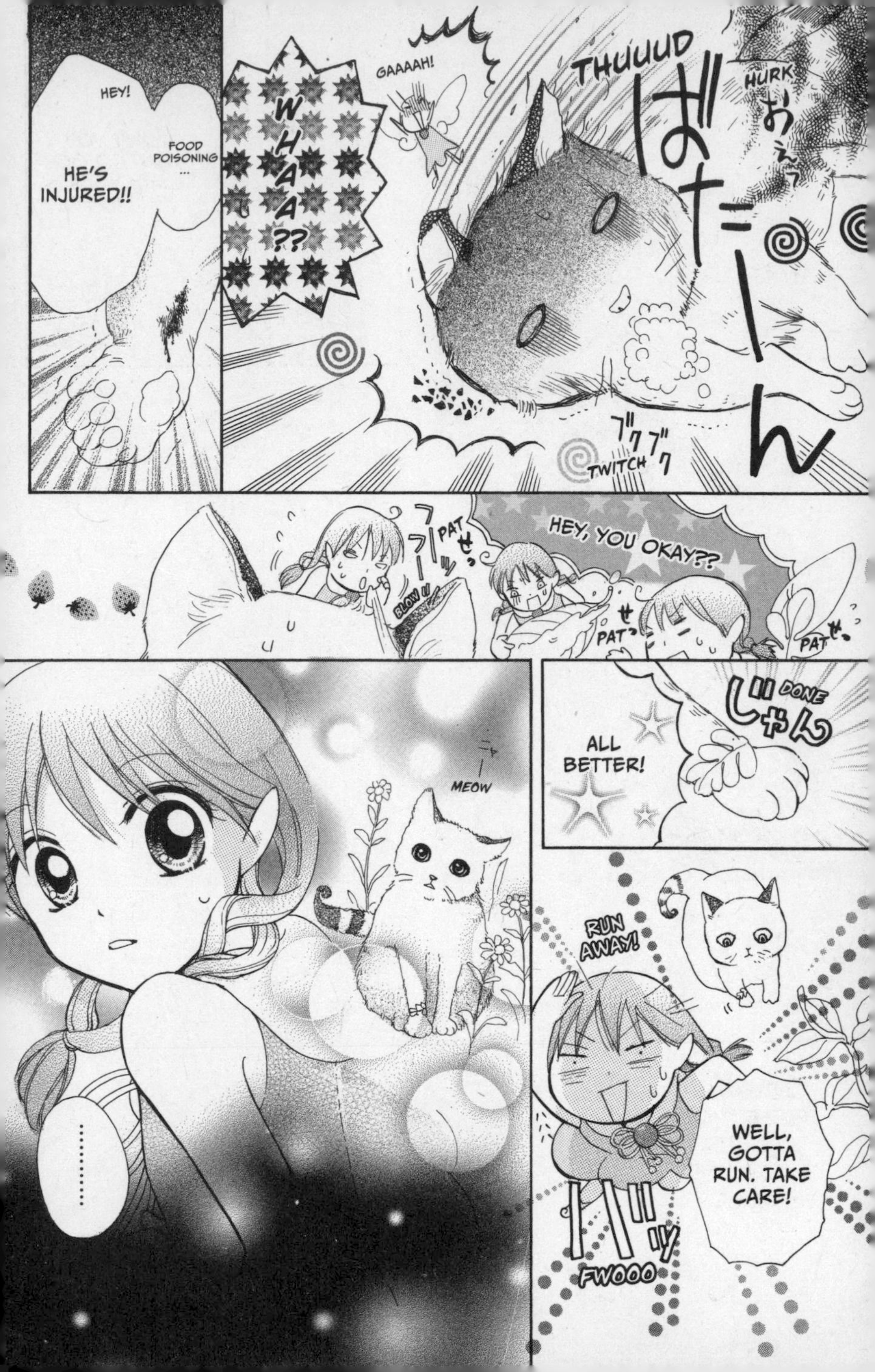
HURK
おぇっ
THUUUD
ばたーん
GAAAAH!
WHAA??
TWITCH
ブクブク
HEY!
FOOD POISONING ...
HE'S INJURED!!
HEY, YOU OKAY??
PAT
せっ
PAT
せっ
PAT
せっ
フーッ
BLOW!!
じゃん
DONE
ALL BETTER!
RUN AWAY!
WELL, GOTTA RUN. TAKE CARE!
バッ
FWOOO
ニャー
MEOW
....

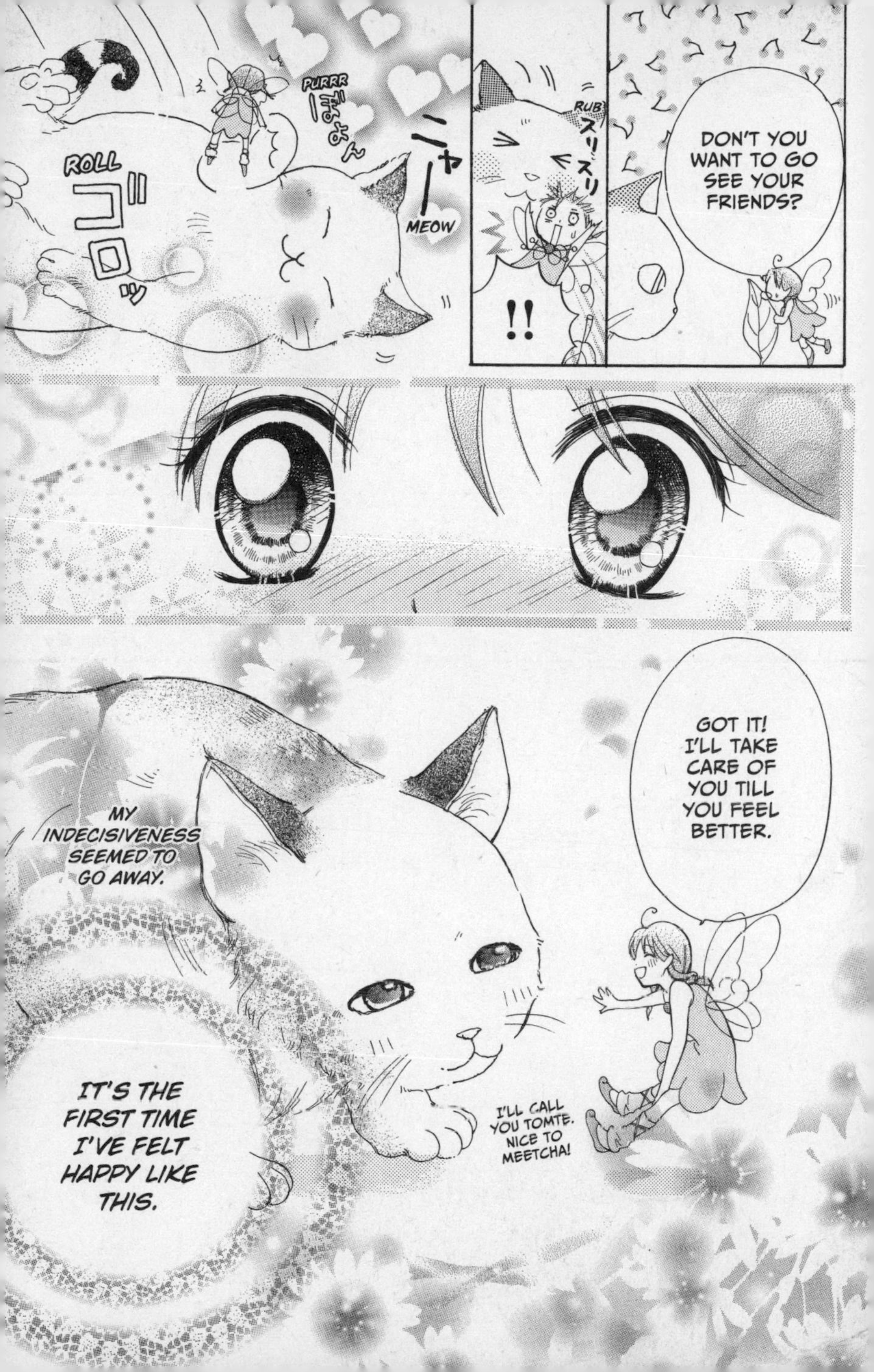
DON'T YOU WANT TO GO SEE YOUR FRIENDS?
RUB スリ スリ
!!
ニャー
MEOW
PURRR ぽよん
ROLL ゴロッ
GOT IT! I'LL TAKE CARE OF YOU TILL YOU FEEL BETTER.
I'LL CALL YOU TOMTE. NICE TO MEETCHA!
MY INDECISIVENESS SEEMED TO GO AWAY.
IT'S THE FIRST TIME I'VE FELT HAPPY LIKE THIS.

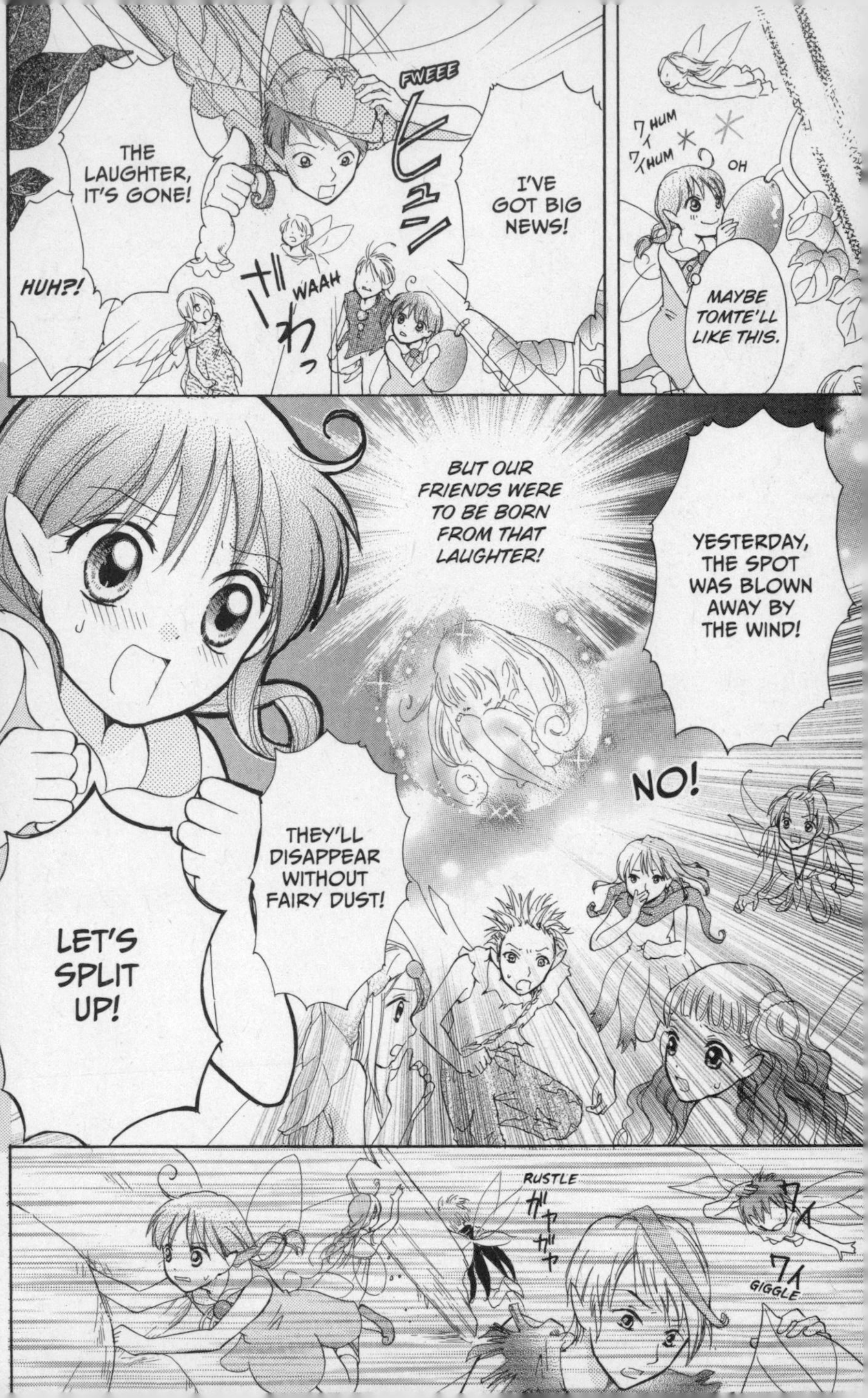
HUM HUM
OH
MAYBE TOMTE'LL LIKE THIS.
FWEEE
I'VE GOT BIG NEWS!
THE LAUGHTER, IT'S GONE!
HUH?!
WAAH
YESTERDAY, THE SPOT WAS BLOWN AWAY BY THE WIND!
BUT OUR FRIENDS WERE TO BE BORN FROM THAT LAUGHTER!
NO!
THEY'LL DISAPPEAR WITHOUT FAIRY DUST!
LET'S SPLIT UP!
GIGGLE
RUSTLE

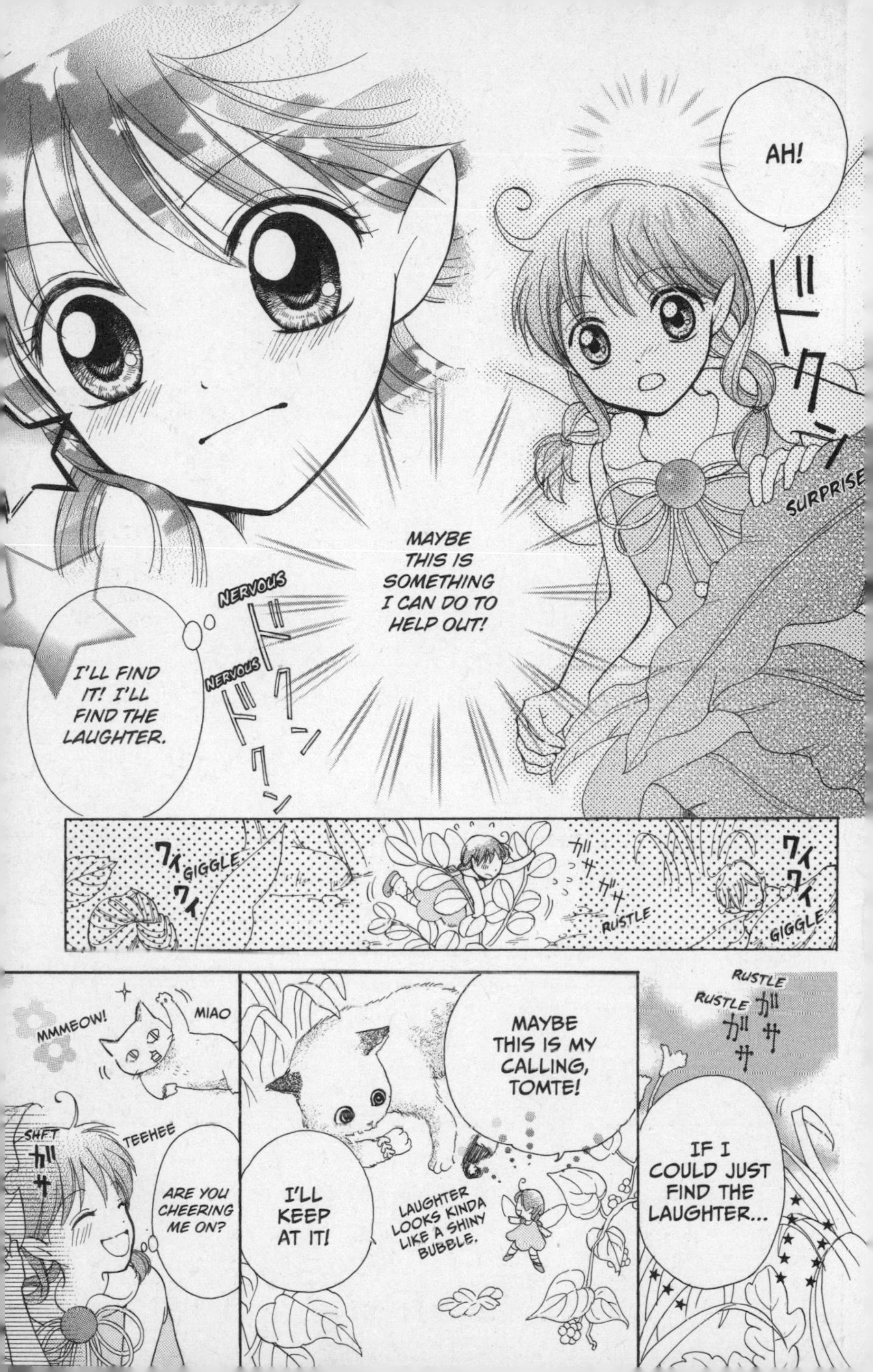
AH!
SURPRISE
MAYBE THIS IS SOMETHING I CAN DO TO HELP OUT!
NERVOUS
NERVOUS
I'LL FIND IT! I'LL FIND THE LAUGHTER.
GIGGLE
RUSTLE
GIGGLE
RUSTLE
RUSTLE
IF I COULD JUST FIND THE LAUGHTER...
MAYBE THIS IS MY CALLING, TOMTE!
LAUGHTER LOOKS KINDA LIKE A SHINY BUBBLE.
I'LL KEEP AT IT!
MIAO
MMMEOW!
TEEHEE
SHFT
ARE YOU CHEERING ME ON?

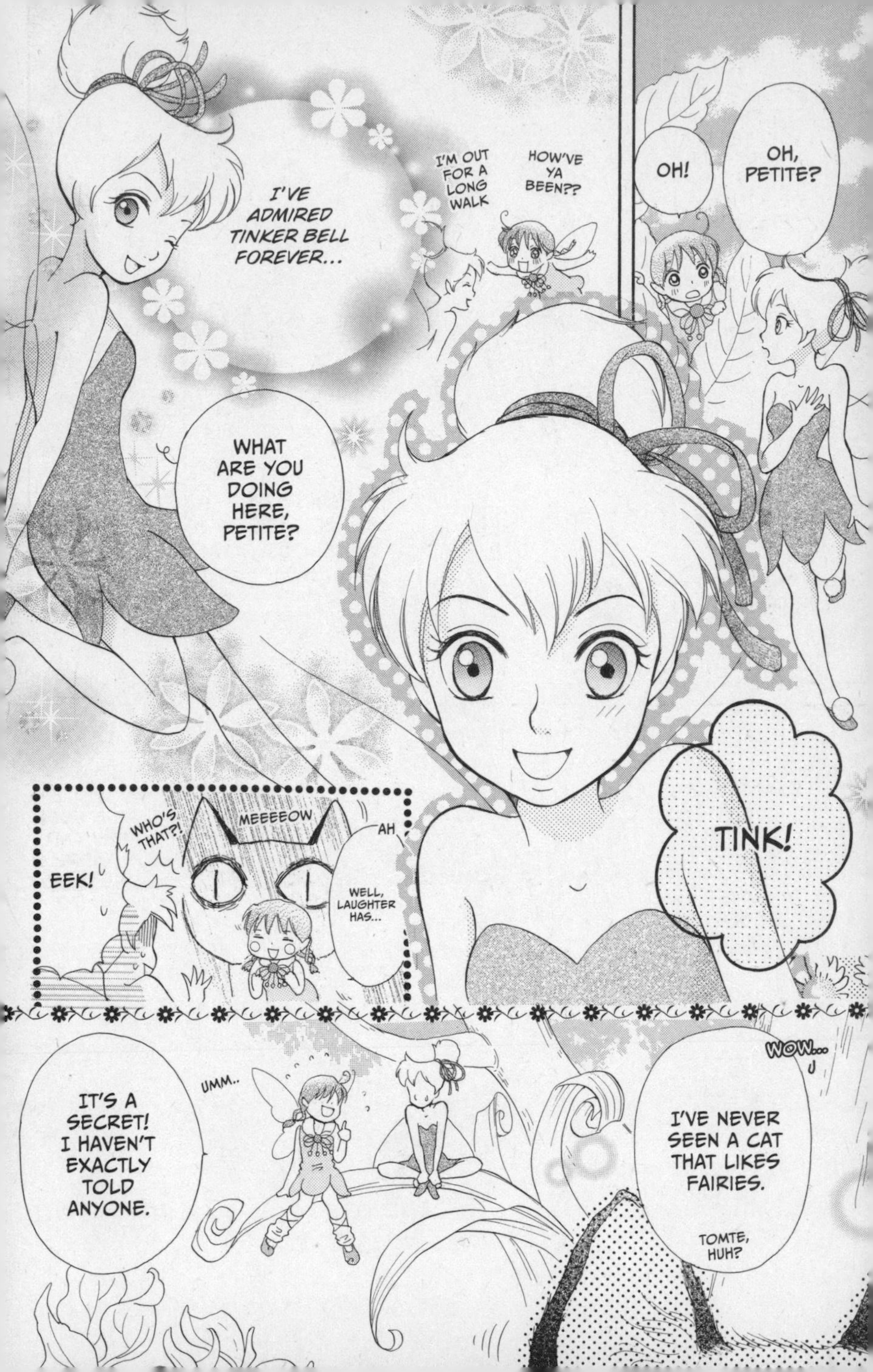
OH, PETITE?
OH!
TINK!
WHAT ARE YOU DOING HERE, PETITE?
HOW'VE YA BEEN??
I'M OUT FOR A LONG WALK
I'VE ADMIRED TINKER BELL FOREVER...
AH
WELL, LAUGHTER HAS...
MEEEEOW
WHO'S THAT?!
EEK!
WOW...
I'VE NEVER SEEN A CAT THAT LIKES FAIRIES.
TOMTE, HUH?
UMM..
IT'S A SECRET! I HAVEN'T EXACTLY TOLD ANYONE.

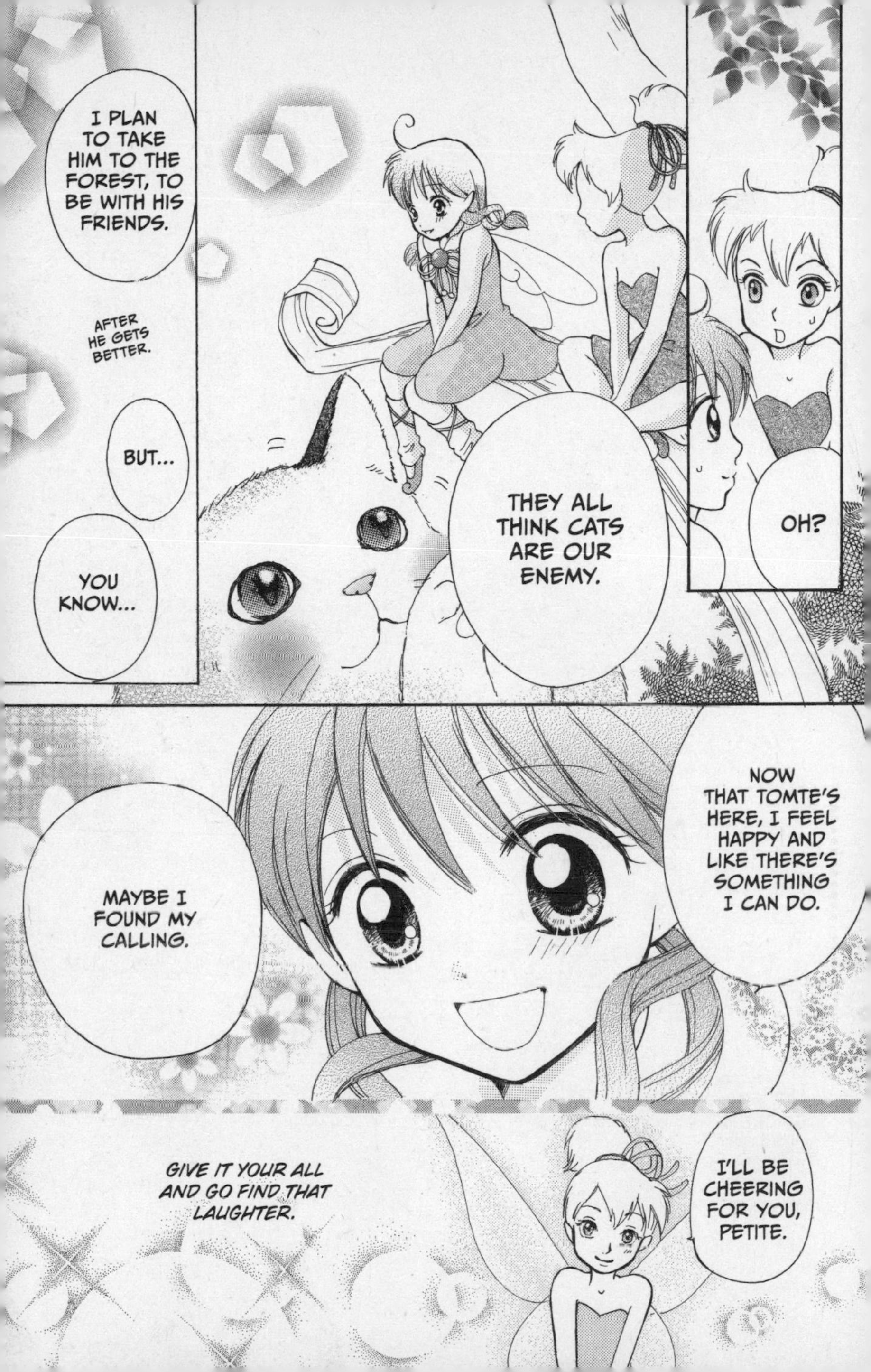
OH?
I PLAN TO TAKE HIM TO THE FOREST, TO BE WITH HIS FRIENDS.
AFTER HE GETS BETTER.
BUT...
YOU KNOW...
THEY ALL THINK CATS ARE OUR ENEMY.
NOW THAT TOMTE'S HERE, I FEEL HAPPY AND LIKE THERE'S SOMETHING I CAN DO.
MAYBE I FOUND MY CALLING.
I'LL BE CHEERING FOR YOU, PETITE.
GIVE IT YOUR ALL AND GO FIND THAT LAUGHTER.

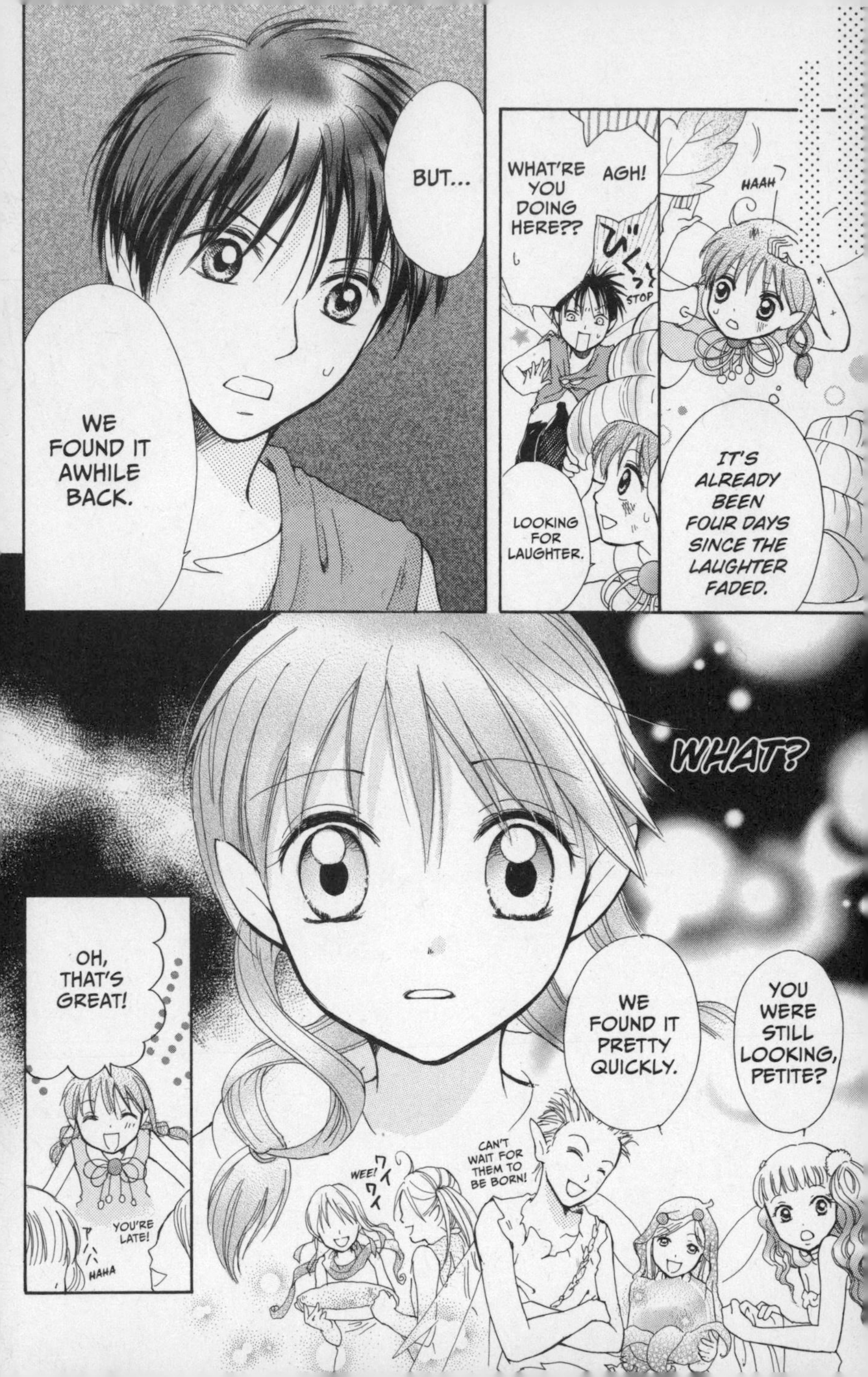
HAAH
IT'S ALREADY BEEN FOUR DAYS SINCE THE LAUGHTER FADED.
AGH!
WHAT'RE YOU DOING HERE??
STOP
LOOKING FOR LAUGHTER.
BUT...
WE FOUND IT AWHILE BACK.
WHAT?
YOU WERE STILL LOOKING, PETITE?
WE FOUND IT PRETTY QUICKLY.
CAN'T WAIT FOR THEM TO BE BORN!
WEE!
OH, THAT'S GREAT!
YOU'RE LATE!
HAHA

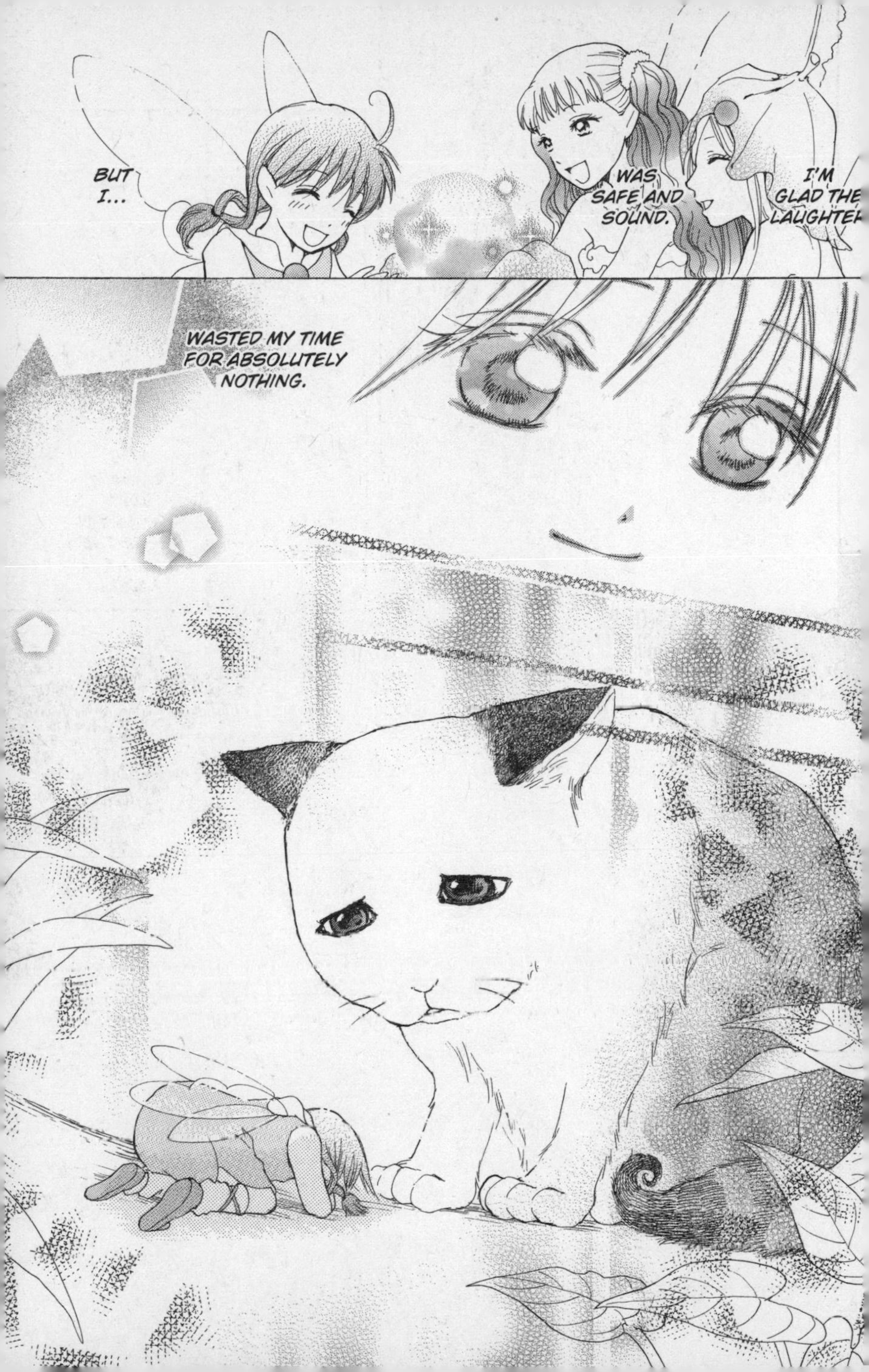
I'M GLAD THE LAUGHTE
WAS SAFE AND SOUND.
BUT I...
WASTED MY TIME FOR ABSOLUTELY NOTHING.

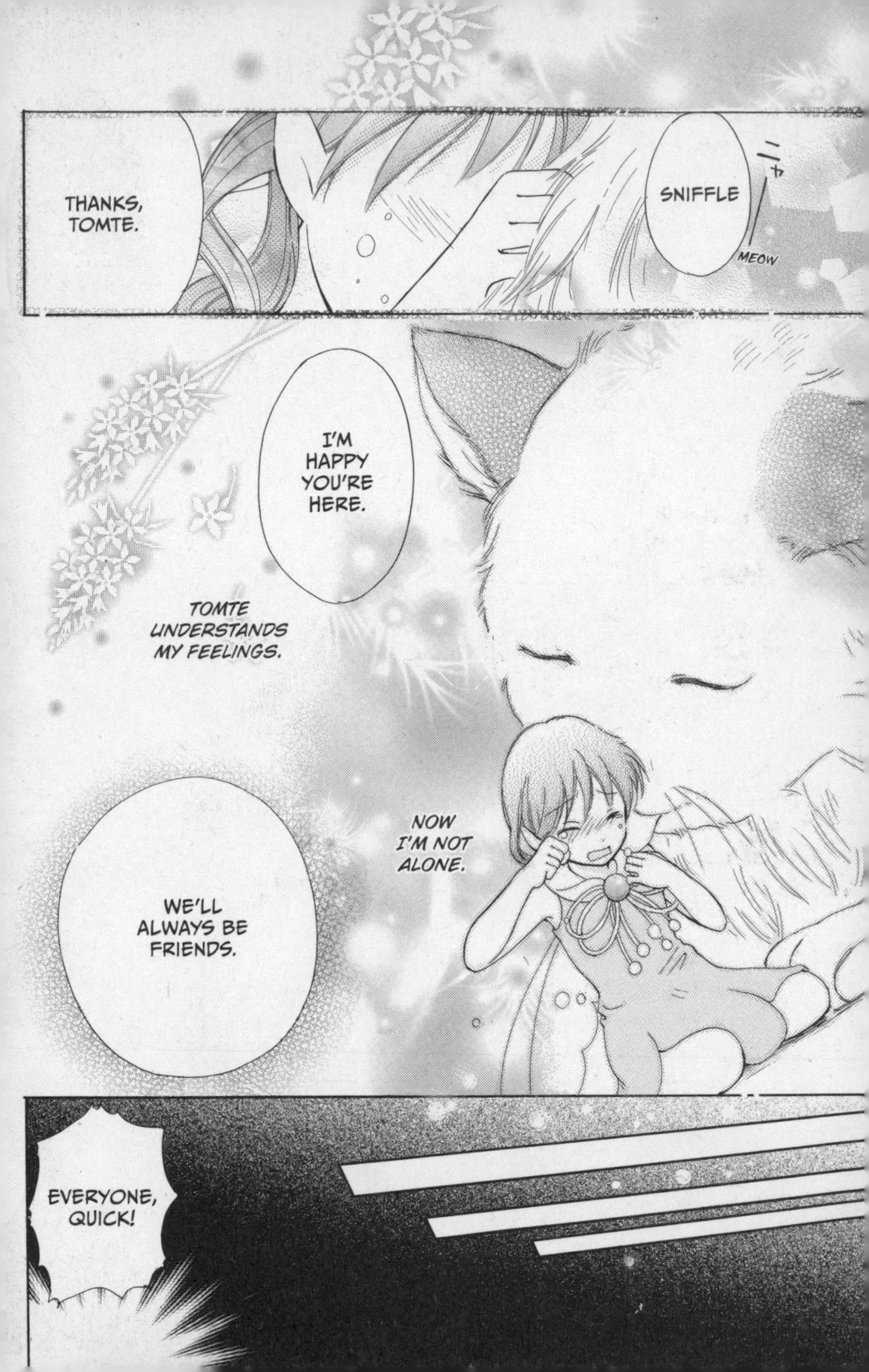
SNIFFLE
MEOW
THANKS, TOMTE.
I'M HAPPY YOU'RE HERE.
TOMTE UNDERSTANDS MY FEELINGS.
NOW I'M NOT ALONE.
WE'LL ALWAYS BE FRIENDS.
EVERYONE, QUICK!

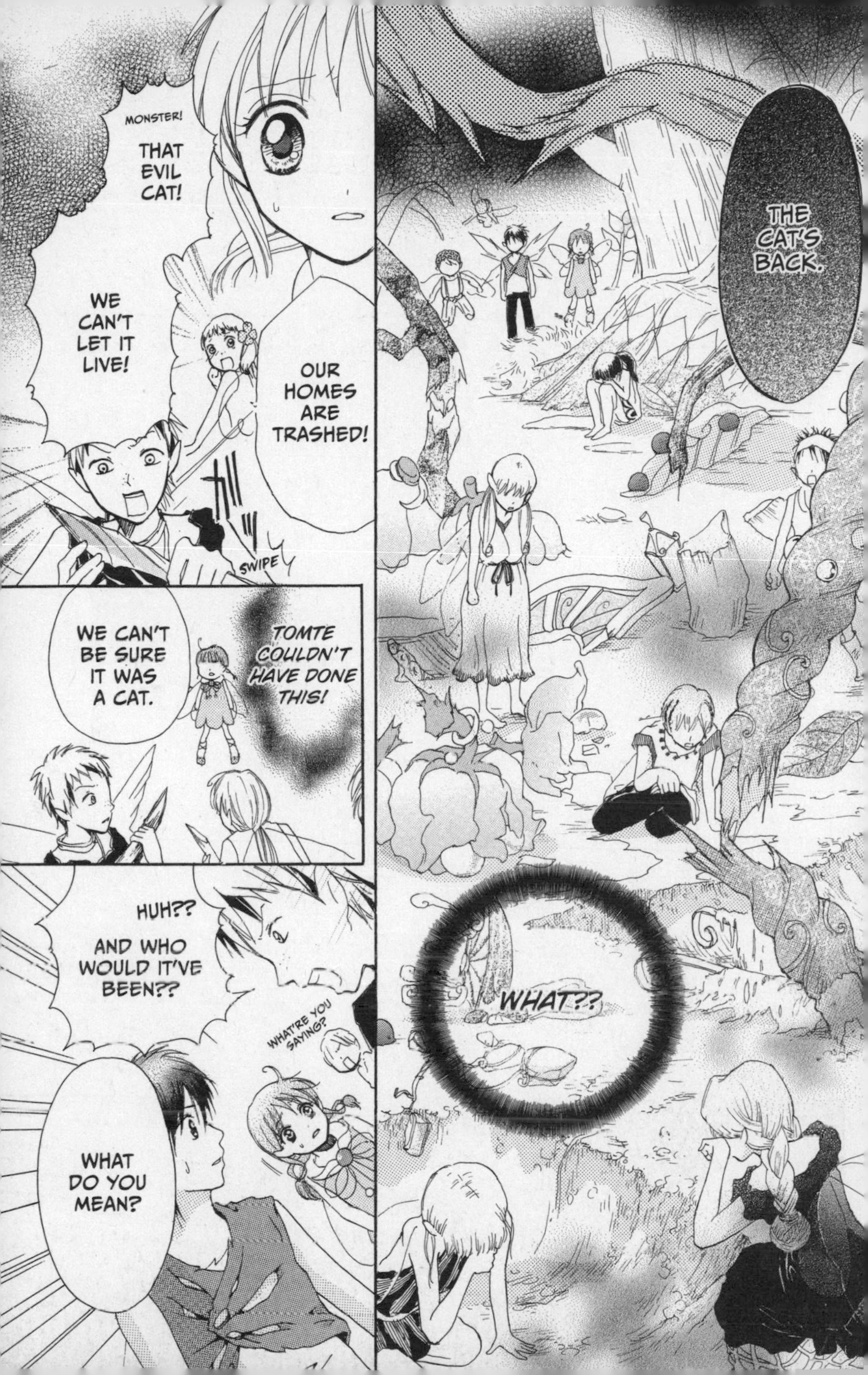
THE CAT'S BACK.
WHAT??
MONSTER!
THAT EVIL CAT!
WE CAN'T LET IT LIVE!
OUR HOMES ARE TRASHED!
SWIPE
TOMTE COULDN'T HAVE DONE THIS!
WE CAN'T BE SURE IT WAS A CAT.
HUH??
AND WHO WOULD IT'VE BEEN??
WHAT'RE YOU SAYING?
WHAT DO YOU MEAN?

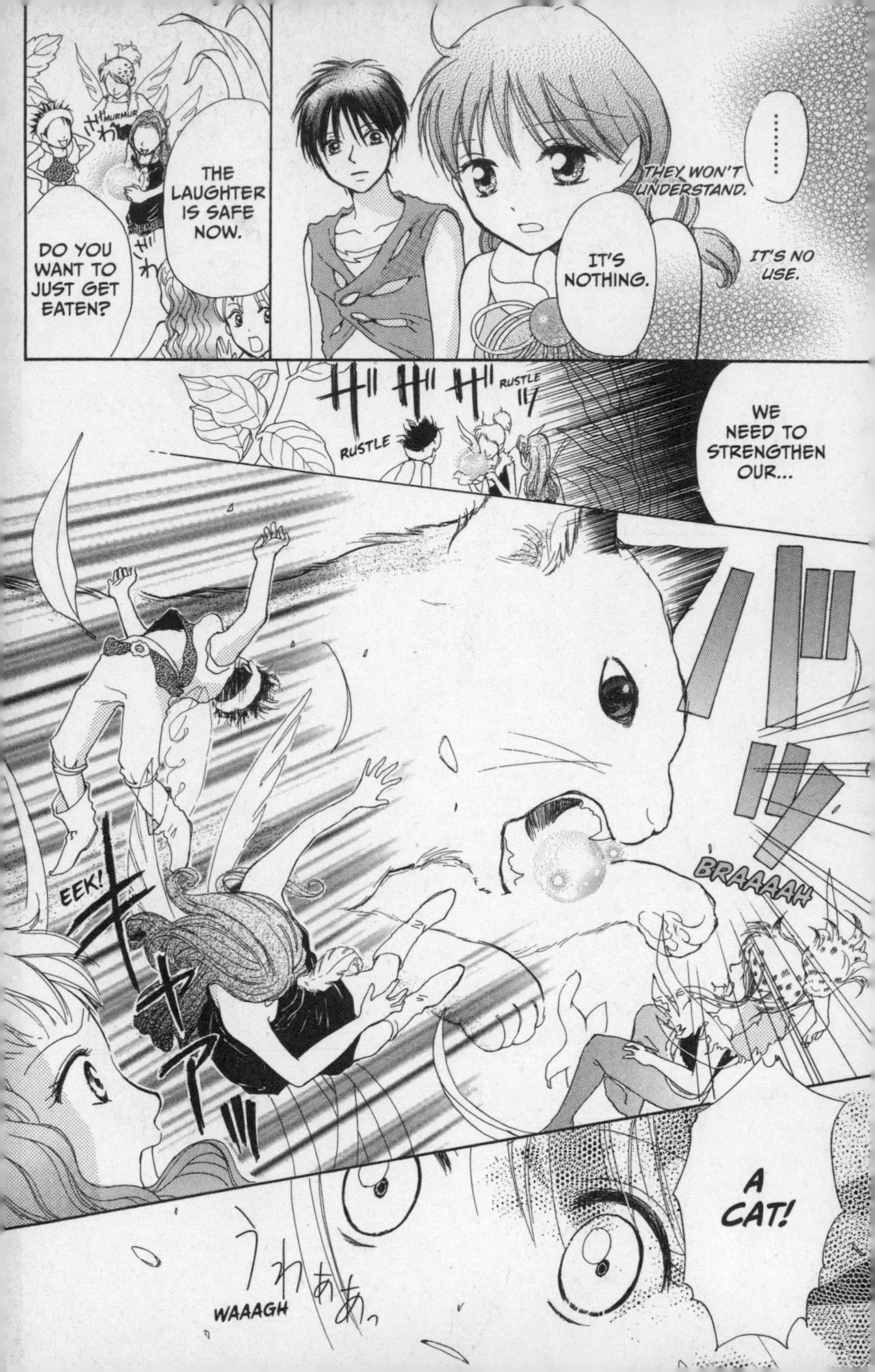
......
THEY WON'T UNDERSTAND.
IT'S NO USE.
IT'S NOTHING.
MURMUR
THE LAUGHTER IS SAFE NOW.
MURMUR
DO YOU WANT TO JUST GET EATEN?
WE NEED TO STRENGTHEN OUR...
RUSTLE
RUSTLE
BRAAAAH
EEK!
A CAT!
WAAAGH

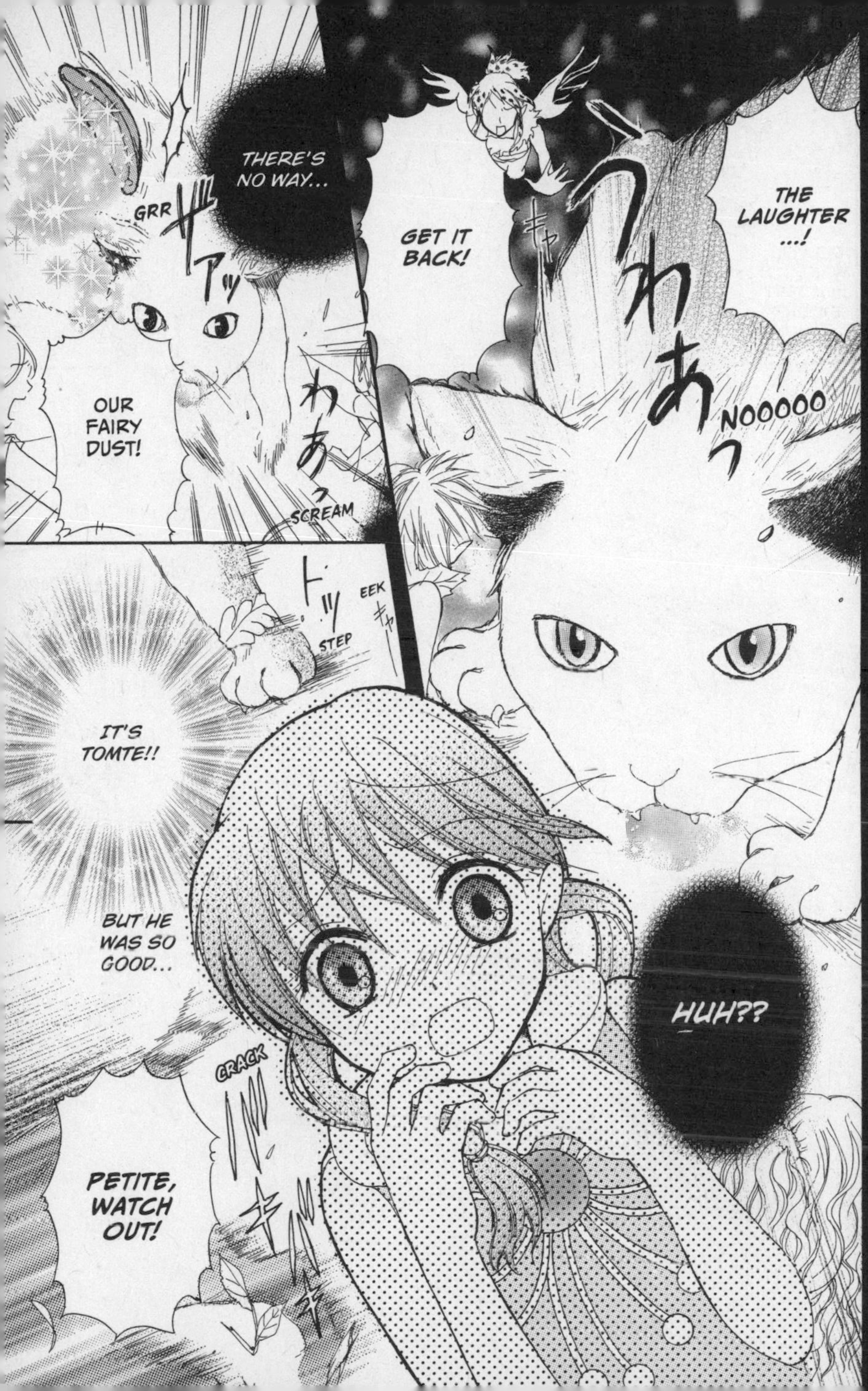
THE LAUGHTER ...!
GET IT BACK!
キャ
うわあっ
NOOOOO
THERE'S NO WAY...
GRR
ザアッ
OUR FAIRY DUST!
わあっ
SCREAM
HUH??
EEK
キャ
ドッ
STEP
IT'S TOMTE!!
BUT HE WAS SO GOOD...
CRACK
PETITE, WATCH OUT!

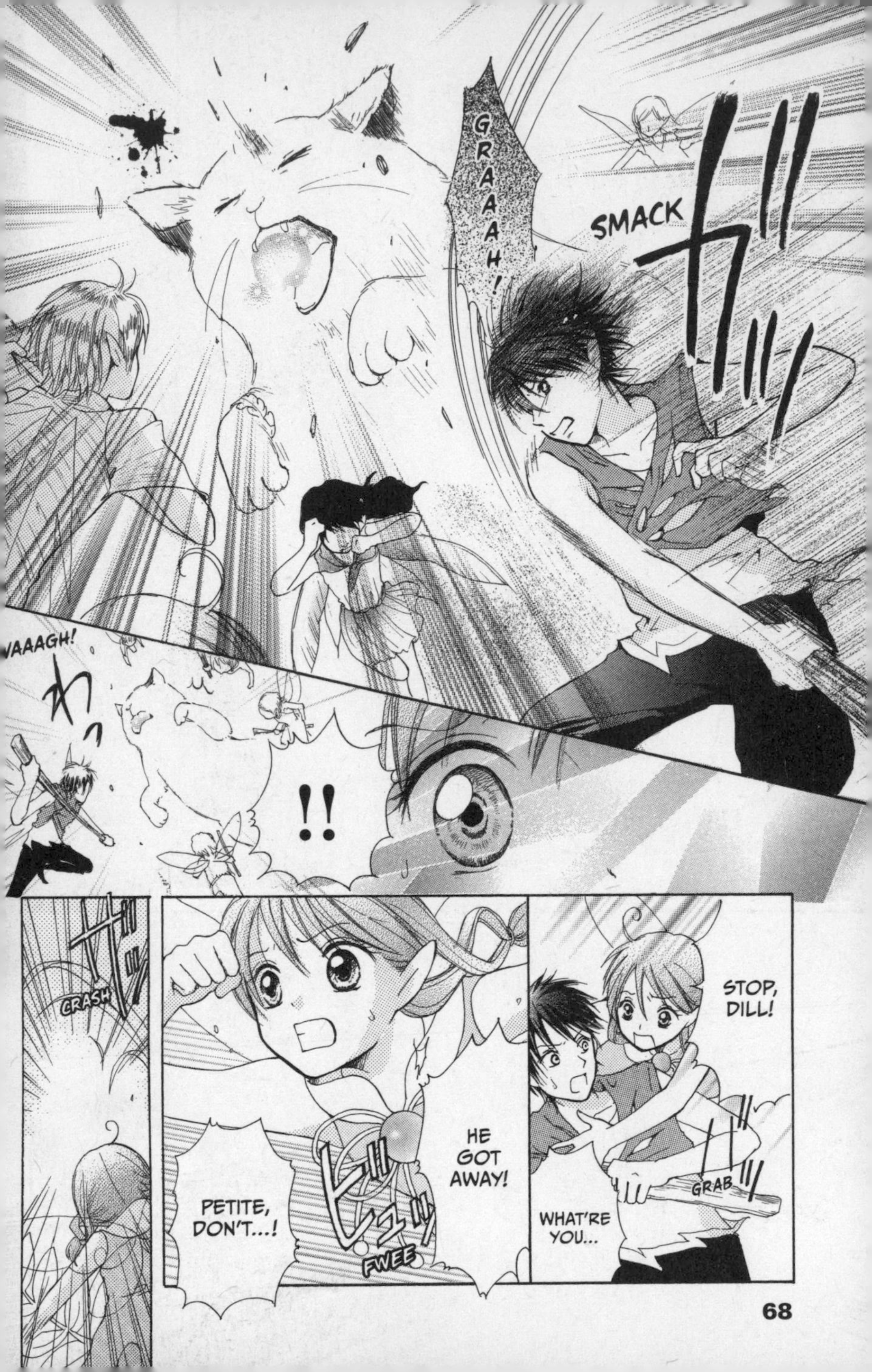
GRAAAH!
SMACK
WAAAGH!
!!
STOP, DILL!
GRAB
WHAT'RE YOU...
HE GOT AWAY!
PETITE, DON'T...!
FWEE
CRASH

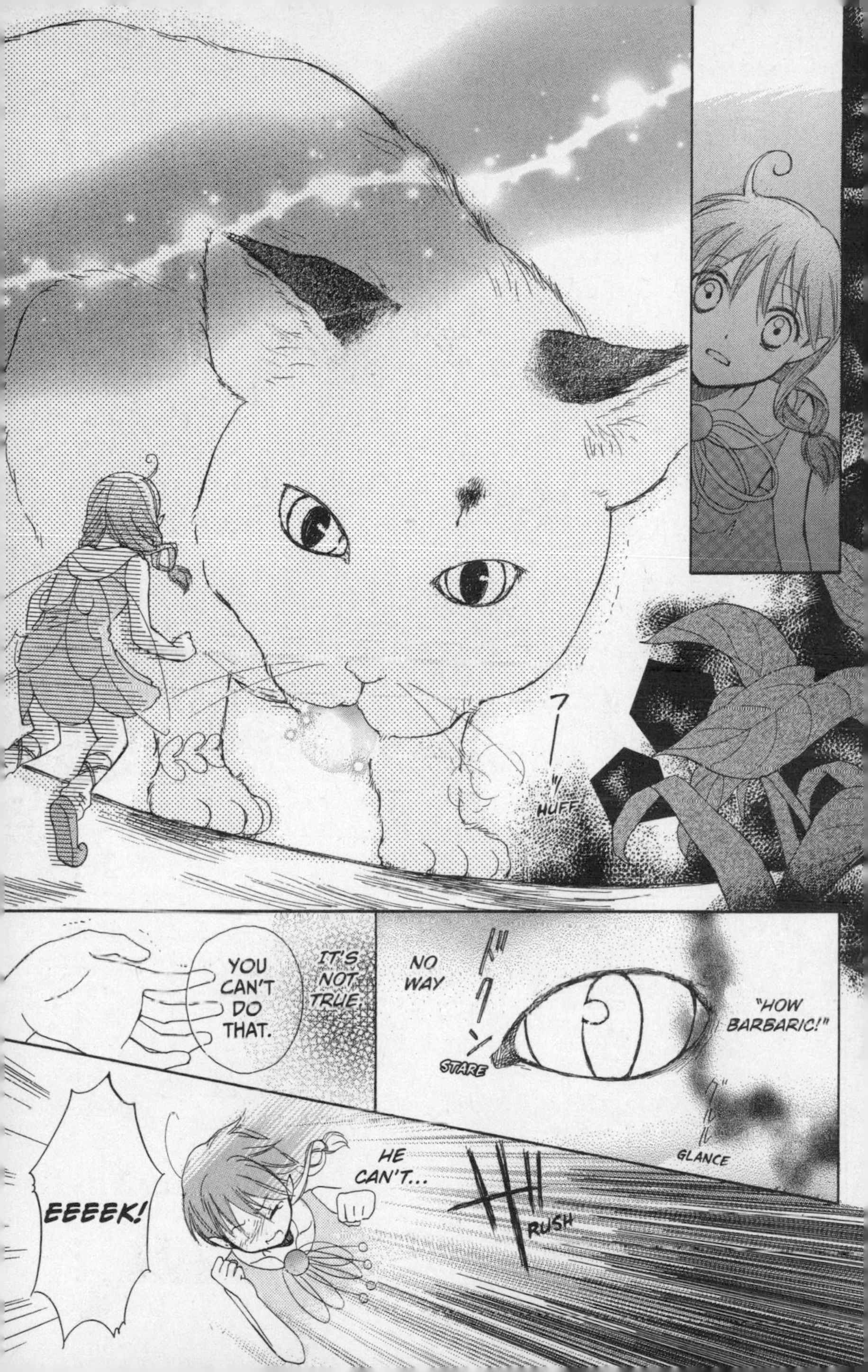
HUFF
"HOW BARBARIC!"
NO WAY
STARE
GLANCE
IT'S NOT TRUE.
YOU CAN'T DO THAT.
RUSH
HE CAN'T...
EEEEK!

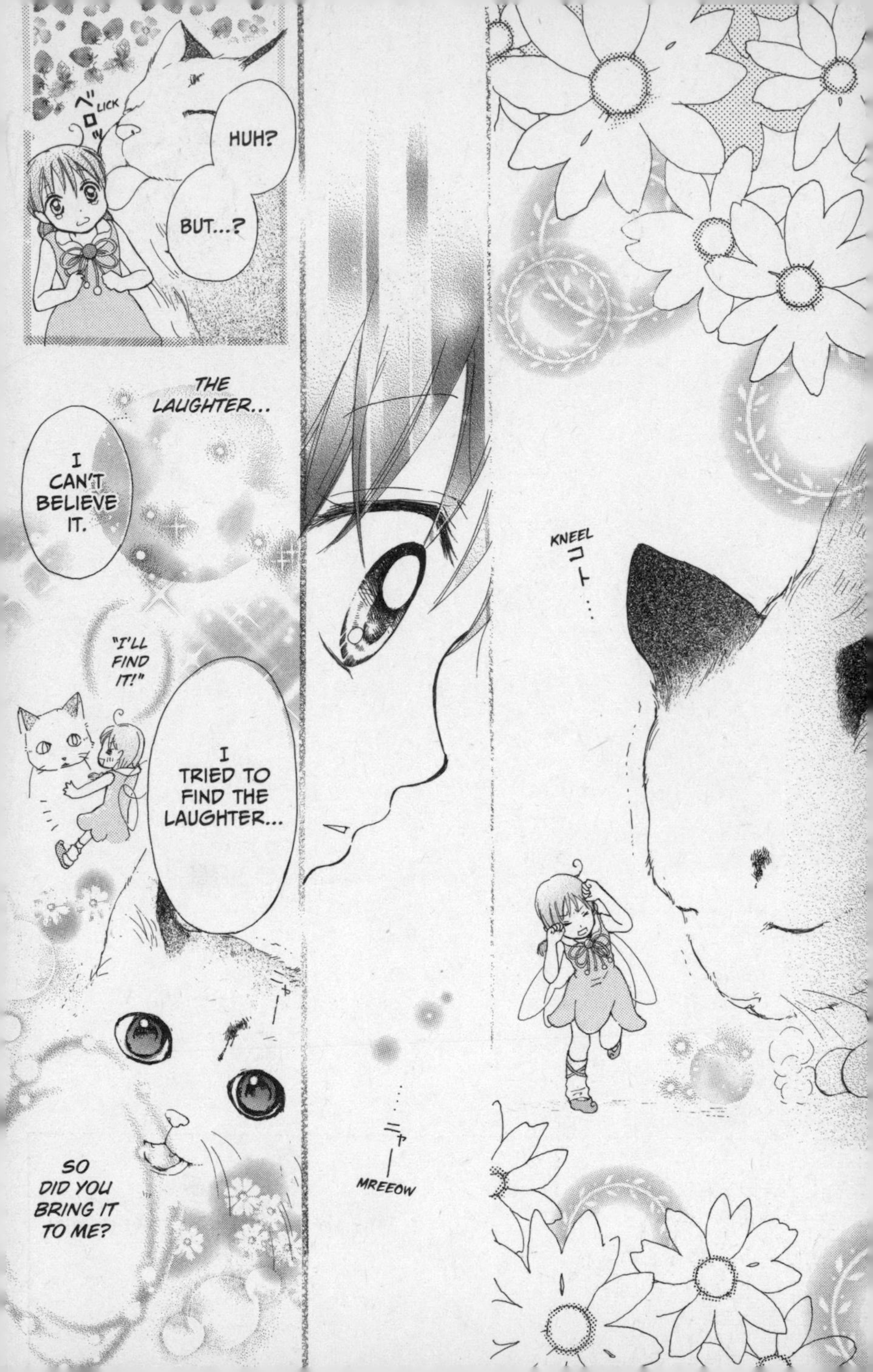
KNEEL
コト…
…ニャー
MREEOW
HUH?
BUT...?
ベロッ
LICK
THE LAUGHTER...
I CAN'T BELIEVE IT.
"I'LL FIND IT!"
I TRIED TO FIND THE LAUGHTER...
ニャー
SO DID YOU BRING IT TO ME?

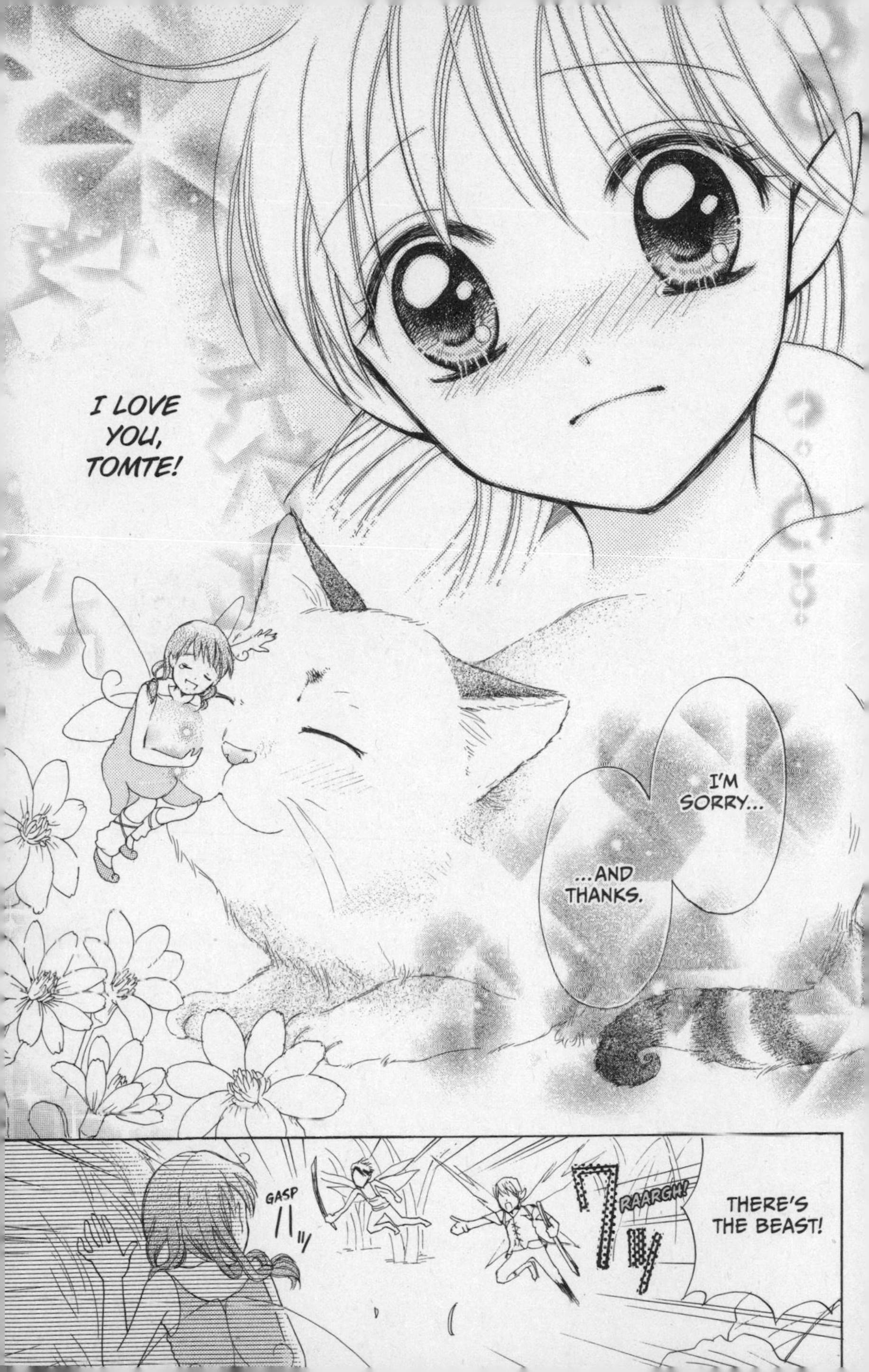
I LOVE YOU, TOMTE!
I'M SORRY...
...AND THANKS.
THERE'S THE BEAST!
RAARGH!
GASP

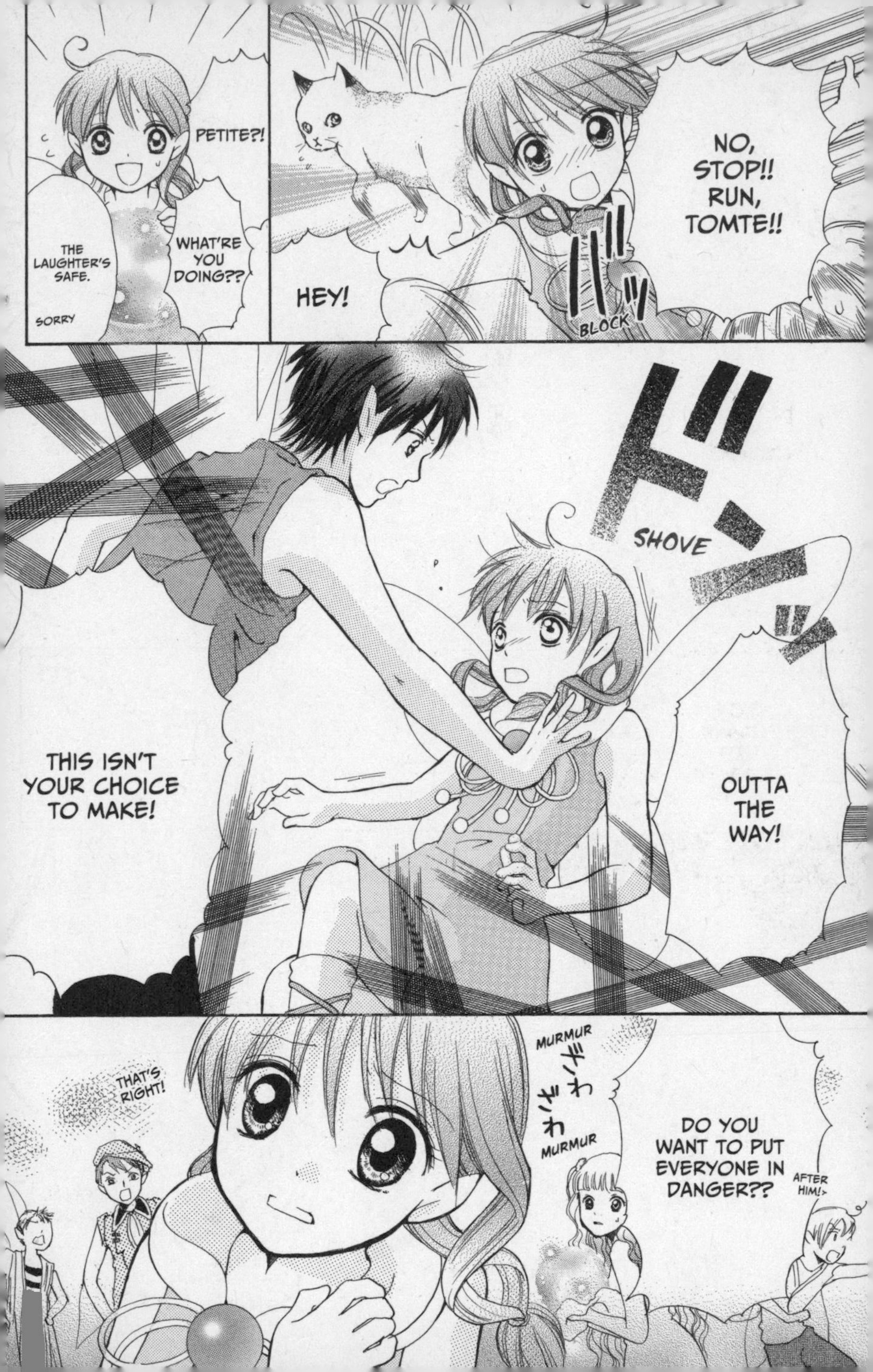
NO, STOP!! RUN, TOMTE!!
バッ
BLOCK
HEY!
PETITE?!
WHAT'RE YOU DOING??
THE LAUGHTER'S SAFE.
SORRY
ドン
SHOVE
OUTTA THE WAY!
THIS ISN'T YOUR CHOICE TO MAKE!
DO YOU WANT TO PUT EVERYONE IN DANGER??
AFTER HIM!>
MURMUR
ざわざわ
MURMUR
THAT'S RIGHT!

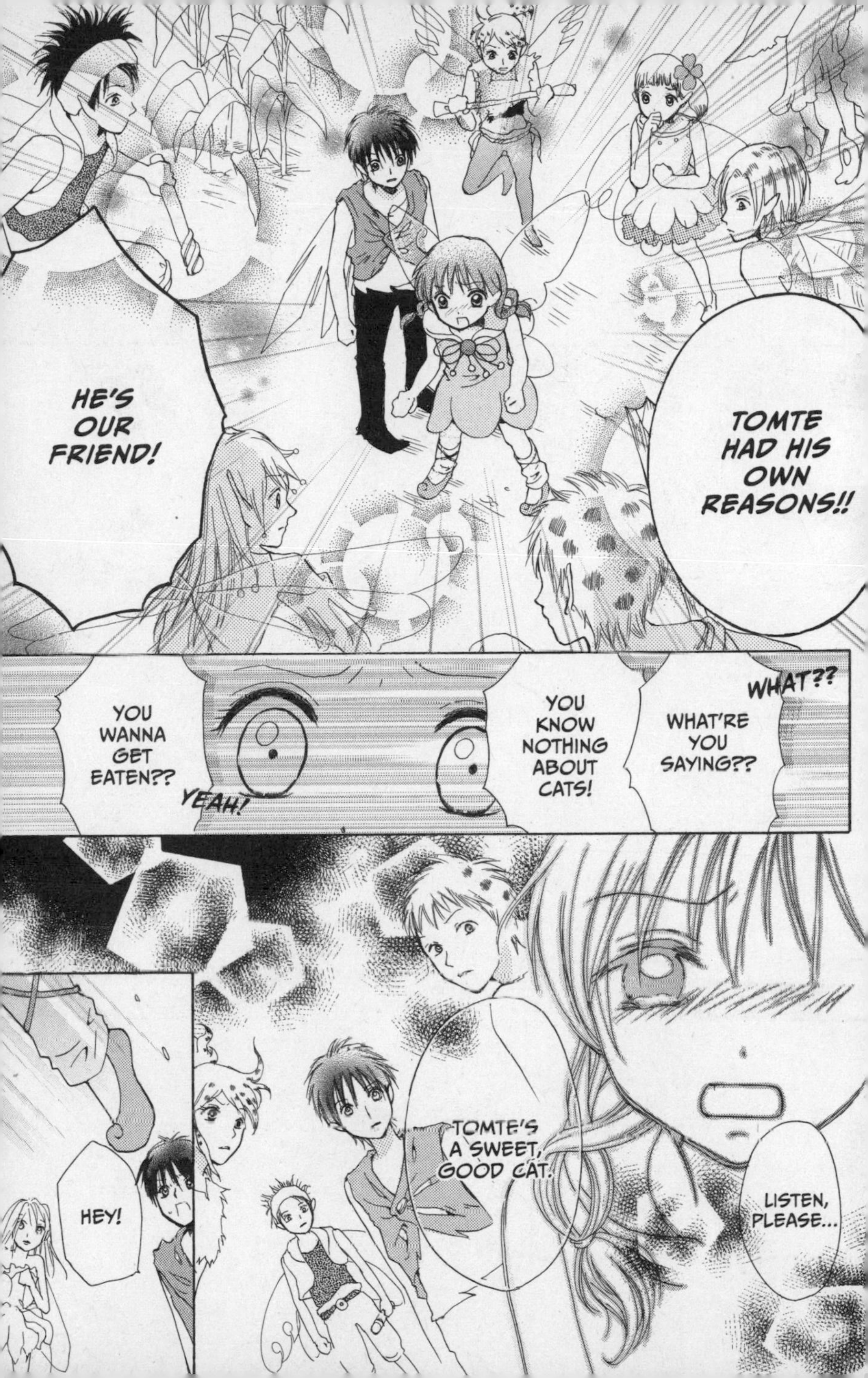
TOMTE HAD HIS OWN REASONS!!
HE'S OUR FRIEND!
WHAT??
WHAT'RE YOU SAYING??
YOU KNOW NOTHING ABOUT CATS!
YOU WANNA GET EATEN??
YEAH!
LISTEN, PLEASE...
TOMTE'S A SWEET, GOOD CAT.
HEY!

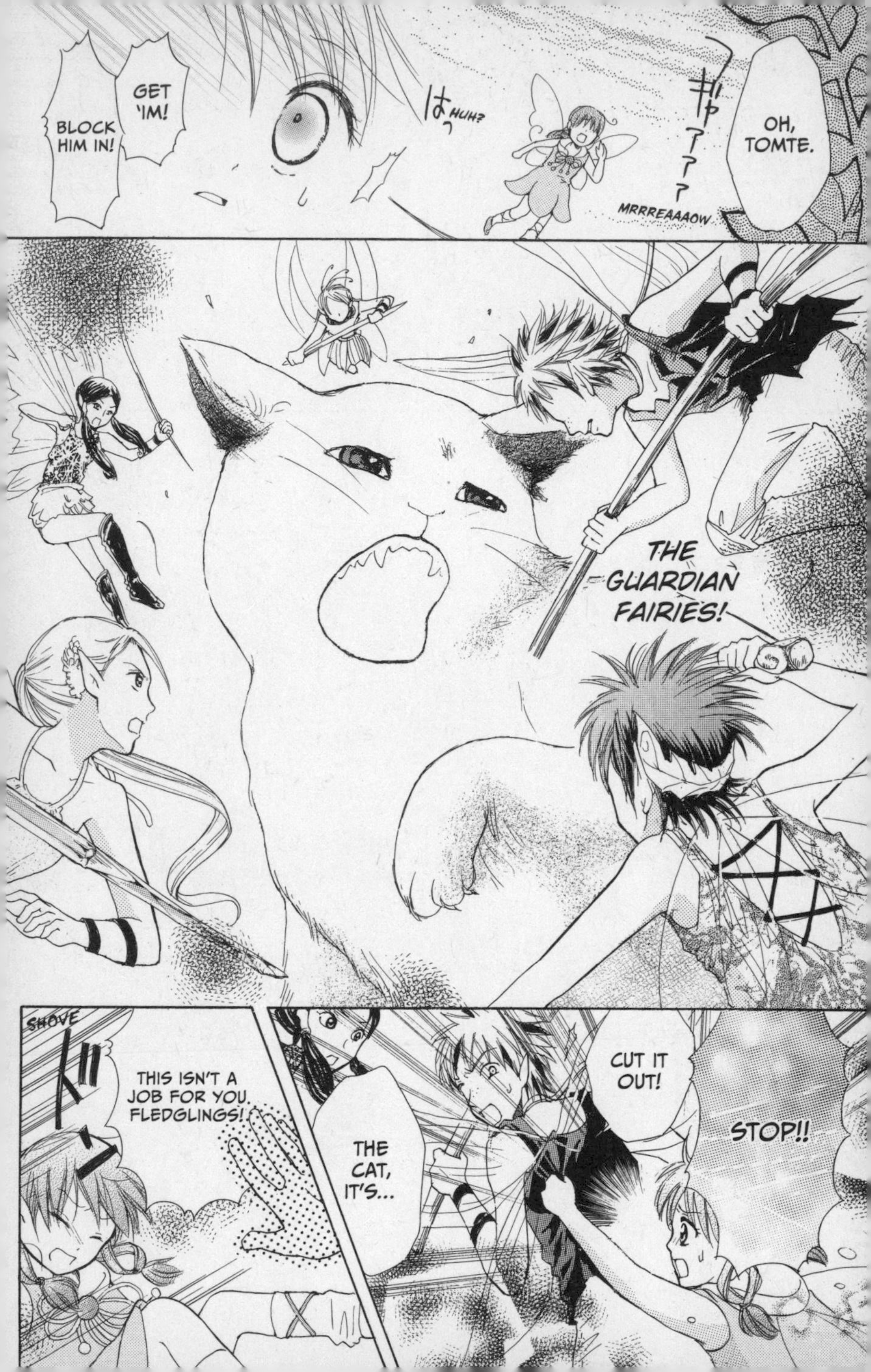
OH, TOMTE.
ギャアアア
MRRREAAAOW
はっ
HUH?
GET 'IM!
BLOCK HIM IN!
THE GUARDIAN FAIRIES!
STOP!!
CUT IT OUT!
THE CAT, IT'S...
SHOVE
THIS ISN'T A JOB FOR YOU FLEDGLINGS!

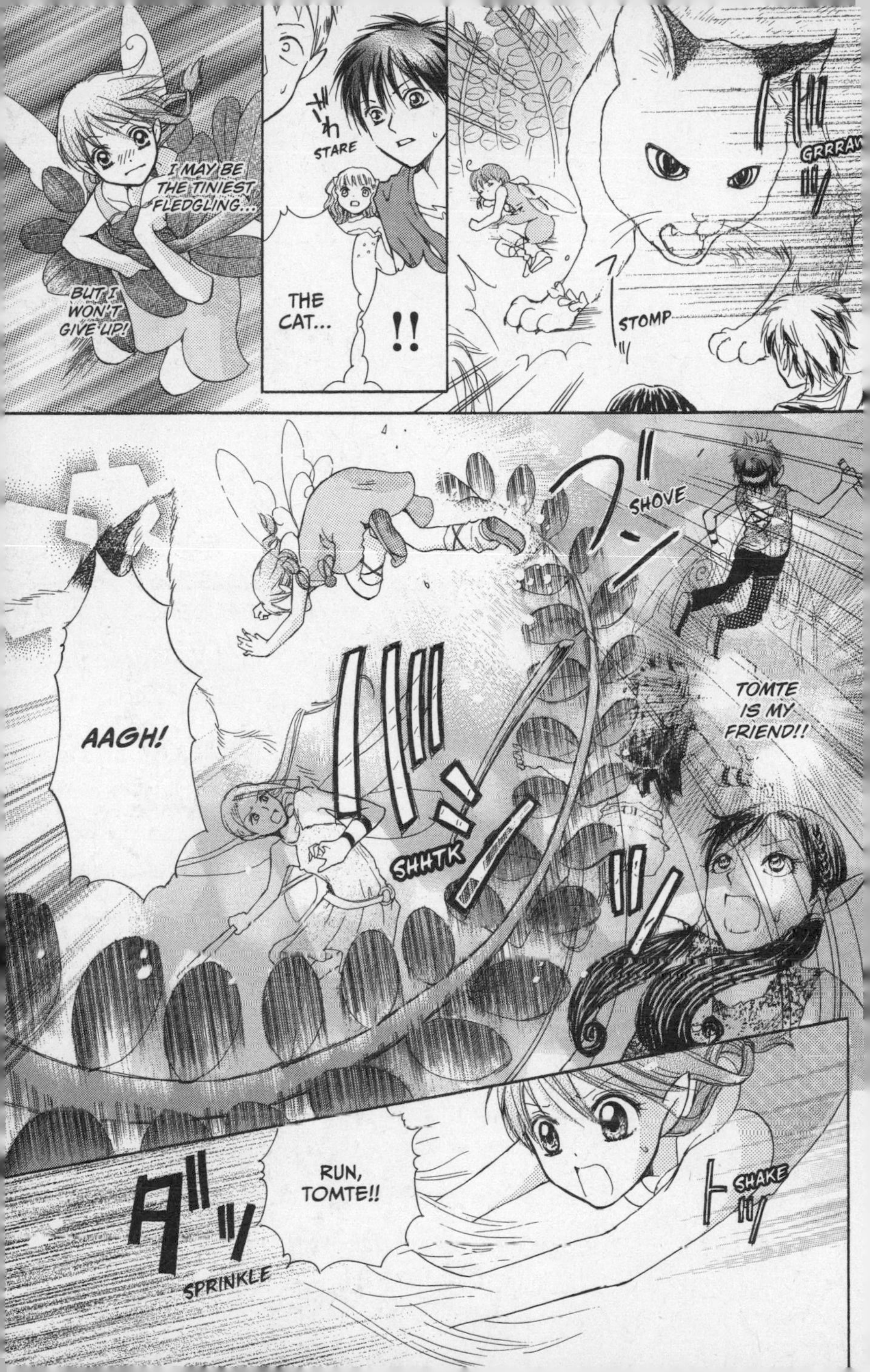
GRRRA
STOMP
STARE
THE CAT...
!!
I MAY BE THE TINIEST FLEDGLING...
BUT I WON'T GIVE UP!
SHOVE
TOMTE IS MY FRIEND!!
AAGH!
SHHTK
SHAKE
RUN, TOMTE!!
SPRINKLE

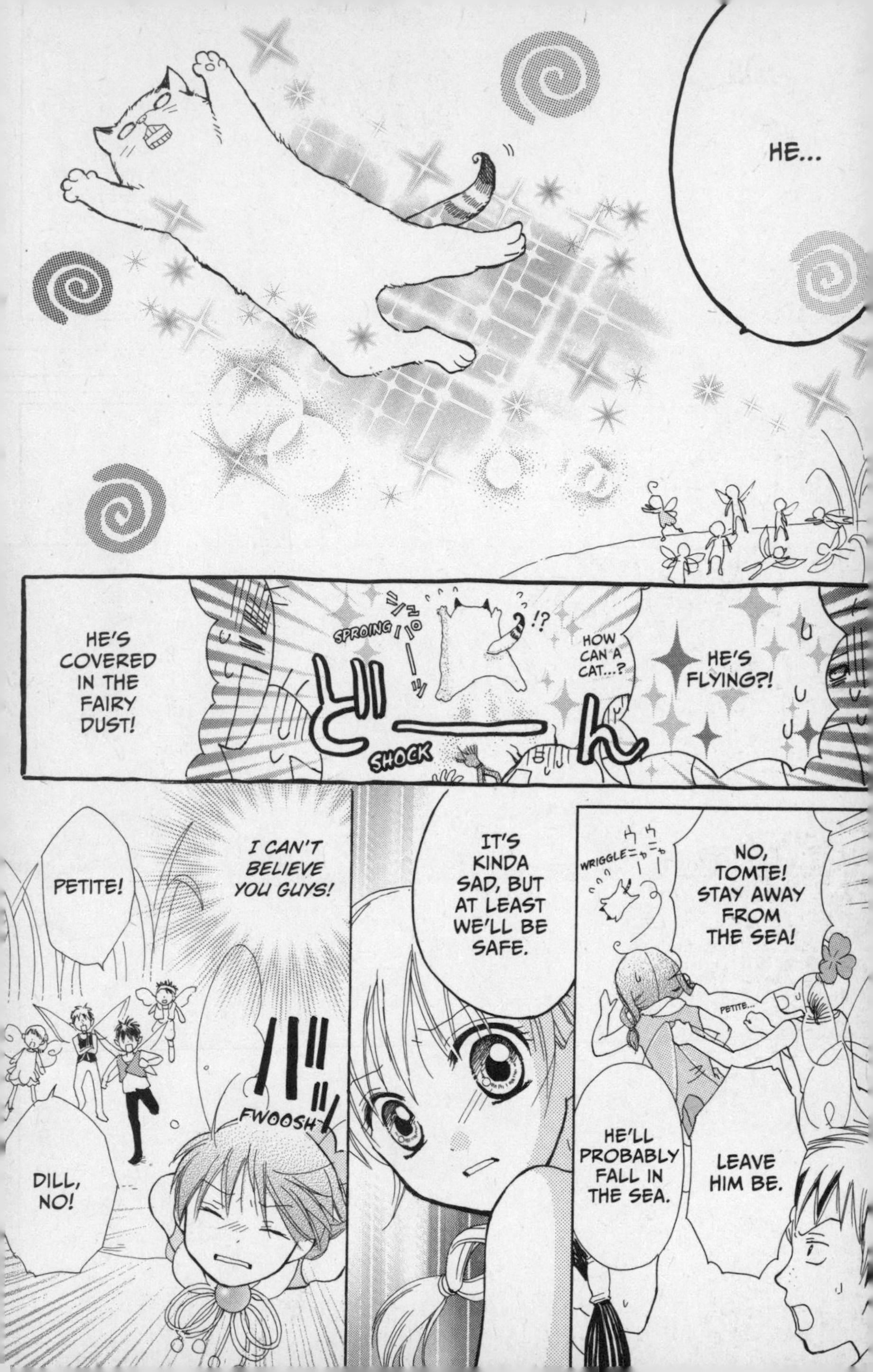
HE...
HE'S FLYING?!
HOW CAN A CAT...?
!?
SPROING
SHOCK
HE'S COVERED IN THE FAIRY DUST!
NO, TOMTE! STAY AWAY FROM THE SEA!
WRIGGLE
PETITE...
LEAVE HIM BE.
HE'LL PROBABLY FALL IN THE SEA.
IT'S KINDA SAD, BUT AT LEAST WE'LL BE SAFE.
I CAN'T BELIEVE YOU GUYS!
PETITE!
FWOOSH
DILL, NO!

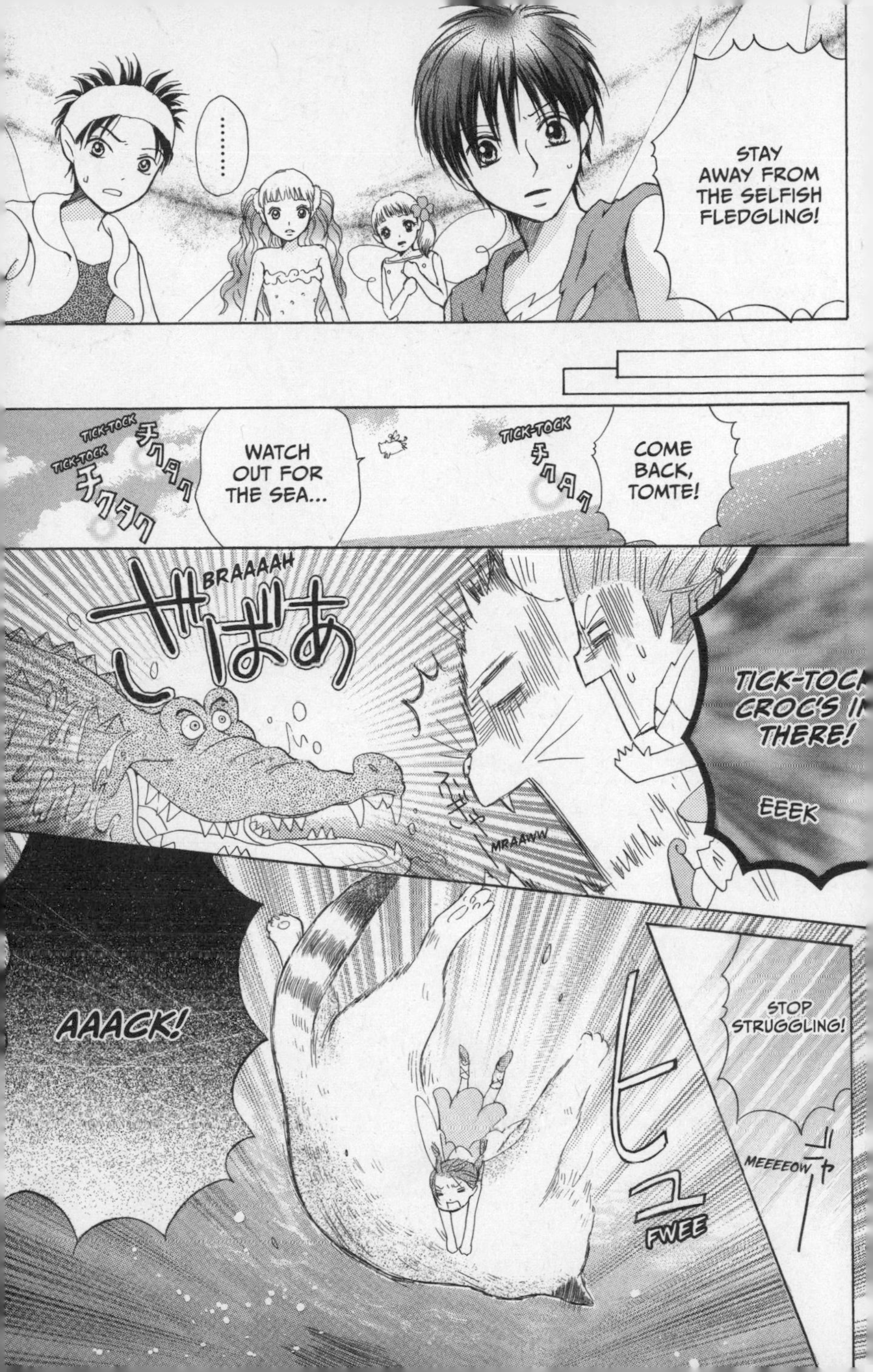
STAY AWAY FROM THE SELFISH FLEDGLING!
......
TICK-TOCK
COME BACK, TOMTE!
TICK-TOCK
TICK-TOCK
WATCH OUT FOR THE SEA...
TICK-TOCK CROC'S IN THERE!
EEEK
BRAAAAH
MRAAWW
STOP STRUGGLING!
MEEEEOW
FWEE
AAACK!

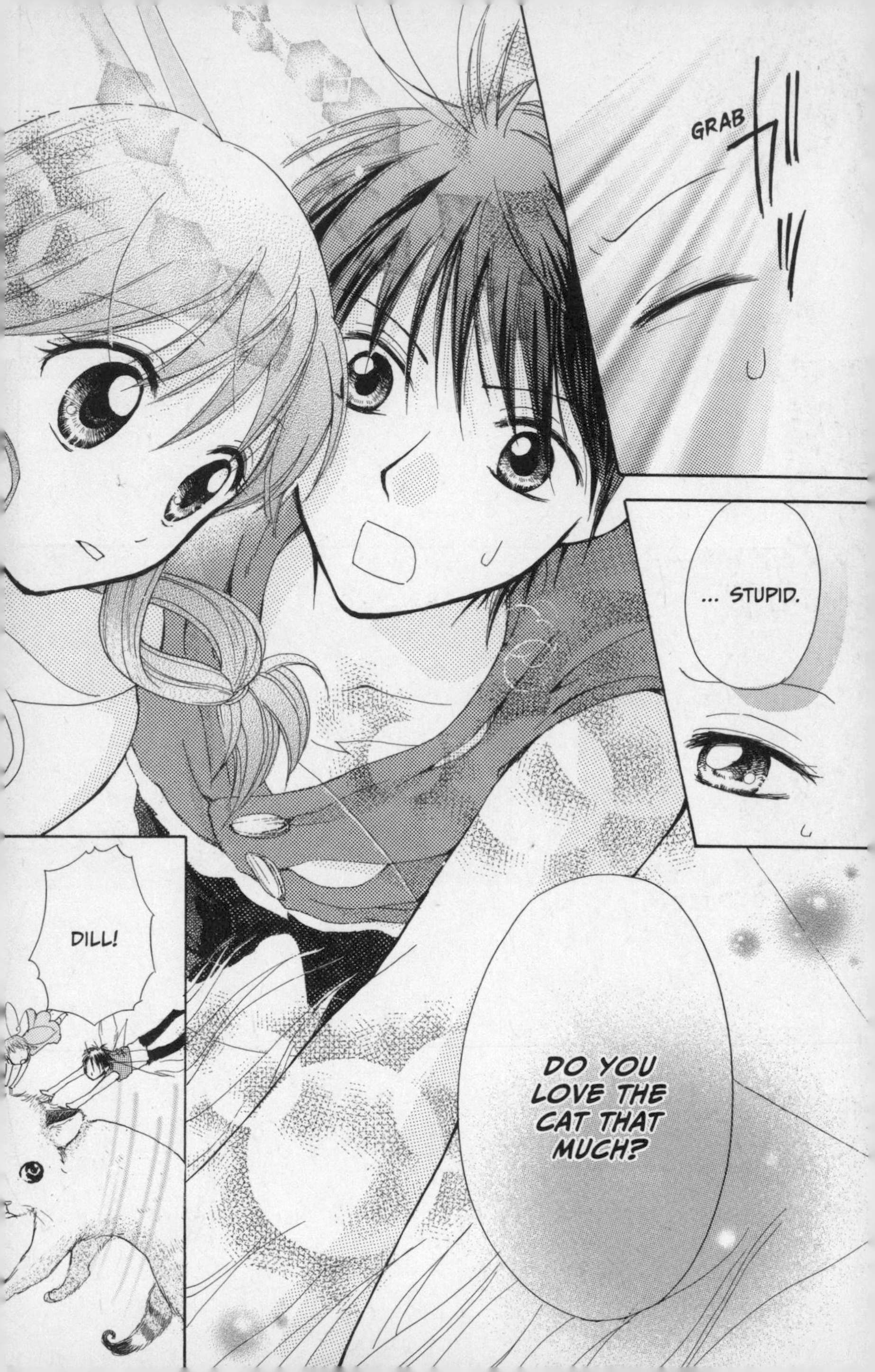
GRAB
... STUPID.
DO YOU LOVE THE CAT THAT MUCH?
DILL!

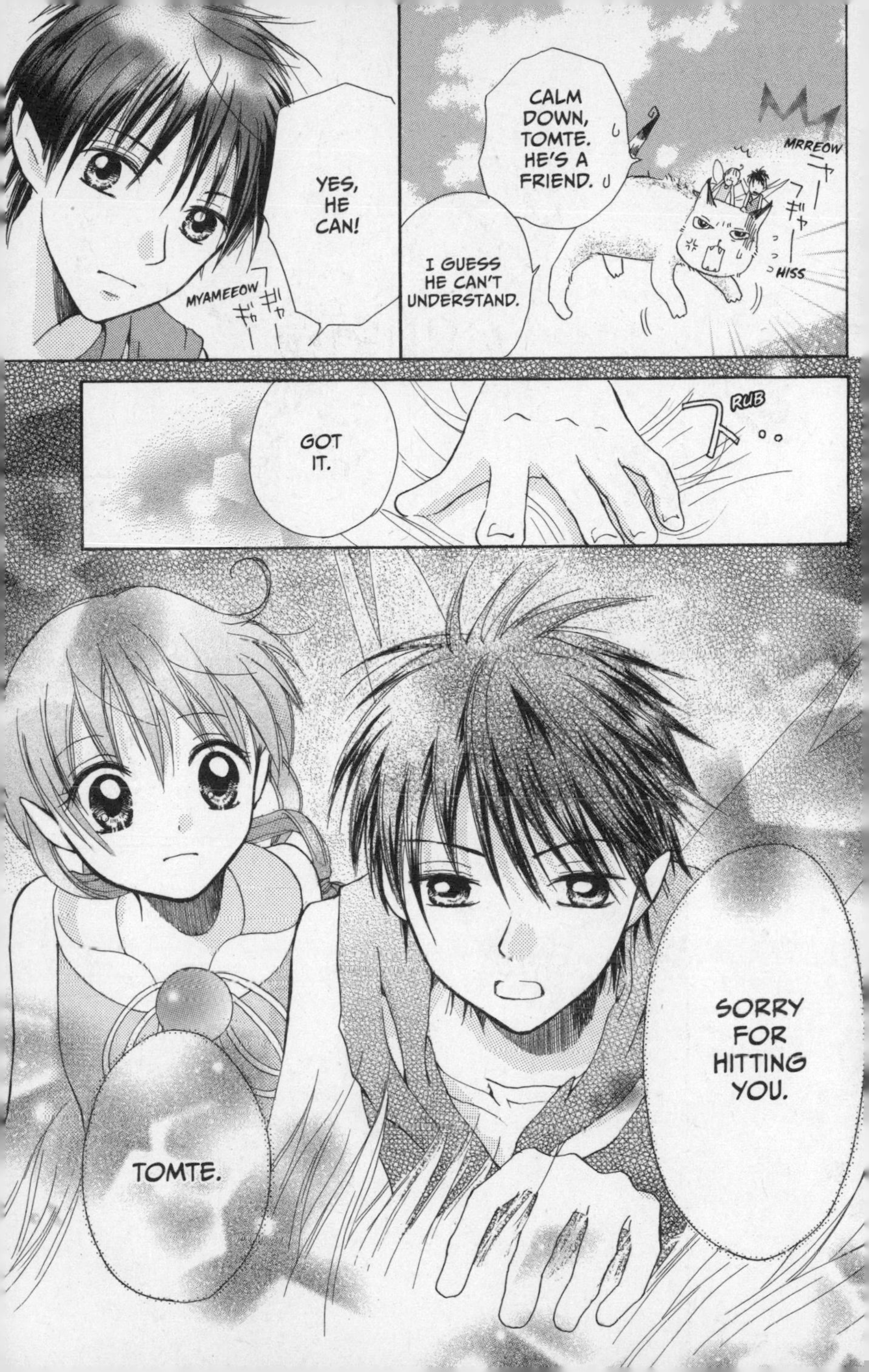
MRREOW
HISS
CALM DOWN, TOMTE. HE'S A FRIEND.
I GUESS HE CAN'T UNDERSTAND.
YES, HE CAN!
MYAMEEOW
RUB
GOT IT.
SORRY FOR HITTING YOU.
TOMTE.

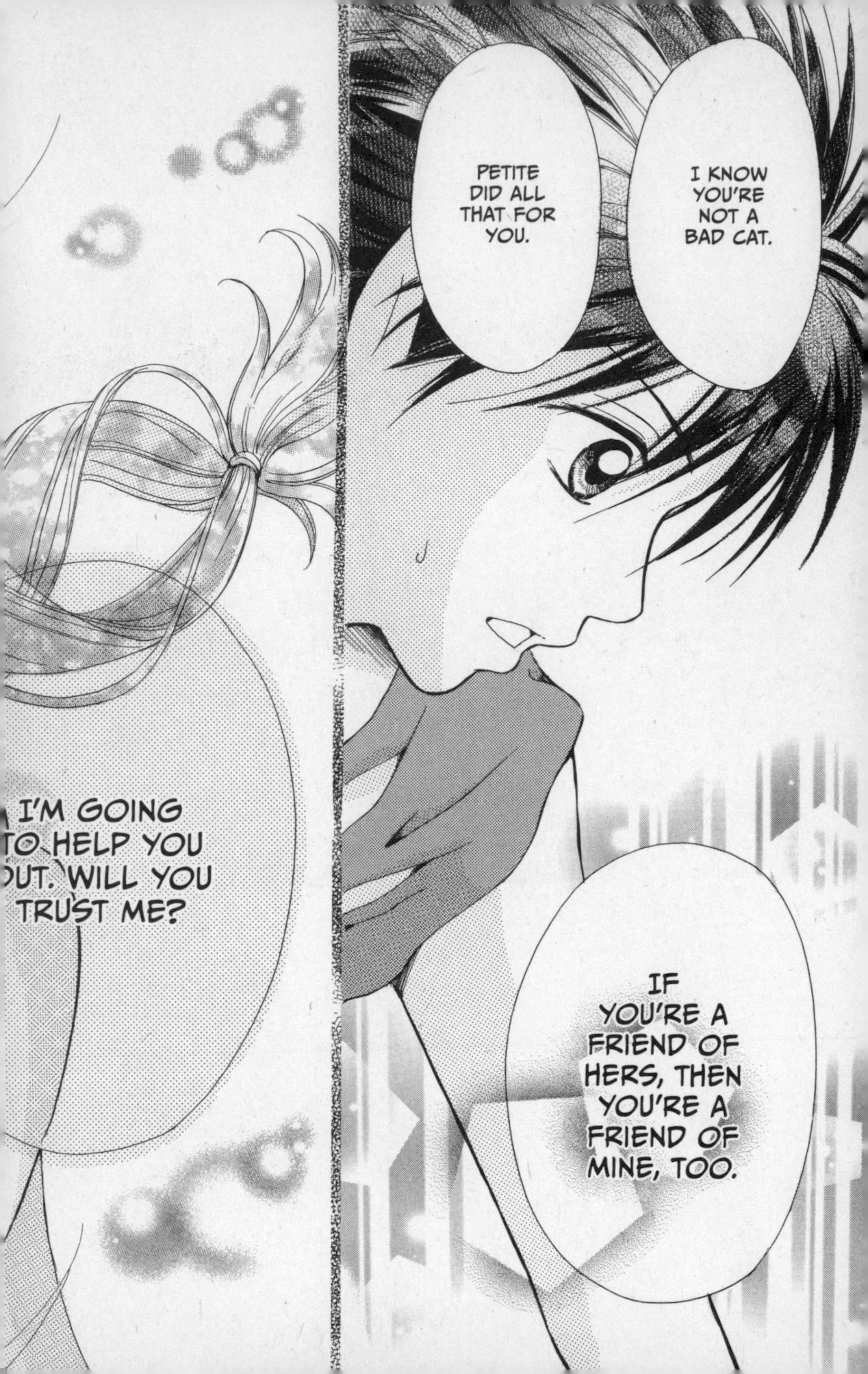
I KNOW YOU'RE NOT A BAD CAT.
PETITE DID ALL THAT FOR YOU.
IF YOU'RE A FRIEND OF HERS, THEN YOU'RE A FRIEND OF MINE, TOO.
I'M GOING TO HELP YOU OUT. WILL YOU TRUST ME?

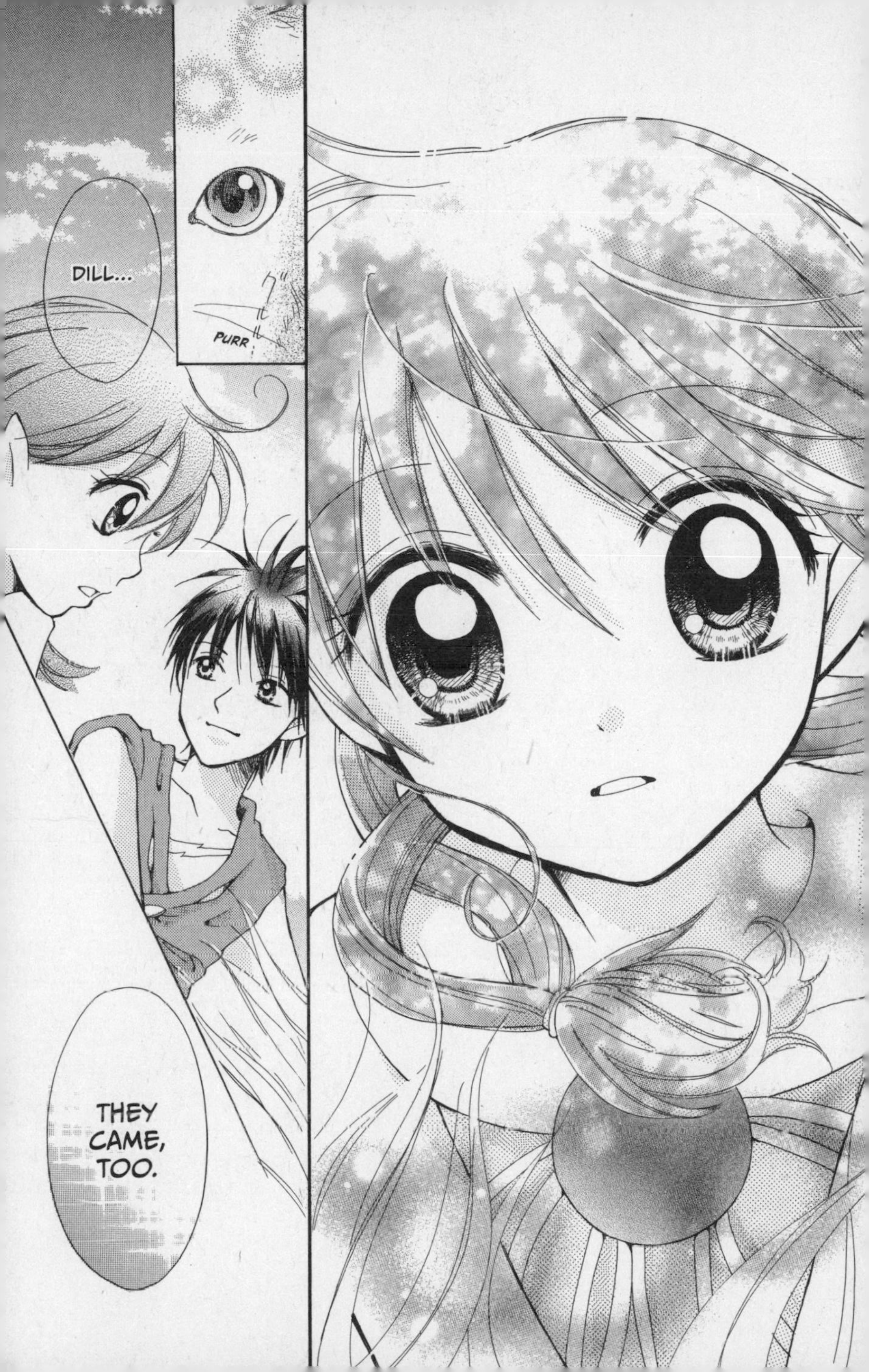
PURR
DILL...
THEY CAME, TOO.

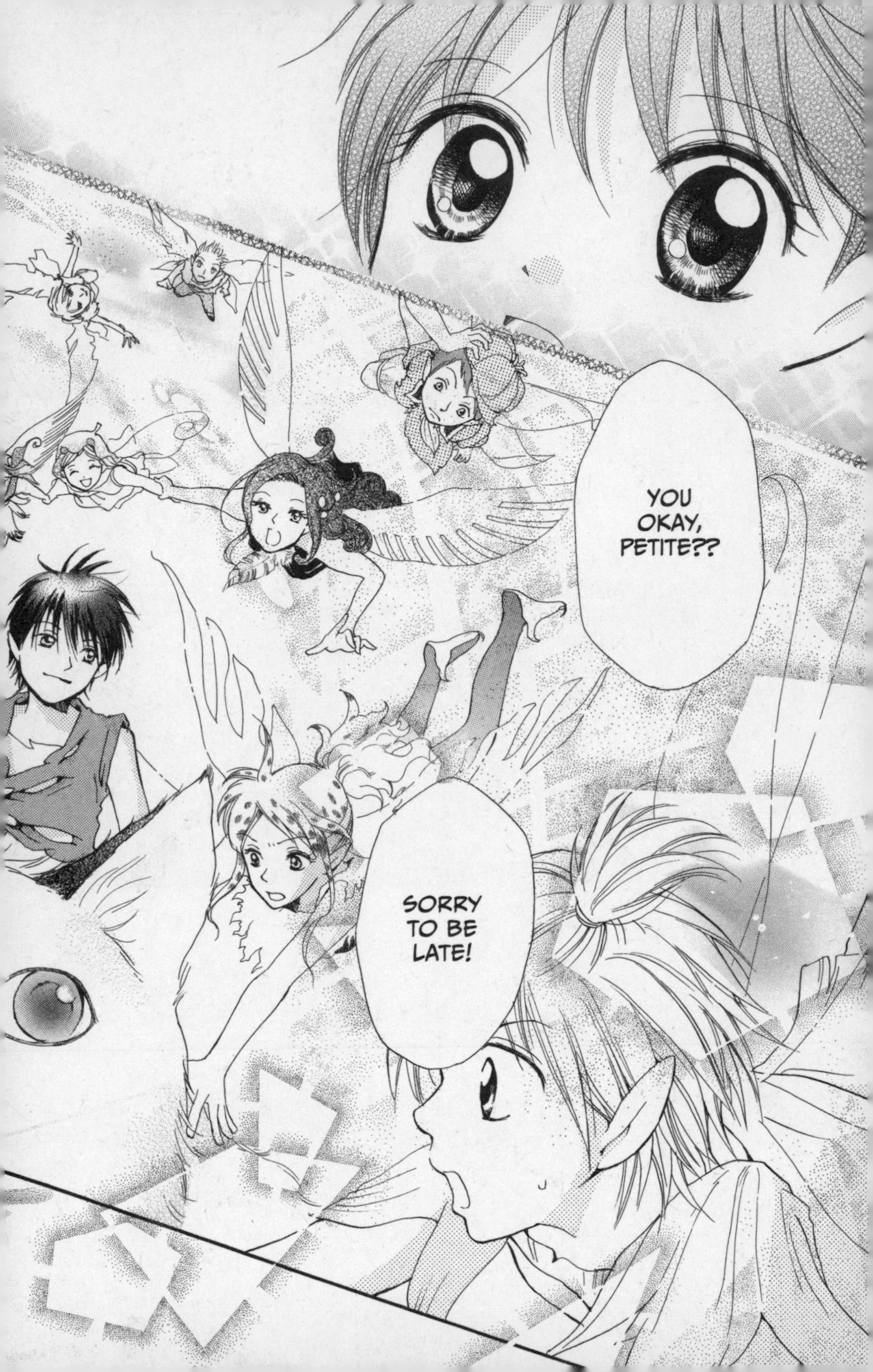
YOU OKAY, PETITE??
SORRY TO BE LATE!

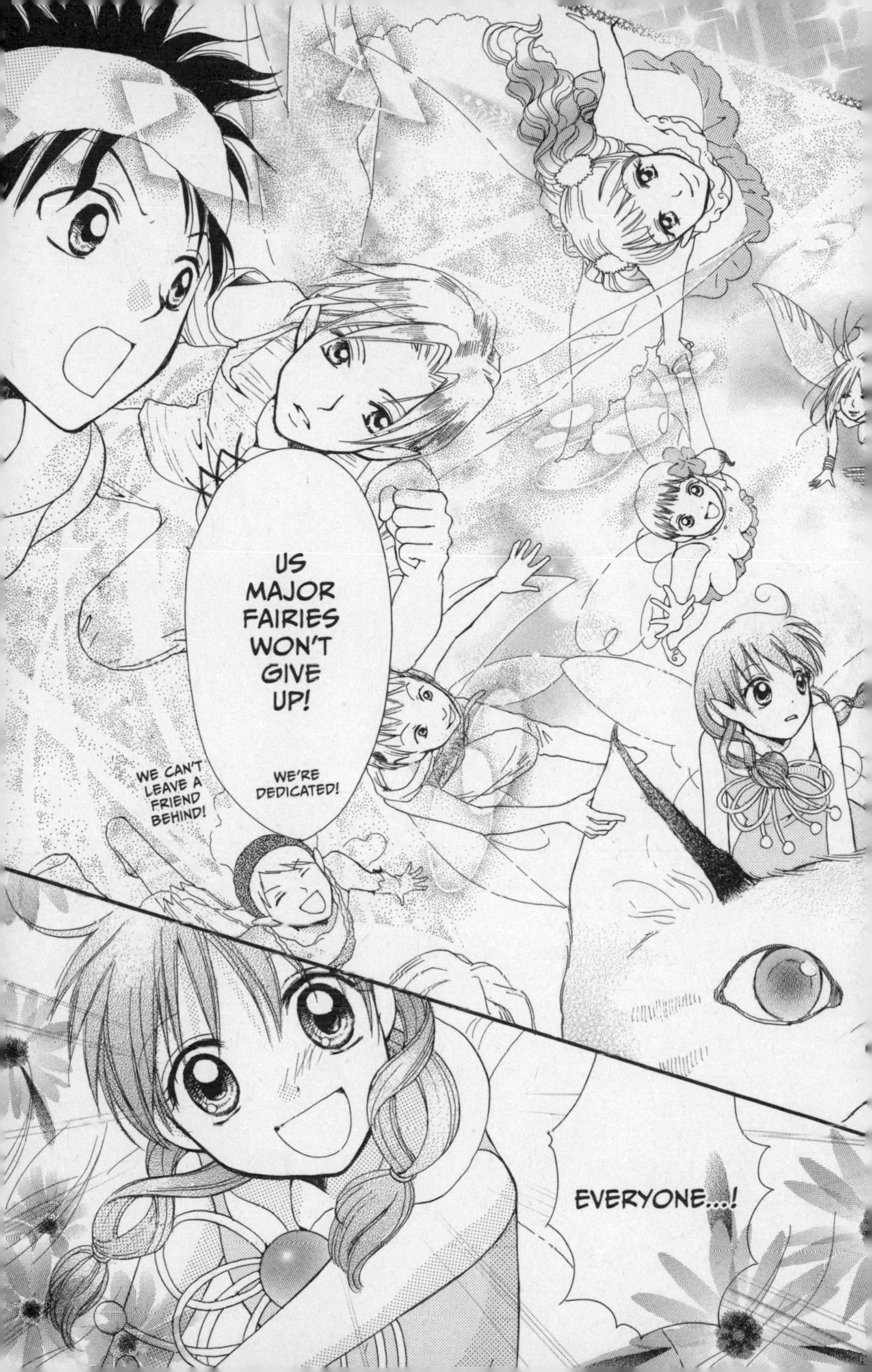
US MAJOR FAIRIES WON'T GIVE UP!
WE'RE DEDICATED!
WE CAN'T LEAVE A FRIEND BEHIND!
EVERYONE...!

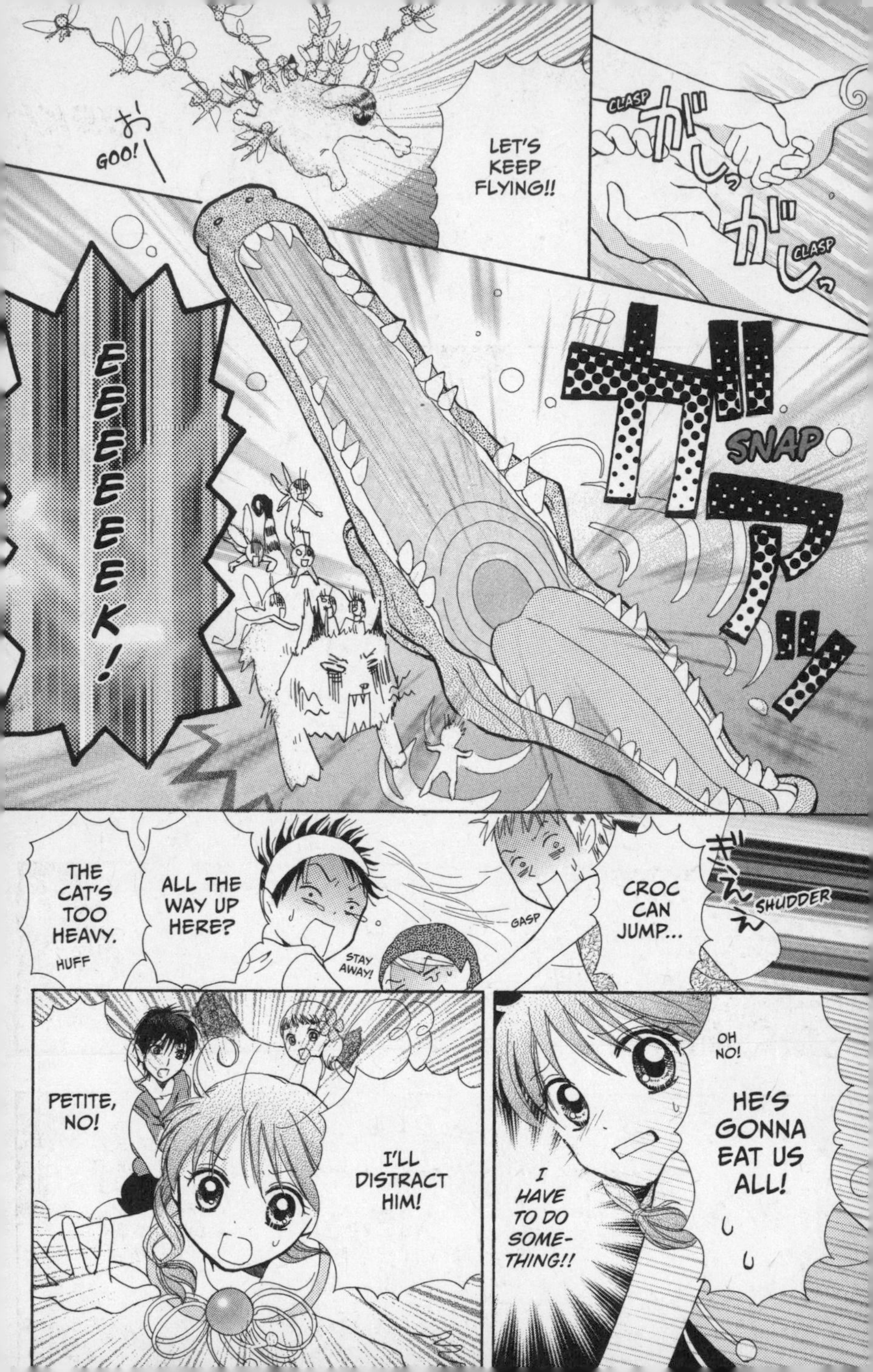
CLASP
CLASP
GOO!
LET'S KEEP FLYING!!
SNAP
EEEEEEEK!
SHUDDER
CROC CAN JUMP...
GASP
STAY AWAY!
ALL THE WAY UP HERE?
THE CAT'S TOO HEAVY.
HUFF
OH NO!
HE'S GONNA EAT US ALL!
I HAVE TO DO SOME-THING!!
I'LL DISTRACT HIM!
PETITE, NO!

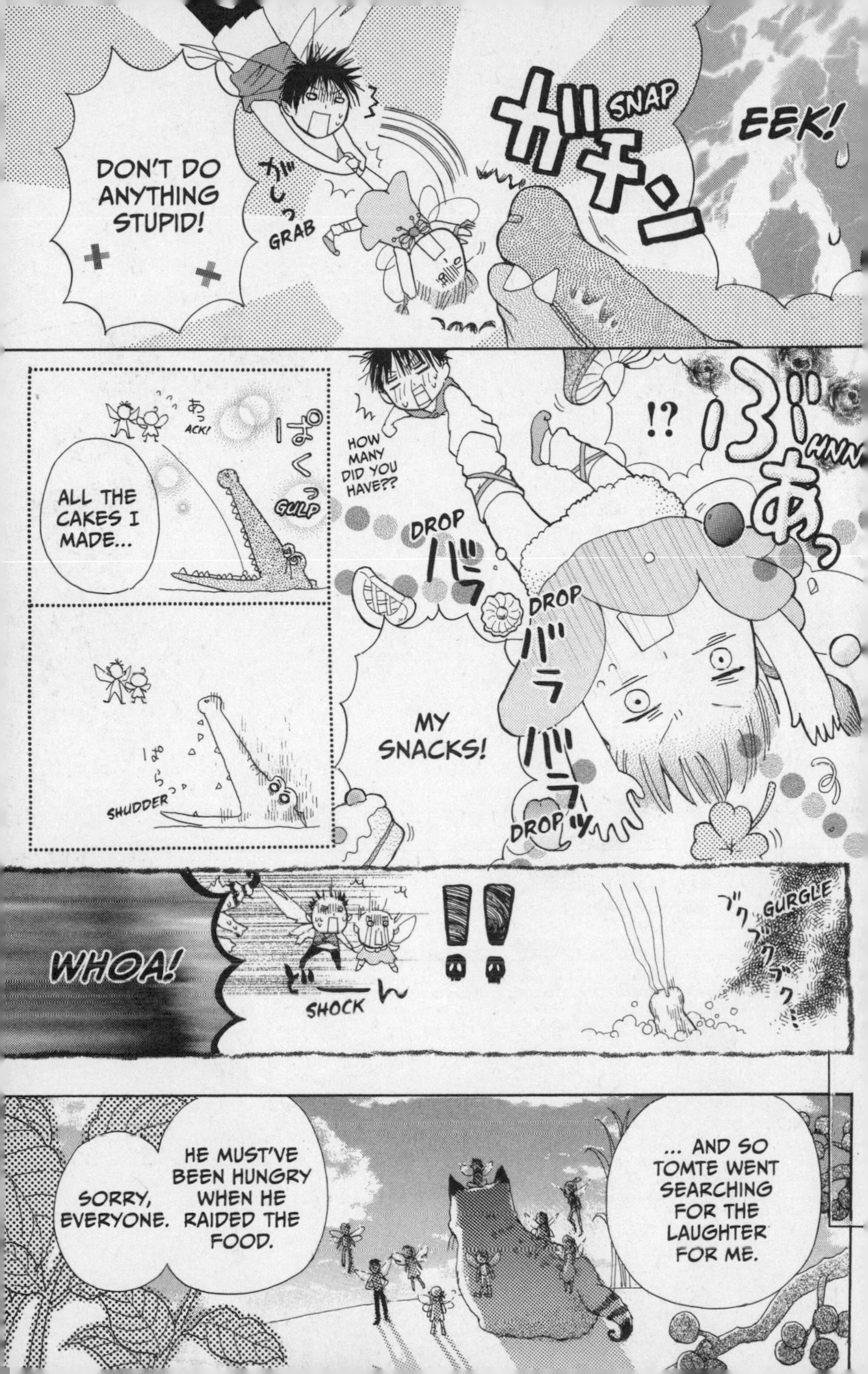
EEK!
SNAP
GRAB
DON'T DO ANYTHING STUPID!
HNN
!?
HOW MANY DID YOU HAVE??
DROP
DROP
DROP
MY SNACKS!
ACK!
GULP
ALL THE CAKES I MADE...
SHUDDER
GURGLE
!!
SHOCK
WHOA!
... AND SO TOMTE WENT SEARCHING FOR THE LAUGHTER FOR ME.
HE MUST'VE BEEN HUNGRY WHEN HE RAIDED THE FOOD.
SORRY, EVERYONE.

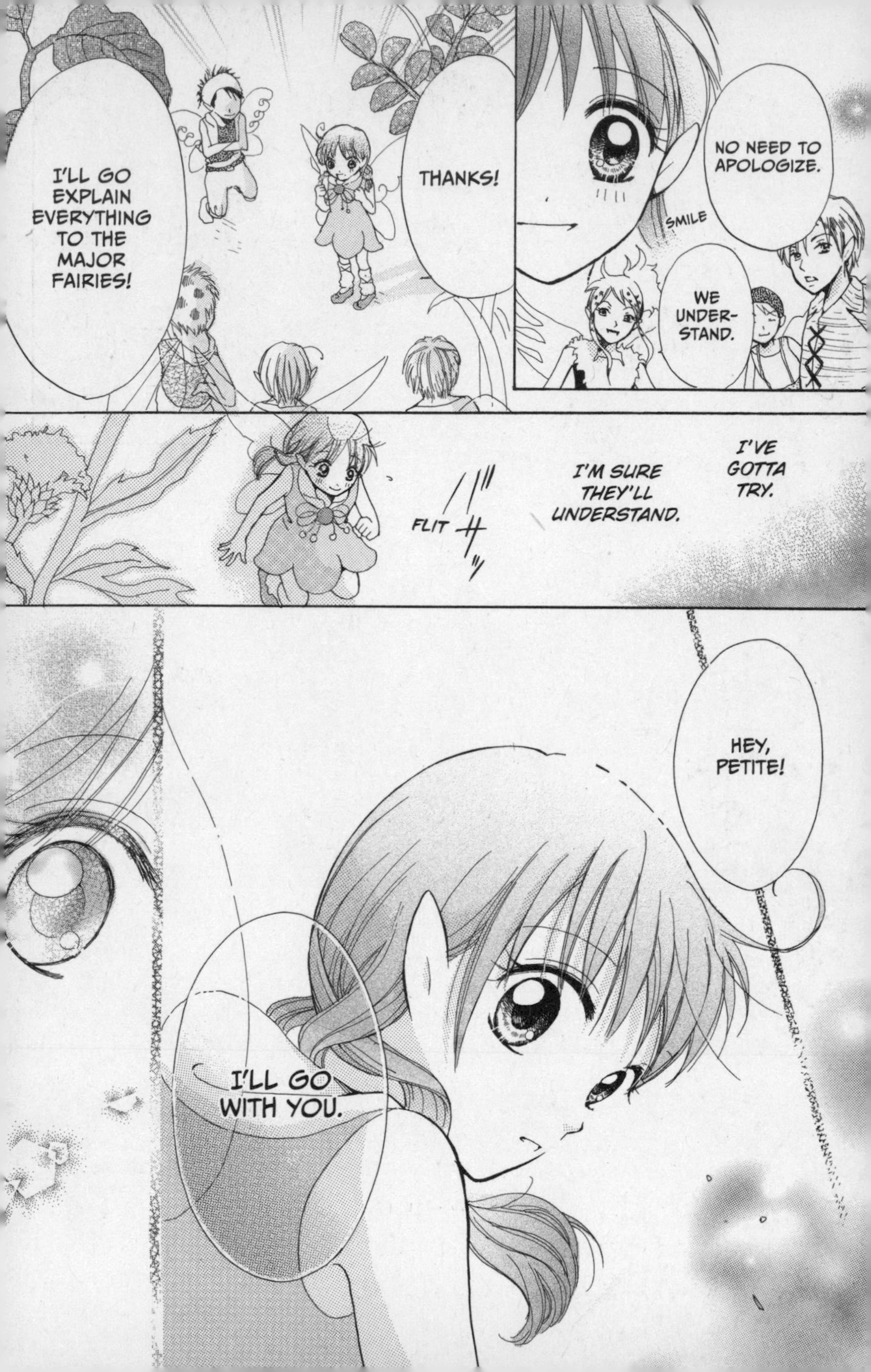
NO NEED TO APOLOGIZE.
SMILE
WE UNDER-STAND.
THANKS!
I'LL GO EXPLAIN EVERYTHING TO THE MAJOR FAIRIES!
I'VE GOTTA TRY.
I'M SURE THEY'LL UNDERSTAND.
FLIT
HEY, PETITE!
I'LL GO WITH YOU.

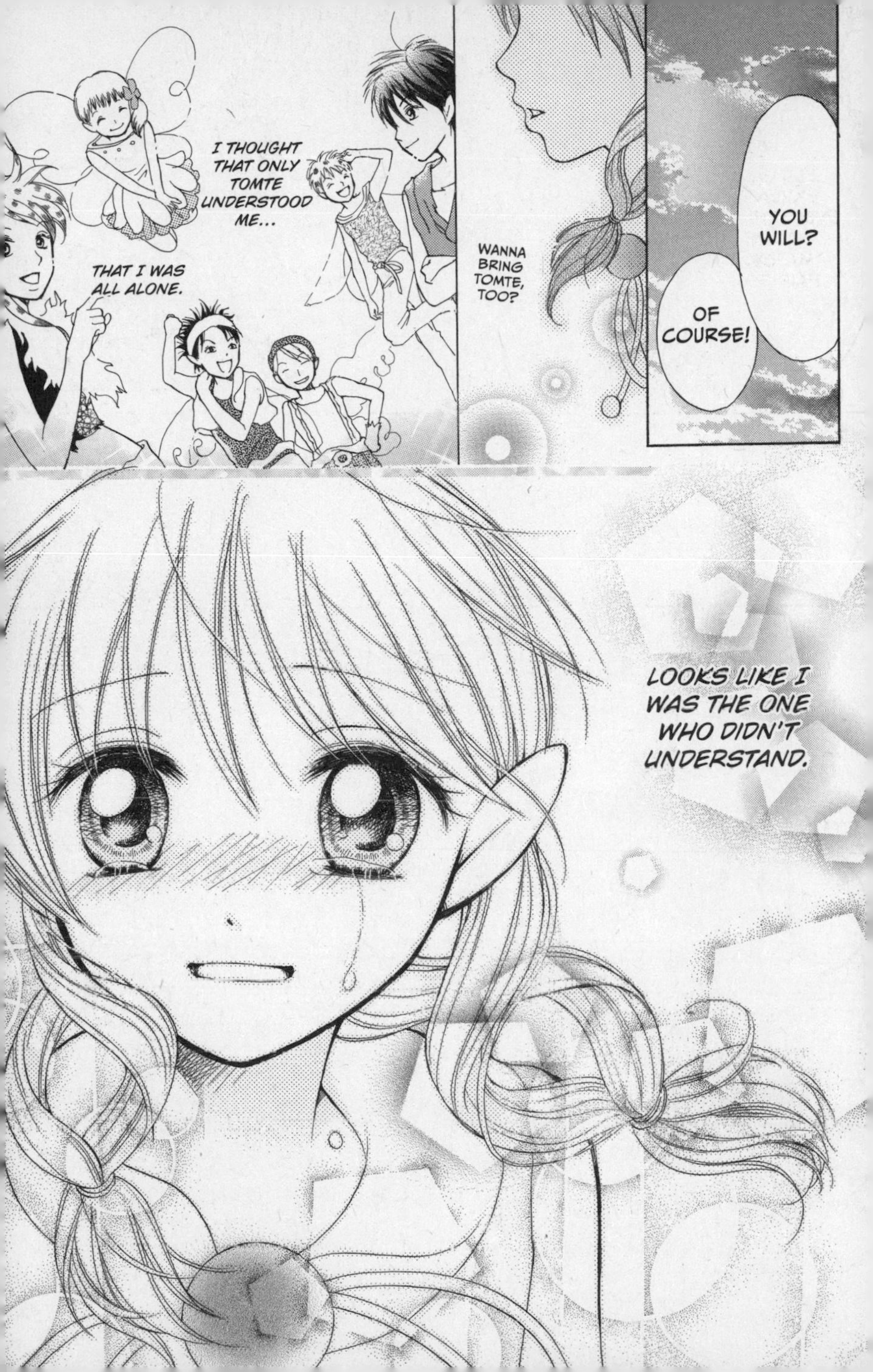
YOU WILL?
OF COURSE!
WANNA BRING TOMTE, TOO?
I THOUGHT THAT ONLY TOMTE UNDERSTOOD ME...
THAT I WAS ALL ALONE.
LOOKS LIKE I WAS THE ONE WHO DIDN'T UNDERSTAND.

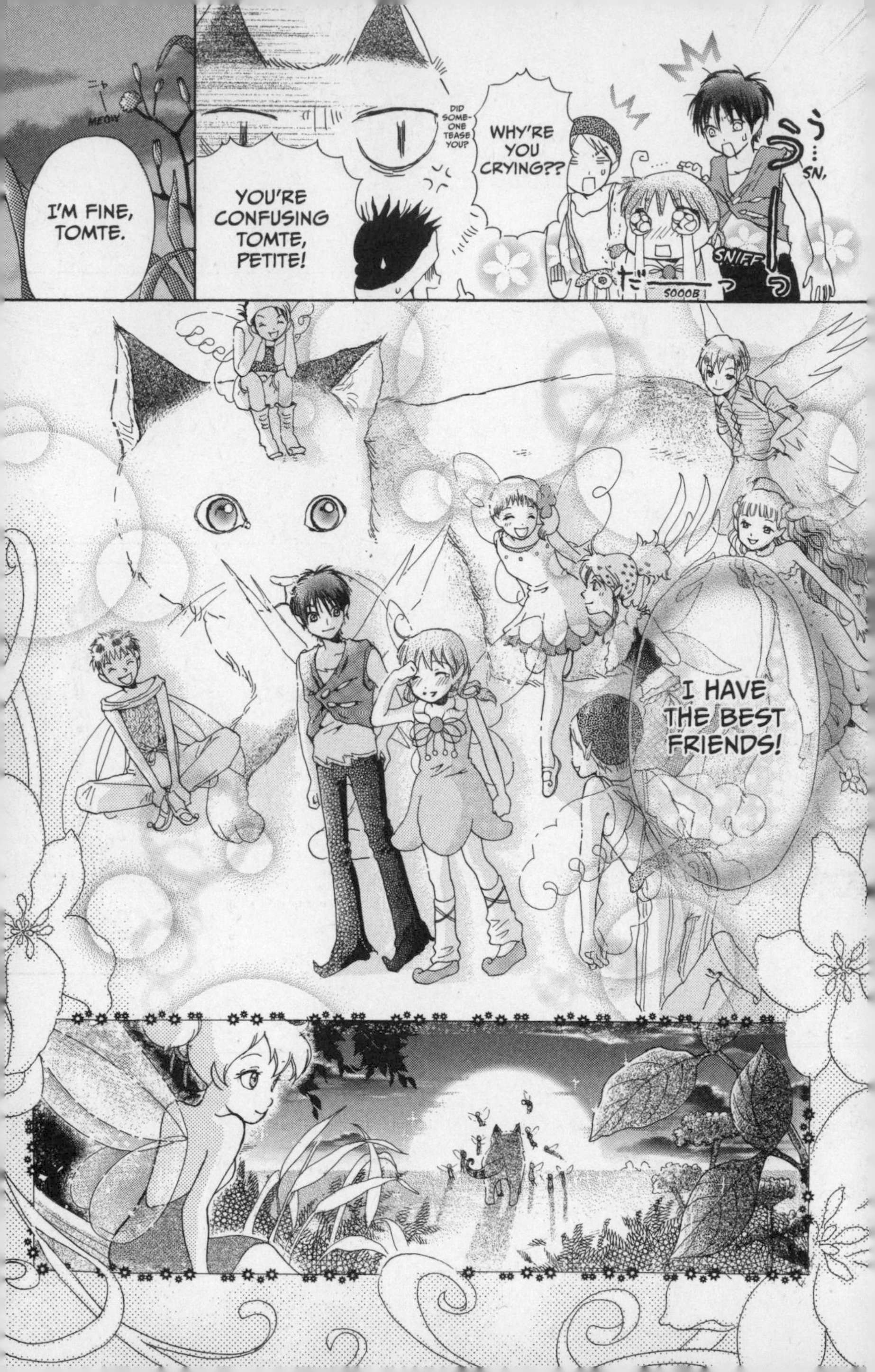
うう…
SN,
WHY'RE YOU CRYING??
DID SOME-ONE TEASE YOU?
SNIFF
だー
SOOOB
YOU'RE CONFUSING TOMTE, PETITE!
ニャ
MEOW
I'M FINE, TOMTE.
I HAVE THE BEST FRIENDS!

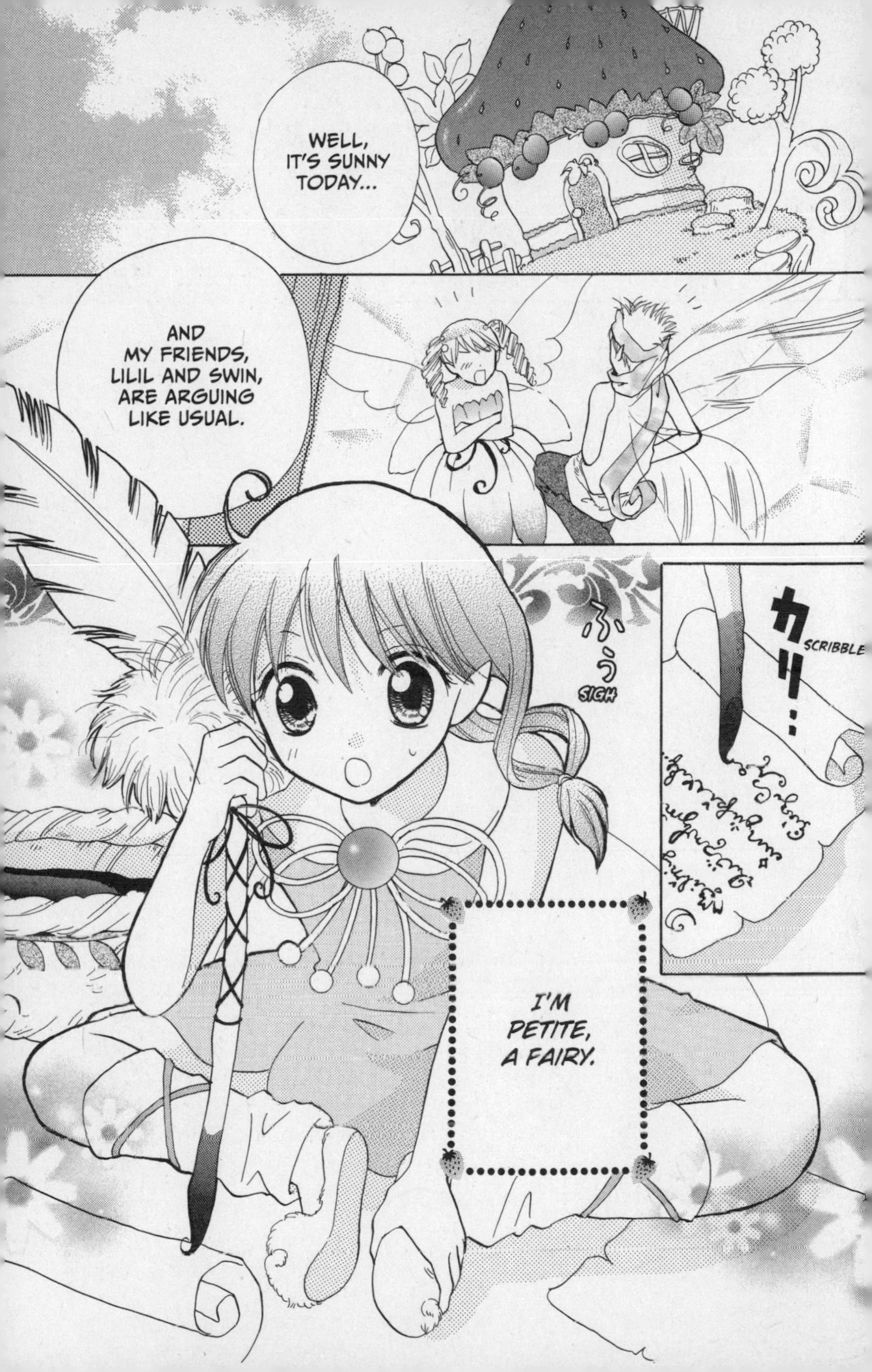
WELL, IT'S SUNNY TODAY...
AND MY FRIENDS, LILIL AND SWIN, ARE ARGUING LIKE USUAL.
カリ… SCRIBBLE
ふう SIGH
I'M PETITE, A FAIRY.

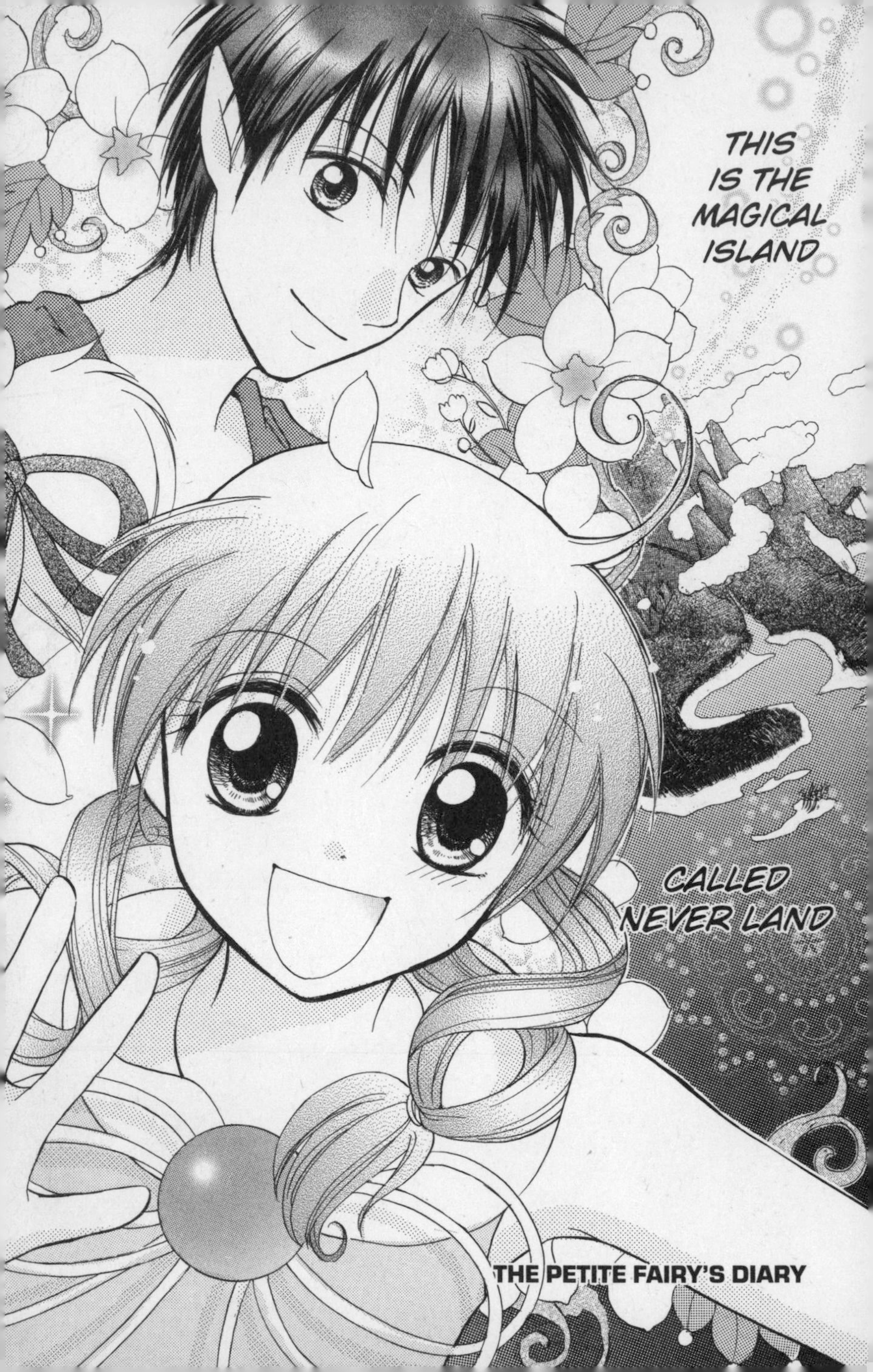
THIS IS THE MAGICAL ISLAND
CALLED NEVER LAND
THE PETITE FAIRY'S DIARY

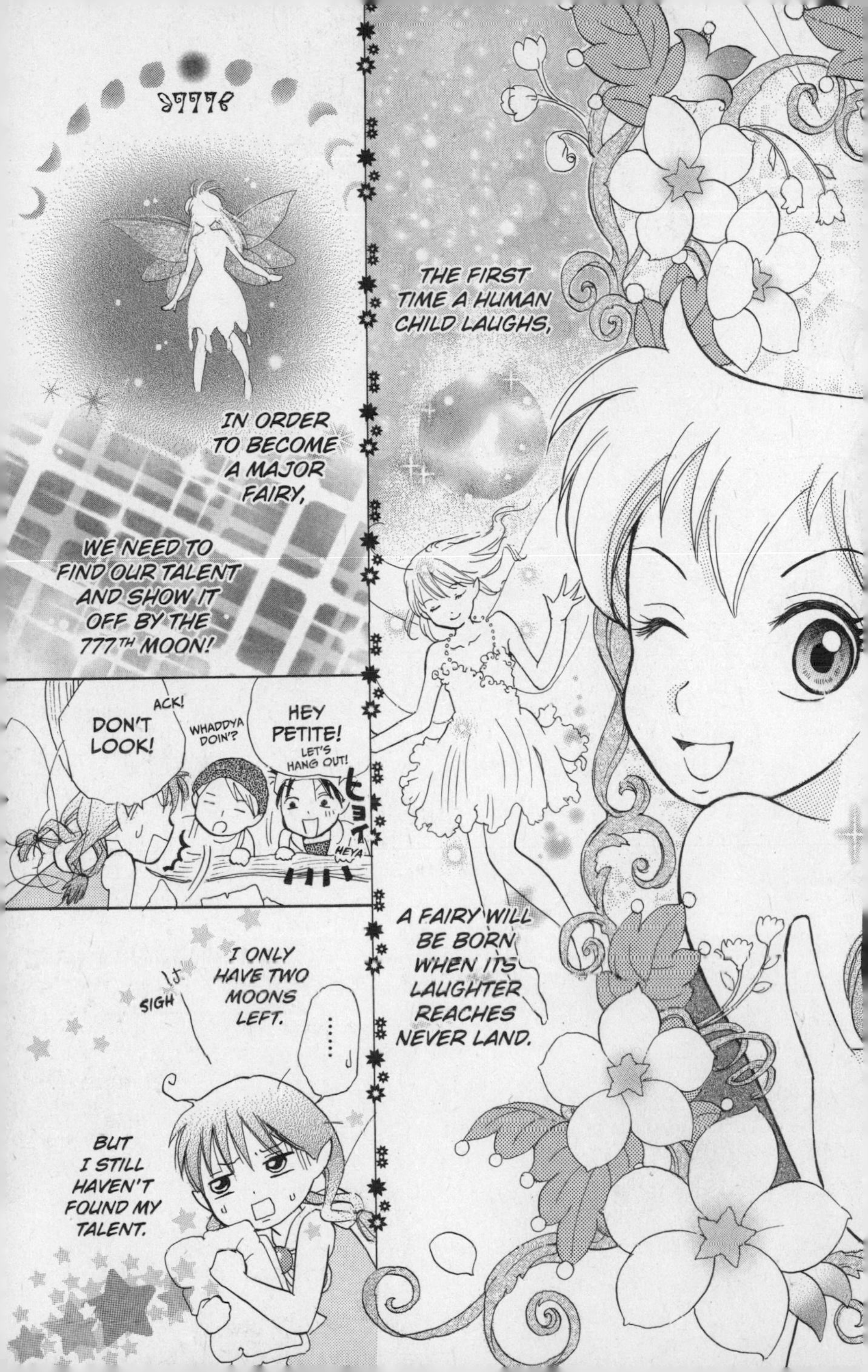
THE FIRST TIME A HUMAN CHILD LAUGHS,
A FAIRY WILL BE BORN WHEN ITS LAUGHTER REACHES NEVER LAND.
IN ORDER TO BECOME A MAJOR FAIRY,
WE NEED TO FIND OUR TALENT AND SHOW IT OFF BY THE 777TH MOON!
HEY PETITE!
LET'S HANG OUT!
ヒョイ
HEYA
WHADDYA DOIN'?
ACK!
DON'T LOOK!
I ONLY HAVE TWO MOONS LEFT.
......
SIGH
BUT I STILL HAVEN'T FOUND MY TALENT.

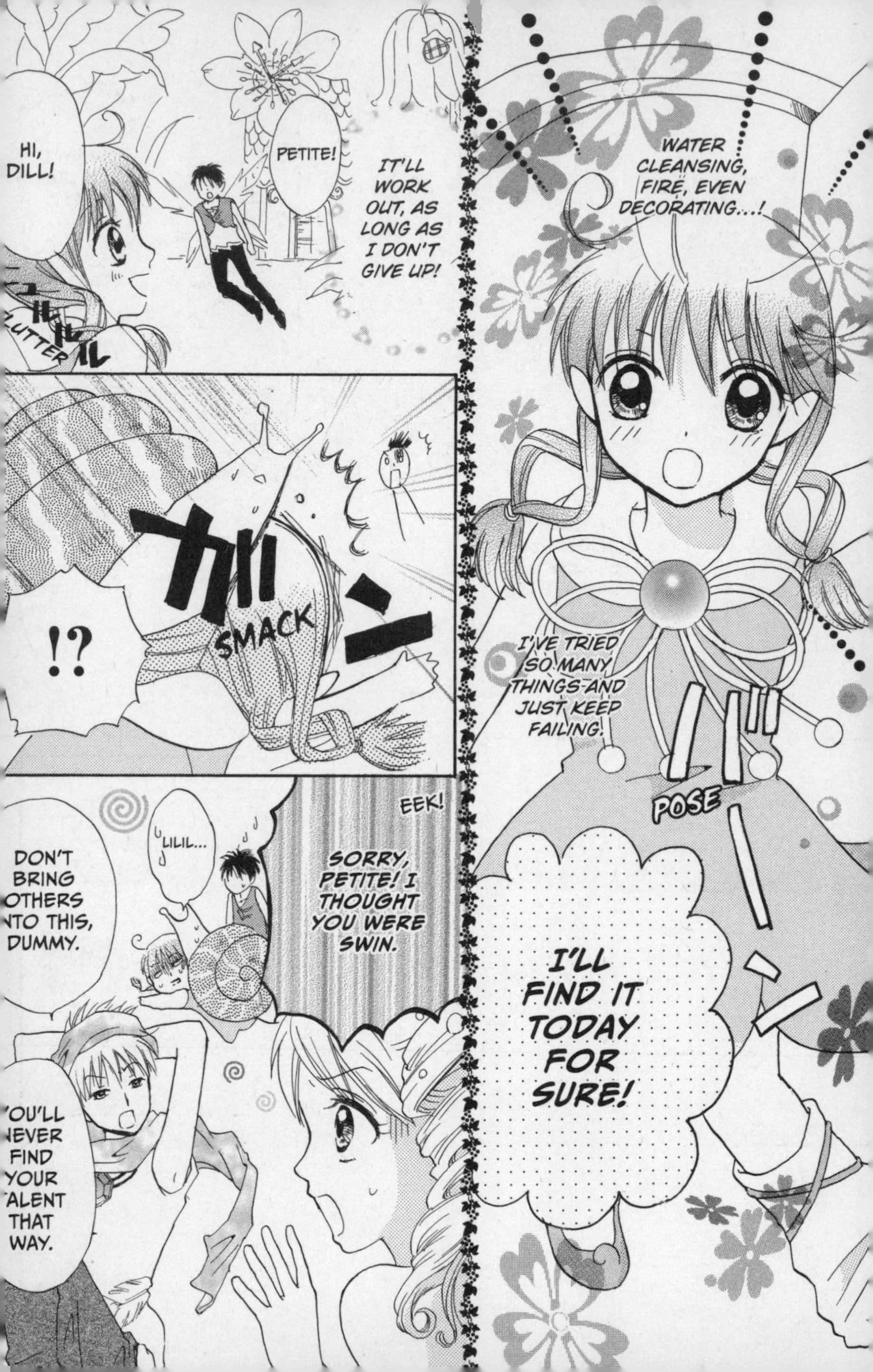
WATER CLEANSING, FIRE, EVEN DECORATING...!
I'VE TRIED SO MANY THINGS AND JUST KEEP FAILING.
POSE
I'LL FIND IT TODAY FOR SURE!
IT'LL WORK OUT, AS LONG AS I DON'T GIVE UP!
PETITE!
HI, DILL!
FLUTTER
SMACK
!?
EEK!
SORRY, PETITE! I THOUGHT YOU WERE SWIN.
LILIL...
DON'T BRING OTHERS NTO THIS, DUMMY.
OU'LL NEVER FIND YOUR ALENT THAT WAY.

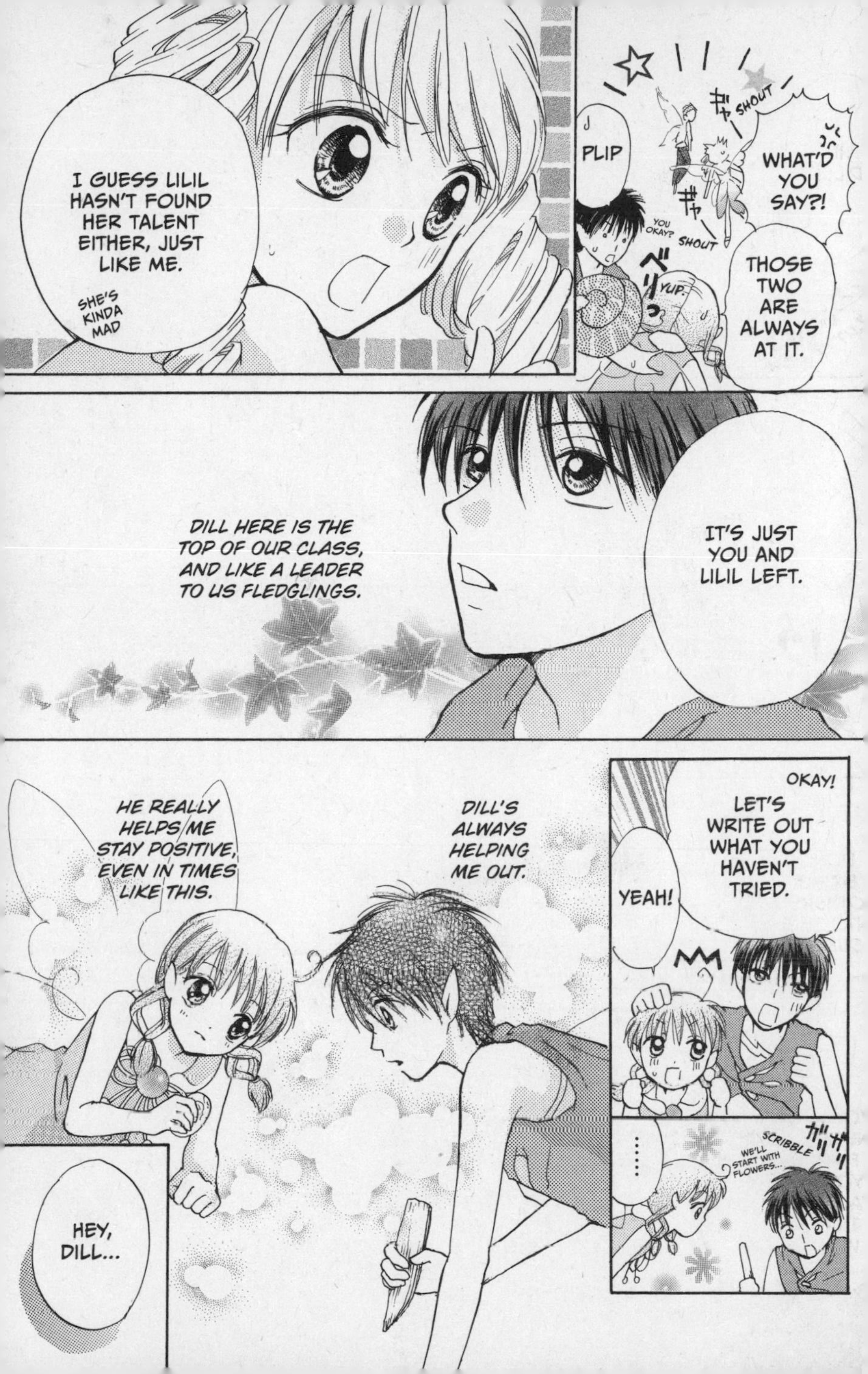
WHAT'D YOU SAY?!
SHOUT
PLIP
SHOUT
YOU OKAY?
THOSE TWO ARE ALWAYS AT IT.
YUP.
I GUESS LILIL HASN'T FOUND HER TALENT EITHER, JUST LIKE ME.
SHE'S KINDA MAD
IT'S JUST YOU AND LILIL LEFT.
DILL HERE IS THE TOP OF OUR CLASS, AND LIKE A LEADER TO US FLEDGLINGS.
OKAY! LET'S WRITE OUT WHAT YOU HAVEN'T TRIED.
YEAH!
SCRIBBLE
WE'LL START WITH FLOWERS...
......
DILL'S ALWAYS HELPING ME OUT.
HE REALLY HELPS ME STAY POSITIVE, EVEN IN TIMES LIKE THIS.
HEY, DILL...

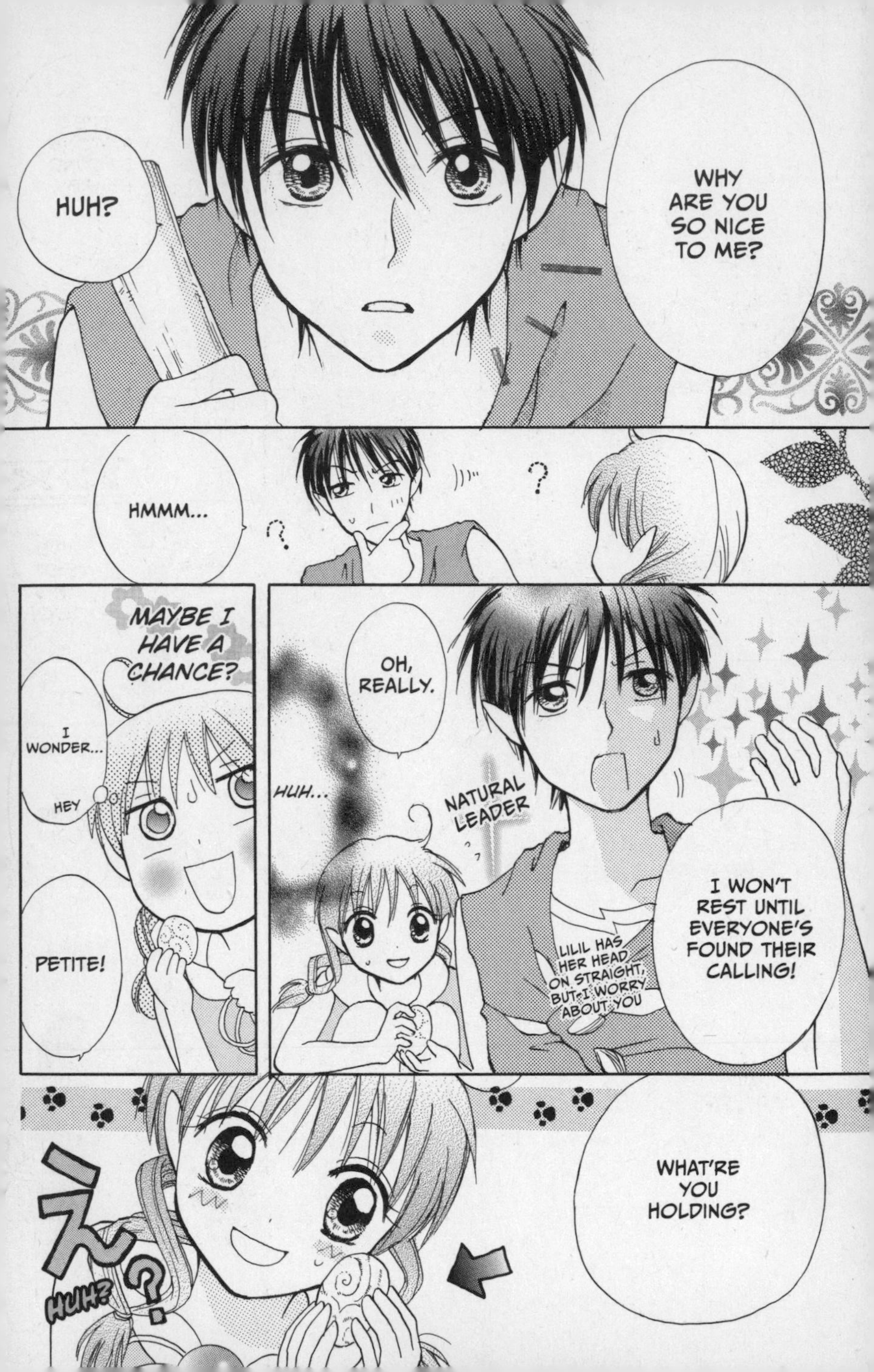
WHY ARE YOU SO NICE TO ME?
HUH?
HMMM...
I WON'T REST UNTIL EVERYONE'S FOUND THEIR CALLING!
LILIL HAS HER HEAD ON STRAIGHT, BUT I WORRY ABOUT YOU
NATURAL LEADER
OH, REALLY.
HUH...
MAYBE I HAVE A CHANCE?
I WONDER...
HEY
PETITE!
WHAT'RE YOU HOLDING?
え?
HUH?

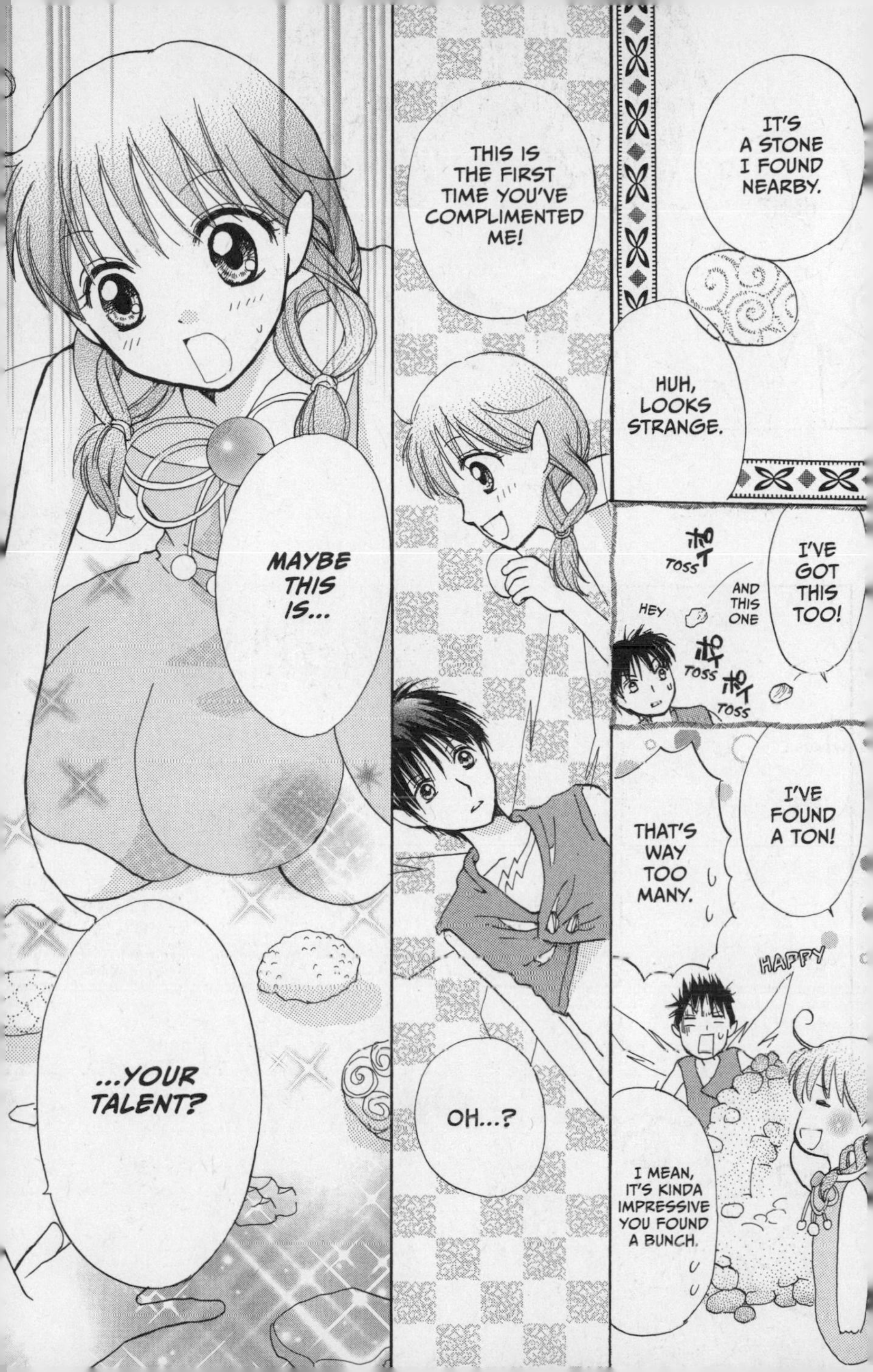
IT'S A STONE I FOUND NEARBY.
HUH, LOOKS STRANGE.
I'VE GOT THIS TOO!
ポイ TOSS
AND THIS ONE
HEY
ポイ TOSS
ポイ TOSS
I'VE FOUND A TON!
THAT'S WAY TOO MANY.
HAPPY
I MEAN, IT'S KINDA IMPRESSIVE YOU FOUND A BUNCH.
THIS IS THE FIRST TIME YOU'VE COMPLIMENTED ME!
OH...?
MAYBE THIS IS...
...YOUR TALENT?

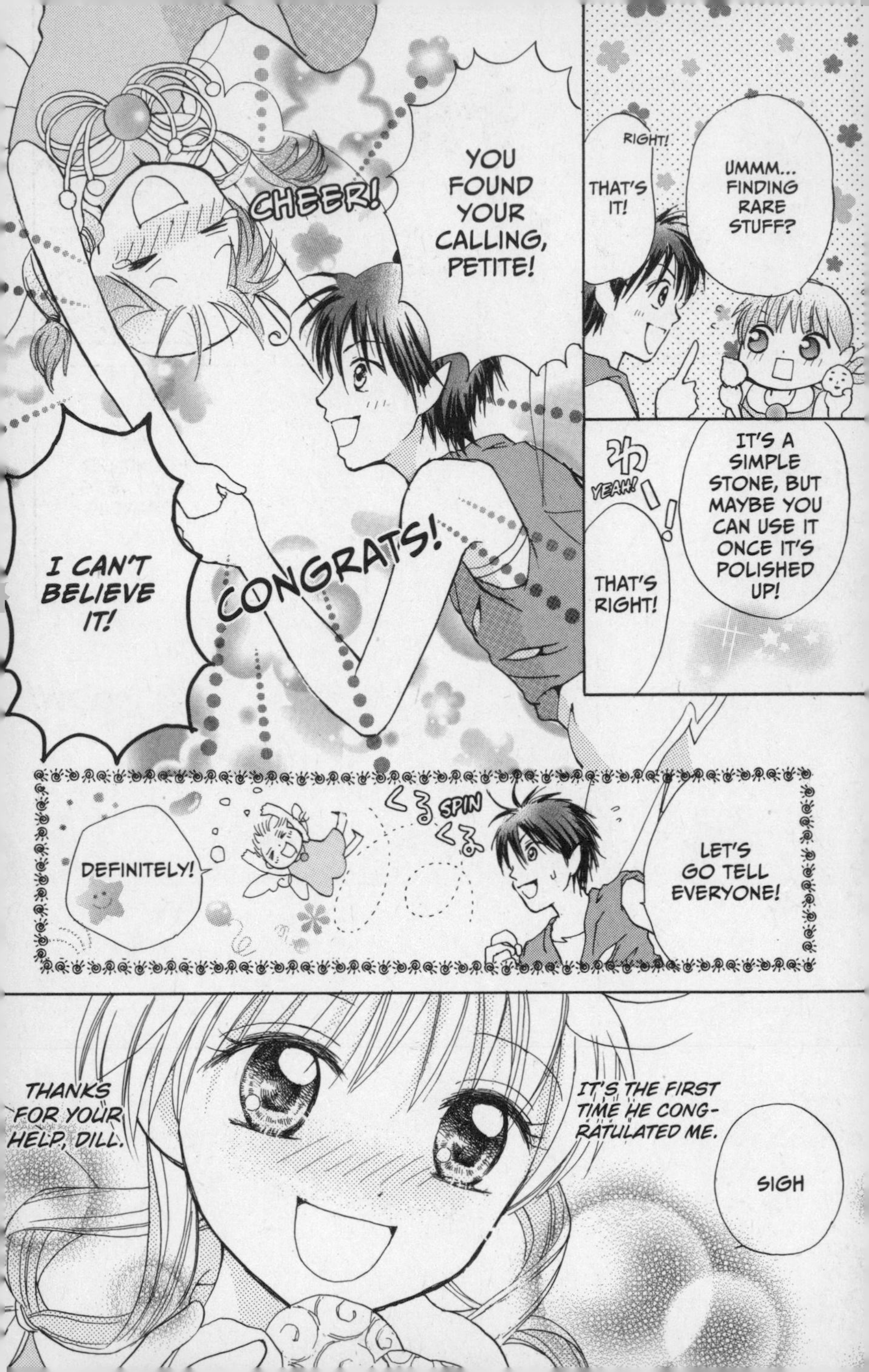
UMMM... FINDING RARE STUFF?
RIGHT!
THAT'S IT!
IT'S A SIMPLE STONE, BUT MAYBE YOU CAN USE IT ONCE IT'S POLISHED UP!
YEAH!
THAT'S RIGHT!
YOU FOUND YOUR CALLING, PETITE!
CHEER!
CONGRATS!
I CAN'T BELIEVE IT!
LET'S GO TELL EVERYONE!
SPIN
DEFINITELY!
SIGH
IT'S THE FIRST TIME HE CONGRATULATED ME.
THANKS FOR YOUR HELP, DILL.

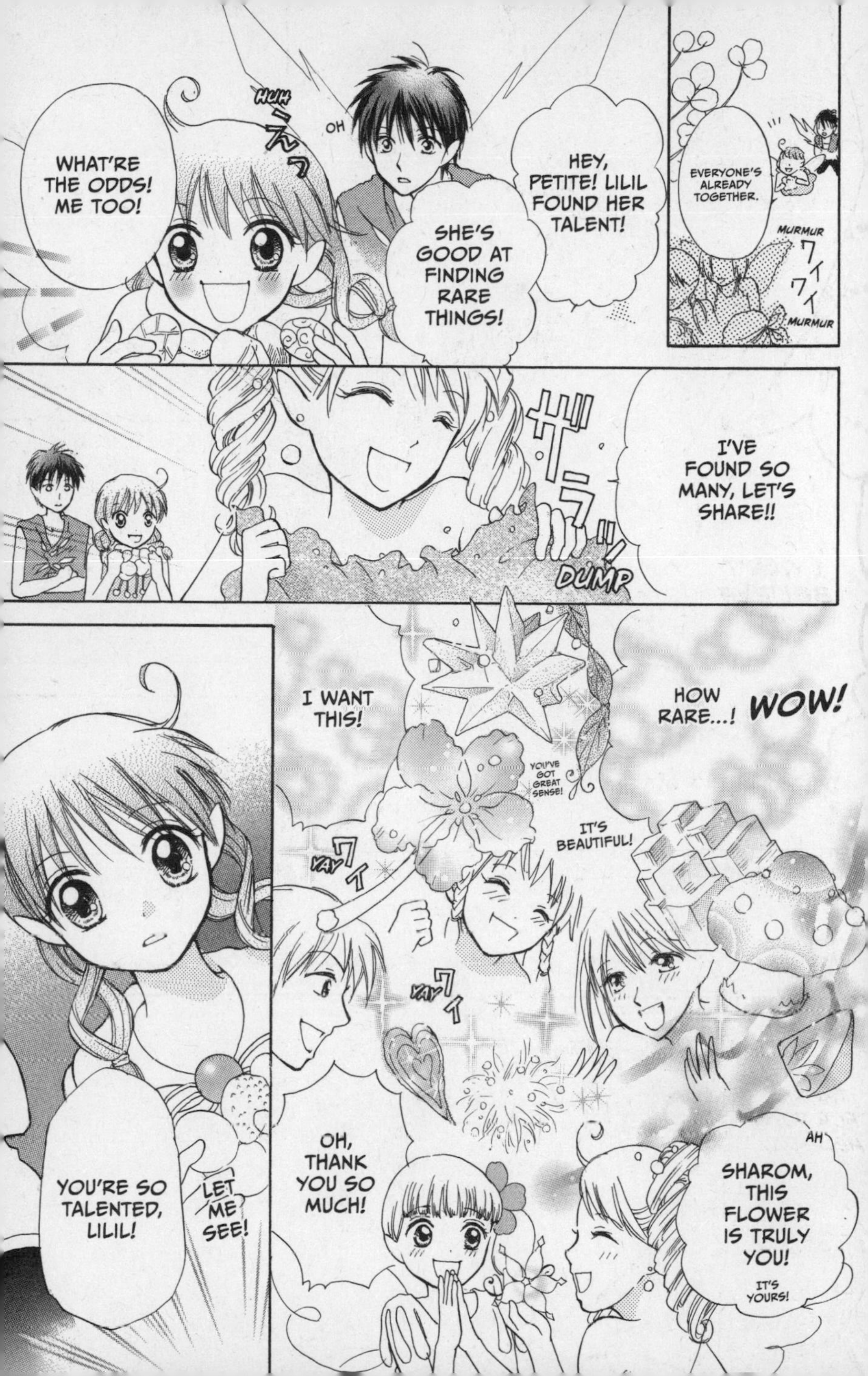
EVERYONE'S ALREADY TOGETHER.
MURMUR
ワイワイ
MURMUR
HEY, PETITE! LILIL FOUND HER TALENT!
SHE'S GOOD AT FINDING RARE THINGS!
OH
HUH
えっ
WHAT'RE THE ODDS! ME TOO!
I'VE FOUND SO MANY, LET'S SHARE!!
ザラッ
DUMP
WOW!
HOW RARE...!
I WANT THIS!
YOU'VE GOT GREAT SENSE!
IT'S BEAUTIFUL!
YAY
ワイ
YAY
ワイ
AH
SHAROM, THIS FLOWER IS TRULY YOU!
IT'S YOURS!
OH, THANK YOU SO MUCH!
LET ME SEE!
YOU'RE SO TALENTED, LILIL!

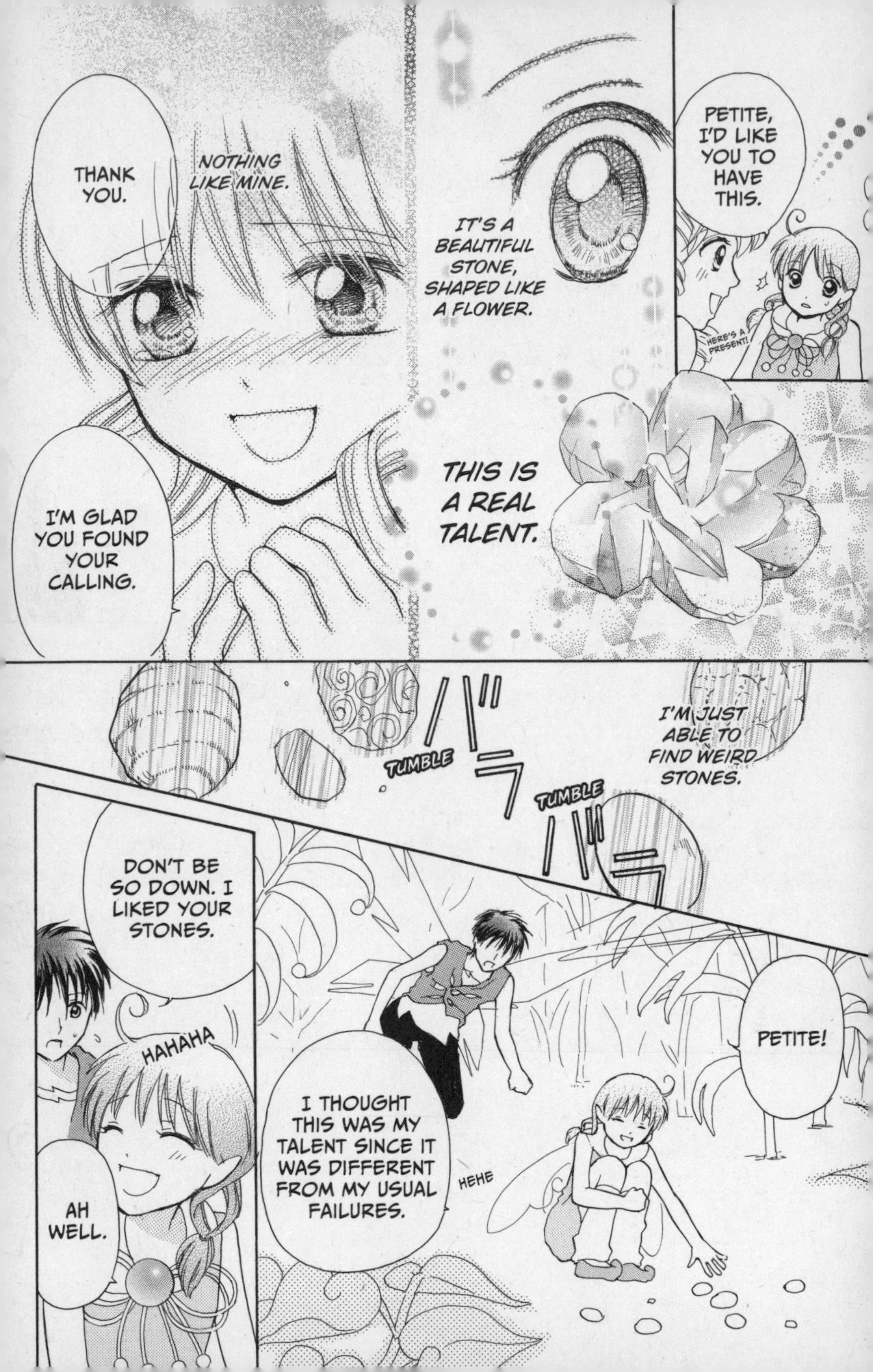
PETITE, I'D LIKE YOU TO HAVE THIS.
HERE'S A PRESENT!
IT'S A BEAUTIFUL STONE, SHAPED LIKE A FLOWER.
THIS IS A REAL TALENT.
THANK YOU.
NOTHING LIKE MINE.
I'M GLAD YOU FOUND YOUR CALLING.
I'M JUST ABLE TO FIND WEIRD STONES.
TUMBLE
TUMBLE
PETITE!
I THOUGHT THIS WAS MY TALENT SINCE IT WAS DIFFERENT FROM MY USUAL FAILURES.
HEHE
DON'T BE SO DOWN. I LIKED YOUR STONES.
HAHAHA
AH WELL.

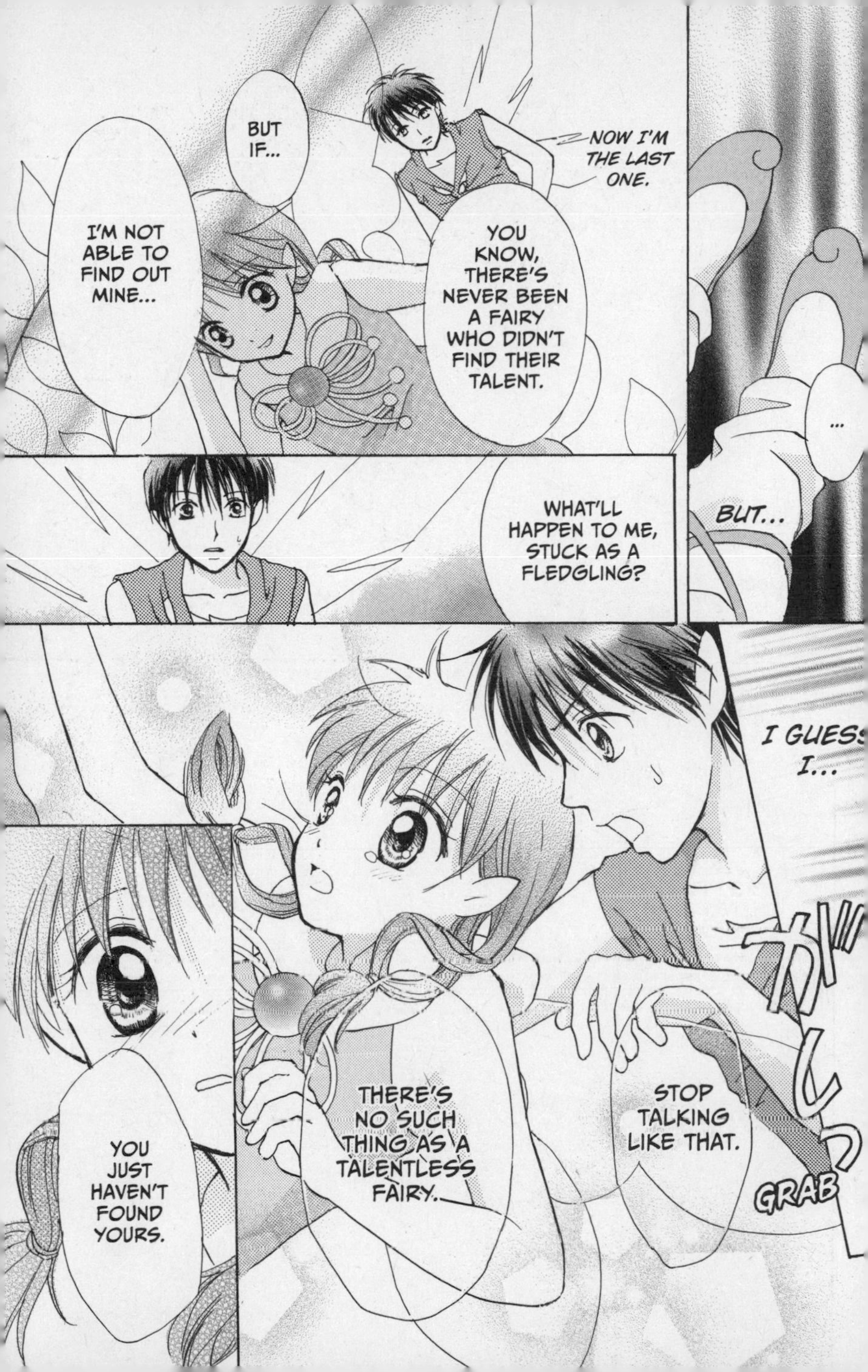
...
BUT...
NOW I'M THE LAST ONE.
YOU KNOW, THERE'S NEVER BEEN A FAIRY WHO DIDN'T FIND THEIR TALENT.
BUT IF...
I'M NOT ABLE TO FIND OUT MINE...
WHAT'LL HAPPEN TO ME, STUCK AS A FLEDGLING?
I GUESS I...
GRAB
STOP TALKING LIKE THAT.
THERE'S NO SUCH THING AS A TALENTLESS FAIRY.
YOU JUST HAVEN'T FOUND YOURS.

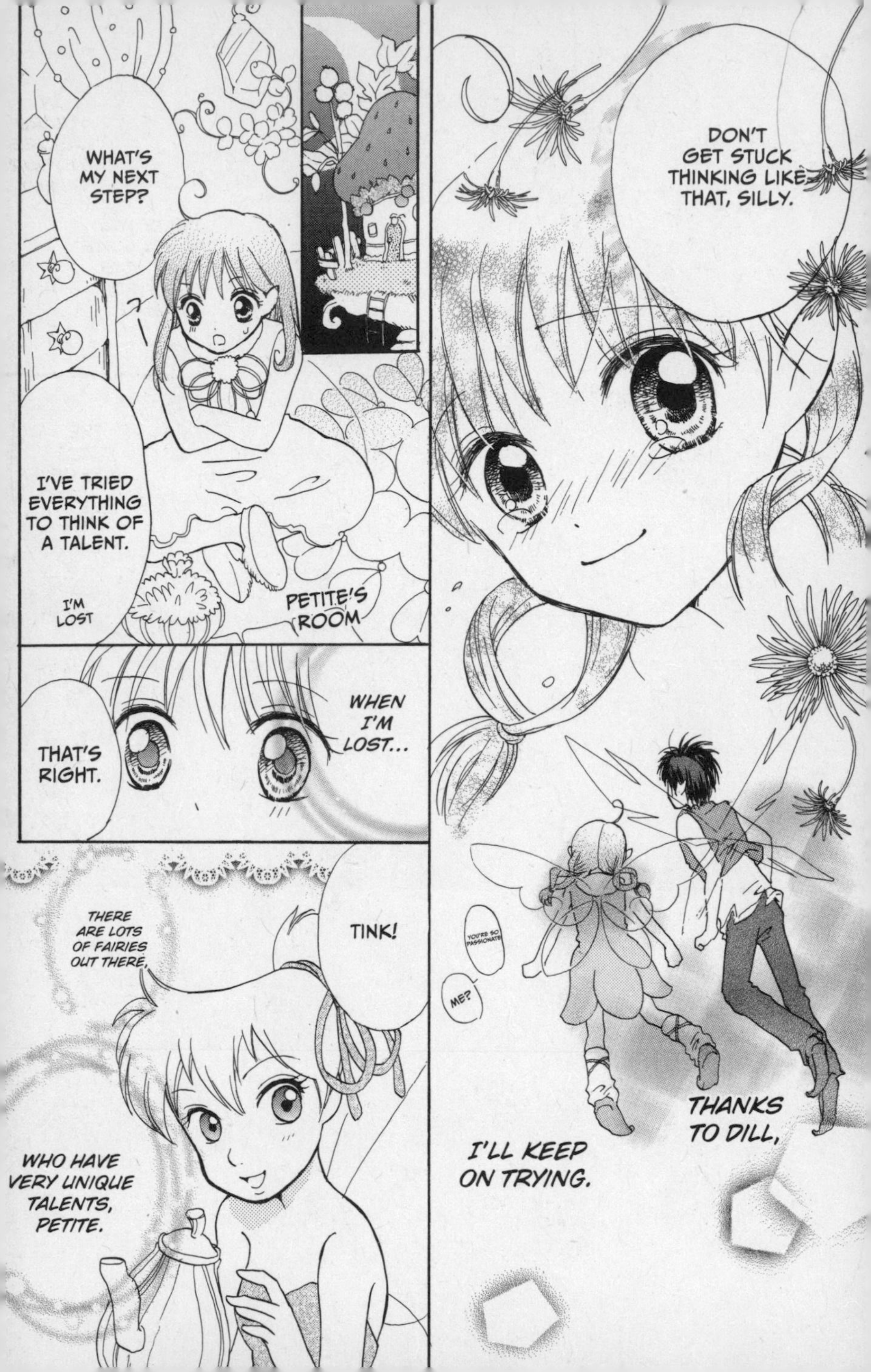
DON'T GET STUCK THINKING LIKE THAT, SILLY.
YOU'RE SO PASSIONATE
ME?
THANKS TO DILL,
I'LL KEEP ON TRYING.
WHAT'S MY NEXT STEP?
I'VE TRIED EVERYTHING TO THINK OF A TALENT.
I'M LOST
PETITE'S ROOM
WHEN I'M LOST...
THAT'S RIGHT.
TINK!
THERE ARE LOTS OF FAIRIES OUT THERE,
WHO HAVE VERY UNIQUE TALENTS, PETITE.

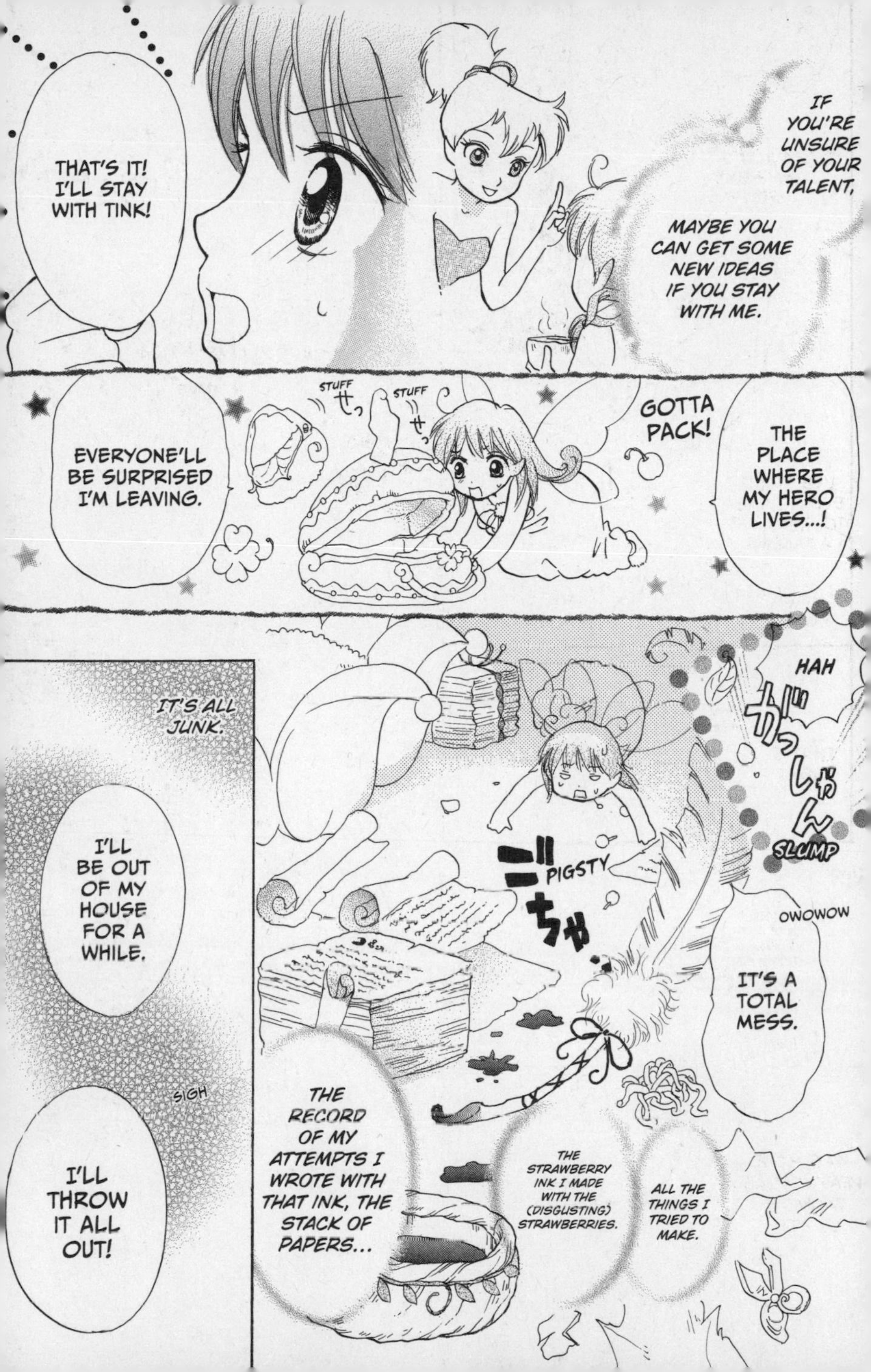

IF YOU'RE UNSURE OF YOUR TALENT,
MAYBE YOU CAN GET SOME NEW IDEAS IF YOU STAY WITH ME.
THAT'S IT! I'LL STAY WITH TINK!
THE PLACE WHERE MY HERO LIVES...!
GOTTA PACK!
STUFF
STUFF
EVERYONE'LL BE SURPRISED I'M LEAVING.
HAH
がっしゃん
SLUMP
OWOWOW
IT'S A TOTAL MESS.
ごちゃ
PIGSTY
ALL THE THINGS I TRIED TO MAKE.
THE STRAWBERRY INK I MADE WITH THE (DISGUSTING) STRAWBERRIES.
THE RECORD OF MY ATTEMPTS I WROTE WITH THAT INK, THE STACK OF PAPERS...
IT'S ALL JUNK.
I'LL BE OUT OF MY HOUSE FOR A WHILE.
SIGH
I'LL THROW IT ALL OUT!

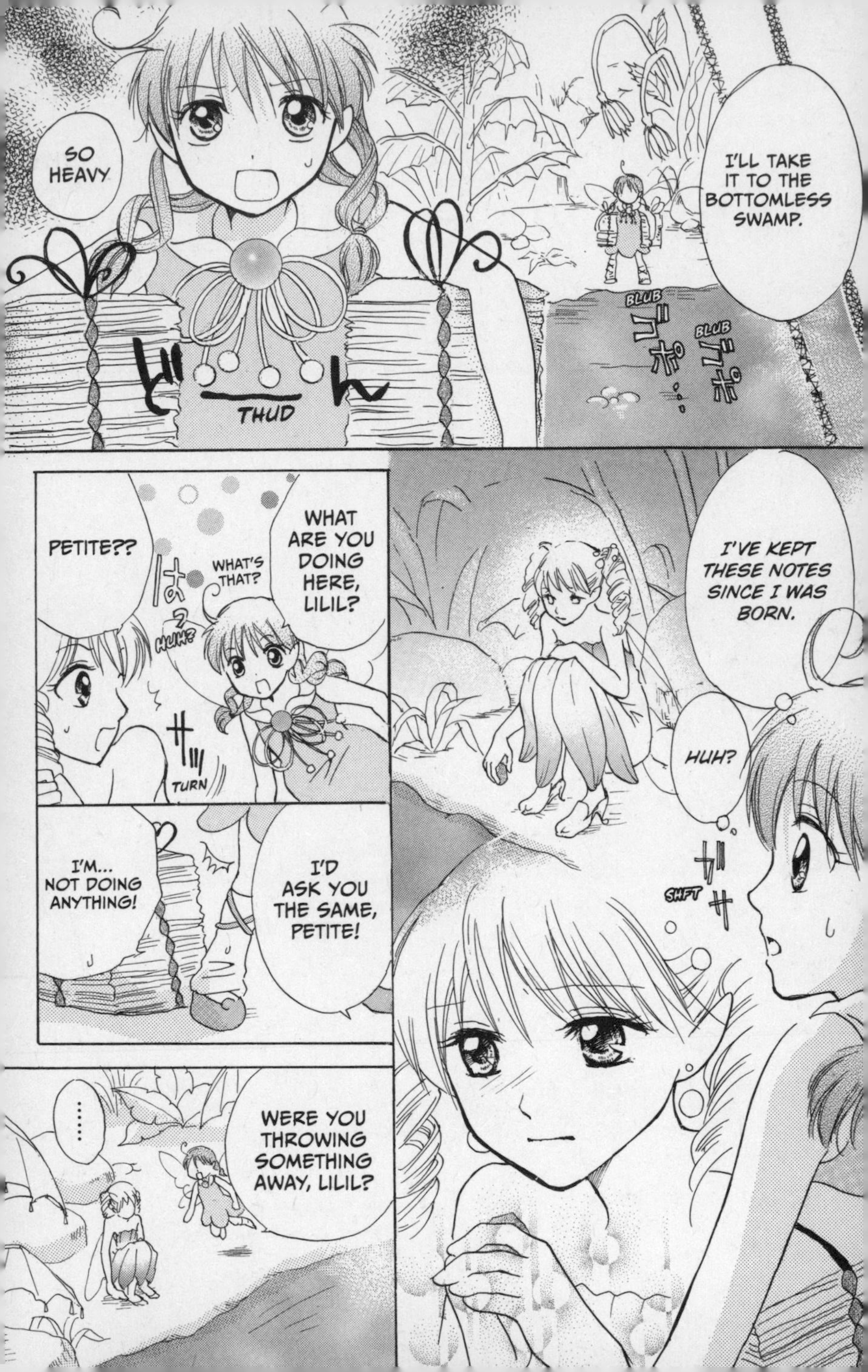
I'LL TAKE IT TO THE BOTTOMLESS SWAMP.
BLUB
BLUB
SO HEAVY
THUD
I'VE KEPT THESE NOTES SINCE I WAS BORN.
HUH?
SHFT
WHAT ARE YOU DOING HERE, LILIL?
WHAT'S THAT?
HUH?
PETITE??
TURN
I'D ASK YOU THE SAME, PETITE!
I'M... NOT DOING ANYTHING!
WERE YOU THROWING SOMETHING AWAY, LILIL?
......

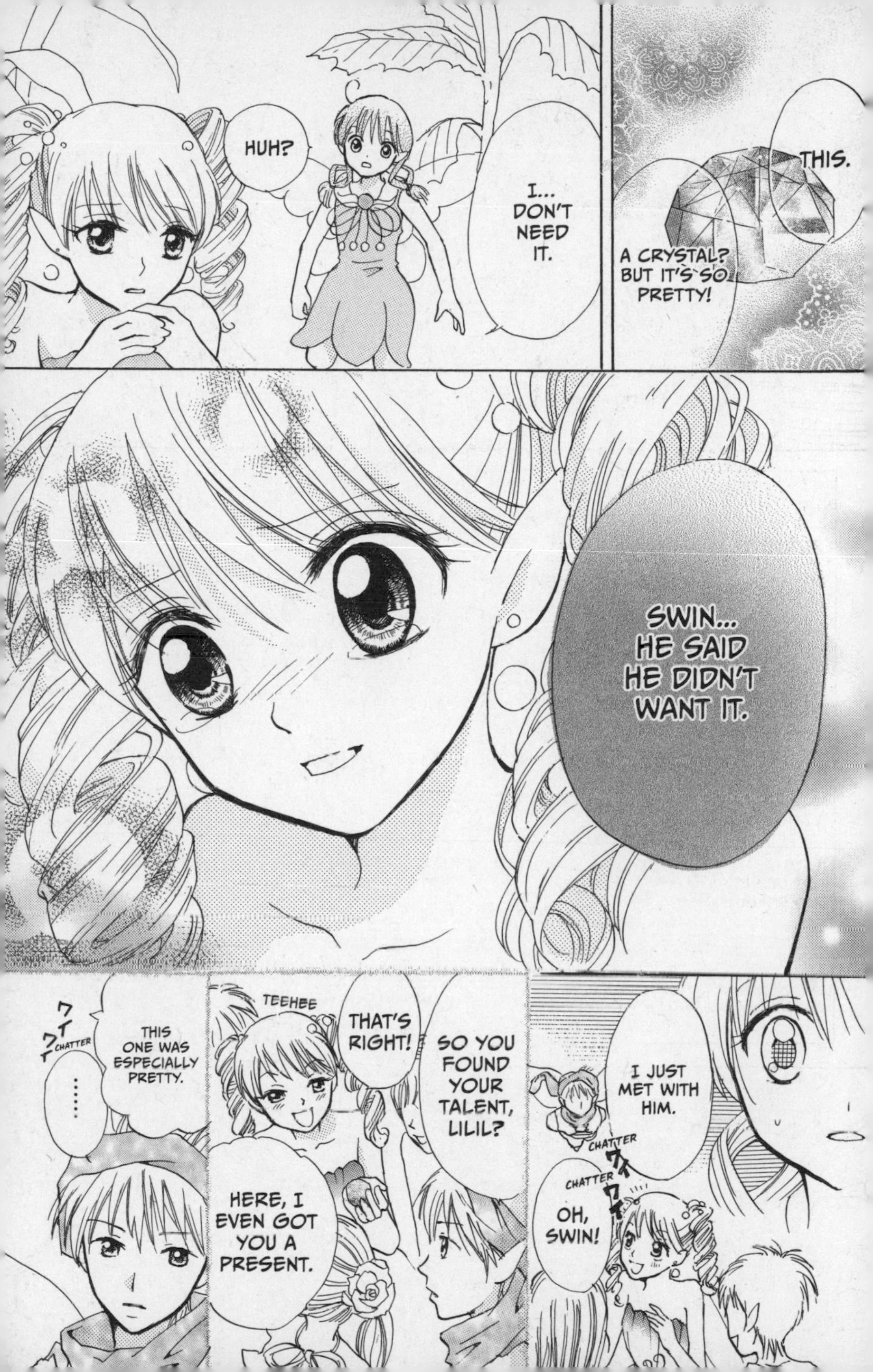
THIS.
A CRYSTAL? BUT IT'S SO PRETTY!
I... DON'T NEED IT.
HUH?
SWIN... HE SAID HE DIDN'T WANT IT.
I JUST MET WITH HIM.
CHATTER
ワイ
CHATTER
ワイ
OH, SWIN!
SO YOU FOUND YOUR TALENT, LILIL?
THAT'S RIGHT!
TEEHEE
HERE, I EVEN GOT YOU A PRESENT.
THIS ONE WAS ESPECIALLY PRETTY.
ワイワイ
CHATTER
......

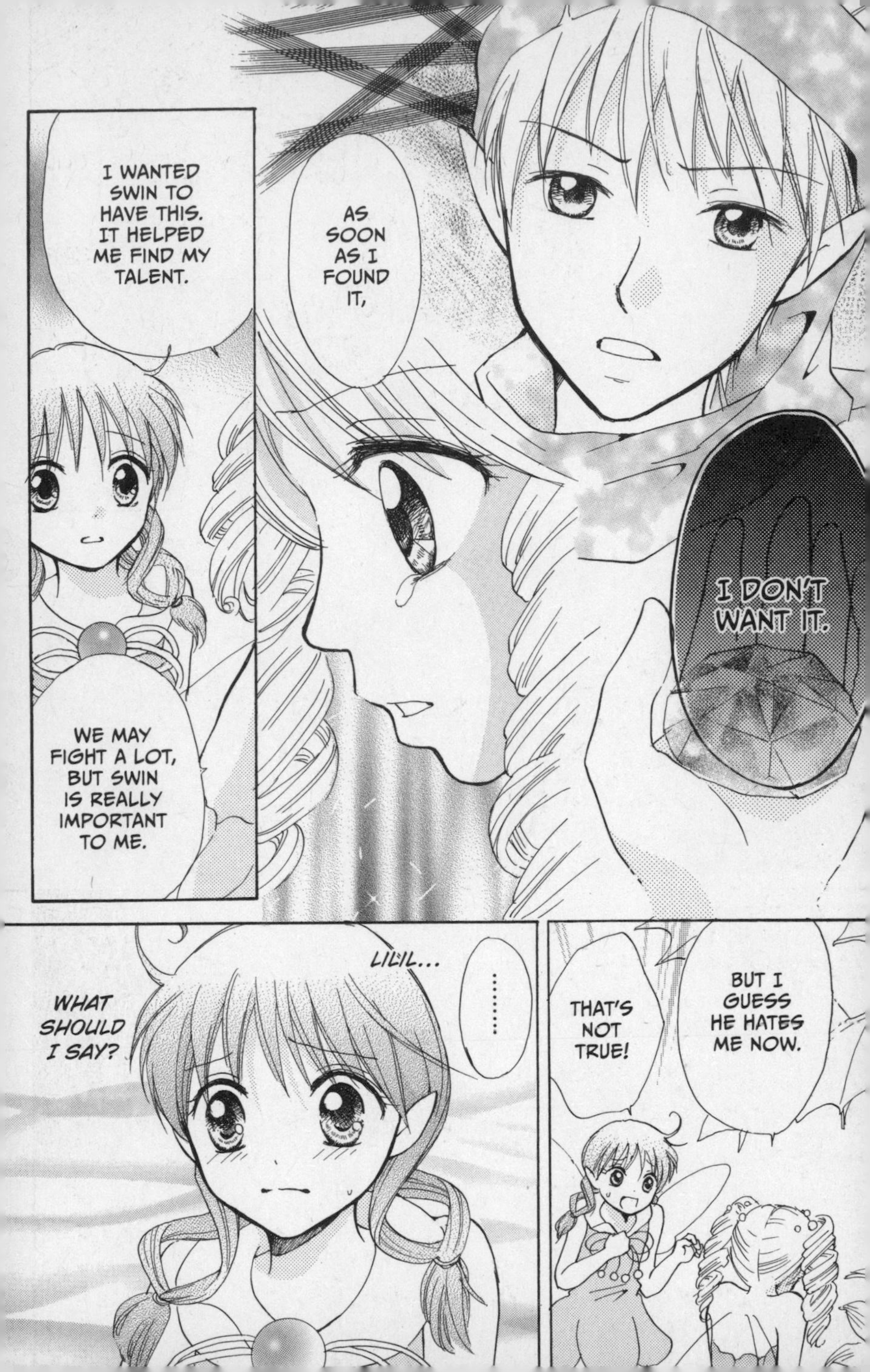
AS SOON AS I FOUND IT,
I DON'T WANT IT.
I WANTED SWIN TO HAVE THIS. IT HELPED ME FIND MY TALENT.
WE MAY FIGHT A LOT, BUT SWIN IS REALLY IMPORTANT TO ME.
BUT I GUESS HE HATES ME NOW.
THAT'S NOT TRUE!
....
LILIL...
WHAT SHOULD I SAY?

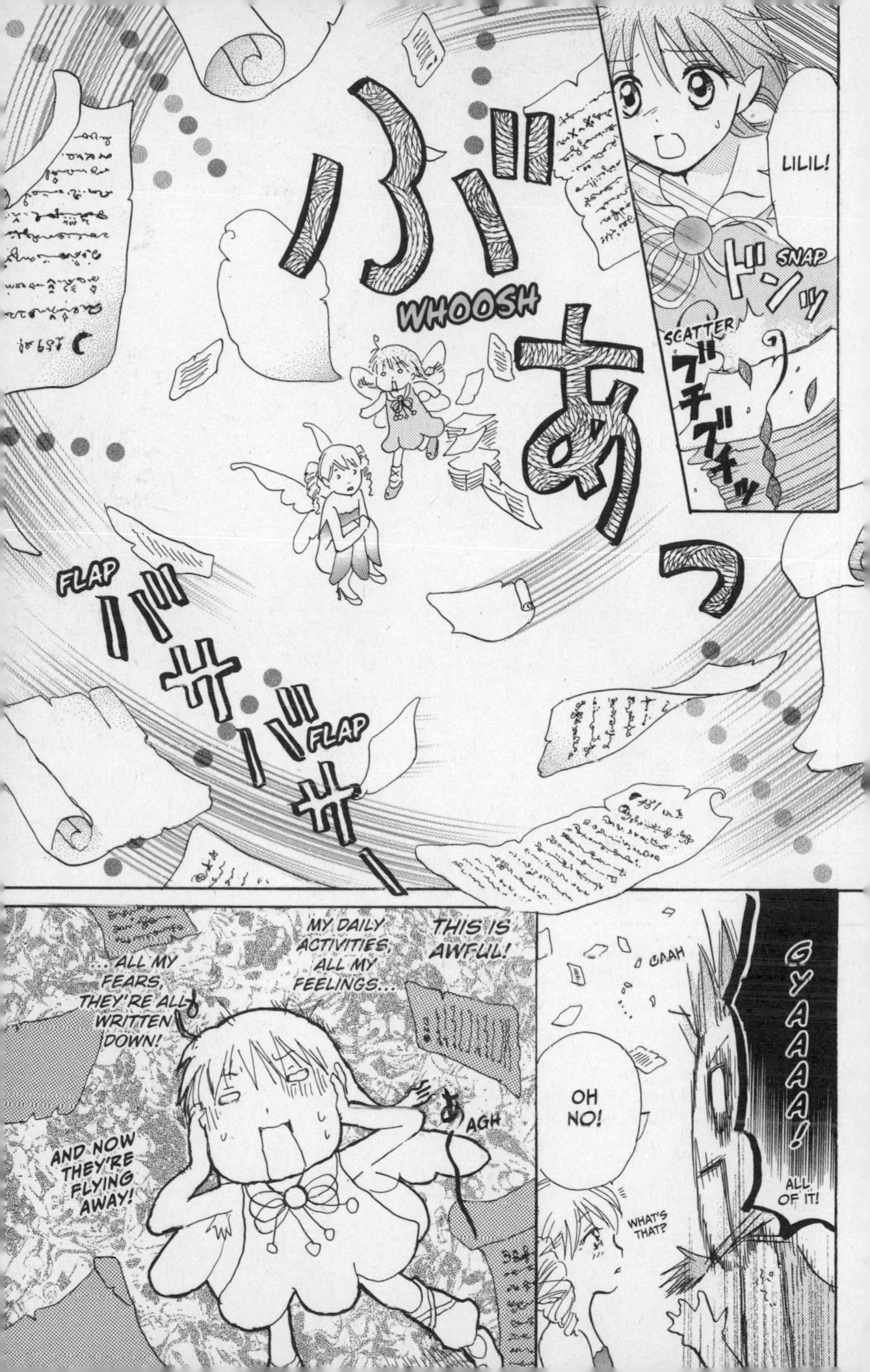
LILIL!
ドンッ
SNAP
ブチブチッ
SCATTER
ぶあっ
WHOOSH
バサ
FLAP
バサー
FLAP
GYAAAAA!
ALL OF IT!
GAAH
OH NO!
WHAT'S THAT?
THIS IS AWFUL!
MY DAILY ACTIVITIES, ALL MY FEELINGS...
...ALL MY FEARS, THEY'RE ALL WRITTEN DOWN!
あ
AGH
AND NOW THEY'RE FLYING AWAY!

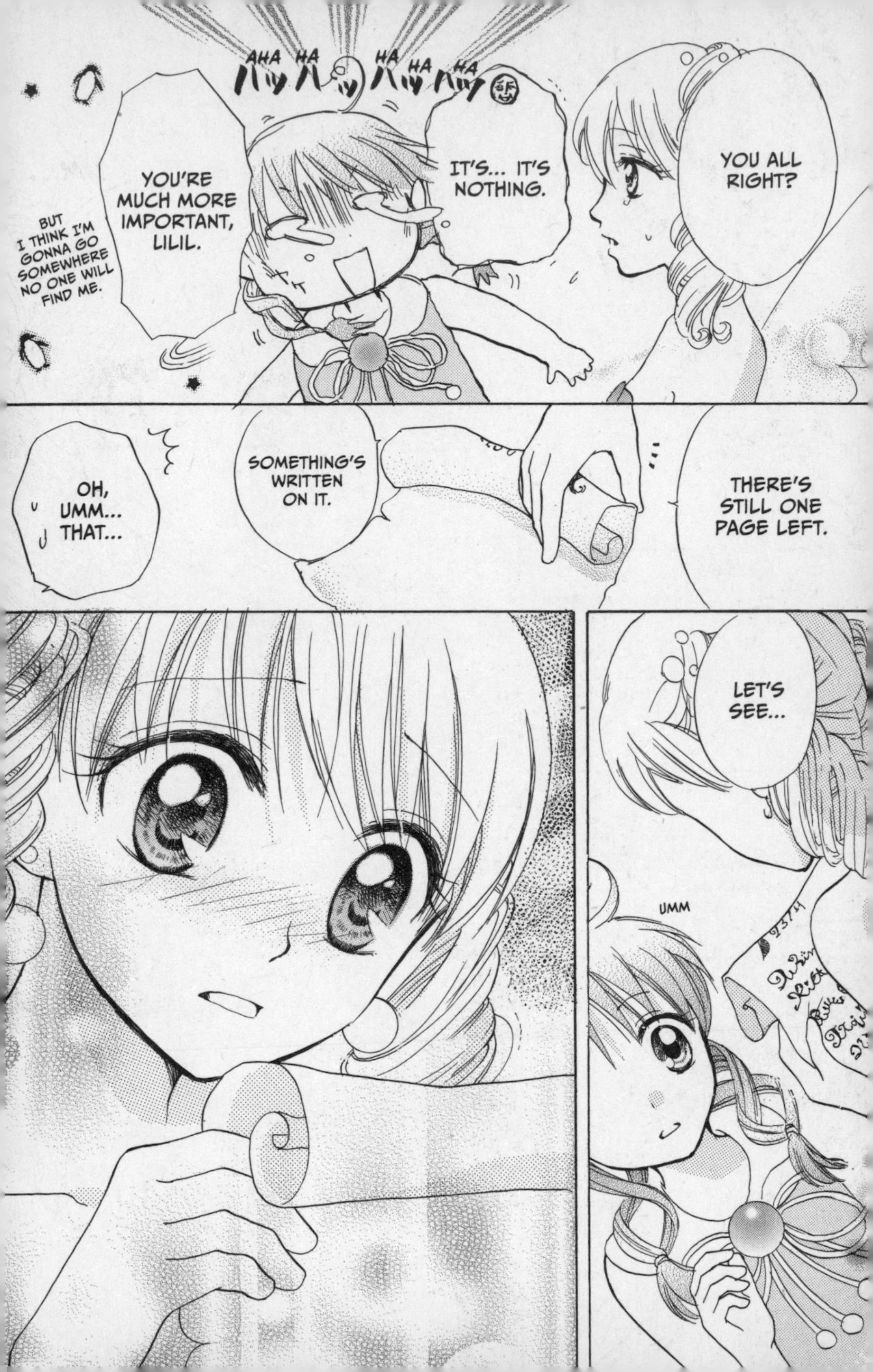
YOU ALL RIGHT?
AHA HA HA HA HA
IT'S... IT'S NOTHING.
YOU'RE MUCH MORE IMPORTANT, LILIL.
BUT I THINK I'M GONNA GO SOMEWHERE NO ONE WILL FIND ME.
THERE'S STILL ONE PAGE LEFT.
SOMETHING'S WRITTEN ON IT.
OH, UMM... THAT...
LET'S SEE...
UMM

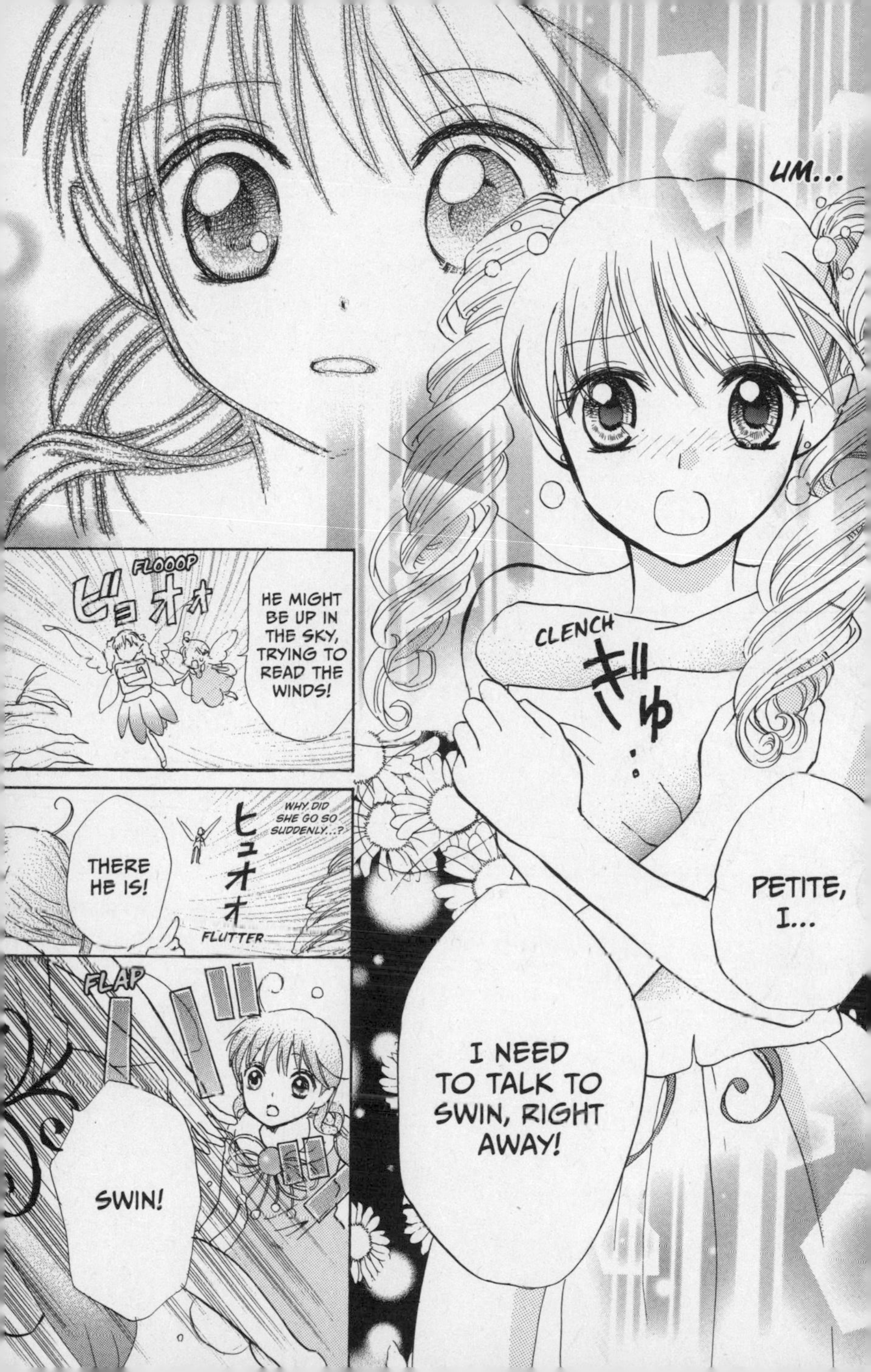
UM...
CLENCH
きゅ
PETITE, I...
I NEED TO TALK TO SWIN, RIGHT AWAY!
FLOOOP
ビョオォ
HE MIGHT BE UP IN THE SKY, TRYING TO READ THE WINDS!
WHY DID SHE GO SO SUDDENLY...?
ヒュオオ
FLUTTER
THERE HE IS!
FLAP
SWIN!

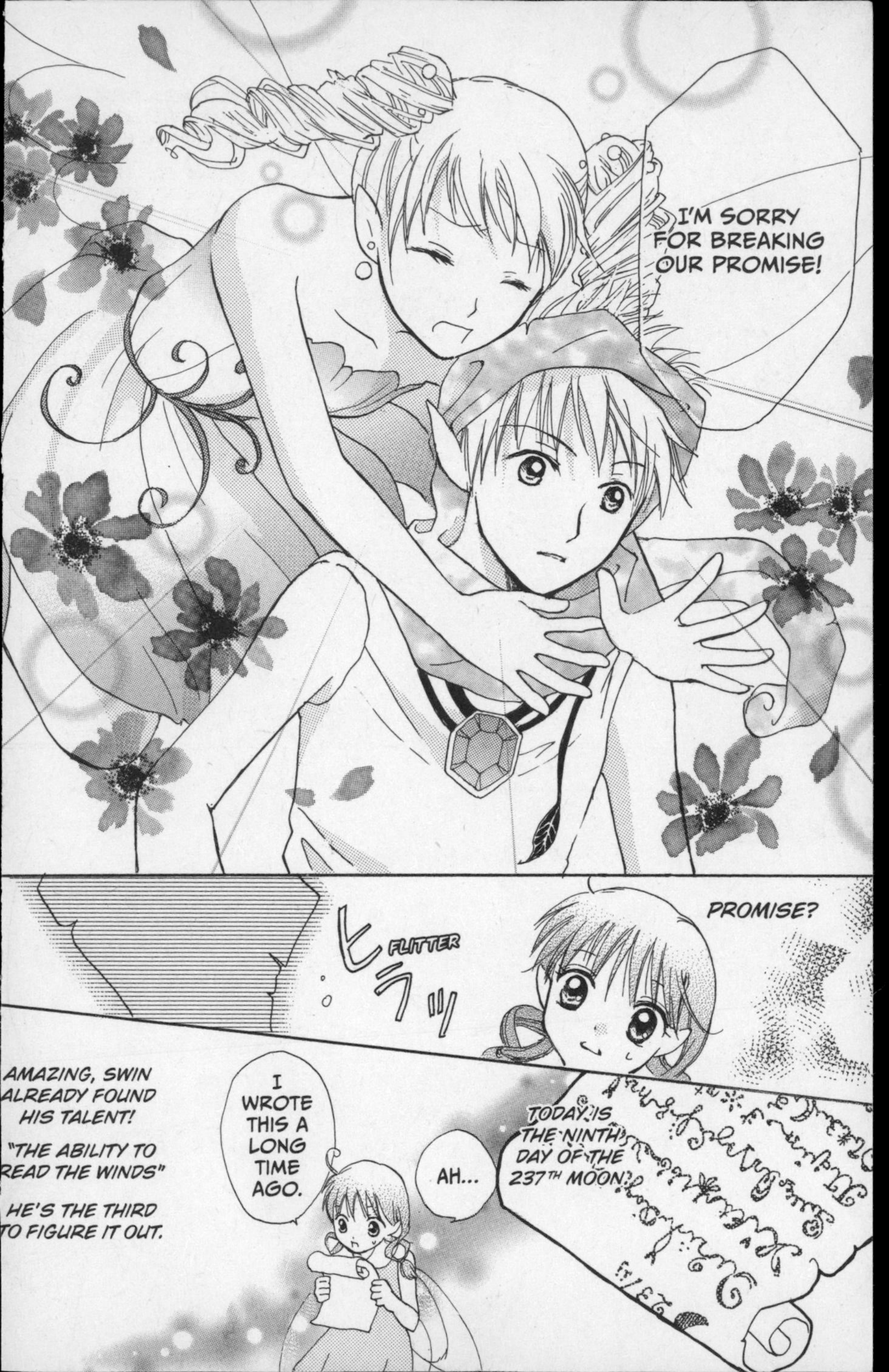
I'M SORRY FOR BREAKING OUR PROMISE!
PROMISE?
FLITTER
TODAY IS THE NINTH DAY OF THE 237TH MOON!
AH...
I WROTE THIS A LONG TIME AGO.
AMAZING, SWIN ALREADY FOUND HIS TALENT!
"THE ABILITY TO READ THE WINDS"
HE'S THE THIRD TO FIGURE IT OUT.

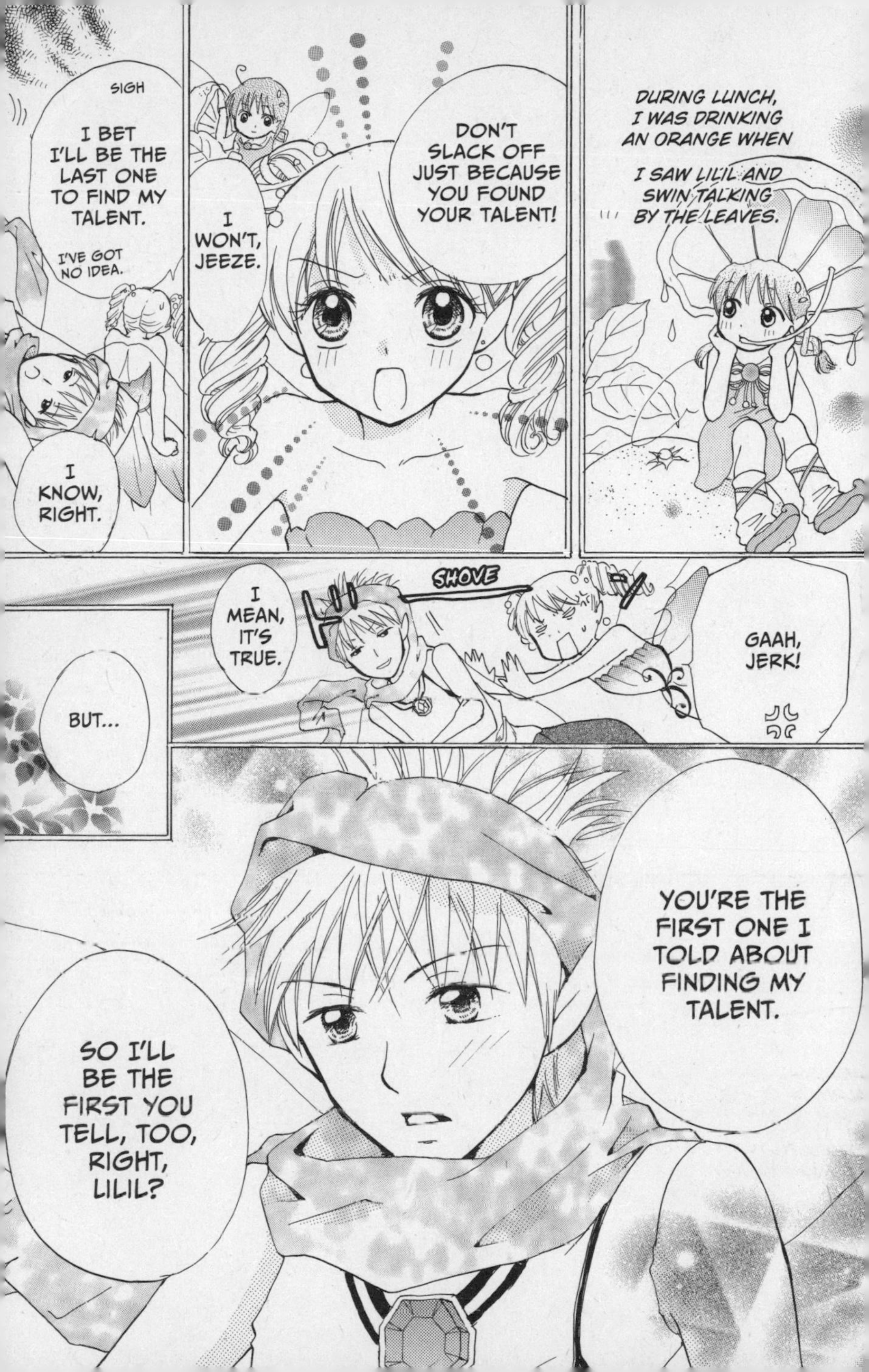
DURING LUNCH, I WAS DRINKING AN ORANGE WHEN
I SAW LILIL AND SWIN TALKING BY THE LEAVES.
DON'T SLACK OFF JUST BECAUSE YOU FOUND YOUR TALENT!
I WON'T, JEEZE.
SIGH
I BET I'LL BE THE LAST ONE TO FIND MY TALENT.
I'VE GOT NO IDEA.
I KNOW, RIGHT.
GAAH, JERK!
SHOVE
I MEAN, IT'S TRUE.
BUT...
YOU'RE THE FIRST ONE I TOLD ABOUT FINDING MY TALENT.
SO I'LL BE THE FIRST YOU TELL, TOO, RIGHT, LILIL?

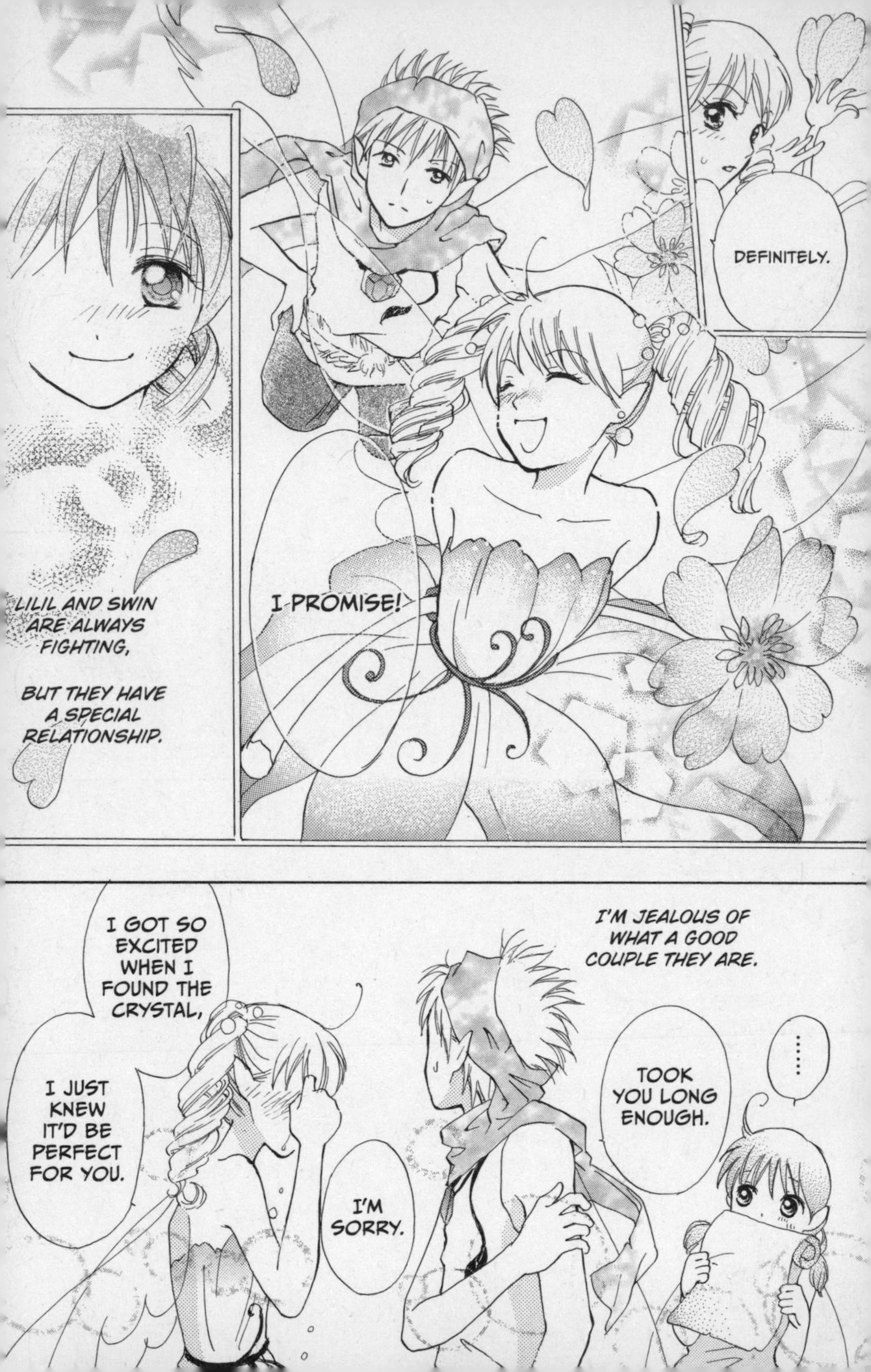
DEFINITELY.
I PROMISE!
LILIL AND SWIN ARE ALWAYS FIGHTING,
BUT THEY HAVE A SPECIAL RELATIONSHIP.
I'M JEALOUS OF WHAT A GOOD COUPLE THEY ARE.
......
TOOK YOU LONG ENOUGH.
I GOT SO EXCITED WHEN I FOUND THE CRYSTAL,
I JUST KNEW IT'D BE PERFECT FOR YOU.
I'M SORRY.

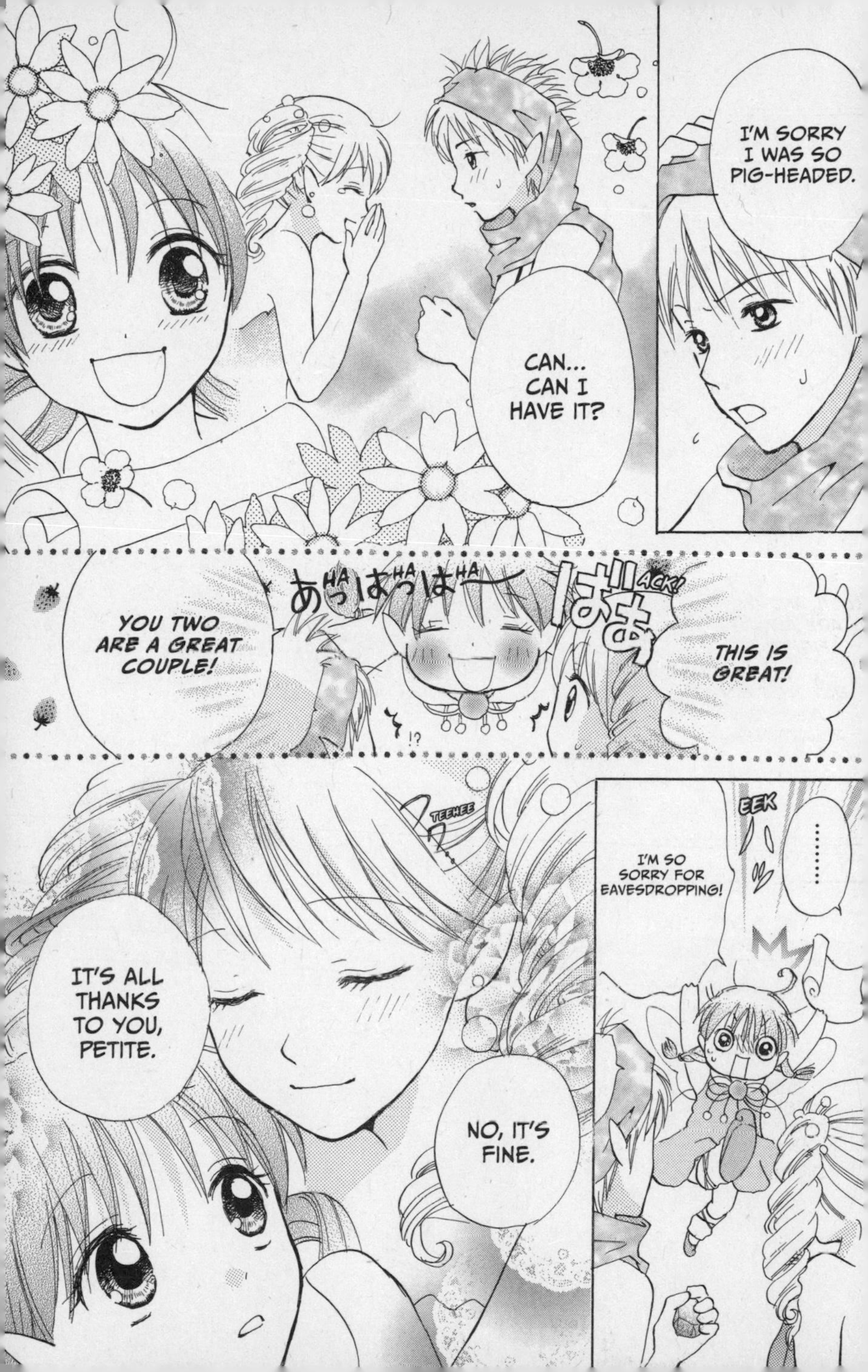
I'M SORRY I WAS SO PIG-HEADED.
CAN... CAN I HAVE IT?
THIS IS GREAT!
ACK!
あっはっはー
HA HA HA
YOU TWO ARE A GREAT COUPLE!
!?
EEK
......
I'M SO SORRY FOR EAVESDROPPING!
TEEHEE
NO, IT'S FINE.
IT'S ALL THANKS TO YOU, PETITE.

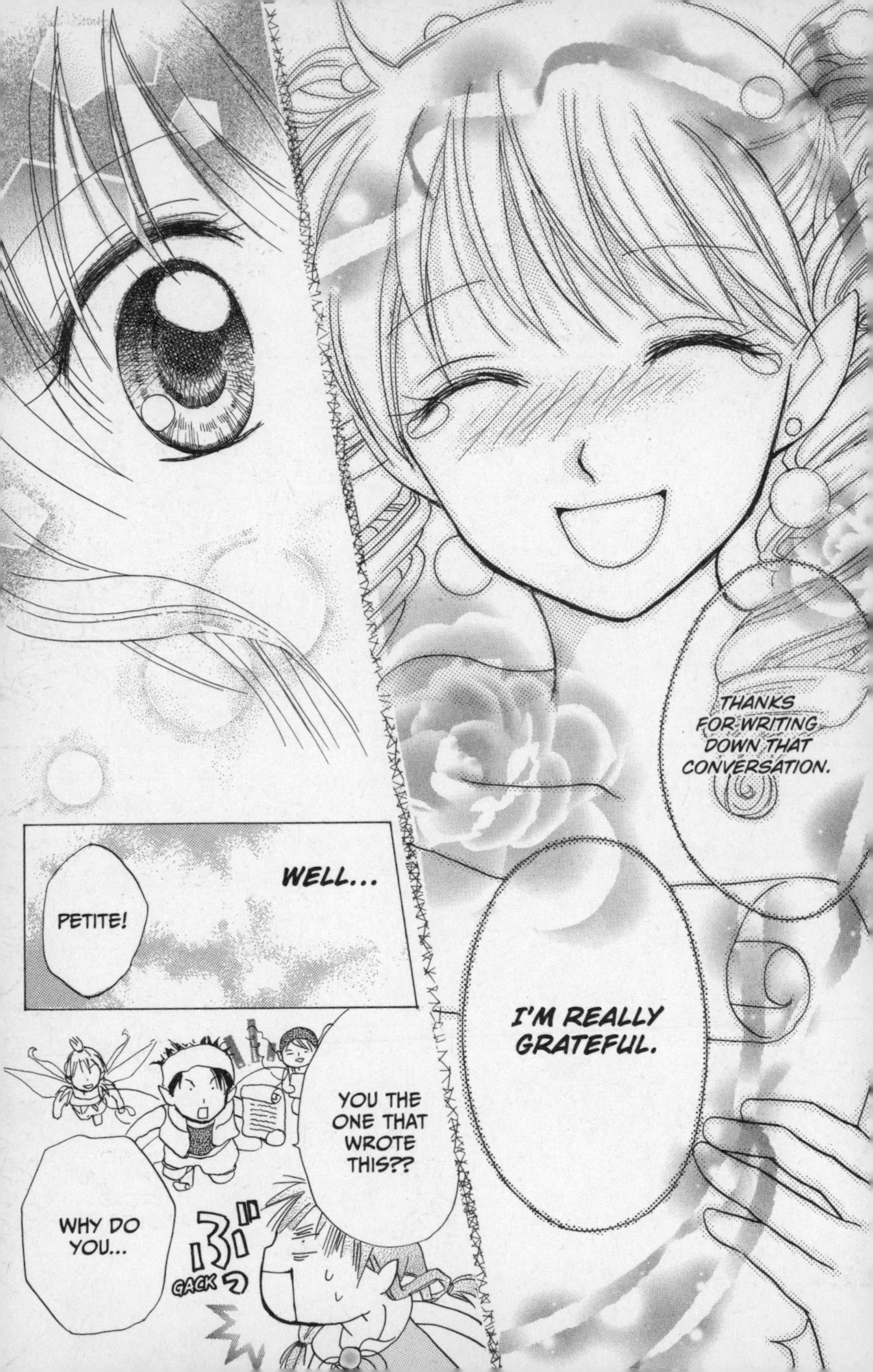
THANKS FOR WRITING DOWN THAT CONVERSATION.
I'M REALLY GRATEFUL.
WELL...
PETITE!
YOU THE ONE THAT WROTE THIS??
WHY DO YOU...
GACK

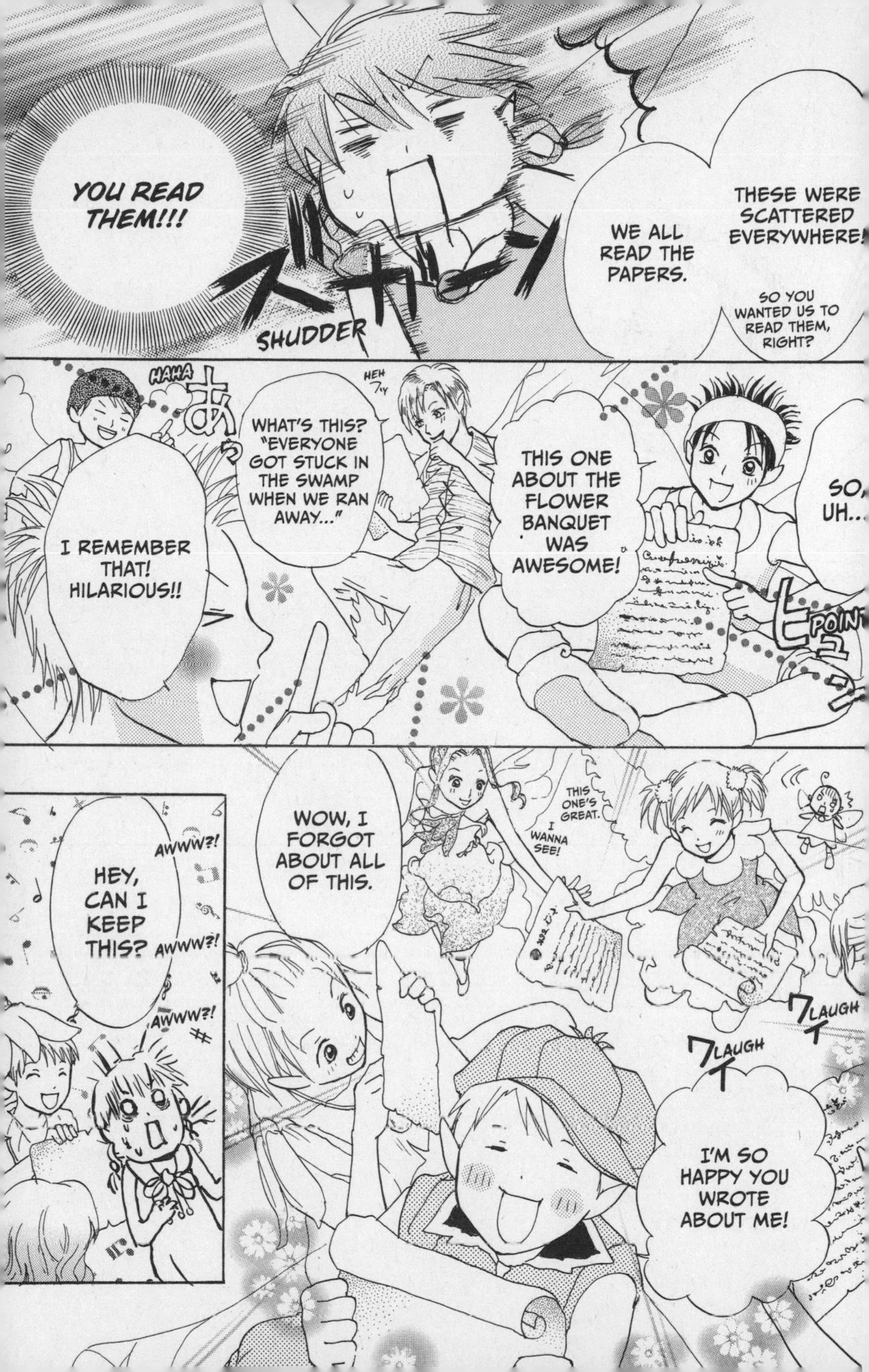
THESE WERE SCATTERED EVERYWHERE!
WE ALL READ THE PAPERS.
SO YOU WANTED US TO READ THEM, RIGHT?
YOU READ THEM!!!
SHUDDER
SO, UH...
POINT
THIS ONE ABOUT THE FLOWER BANQUET WAS AWESOME!
HEH
WHAT'S THIS? "EVERYONE GOT STUCK IN THE SWAMP WHEN WE RAN AWAY..."
HAHA
I REMEMBER THAT! HILARIOUS!!
LAUGH
LAUGH
I'M SO HAPPY YOU WROTE ABOUT ME!
THIS ONE'S GREAT.
I WANNA SEE!
WOW, I FORGOT ABOUT ALL OF THIS.
HEY, CAN I KEEP THIS?
AWWW?!
AWWW?!
AWWW?!

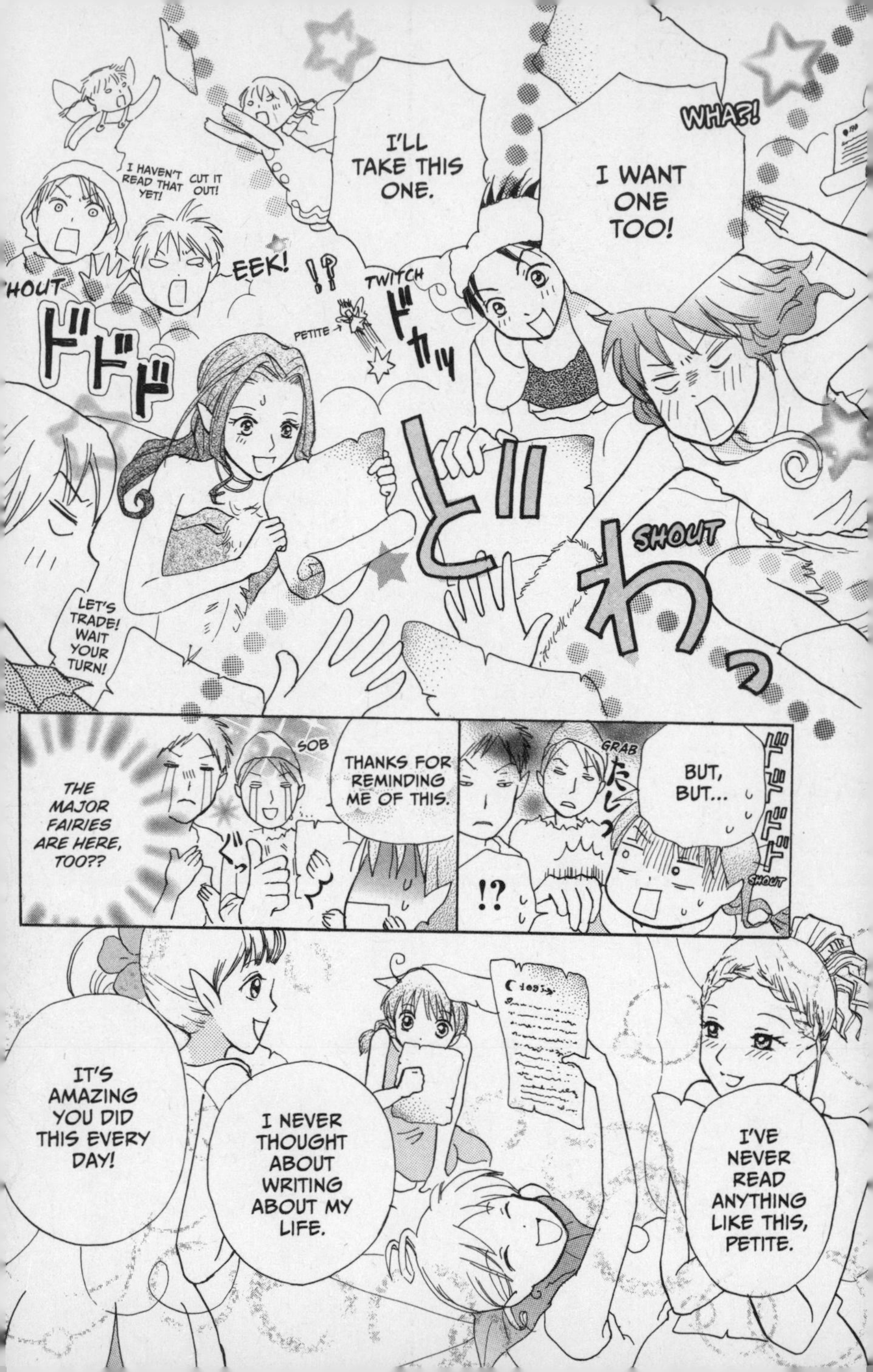
WHA?!
I WANT ONE TOO!
I'LL TAKE THIS ONE.
TWITCH
PETITE
!?
EEK!
CUT IT OUT!
I HAVEN'T READ THAT YET!
HOUT
SHOUT
LET'S TRADE! WAIT YOUR TURN!
BUT, BUT...
GRAB
SHOUT
!?
THANKS FOR REMINDING ME OF THIS.
SOB
THE MAJOR FAIRIES ARE HERE, TOO??
I'VE NEVER READ ANYTHING LIKE THIS, PETITE.
I NEVER THOUGHT ABOUT WRITING ABOUT MY LIFE.
IT'S AMAZING YOU DID THIS EVERY DAY!

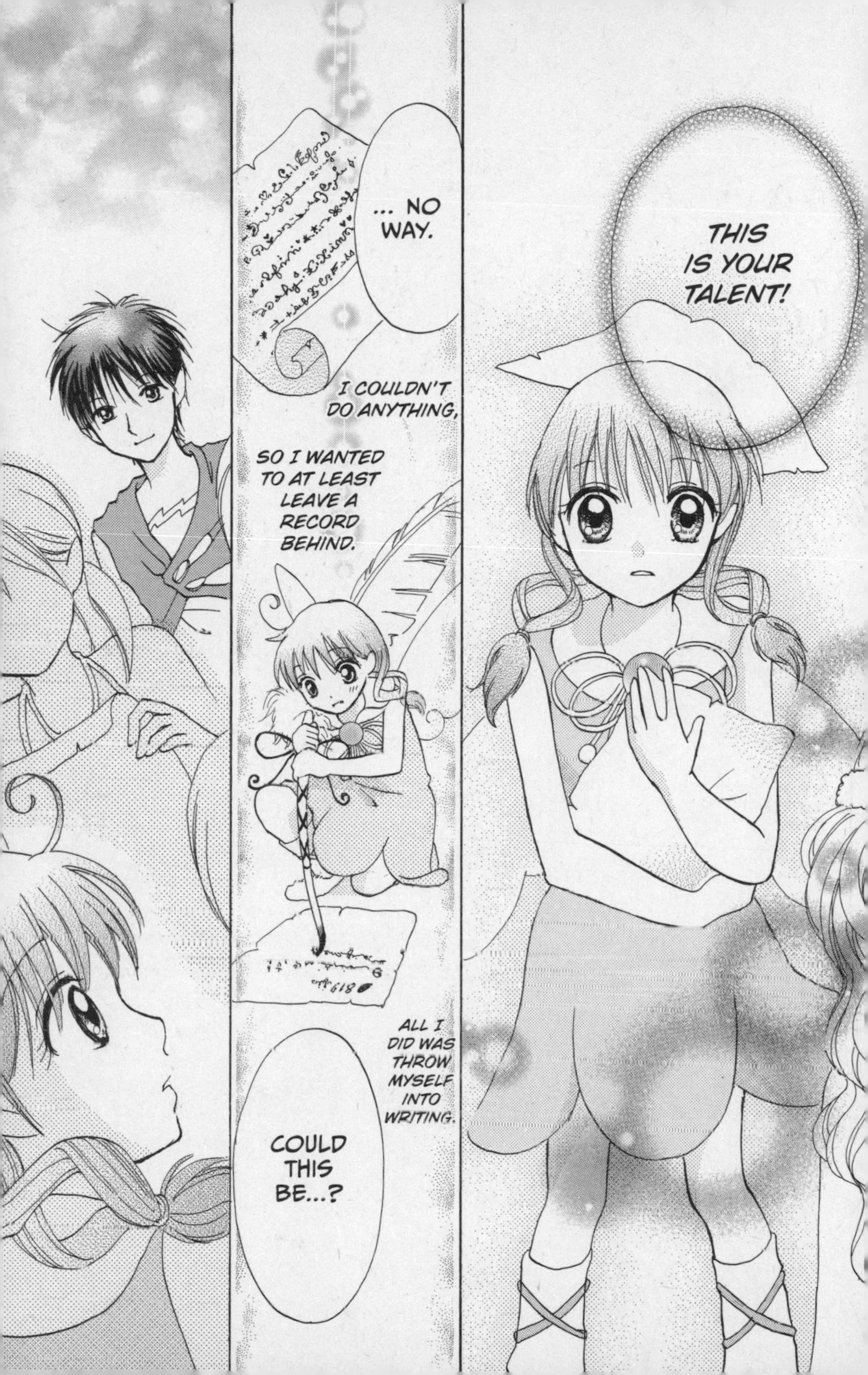
THIS IS YOUR TALENT!
... NO WAY.
I COULDN'T DO ANYTHING,
SO I WANTED TO AT LEAST LEAVE A RECORD BEHIND.
ALL I DID WAS THROW MYSELF INTO WRITING.
COULD THIS BE...?

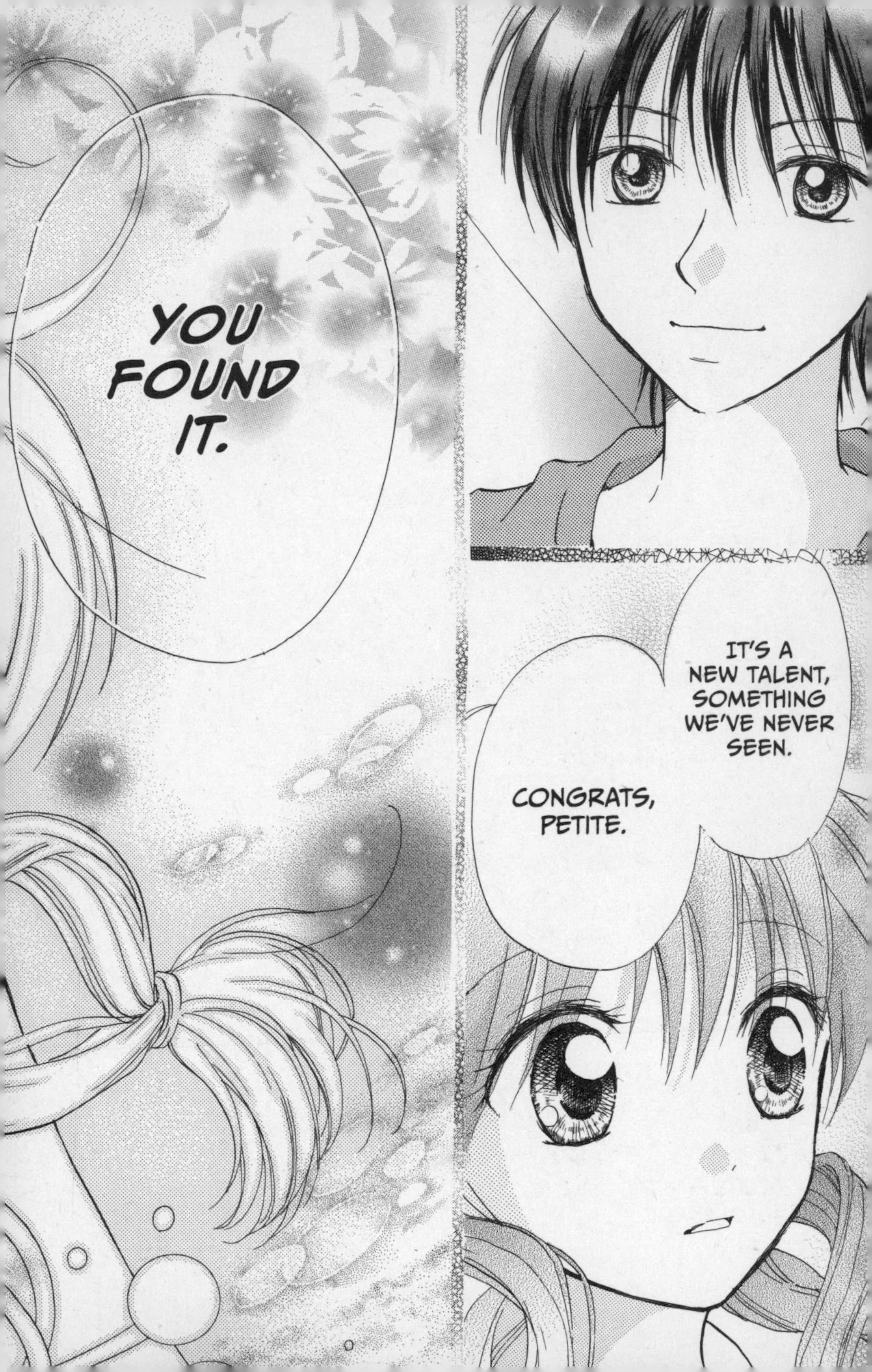
IT'S A NEW TALENT, SOMETHING WE'VE NEVER SEEN.
CONGRATS, PETITE.
YOU FOUND IT.

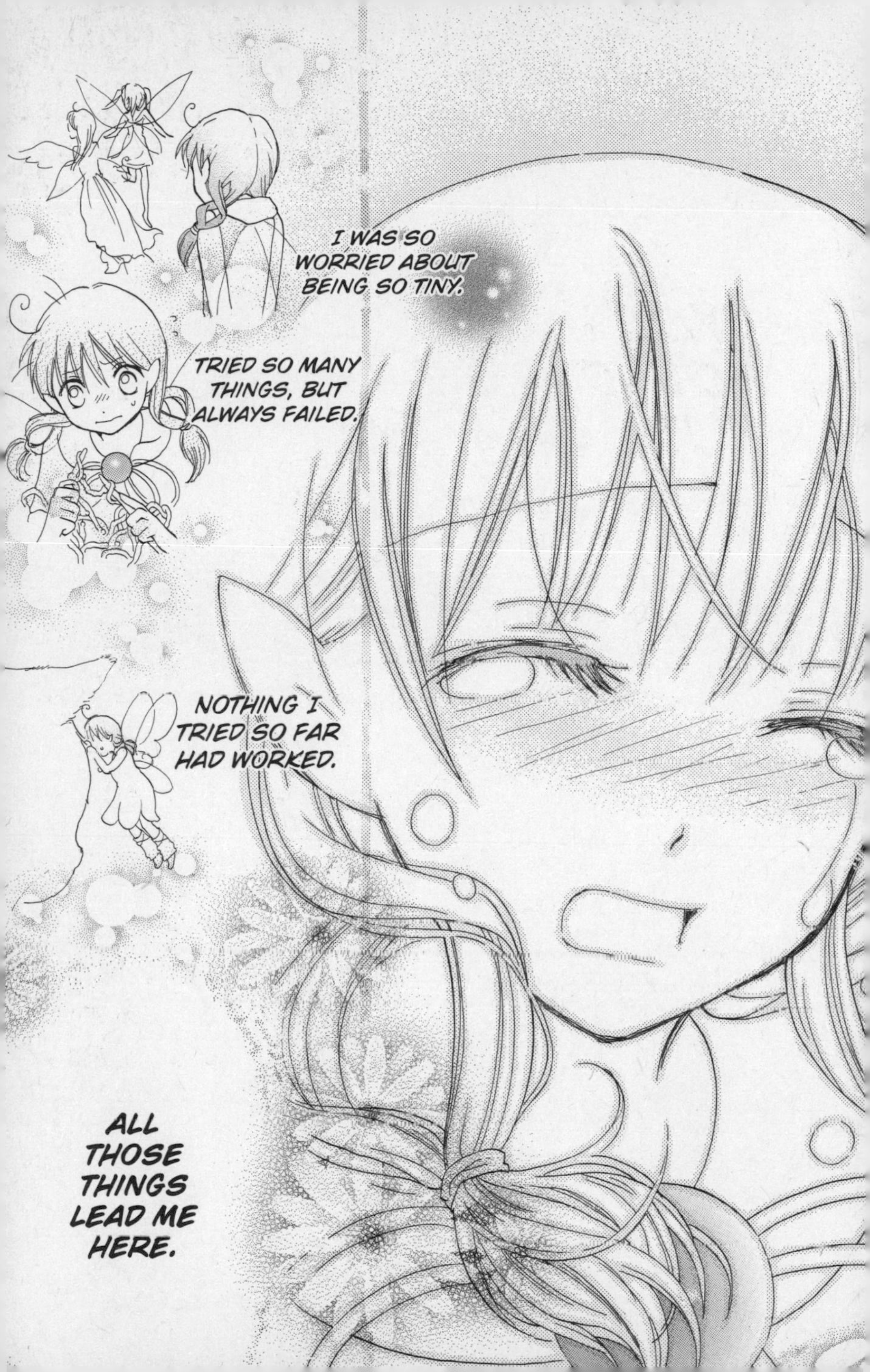
I WAS SO WORRIED ABOUT BEING SO TINY.
TRIED SO MANY THINGS, BUT ALWAYS FAILED.
NOTHING I TRIED SO FAR HAD WORKED.
ALL THOSE THINGS LEAD ME HERE.

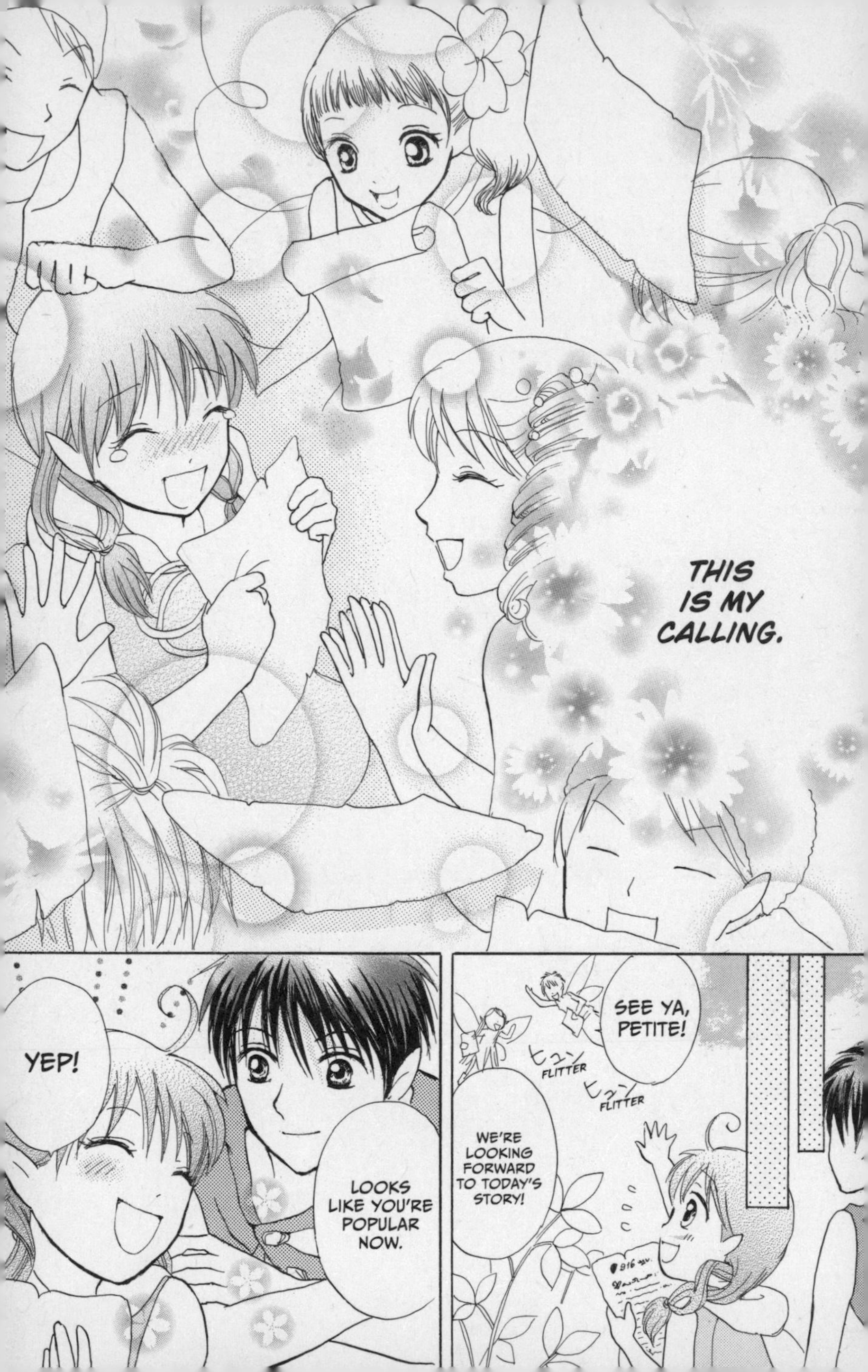
THIS IS MY CALLING.
SEE YA, PETITE!
ヒュン FLITTER
ヒュン FLITTER
WE'RE LOOKING FORWARD TO TODAY'S STORY!
LOOKS LIKE YOU'RE POPULAR NOW.
YEP!

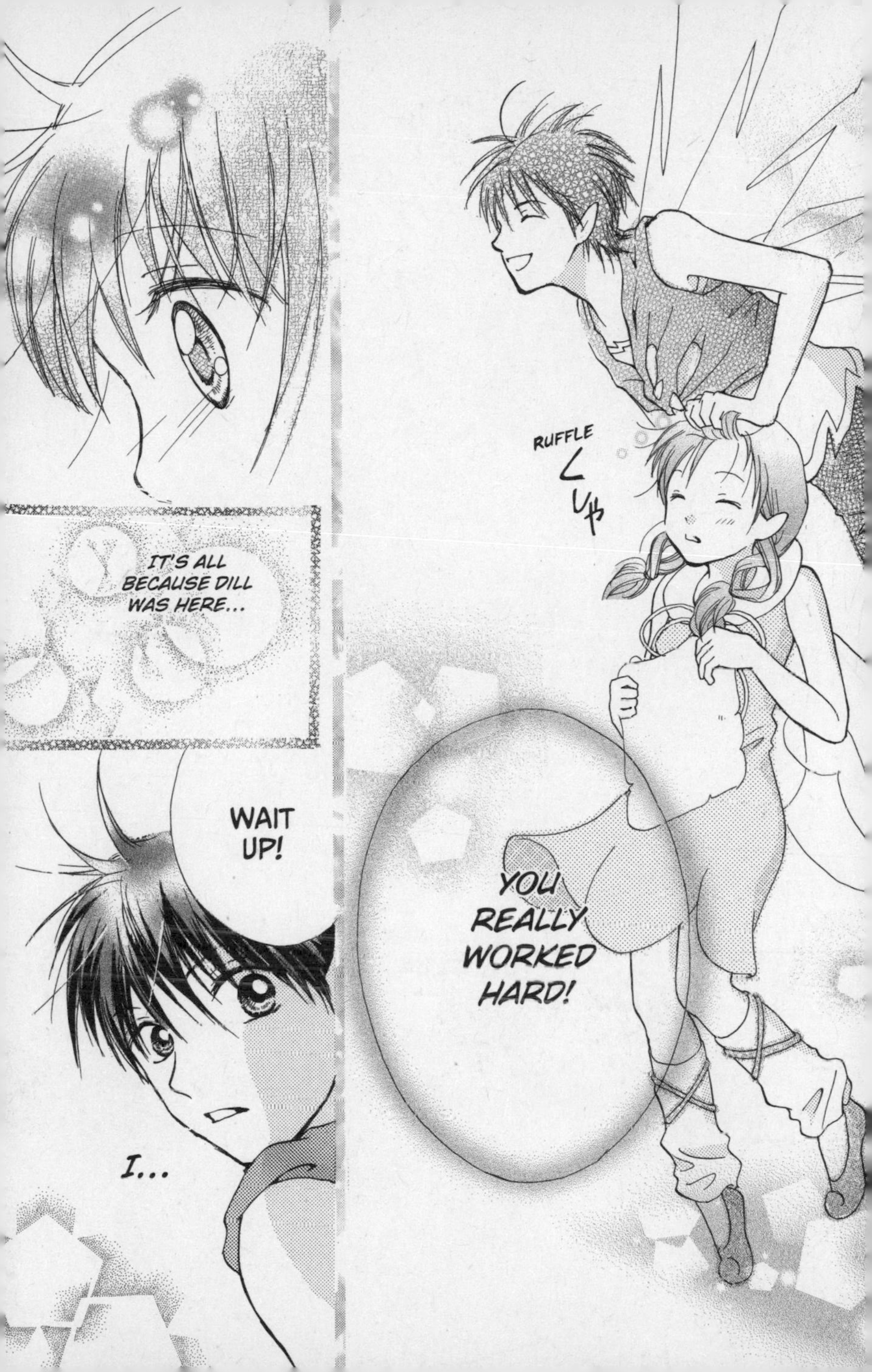
RUFFLE
くしゃ
YOU REALLY WORKED HARD!
IT'S ALL BECAUSE DILL WAS HERE...
WAIT UP!
I...

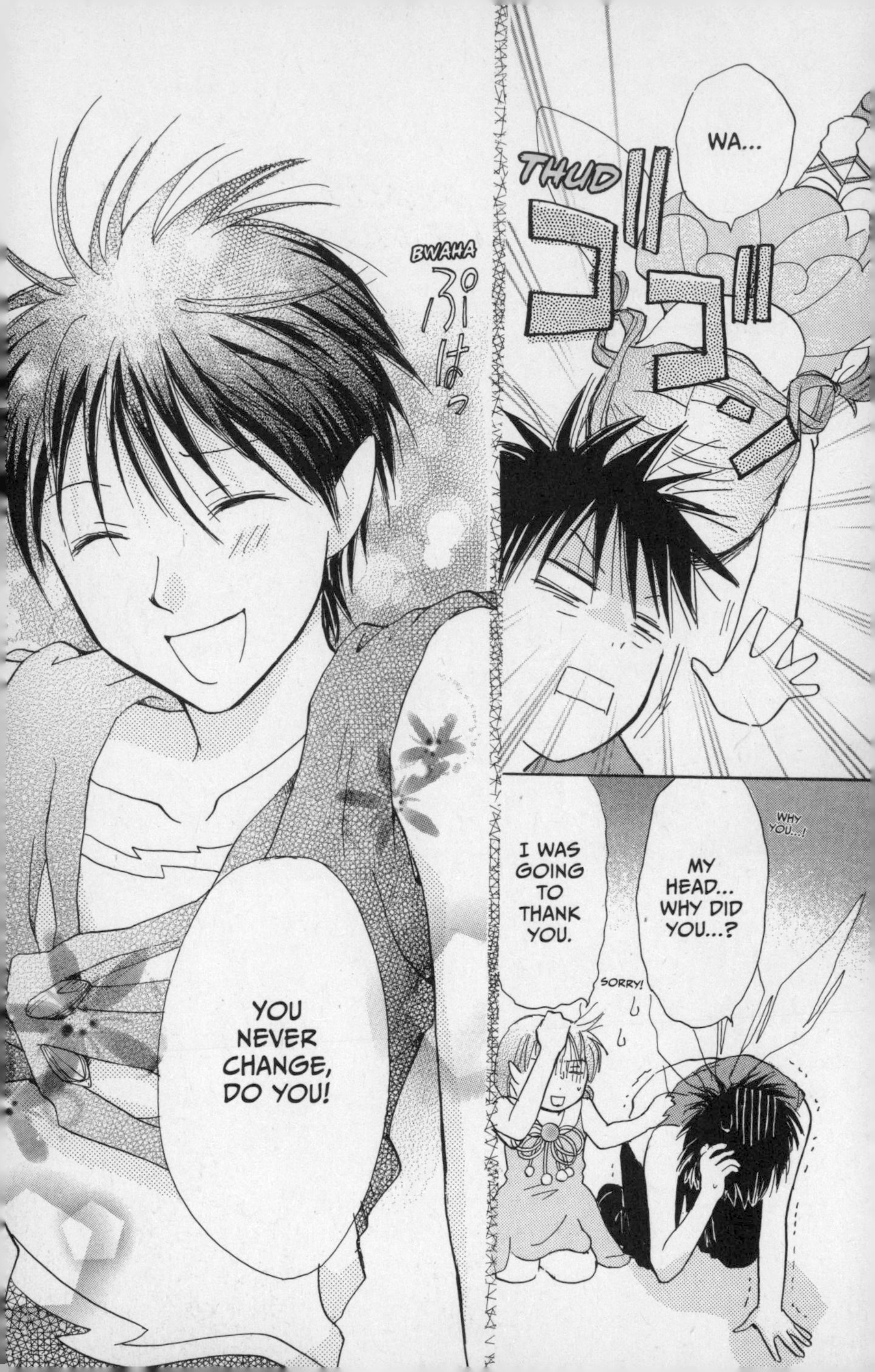
WA...
THUD
ゴゴ
WHY YOU...!
MY HEAD... WHY DID YOU...?
I WAS GOING TO THANK YOU.
SORRY!
BWAHA
ぷはっ
YOU NEVER CHANGE, DO YOU!

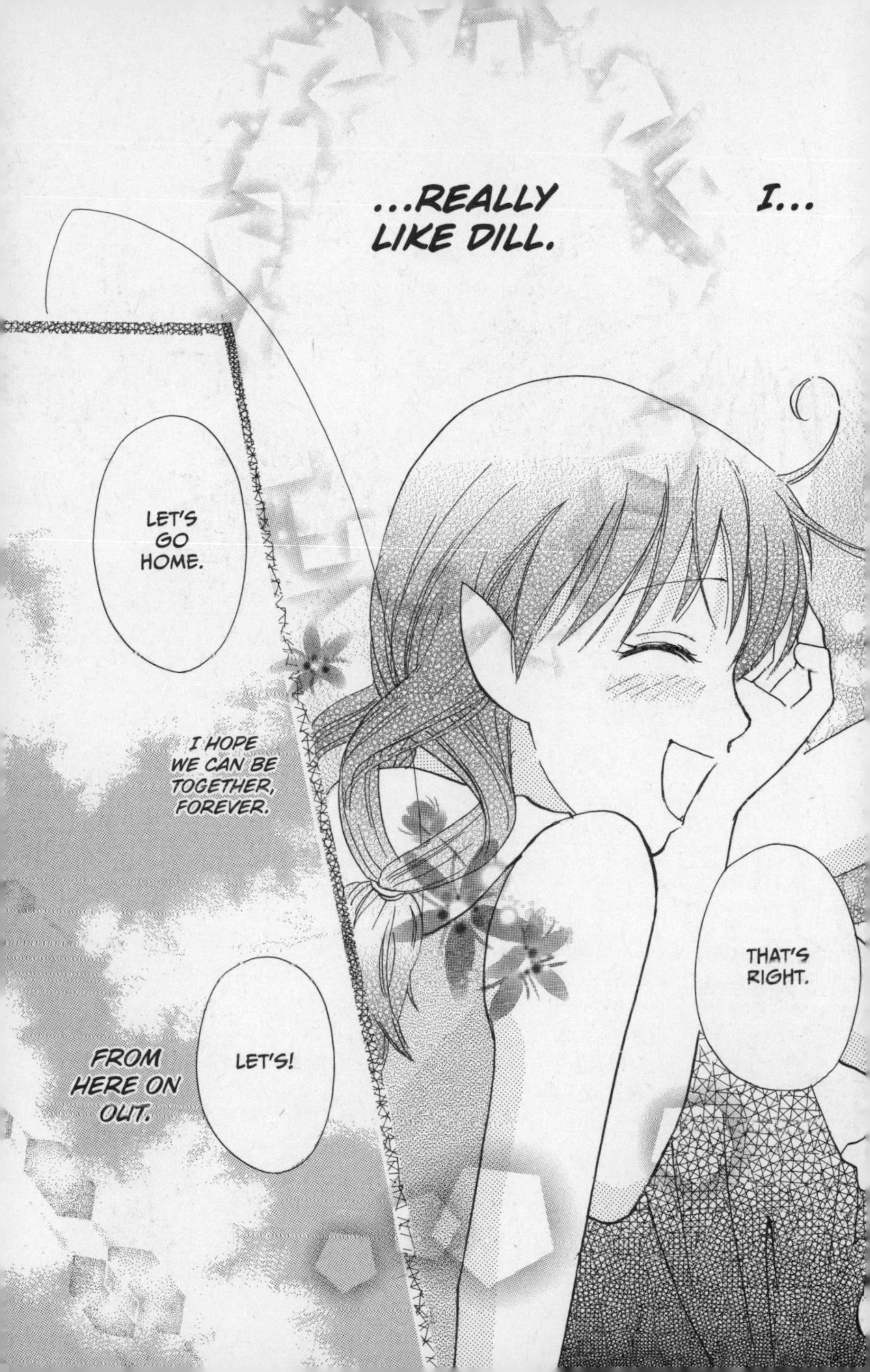
I...
...REALLY LIKE DILL.
THAT'S RIGHT.
LET'S GO HOME.
I HOPE WE CAN BE TOGETHER, FOREVER.
LET'S!
FROM HERE ON OUT.

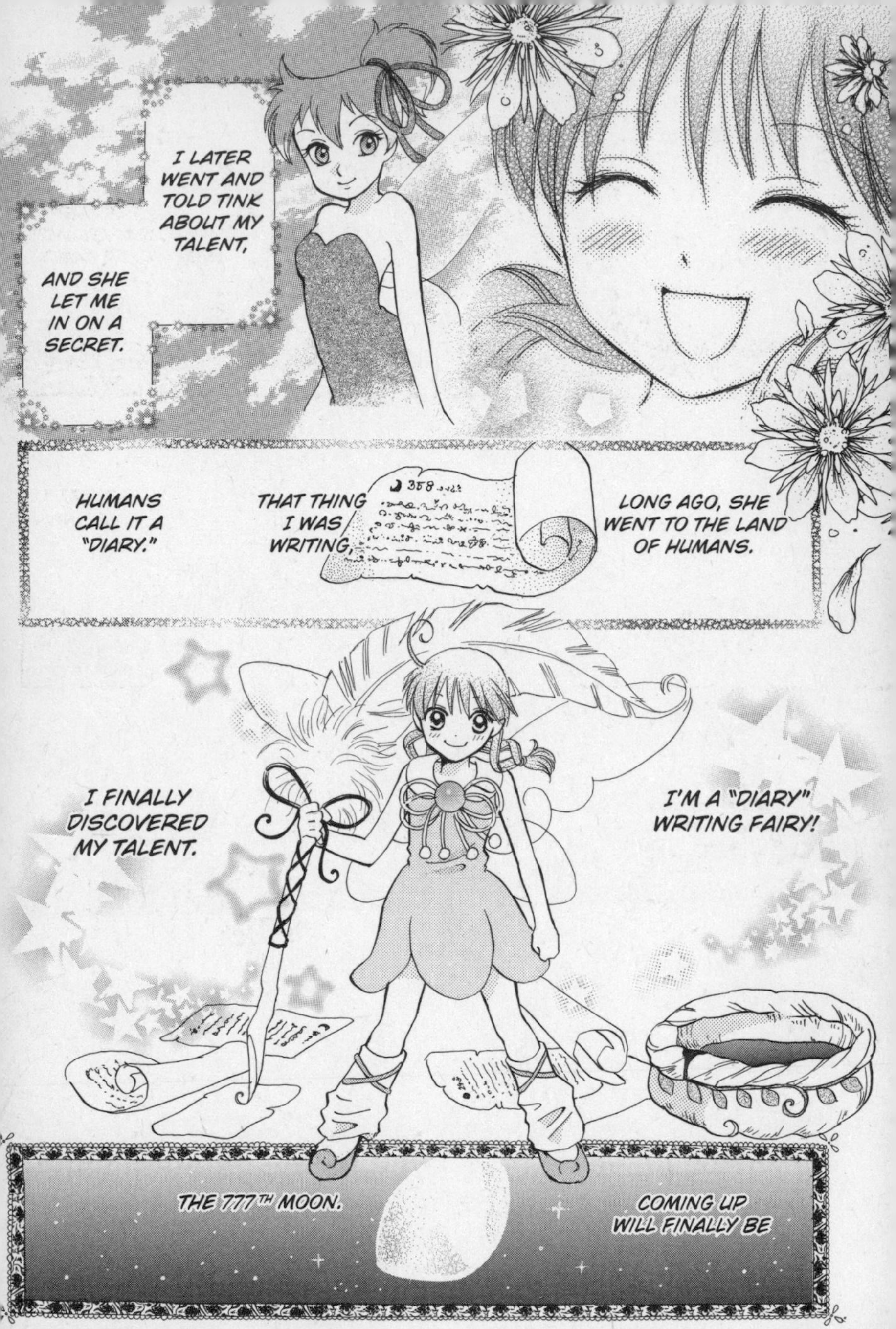
I LATER WENT AND TOLD TINK ABOUT MY TALENT,
AND SHE LET ME IN ON A SECRET.
LONG AGO, SHE WENT TO THE LAND OF HUMANS.
THAT THING I WAS WRITING,
HUMANS CALL IT A "DIARY."
I'M A "DIARY" WRITING FAIRY!
I FINALLY DISCOVERED MY TALENT.
COMING UP WILL FINALLY BE
THE 777TH MOON.

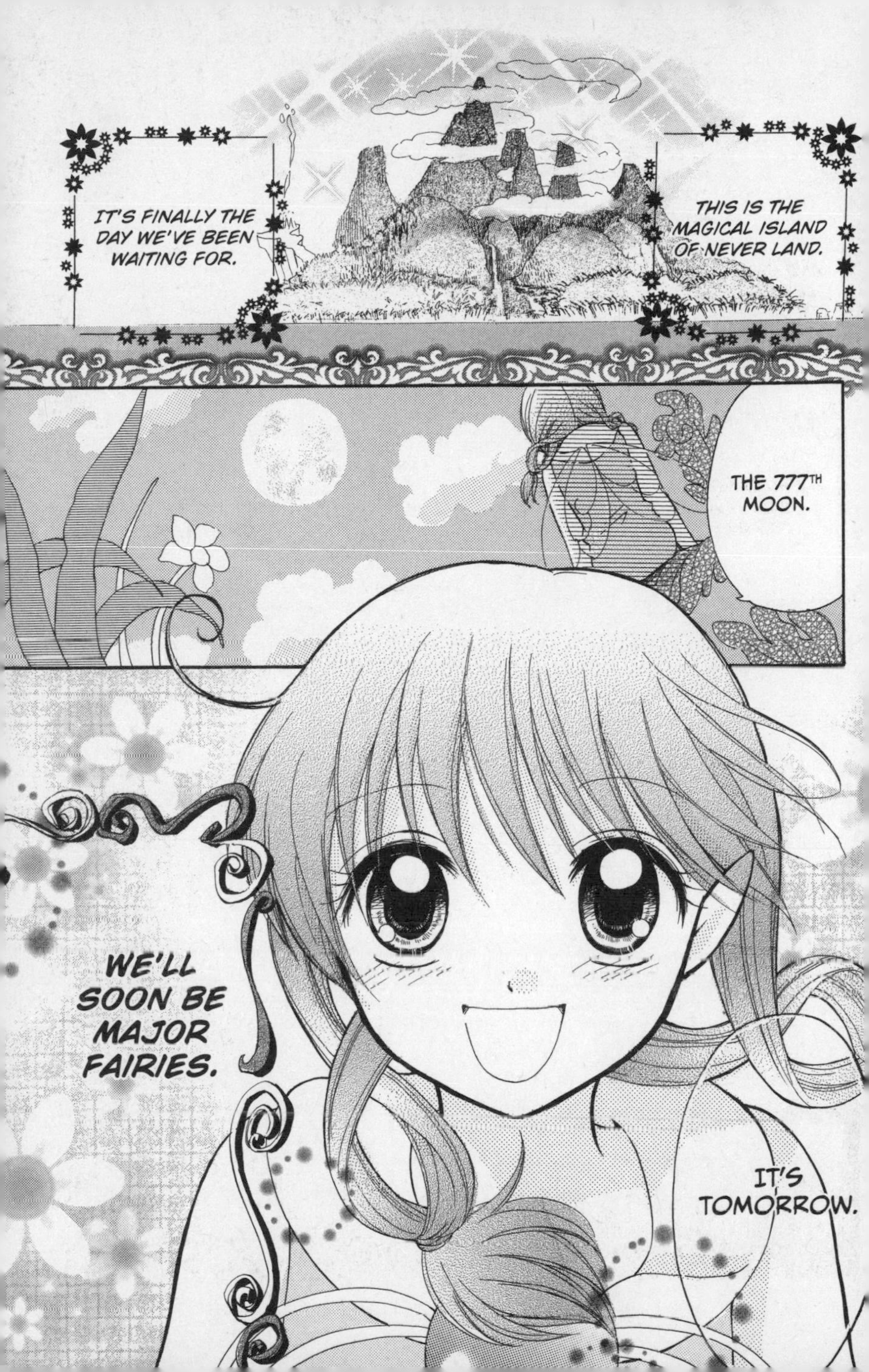
THIS IS THE MAGICAL ISLAND OF NEVER LAND.
IT'S FINALLY THE DAY WE'VE BEEN WAITING FOR.
THE 777TH MOON.
IT'S TOMORROW.
WE'LL SOON BE MAJOR FAIRIES.

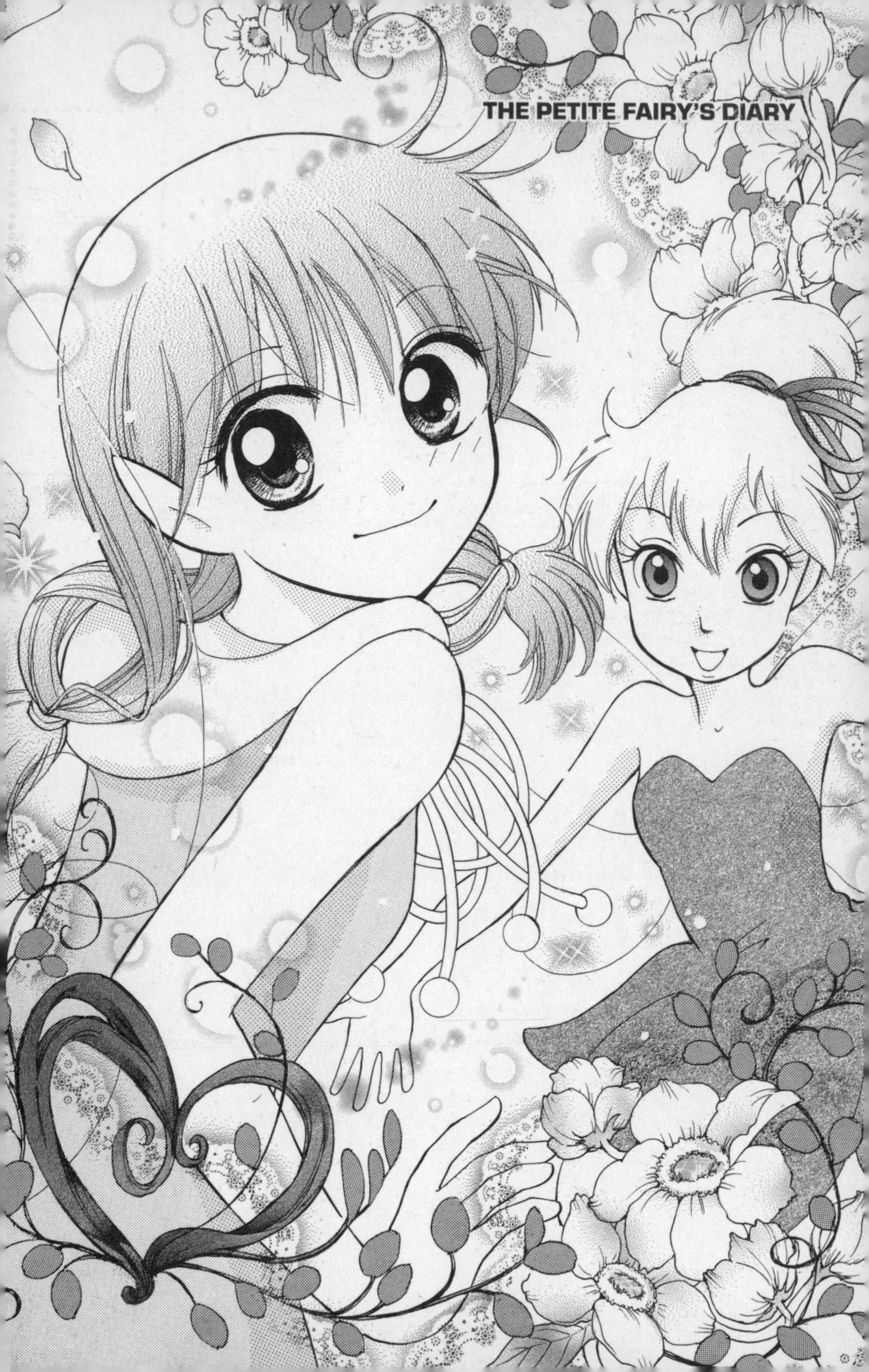
THE PETITE FAIRY'S DIARY

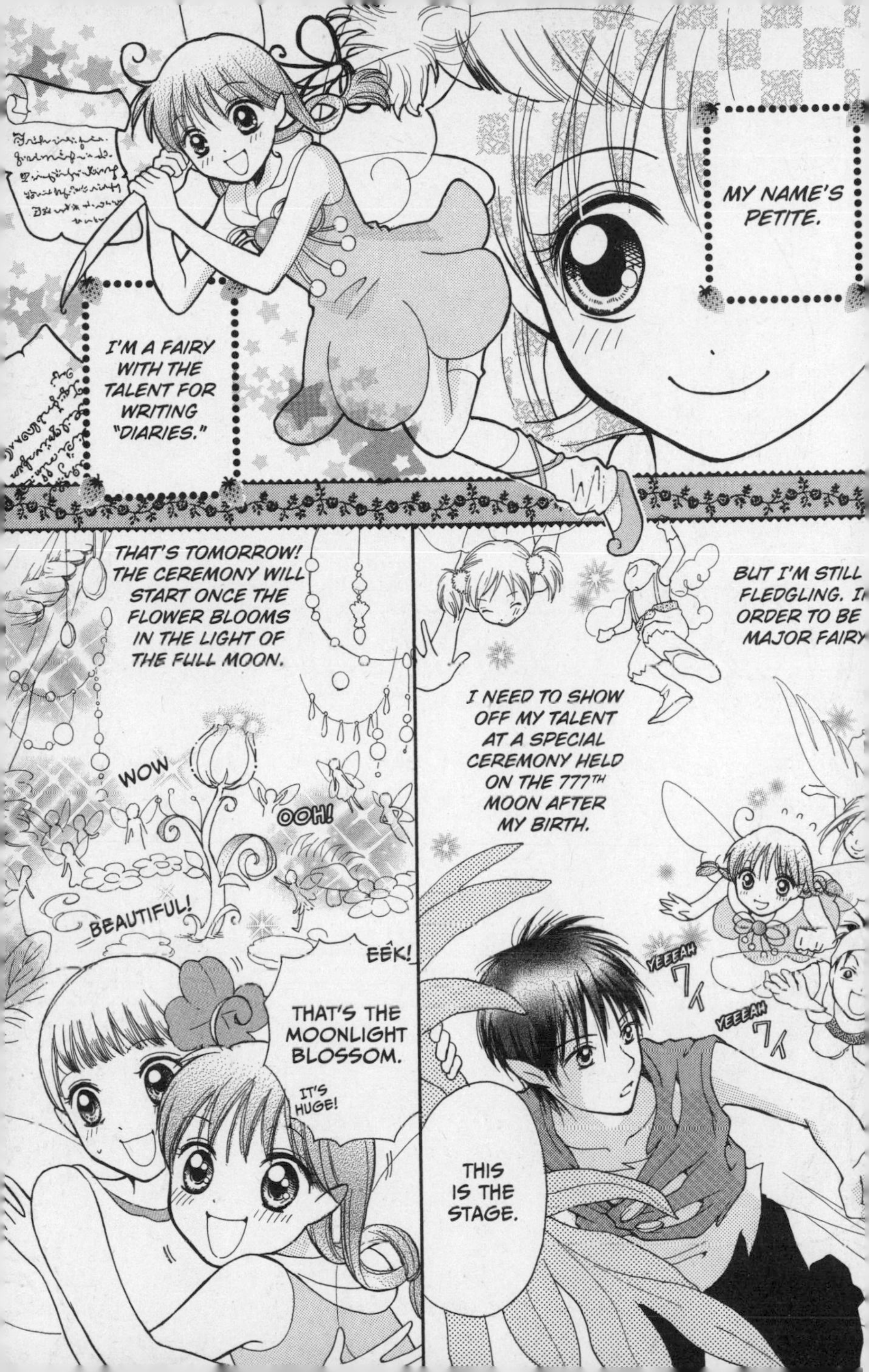
MY NAME'S PETITE.
I'M A FAIRY WITH THE TALENT FOR WRITING "DIARIES."
BUT I'M STILL FLEDGLING. I ORDER TO BE MAJOR FAIRY
I NEED TO SHOW OFF MY TALENT AT A SPECIAL CEREMONY HELD ON THE 777TH MOON AFTER MY BIRTH.
YEEEAH ワイ
YEEEAH ワイ
THIS IS THE STAGE.
THAT'S TOMORROW! THE CEREMONY WILL START ONCE THE FLOWER BLOOMS IN THE LIGHT OF THE FULL MOON.
WOW
OOH!
BEAUTIFUL!
EEK!
THAT'S THE MOONLIGHT BLOSSOM.
IT'S HUGE!

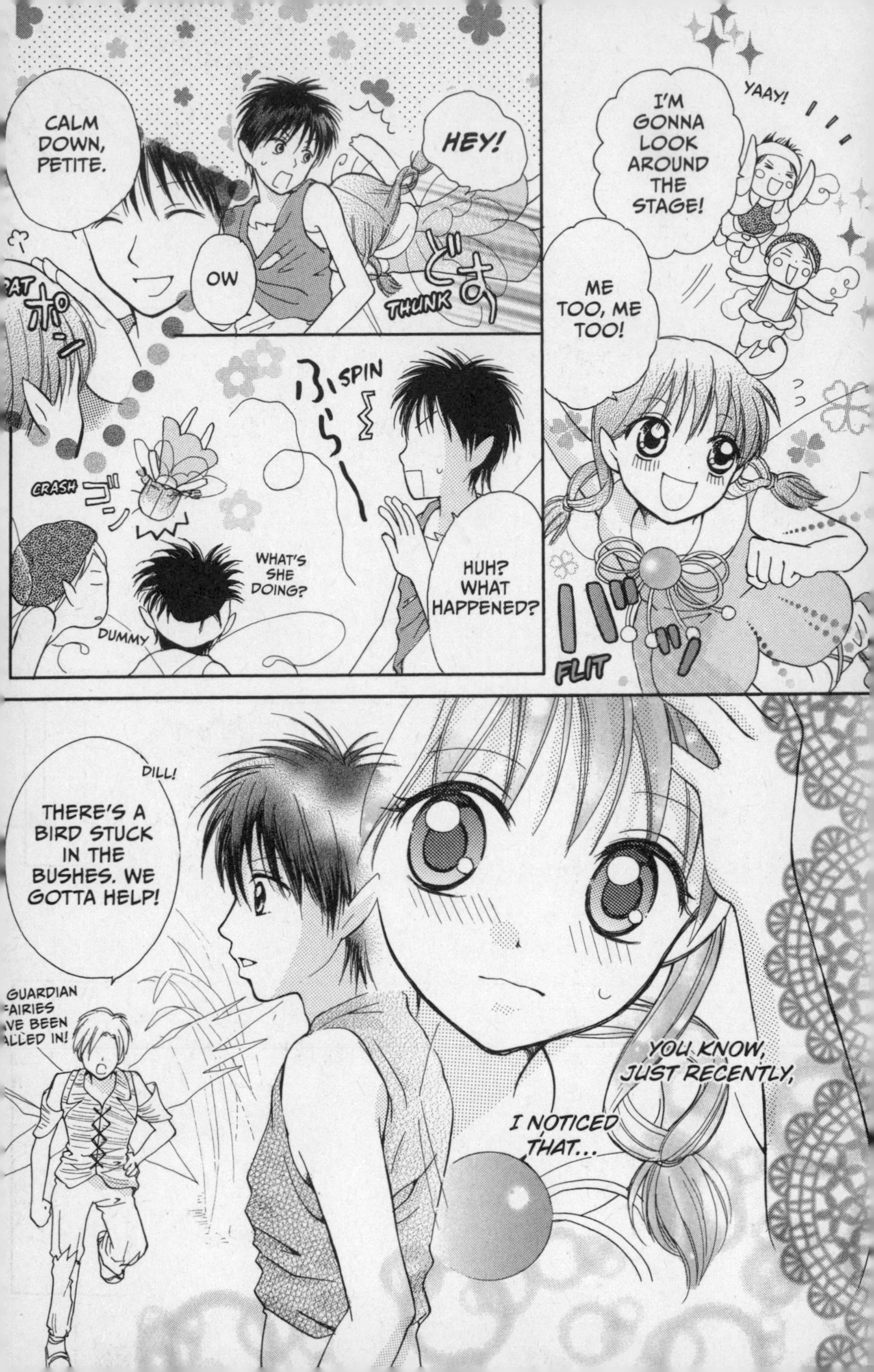
I'M GONNA LOOK AROUND THE STAGE!
YAAY!
ME TOO, ME TOO!
FLIT
HEY!
CALM DOWN, PETITE.
OW
THUNK
PAT
SPIN
HUH? WHAT HAPPENED?
WHAT'S SHE DOING?
CRASH
DUMMY
YOU KNOW, JUST RECENTLY,
I NOTICED THAT...
DILL!
THERE'S A BIRD STUCK IN THE BUSHES. WE GOTTA HELP!
GUARDIAN
FAIRIES

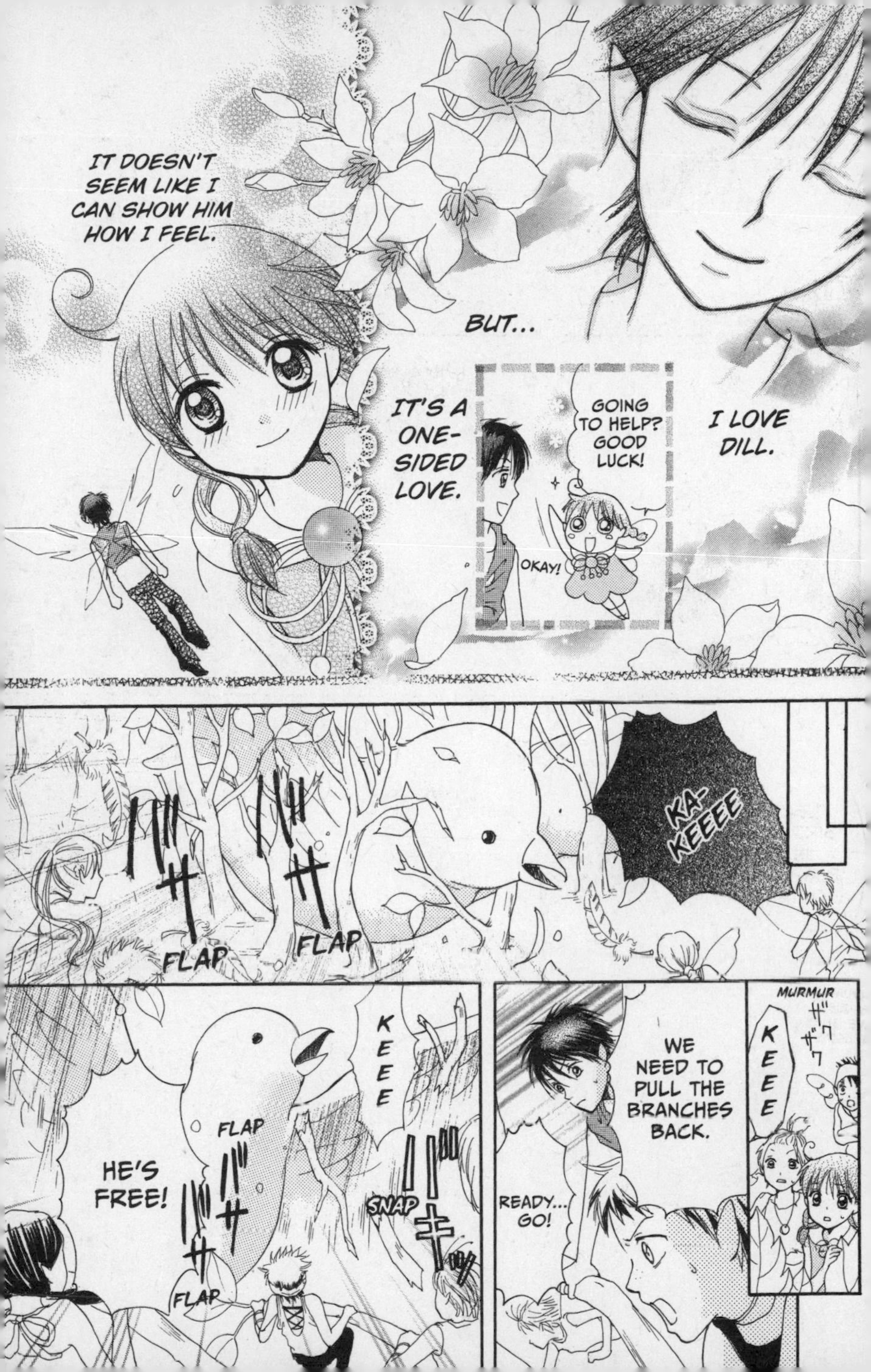
I LOVE DILL.
GOING TO HELP? GOOD LUCK!
OKAY!
BUT...
IT'S A ONE-SIDED LOVE.
IT DOESN'T SEEM LIKE I CAN SHOW HIM HOW I FEEL.
KA-KEEEE
FLAP
FLAP
MURMUR
KEEE
WE NEED TO PULL THE BRANCHES BACK.
READY... GO!
KEEE
SNAP
FLAP
HE'S FREE!
FLAP

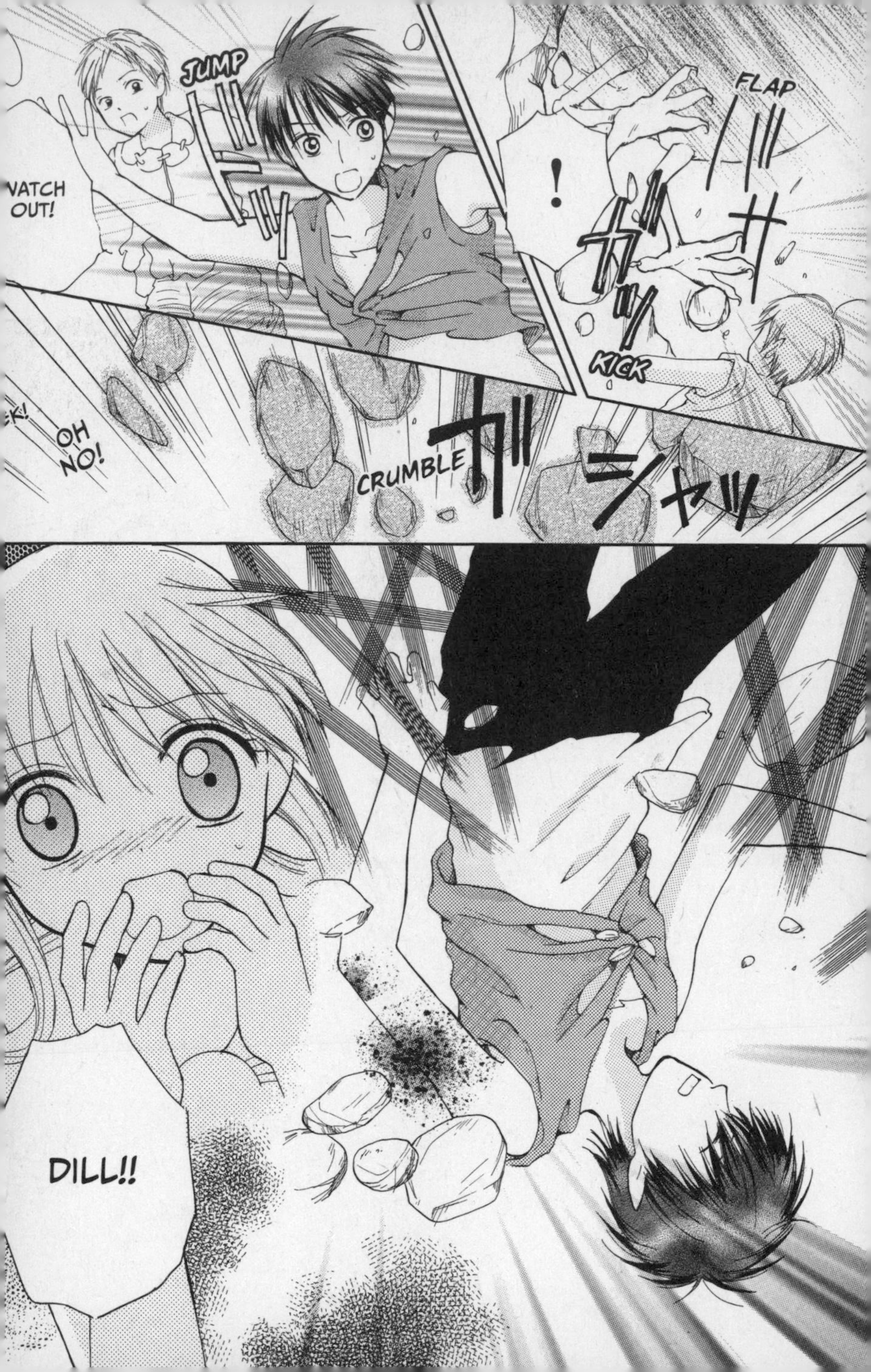

!
FLAP
KICK
JUMP
WATCH OUT!
CRUMBLE
OH NO!
EK!
DILL!!

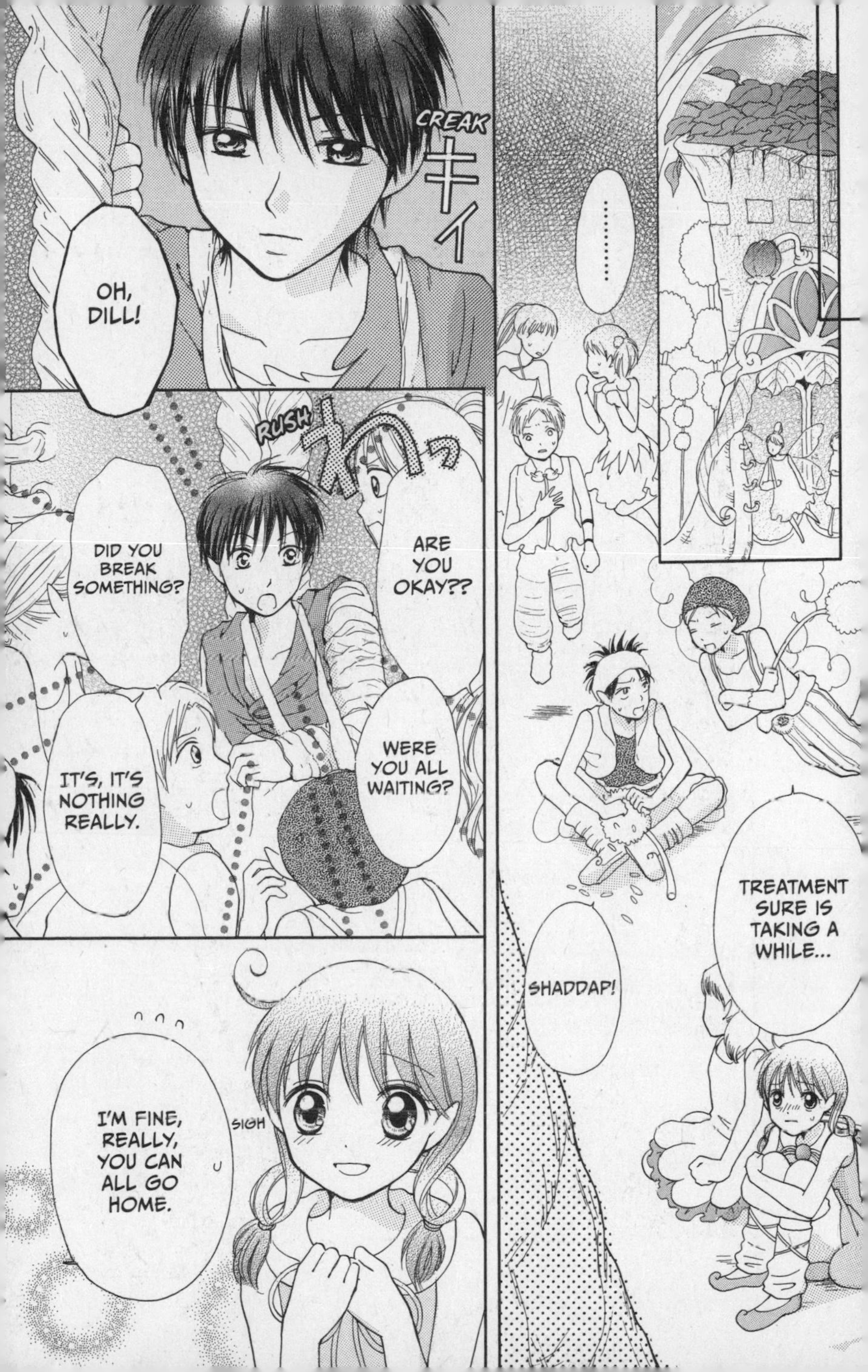
......
TREATMENT SURE IS TAKING A WHILE...
SHADDAP!
CREAK
キィ
OH, DILL!
RUSH
わっ
ARE YOU OKAY??
DID YOU BREAK SOMETHING?
WERE YOU ALL WAITING?
IT'S, IT'S NOTHING REALLY.
SIGH
I'M FINE, REALLY, YOU CAN ALL GO HOME.

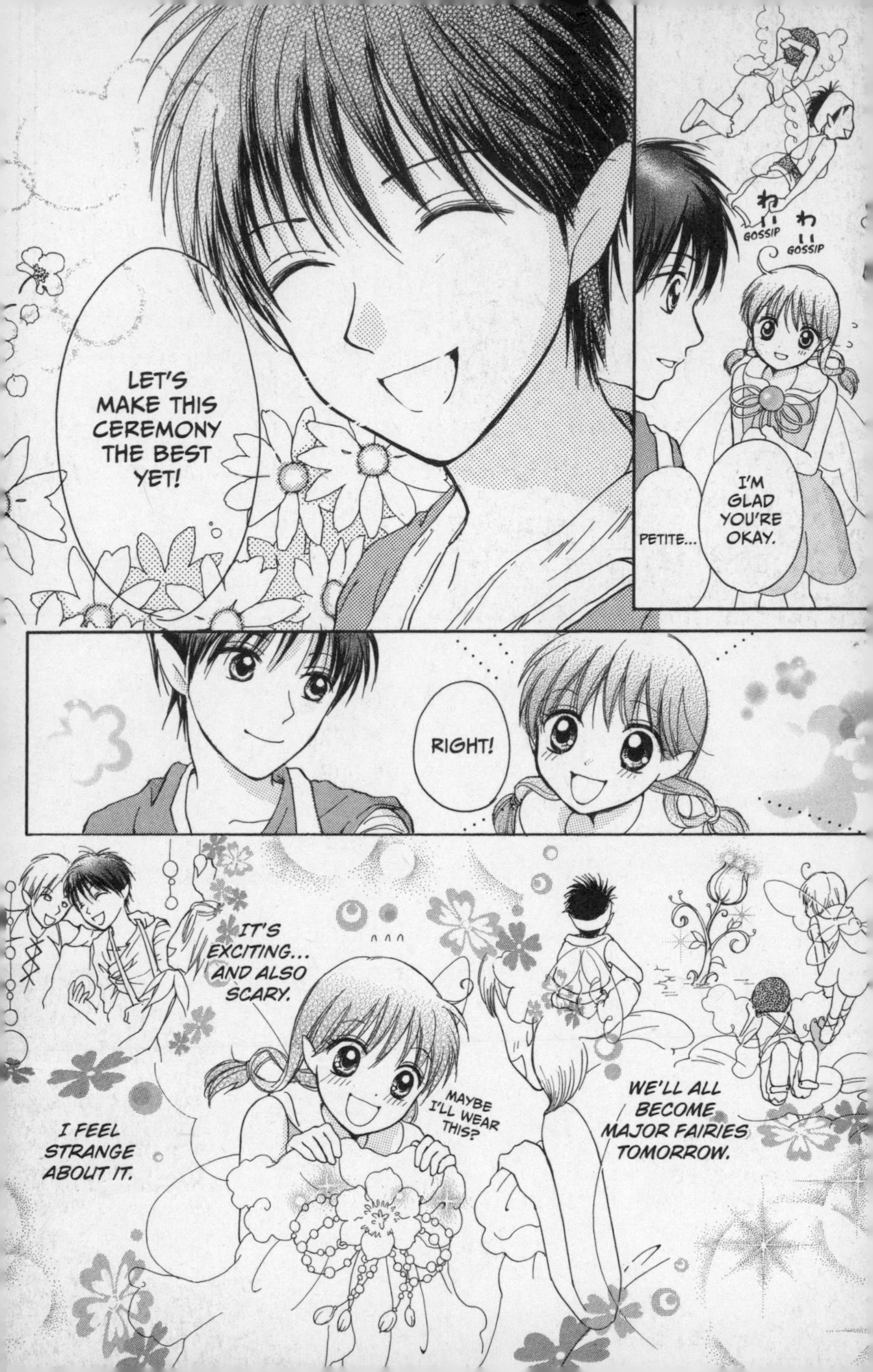
わい GOSSIP
わい GOSSIP
I'M GLAD YOU'RE OKAY.
PETITE...
LET'S MAKE THIS CEREMONY THE BEST YET!
RIGHT!
WE'LL ALL BECOME MAJOR FAIRIES TOMORROW.
MAYBE I'LL WEAR THIS?
IT'S EXCITING... AND ALSO SCARY.
I FEEL STRANGE ABOUT IT.

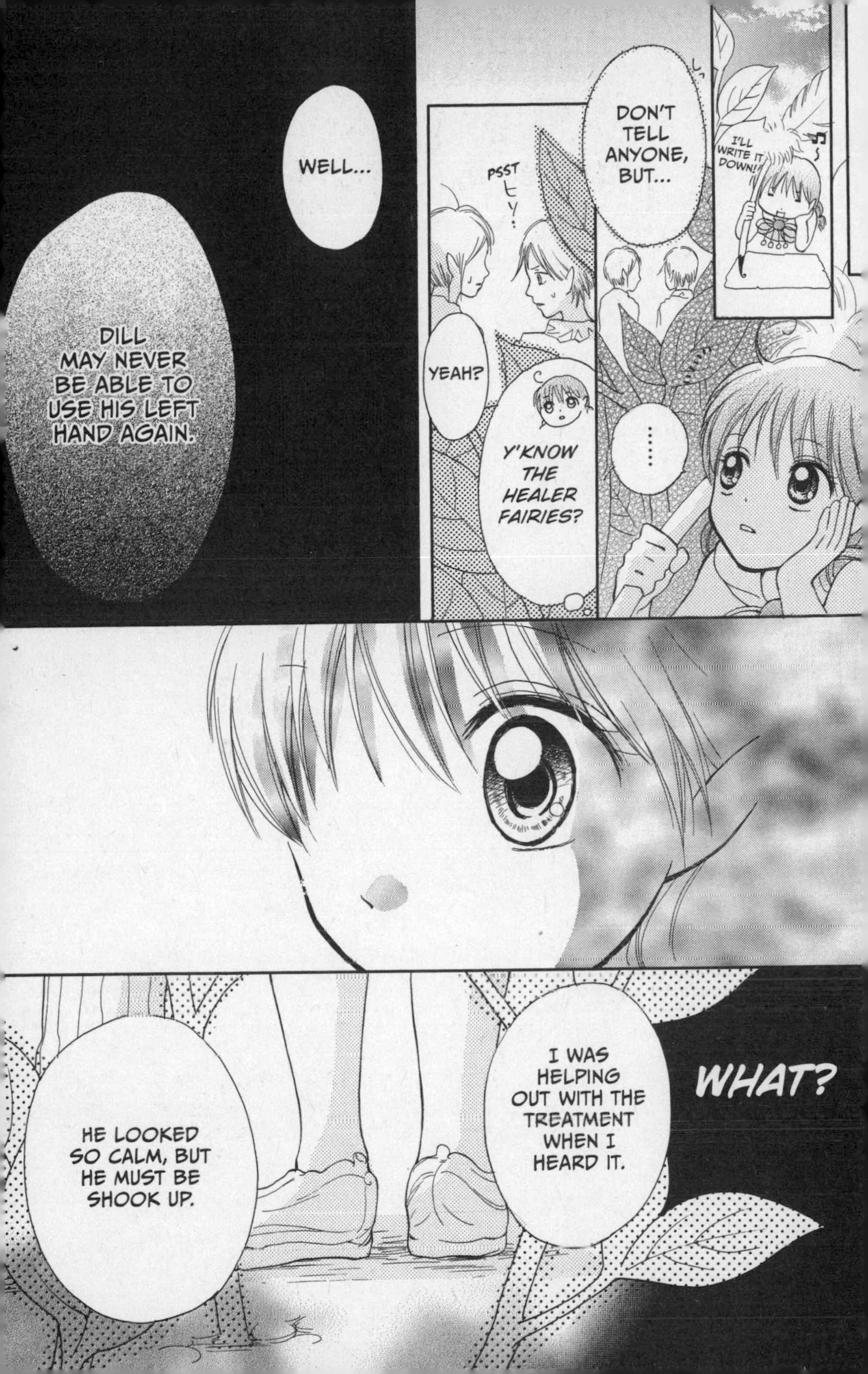
I'LL WRITE IT DOWN!
DON'T TELL ANYONE, BUT...
PSST
YEAH?
Y'KNOW THE HEALER FAIRIES?
......
WELL...
DILL MAY NEVER BE ABLE TO USE HIS LEFT HAND AGAIN.
WHAT?
I WAS HELPING OUT WITH THE TREATMENT WHEN I HEARD IT.
HE LOOKED SO CALM, BUT HE MUST BE SHOOK UP.

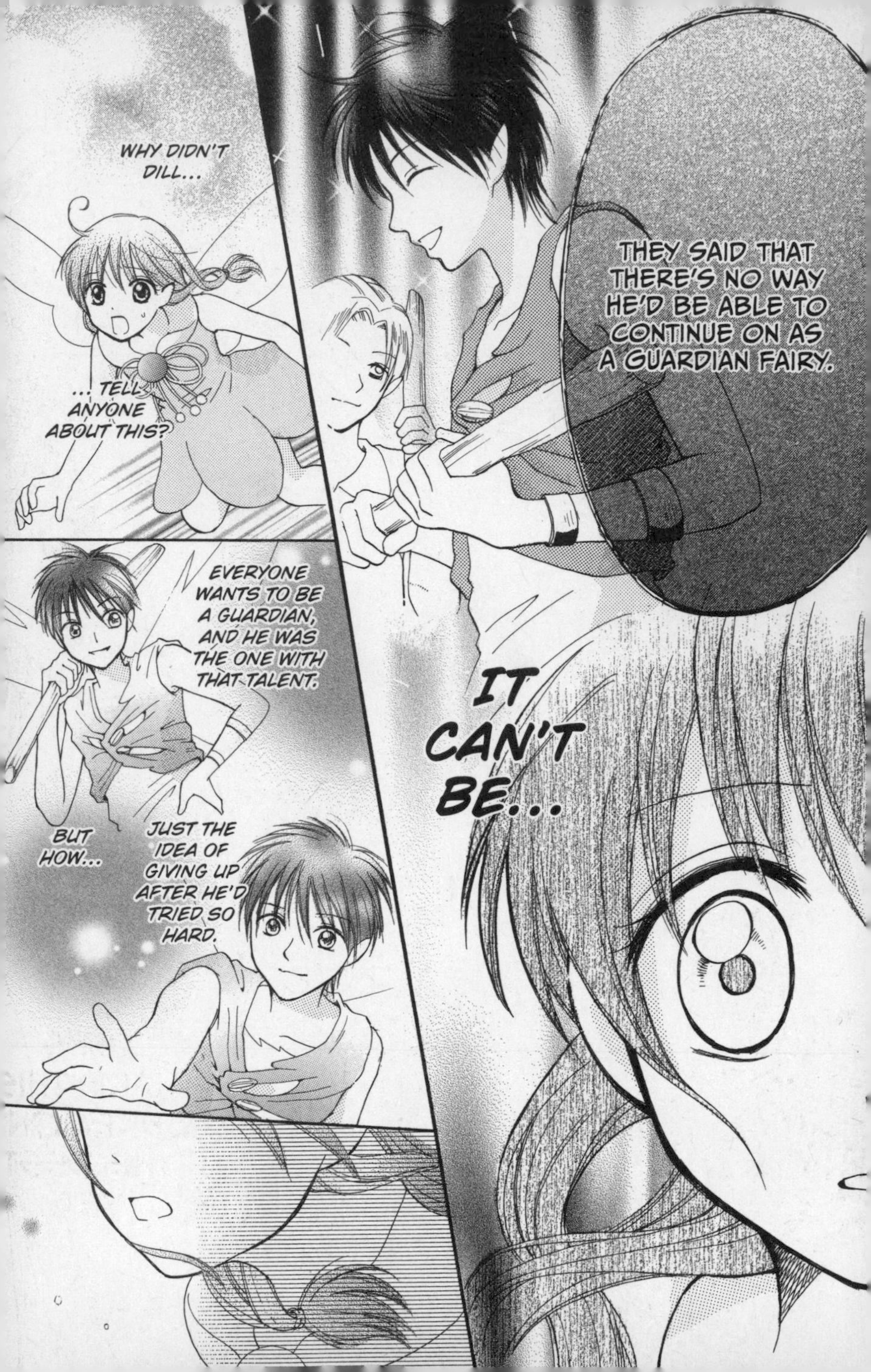
THEY SAID THAT THERE'S NO WAY HE'D BE ABLE TO CONTINUE ON AS A GUARDIAN FAIRY.
IT CAN'T BE...
WHY DIDN'T DILL...
... TELL ANYONE ABOUT THIS?
EVERYONE WANTS TO BE A GUARDIAN, AND HE WAS THE ONE WITH THAT TALENT.
JUST THE IDEA OF GIVING UP AFTER HE'D TRIED SO HARD.
BUT HOW...

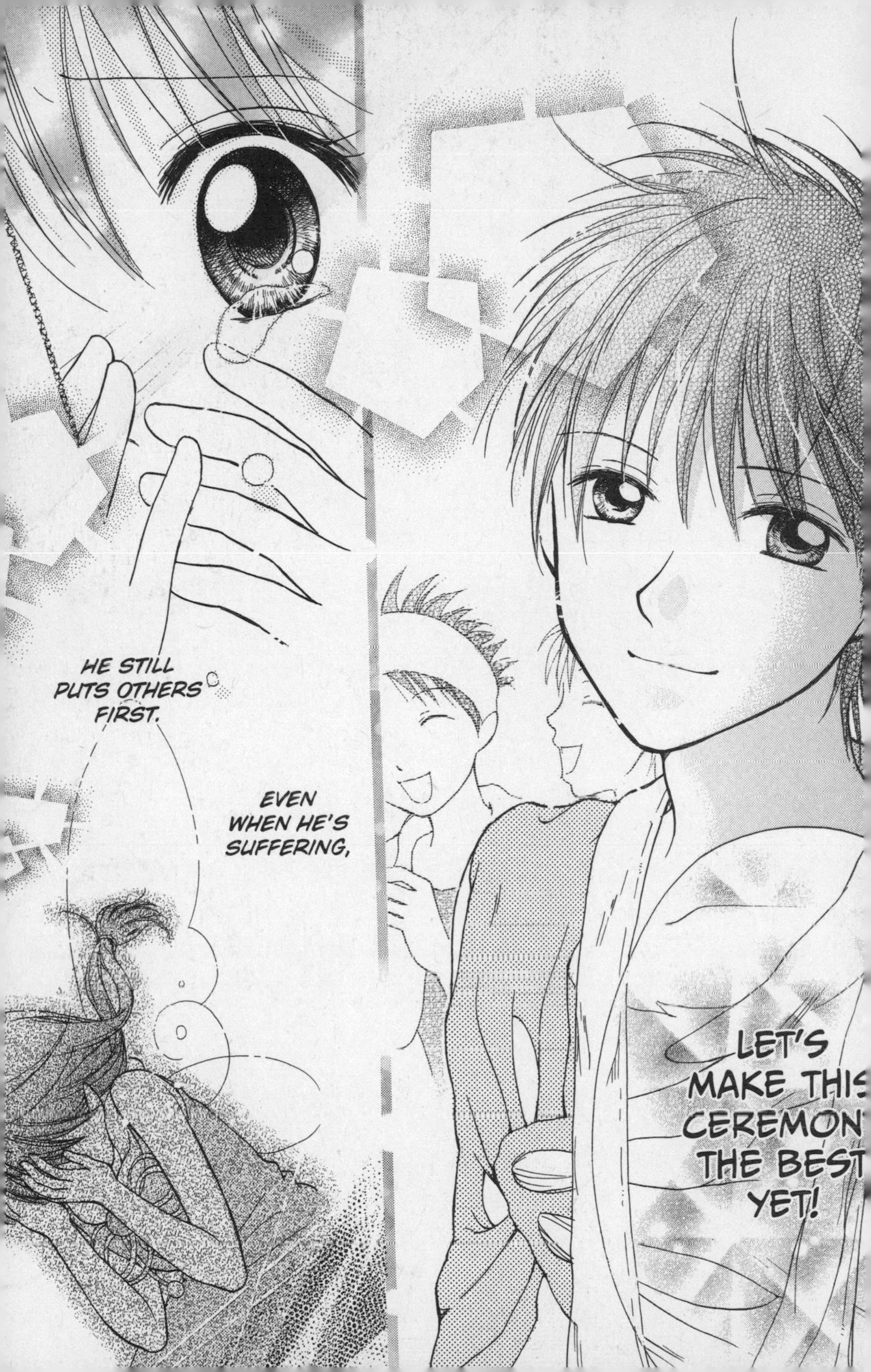
LET'S MAKE THIS CEREMON THE BEST YET!
HE STILL PUTS OTHERS FIRST.
EVEN WHEN HE'S SUFFERING,

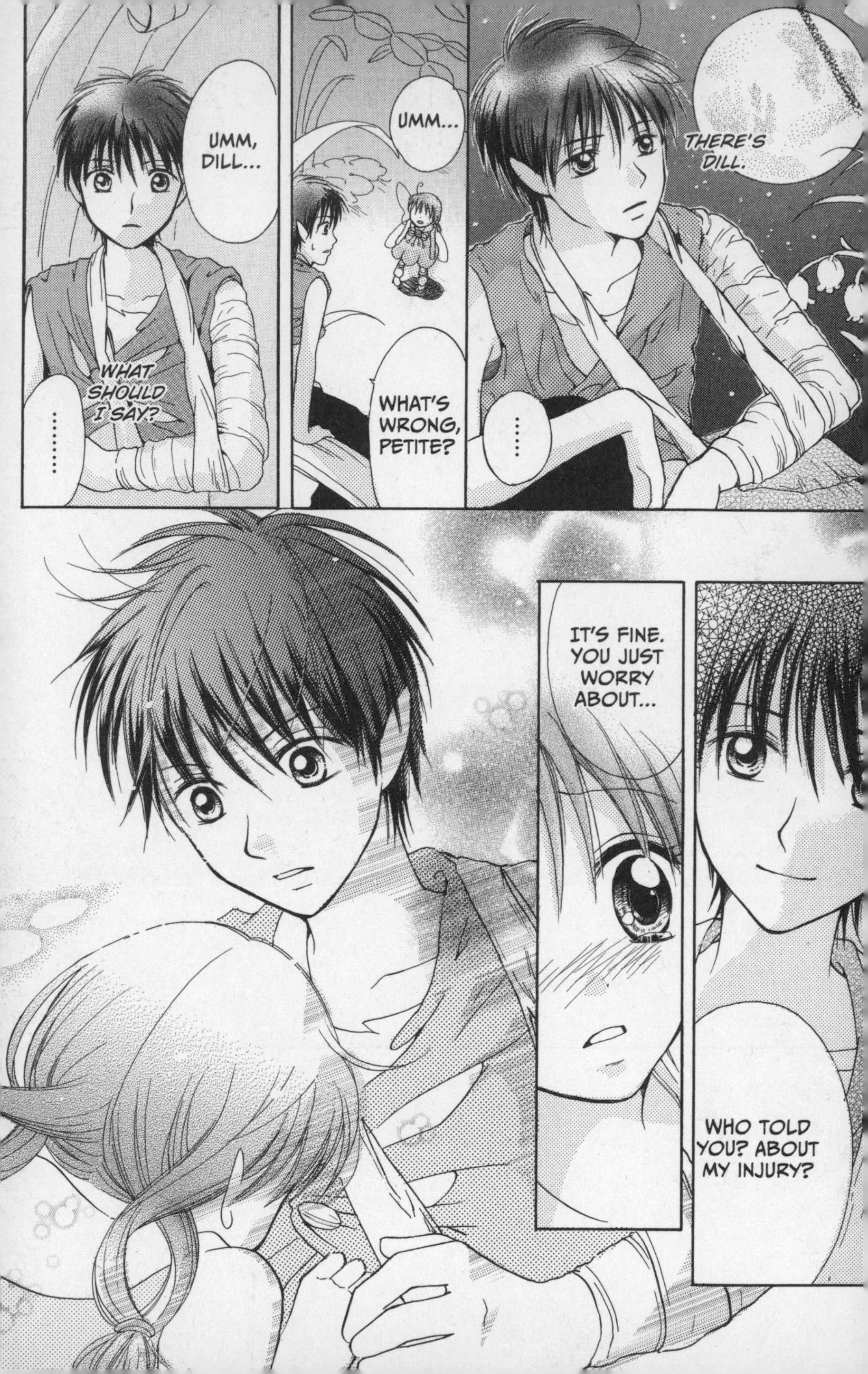
THERE'S DILL.
......
UMM...
WHAT'S WRONG, PETITE?
UMM, DILL...
WHAT SHOULD I SAY?
......
WHO TOLD YOU? ABOUT MY INJURY?
IT'S FINE. YOU JUST WORRY ABOUT...

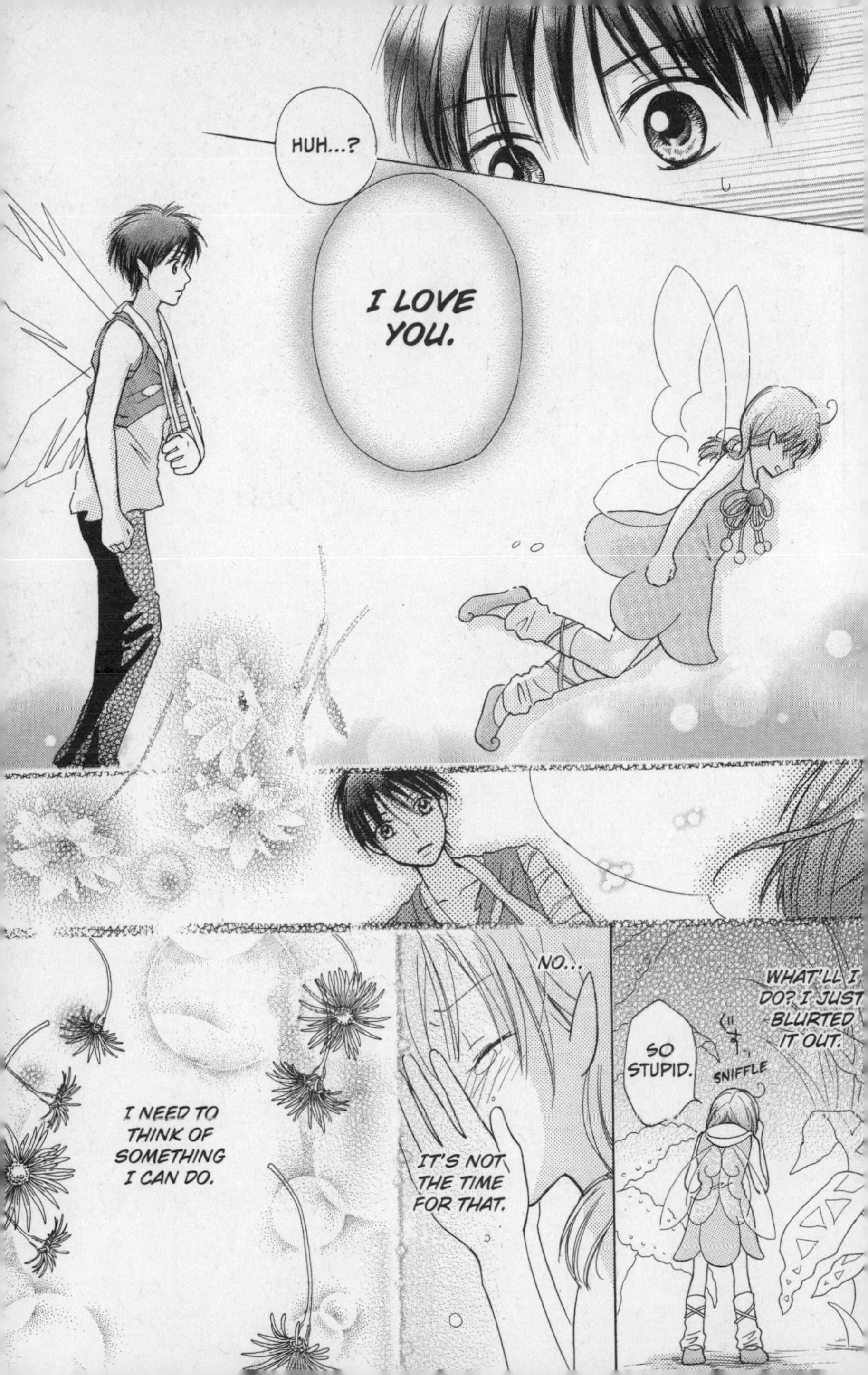
HUH...?
I LOVE YOU.
WHAT'LL I DO? I JUST BLURTED IT OUT.
SO STUPID.
SNIFFLE
NO...
IT'S NOT THE TIME FOR THAT.
I NEED TO THINK OF SOMETHING I CAN DO.

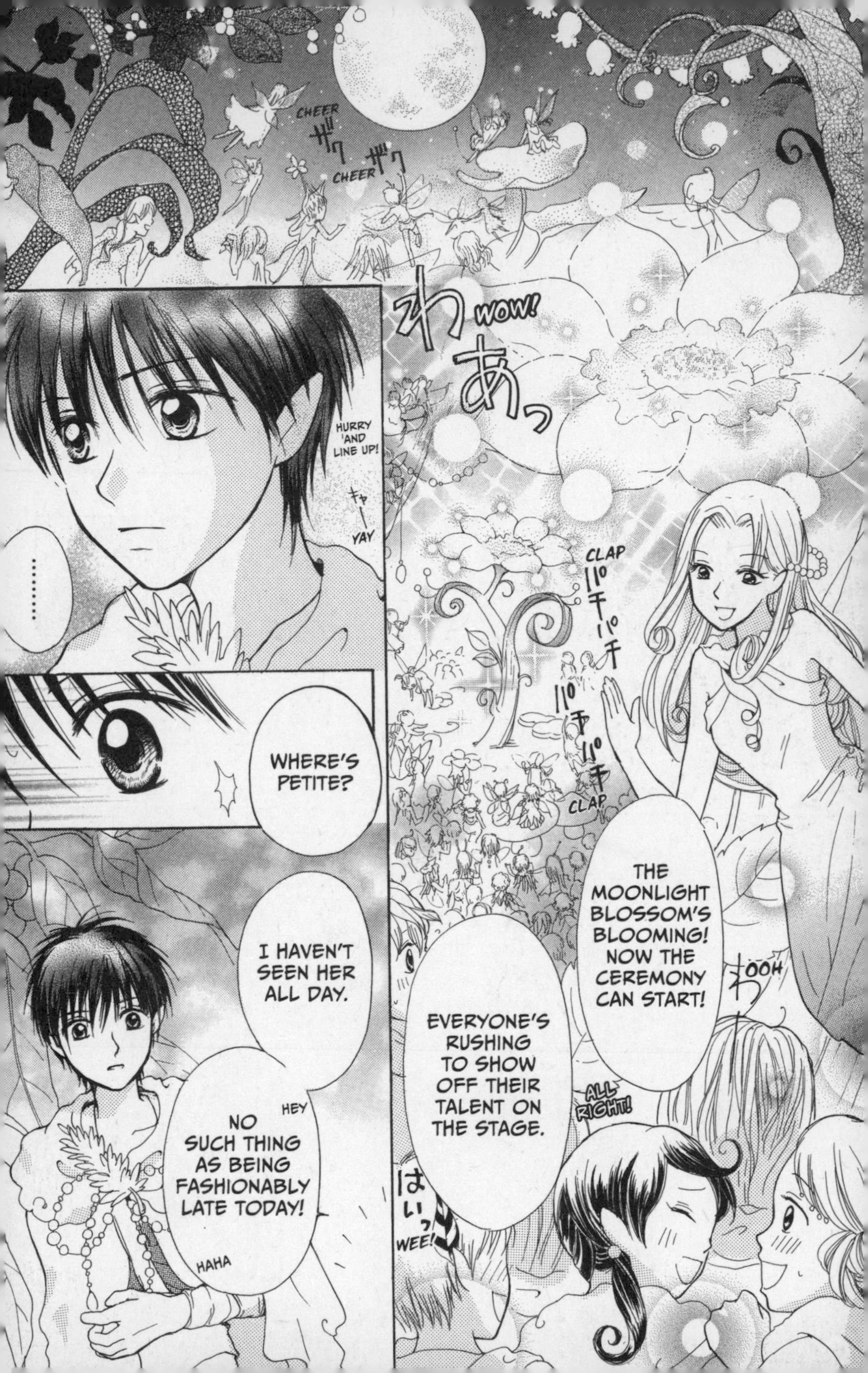

CHEER
CHEER
わあっ WOW!
CLAP パチパチ
パチパチ CLAP
THE MOONLIGHT BLOSSOM'S BLOOMING! NOW THE CEREMONY CAN START!
わ OOH
EVERYONE'S RUSHING TO SHOW OFF THEIR TALENT ON THE STAGE.
ALL RIGHT!
はいっ WEE!
HURRY 'AND LINE UP!
キャー YAY
......
WHERE'S PETITE?
I HAVEN'T SEEN HER ALL DAY.
HEY
NO SUCH THING AS BEING FASHIONABLY LATE TODAY!
HAHA

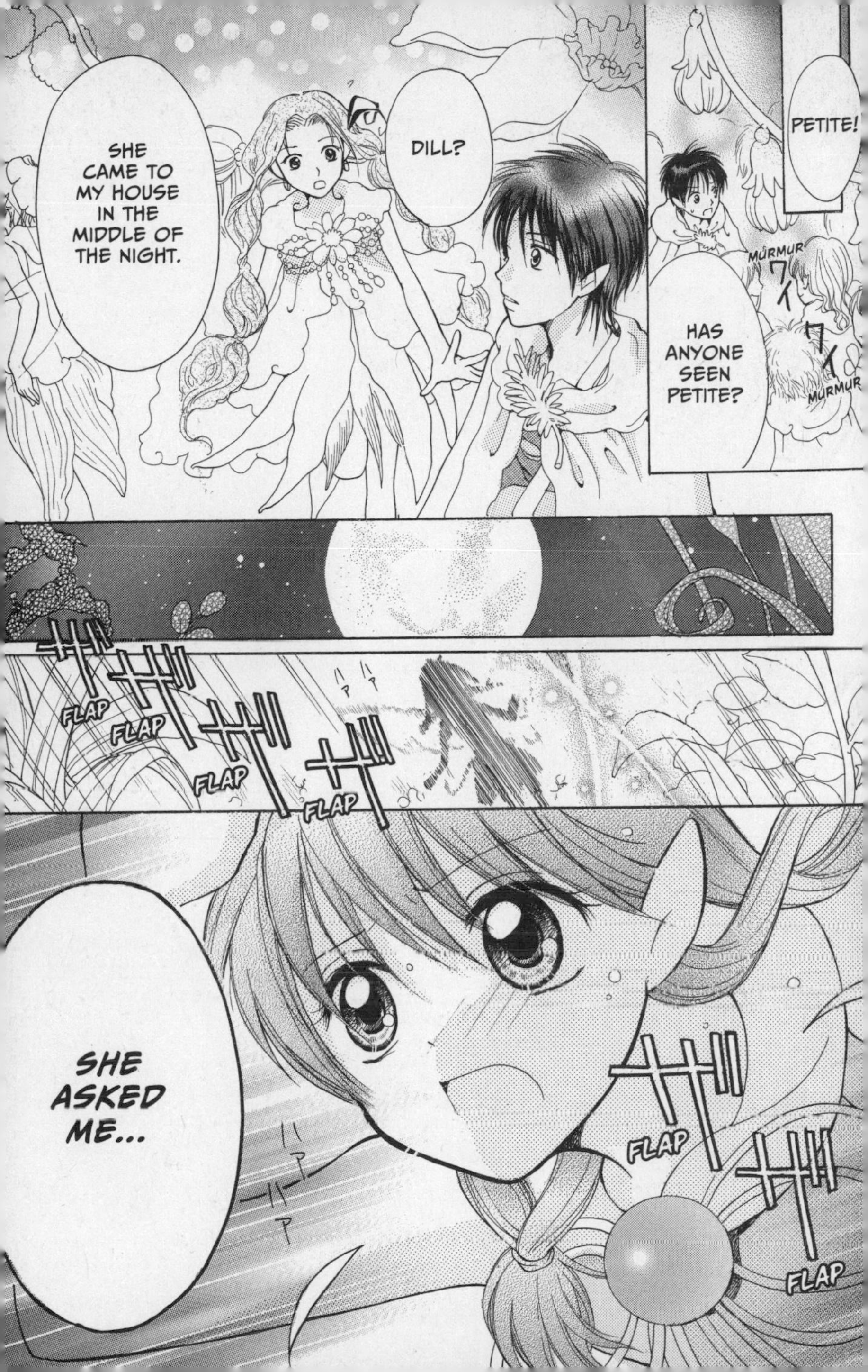
PETITE!
HAS ANYONE SEEN PETITE?
MURMUR
MURMUR
DILL?
SHE CAME TO MY HOUSE IN THE MIDDLE OF THE NIGHT.
FLAP
FLAP
FLAP
FLAP
FLAP
FLAP
SHE ASKED ME...

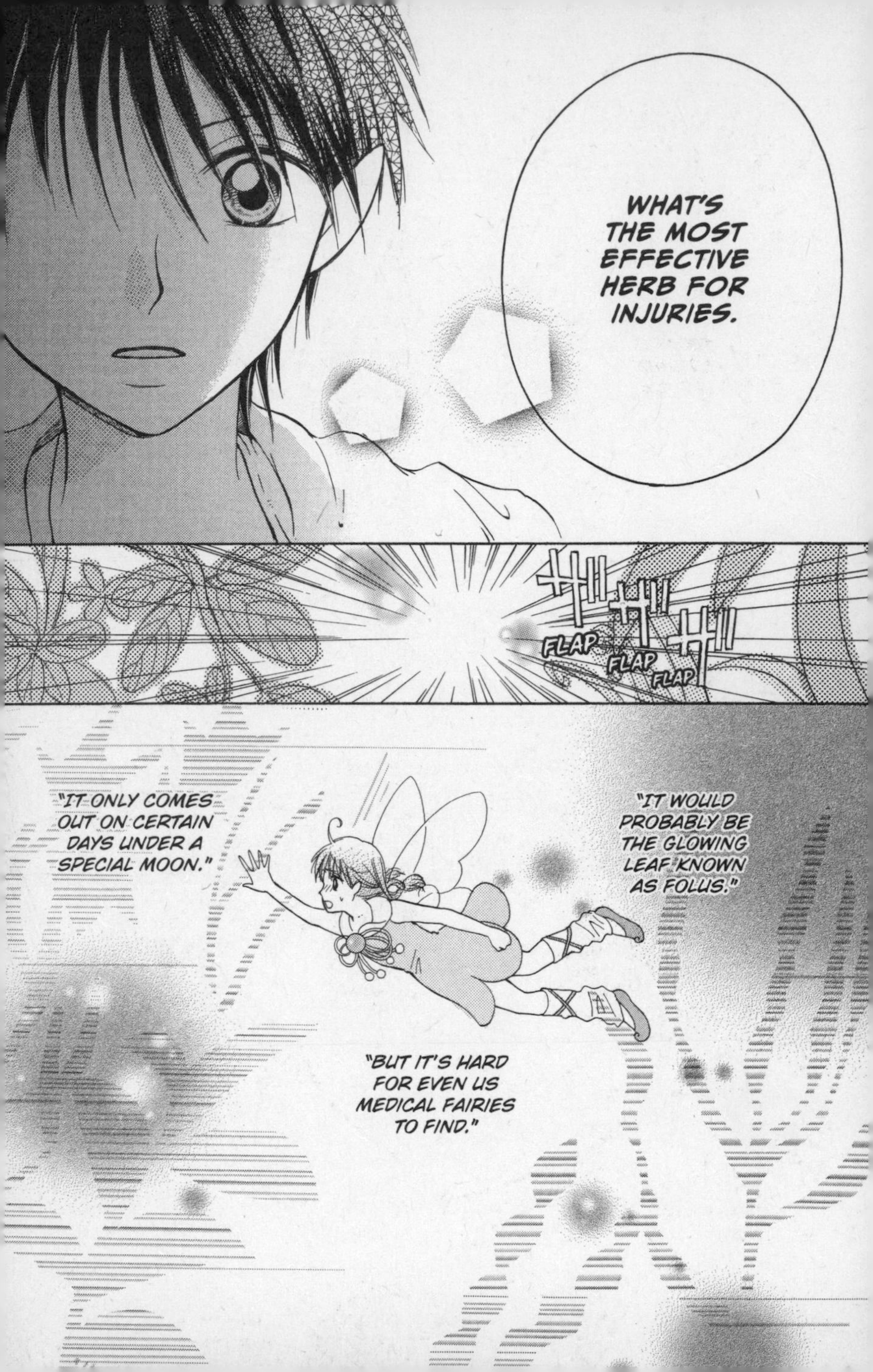
WHAT'S THE MOST EFFECTIVE HERB FOR INJURIES.
FLAP FLAP FLAP
"IT WOULD PROBABLY BE THE GLOWING LEAF KNOWN AS FOLUS."
"IT ONLY COMES OUT ON CERTAIN DAYS UNDER A SPECIAL MOON."
"BUT IT'S HARD FOR EVEN US MEDICAL FAIRIES TO FIND."

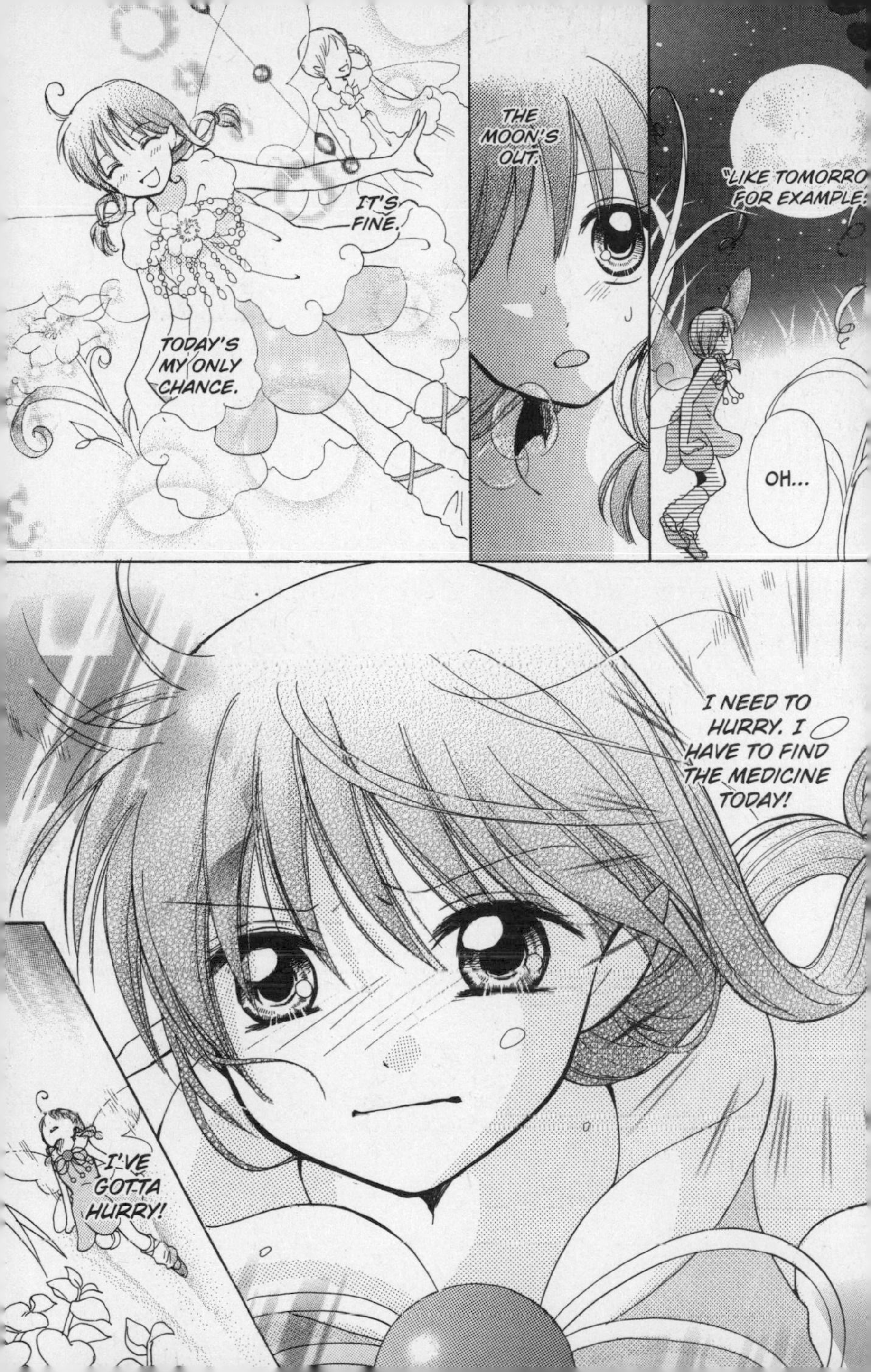
"LIKE TOMORRO FOR EXAMPLE."
OH...
THE MOON'S OUT.
IT'S FINE.
TODAY'S MY ONLY CHANCE.
I NEED TO HURRY. I HAVE TO FIND THE MEDICINE TODAY!
I'VE GOTTA HURRY!

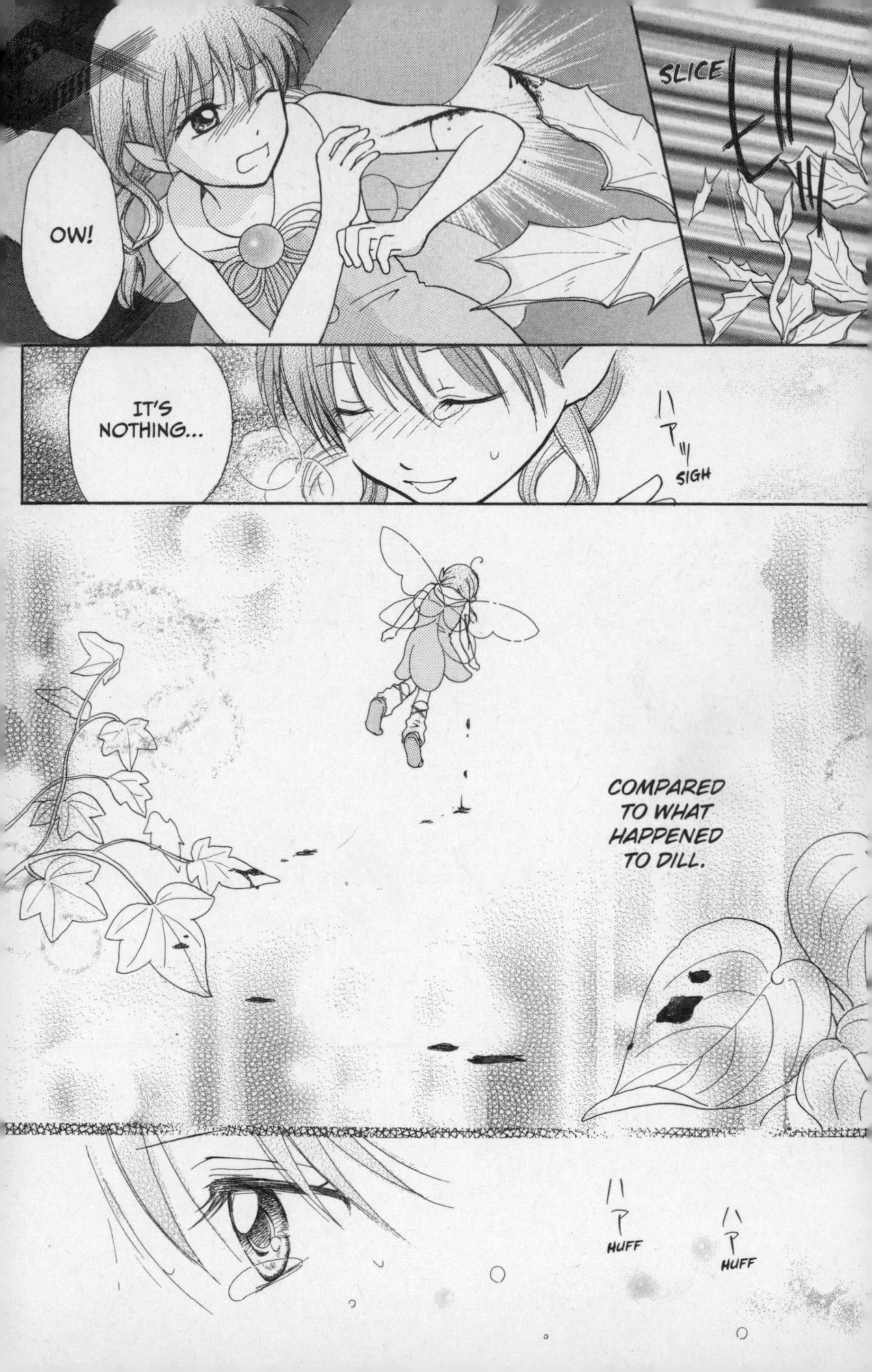
SLICE
OW!
IT'S NOTHING...
SIGH
COMPARED TO WHAT HAPPENED TO DILL.
HUFF
HUFF

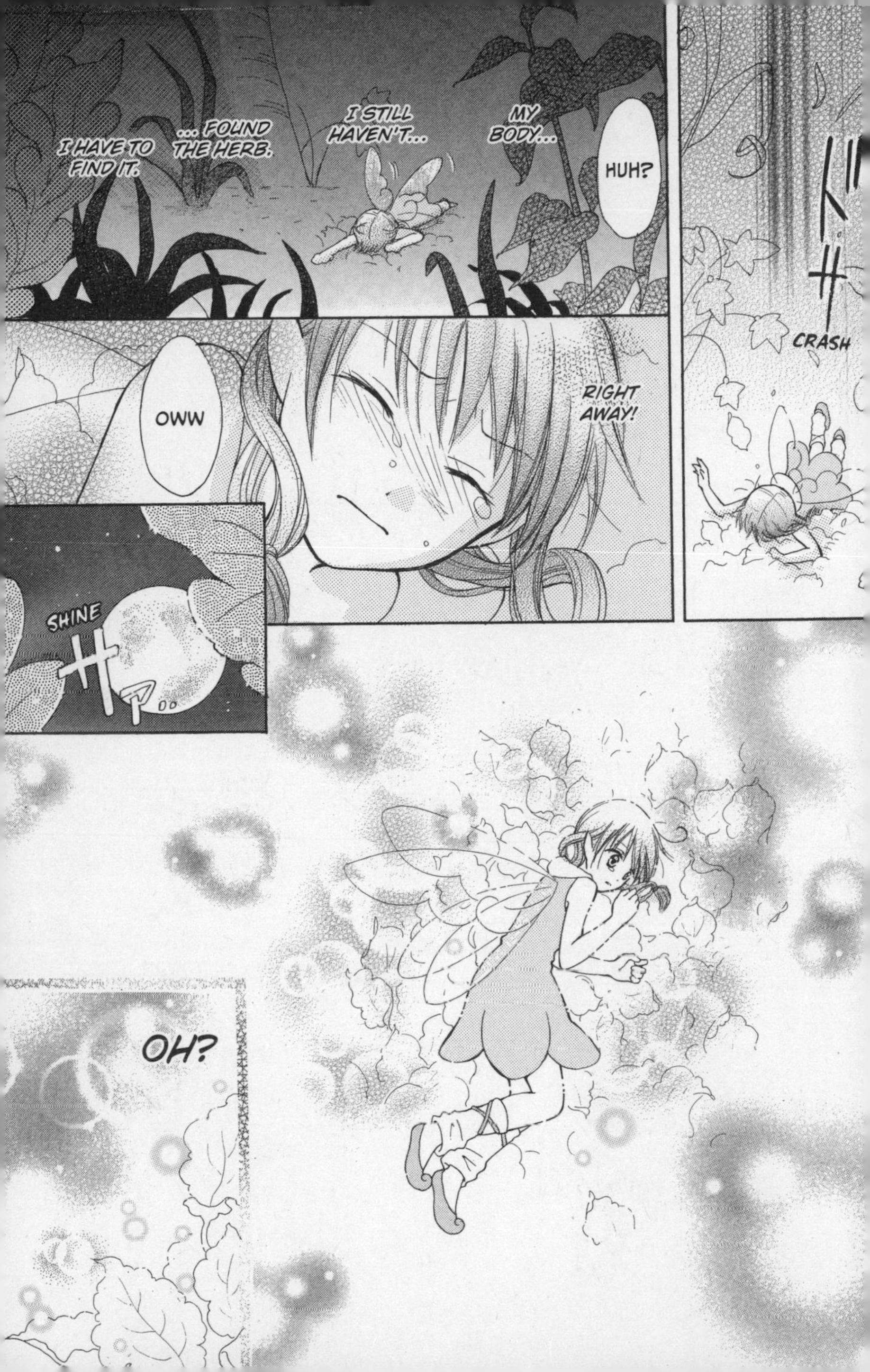
CRASH
HUH?
MY BODY...
I STILL HAVEN'T...
... FOUND THE HERB.
I HAVE TO FIND IT.
RIGHT AWAY!
OWW
SHINE
OH?

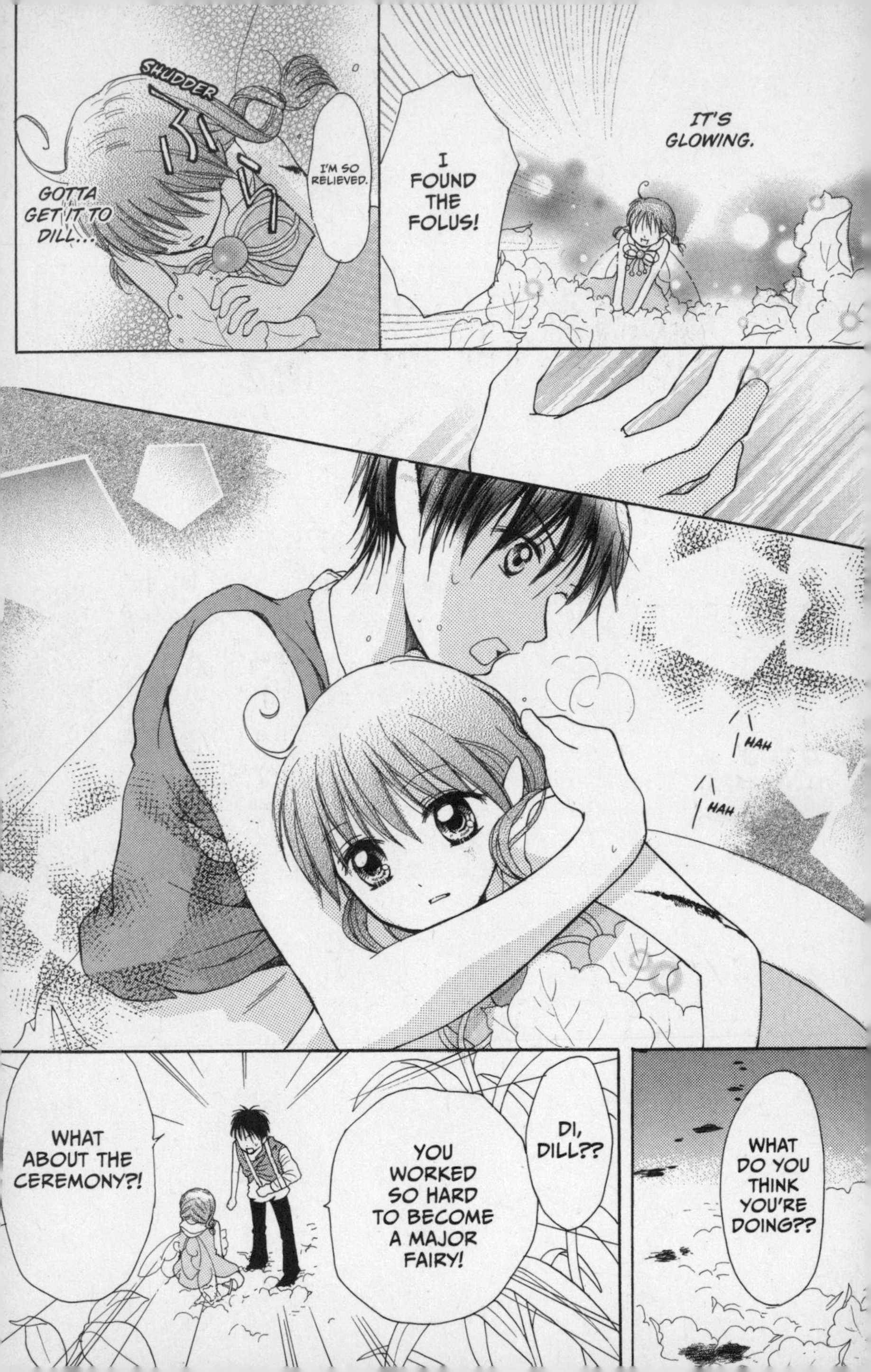
IT'S GLOWING.
I FOUND THE FOLUS!
I'M SO RELIEVED.
SHUDDER
GOTTA GET IT TO DILL...
HAH
HAH
WHAT DO YOU THINK YOU'RE DOING??
DI, DILL??
YOU WORKED SO HARD TO BECOME A MAJOR FAIRY!
WHAT ABOUT THE CEREMONY?!

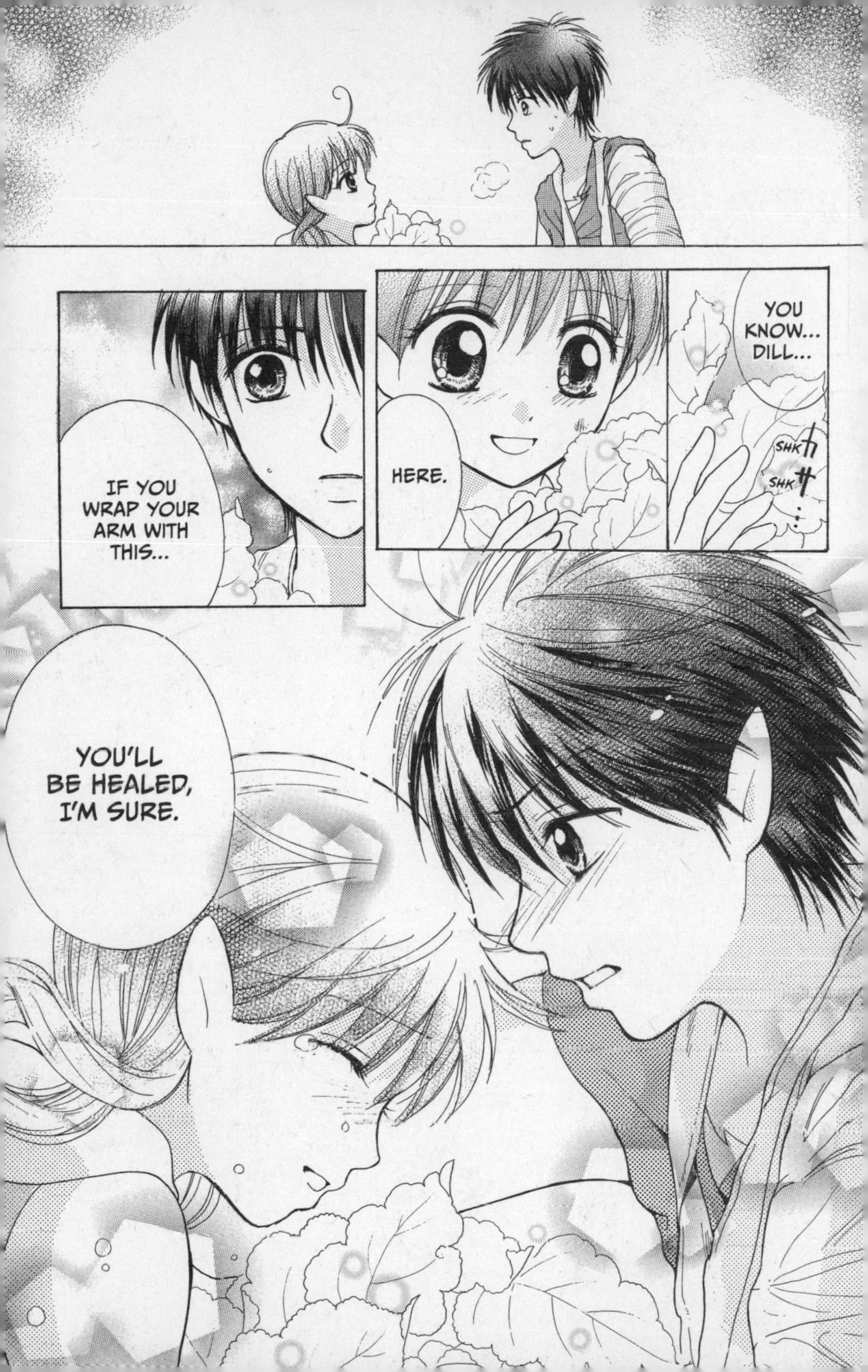
YOU KNOW... DILL...
SHK
SHK
HERE.
IF YOU WRAP YOUR ARM WITH THIS...
YOU'LL BE HEALED, I'M SURE.

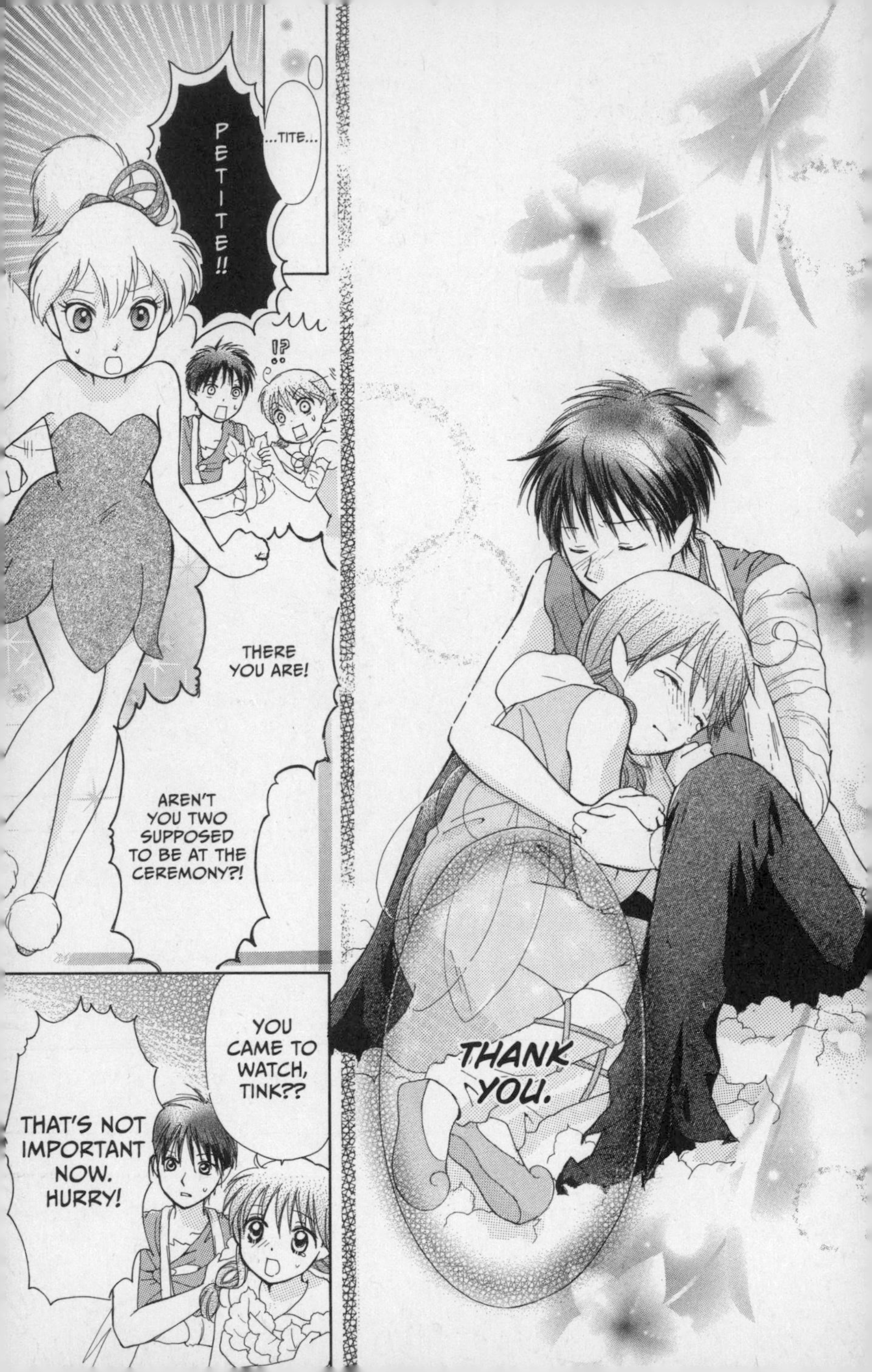
THANK YOU.
...TITE...
PETITE!!
!?
THERE YOU ARE!
AREN'T YOU TWO SUPPOSED TO BE AT THE CEREMONY?!
YOU CAME TO WATCH, TINK??
THAT'S NOT IMPORTANT NOW. HURRY!

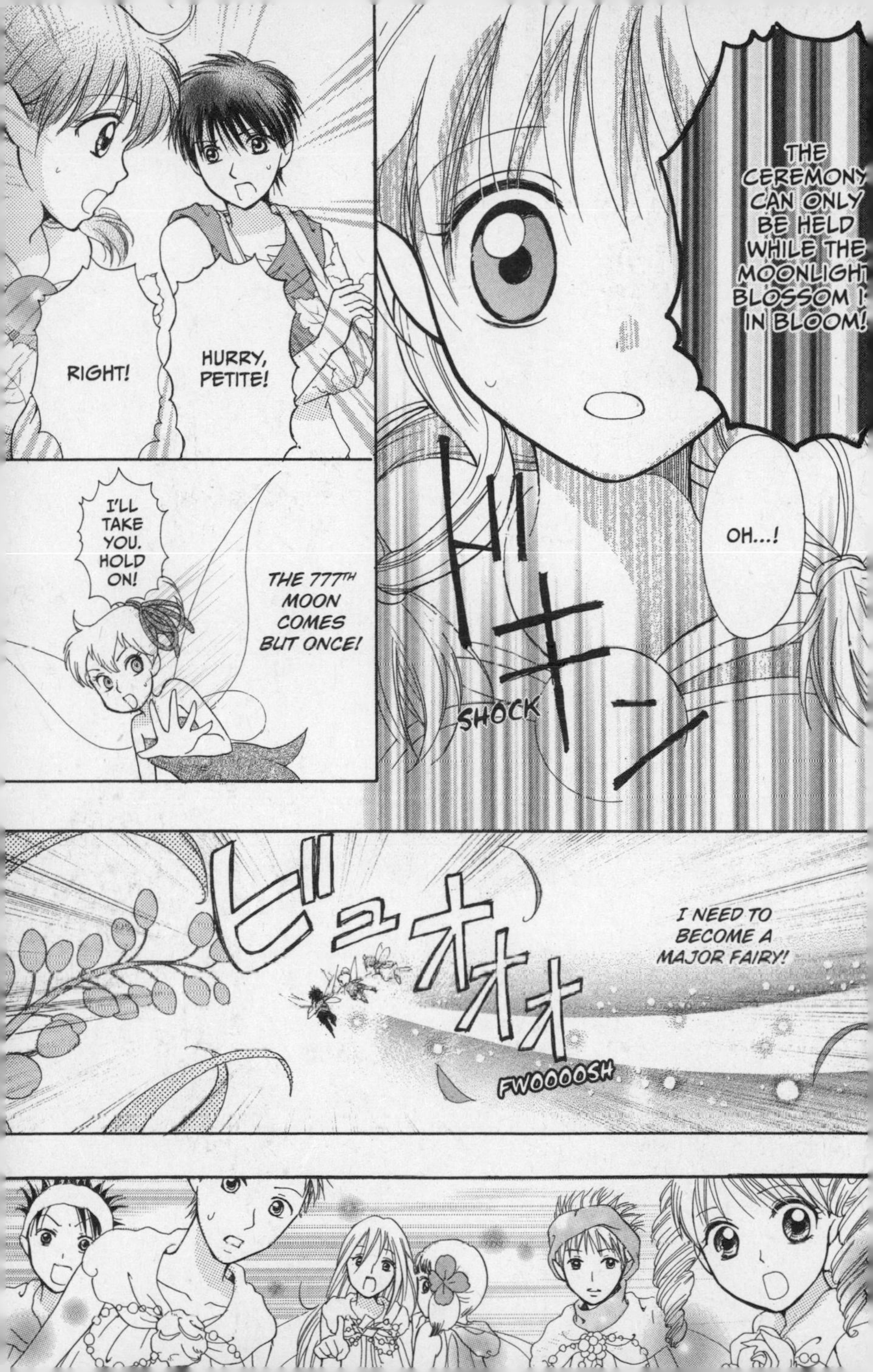
THE CEREMONY CAN ONLY BE HELD WHILE THE MOONLIGHT BLOSSOM IS IN BLOOM!
OH...!
ドキーン
SHOCK
HURRY, PETITE!
RIGHT!
I'LL TAKE YOU. HOLD ON!
THE 777TH MOON COMES BUT ONCE!
I NEED TO BECOME A MAJOR FAIRY!
ビュオオオ
FWOOOOSH

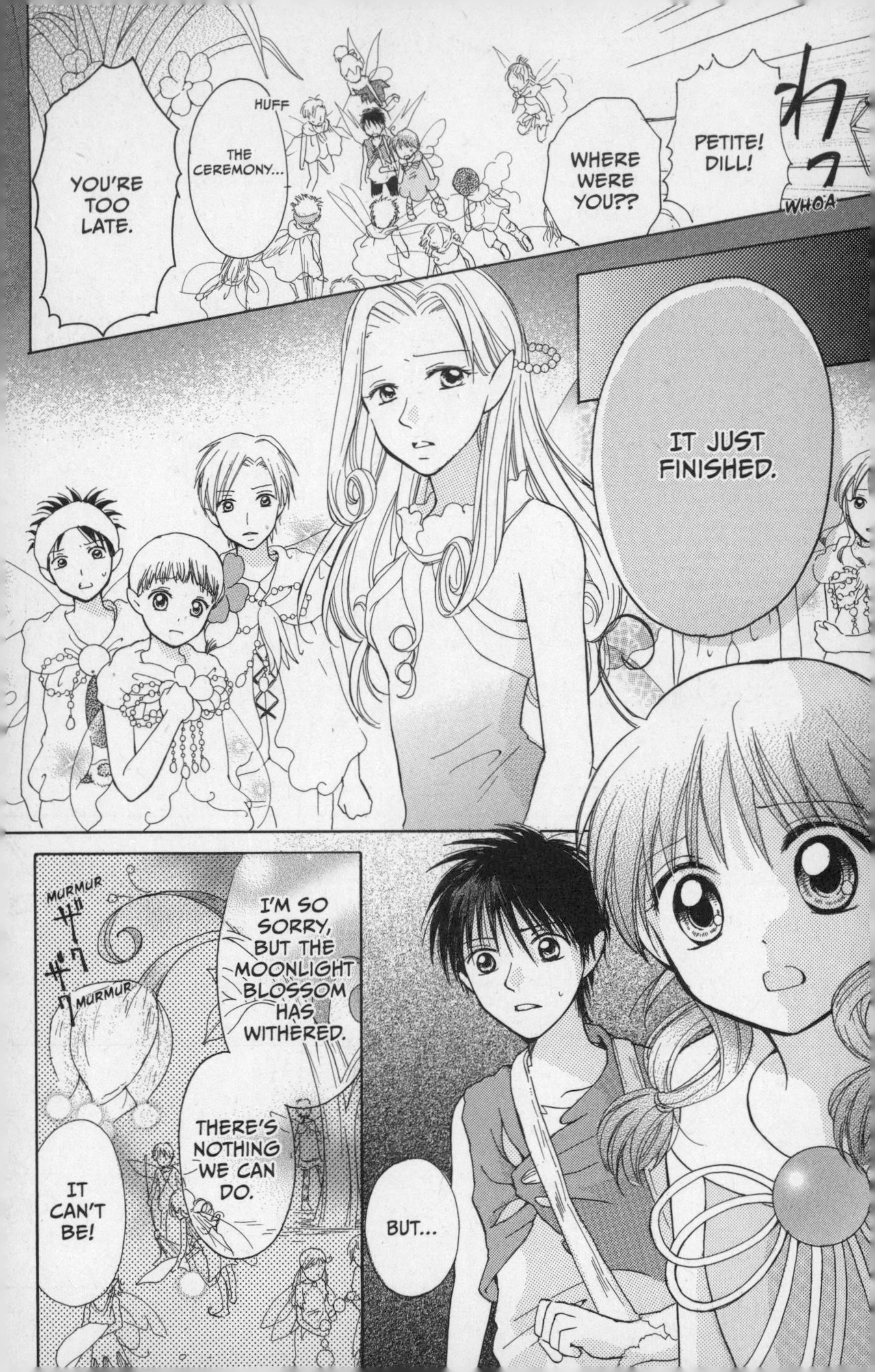
わっ
WHOA
PETITE! DILL!
WHERE WERE YOU??
HUFF
THE CEREMONY...
YOU'RE TOO LATE.
IT JUST FINISHED.
BUT...
I'M SO SORRY, BUT THE MOONLIGHT BLOSSOM HAS WITHERED.
MURMUR
MURMUR
THERE'S NOTHING WE CAN DO.
IT CAN'T BE!

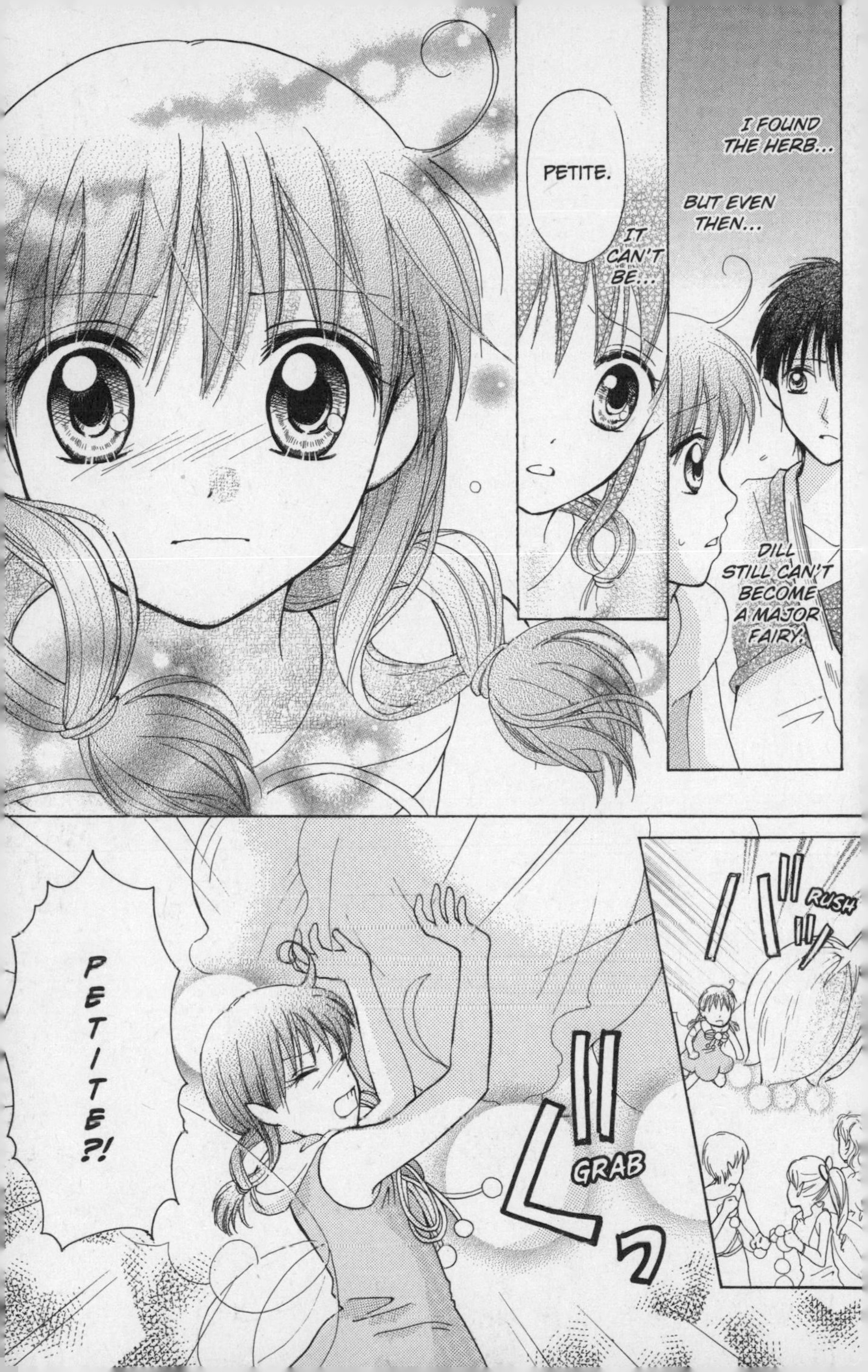
I FOUND THE HERB...
BUT EVEN THEN...
DILL STILL CAN'T BECOME A MAJOR FAIRY.
PETITE.
IT CAN'T BE...
RUSH
GRAB
PETITE?!

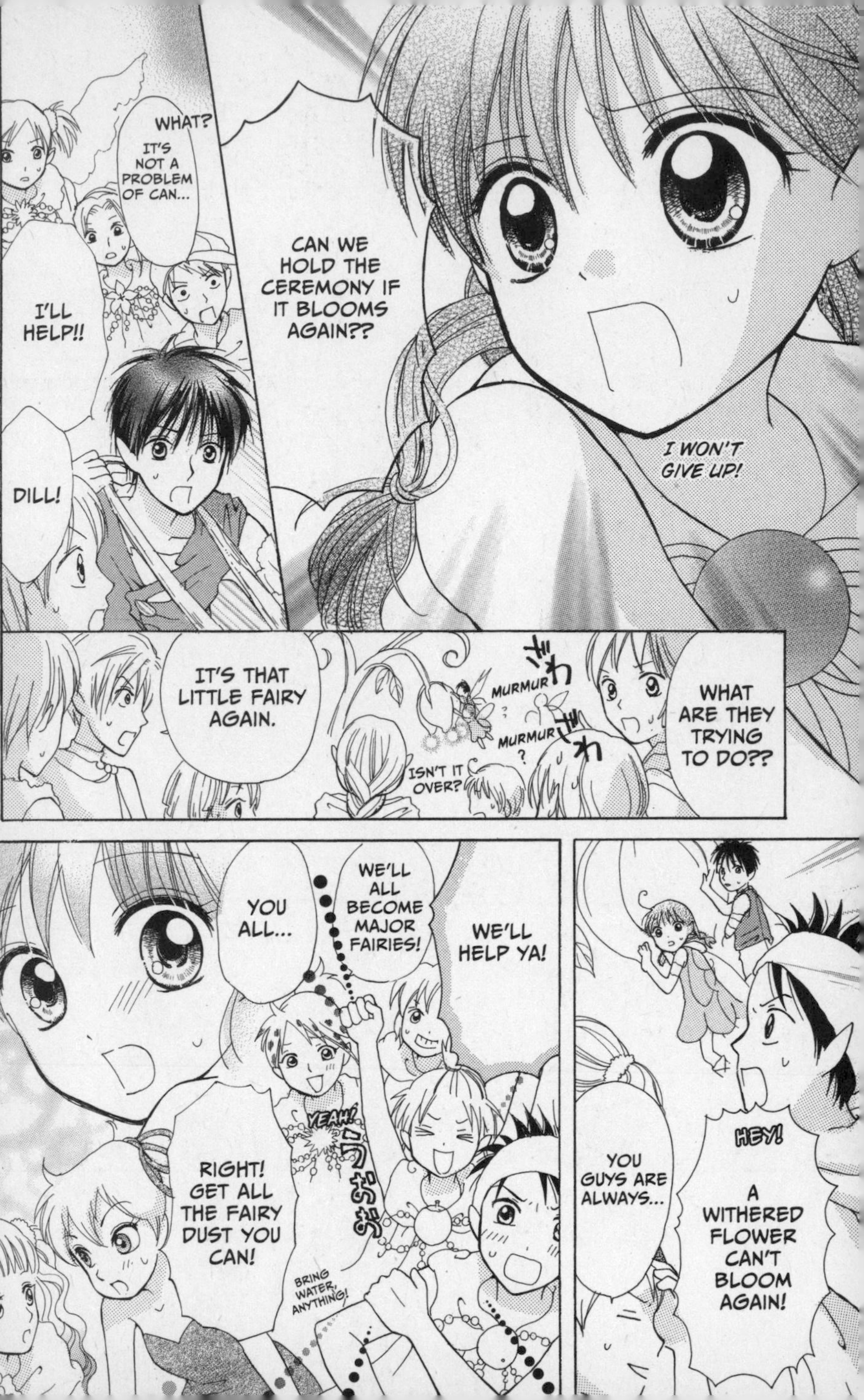
I WON'T GIVE UP!
CAN WE HOLD THE CEREMONY IF IT BLOOMS AGAIN??
WHAT?
IT'S NOT A PROBLEM OF CAN...
I'LL HELP!!
DILL!
WHAT ARE THEY TRYING TO DO??
ざわ ざわ
MURMUR
MURMUR
ISN'T IT OVER?
IT'S THAT LITTLE FAIRY AGAIN.
HEY!
A WITHERED FLOWER CAN'T BLOOM AGAIN!
YOU GUYS ARE ALWAYS...
WE'LL HELP YA!
WE'LL ALL BECOME MAJOR FAIRIES!
YOU ALL...
YEAH!
RIGHT! GET ALL THE FAIRY DUST YOU CAN!
BRING WATER, ANYTHING!

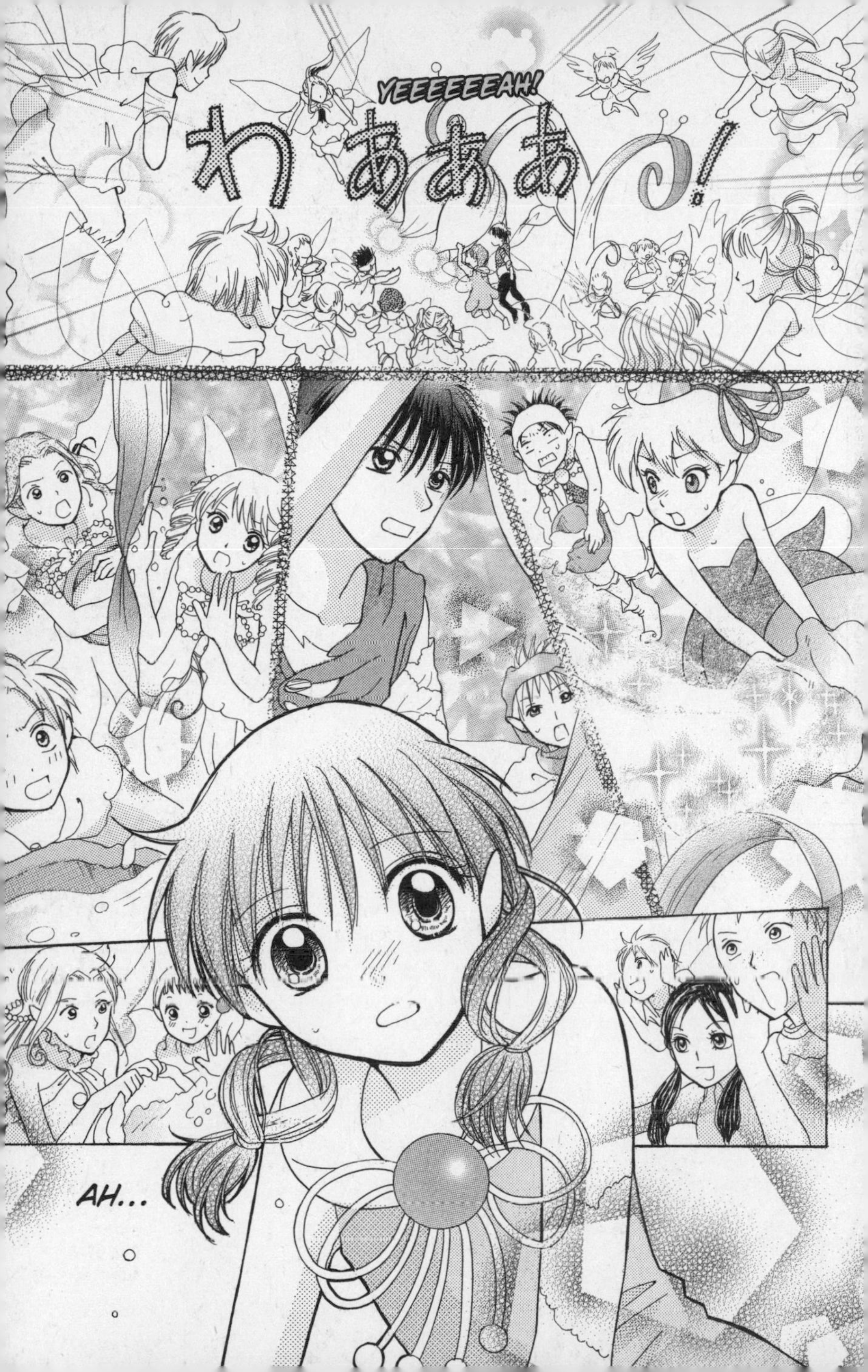
YEEEEEEEAH!
わあああ〜!
AH...

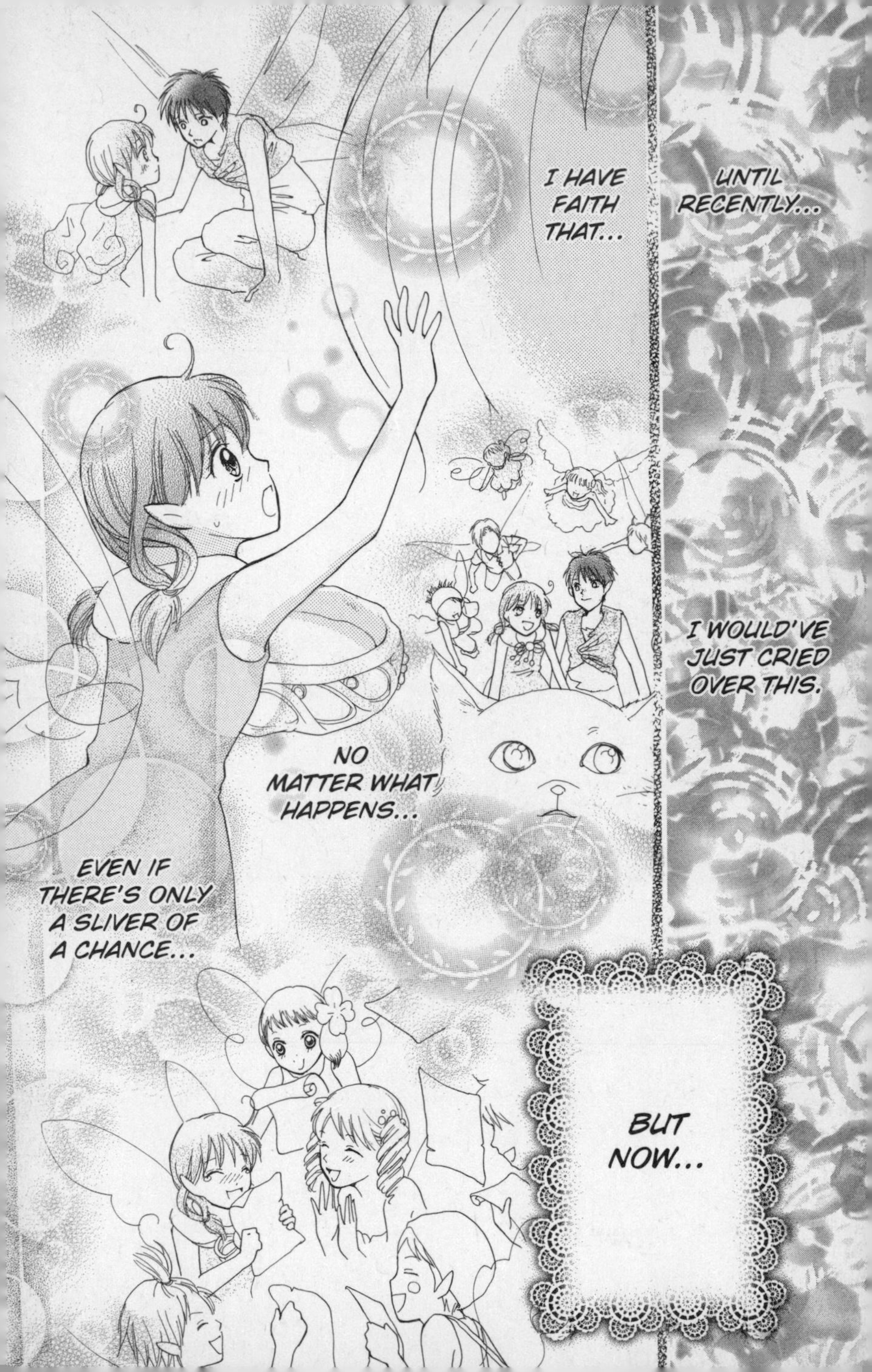
UNTIL RECENTLY...
I WOULD'VE JUST CRIED OVER THIS.
BUT NOW...
I HAVE FAITH THAT...
NO MATTER WHAT HAPPENS...
EVEN IF THERE'S ONLY A SLIVER OF A CHANCE...

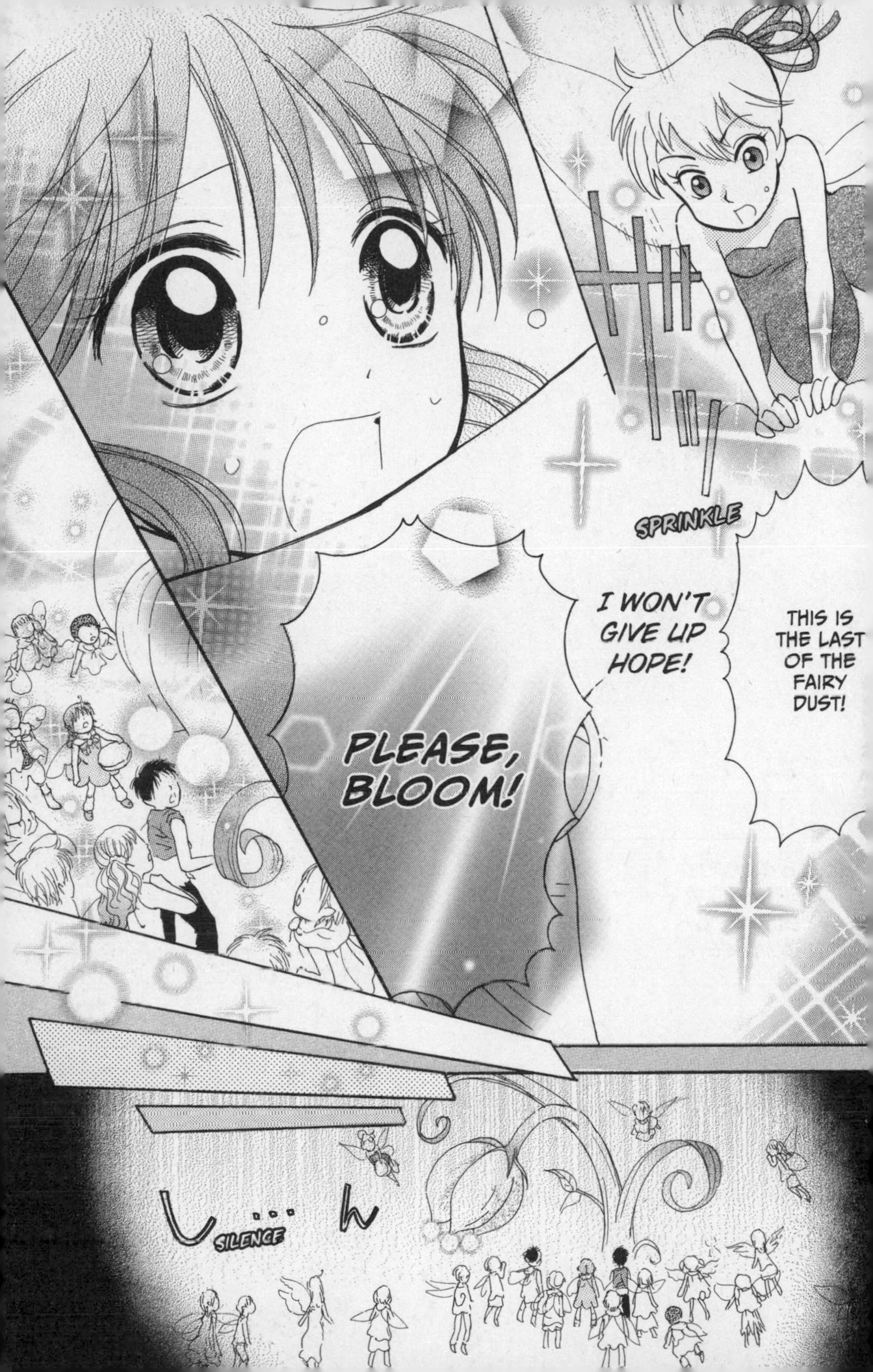
THIS IS THE LAST OF THE FAIRY DUST!
SPRINKLE
I WON'T GIVE UP HOPE!
PLEASE, BLOOM!
SILENCE

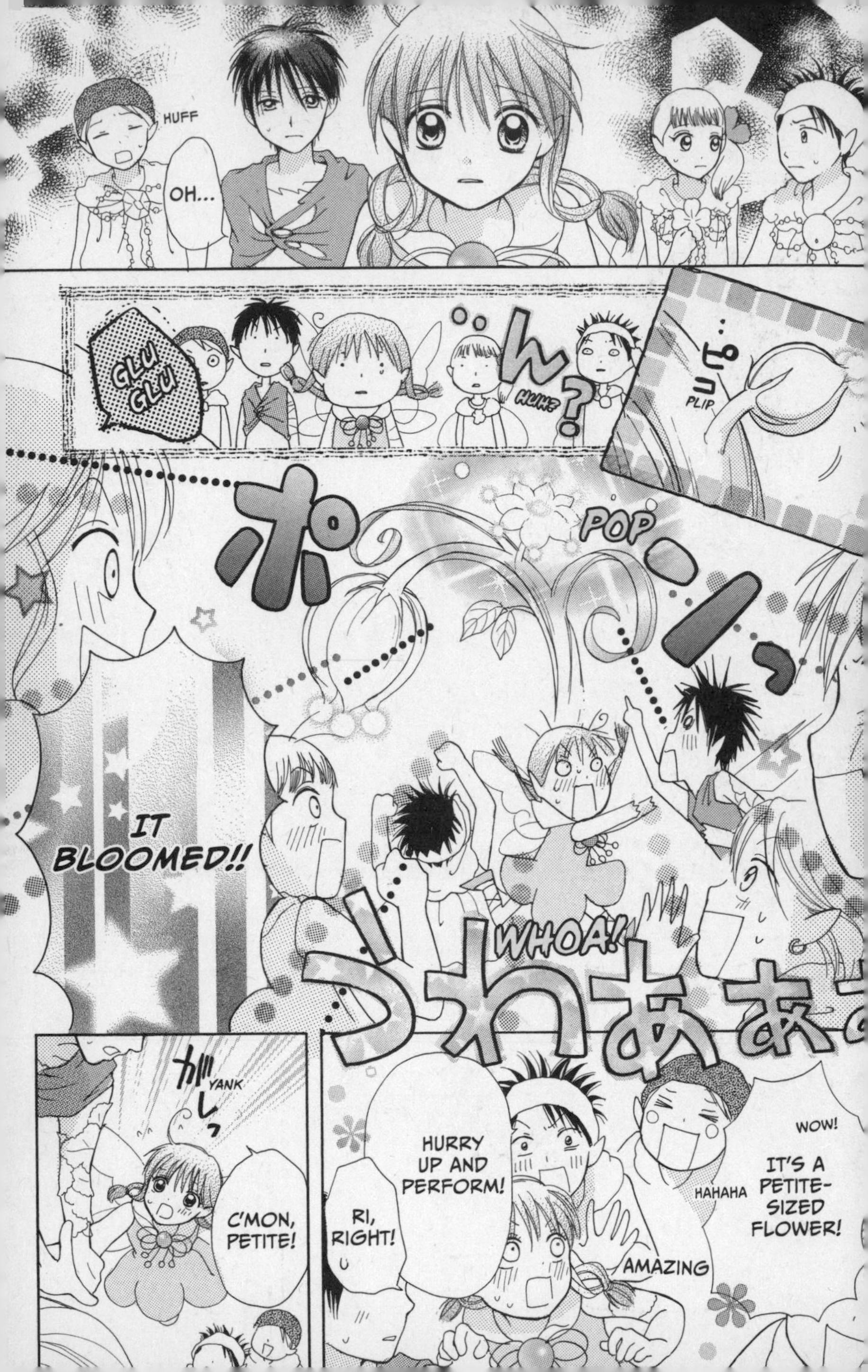
HUFF
OH...
PLIP
HUH?
GLU GLU
POP
IT BLOOMED!!
WHOA!
WOW!
IT'S A PETITE-SIZED FLOWER!
HAHAHA
HURRY UP AND PERFORM!
RI, RIGHT!
AMAZING
YANK
C'MON, PETITE!

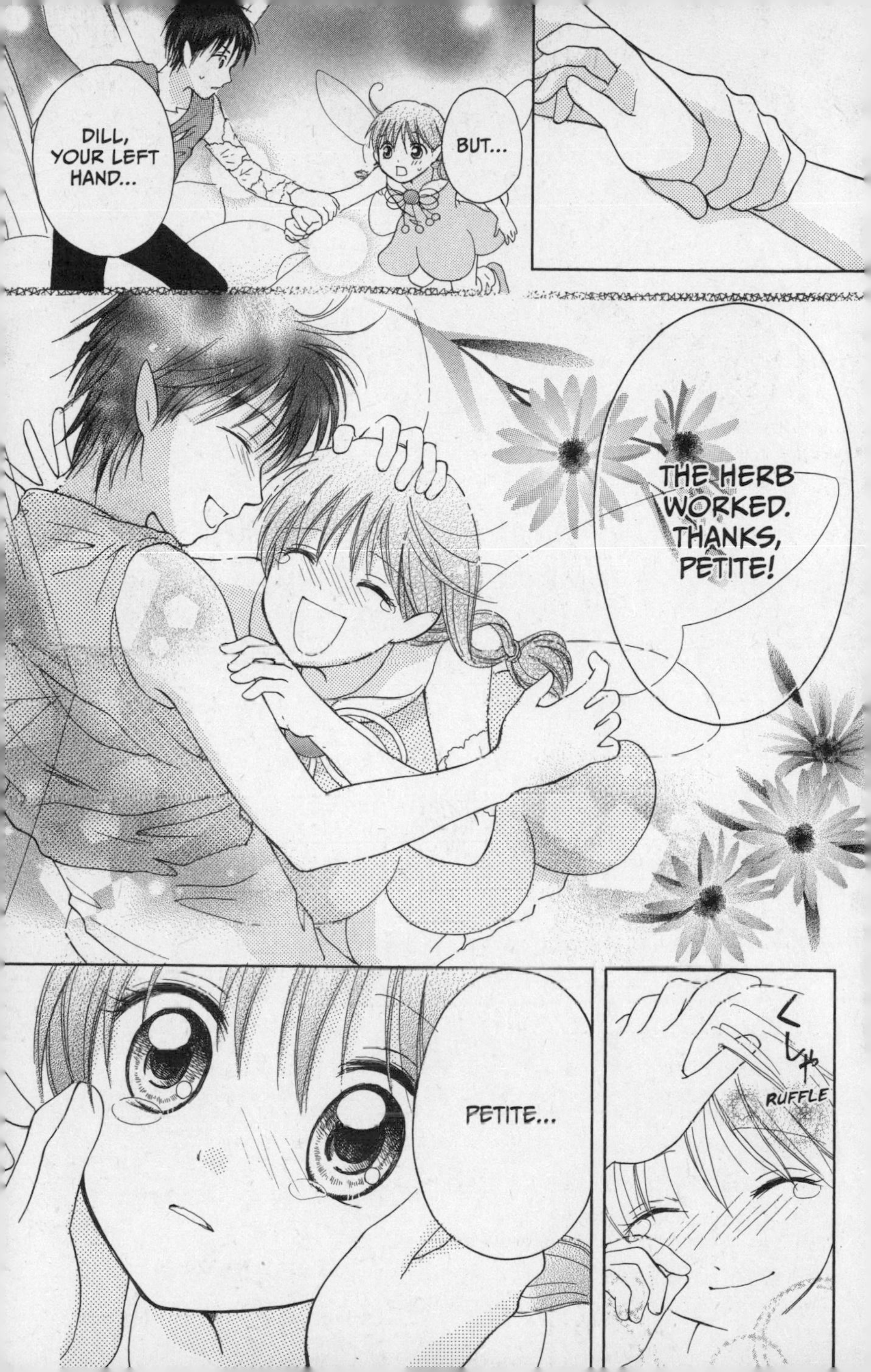
BUT...
DILL, YOUR LEFT HAND...
THE HERB WORKED. THANKS, PETITE!
くしゃ
RUFFLE
PETITE...

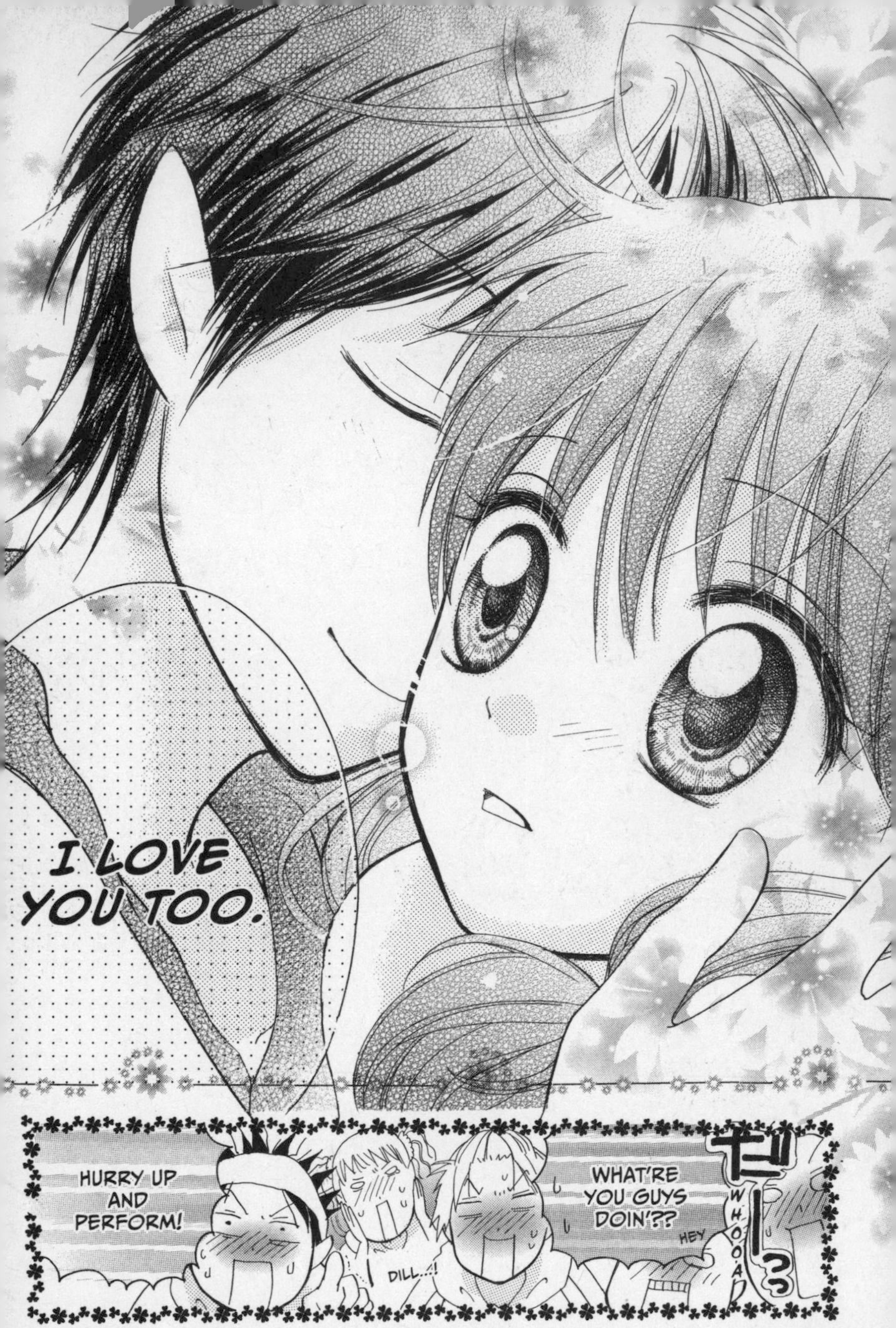
I LOVE YOU TOO.
WHOOA!
HEY
WHAT'RE YOU GUYS DOIN'??
DILL...!
HURRY UP AND PERFORM!

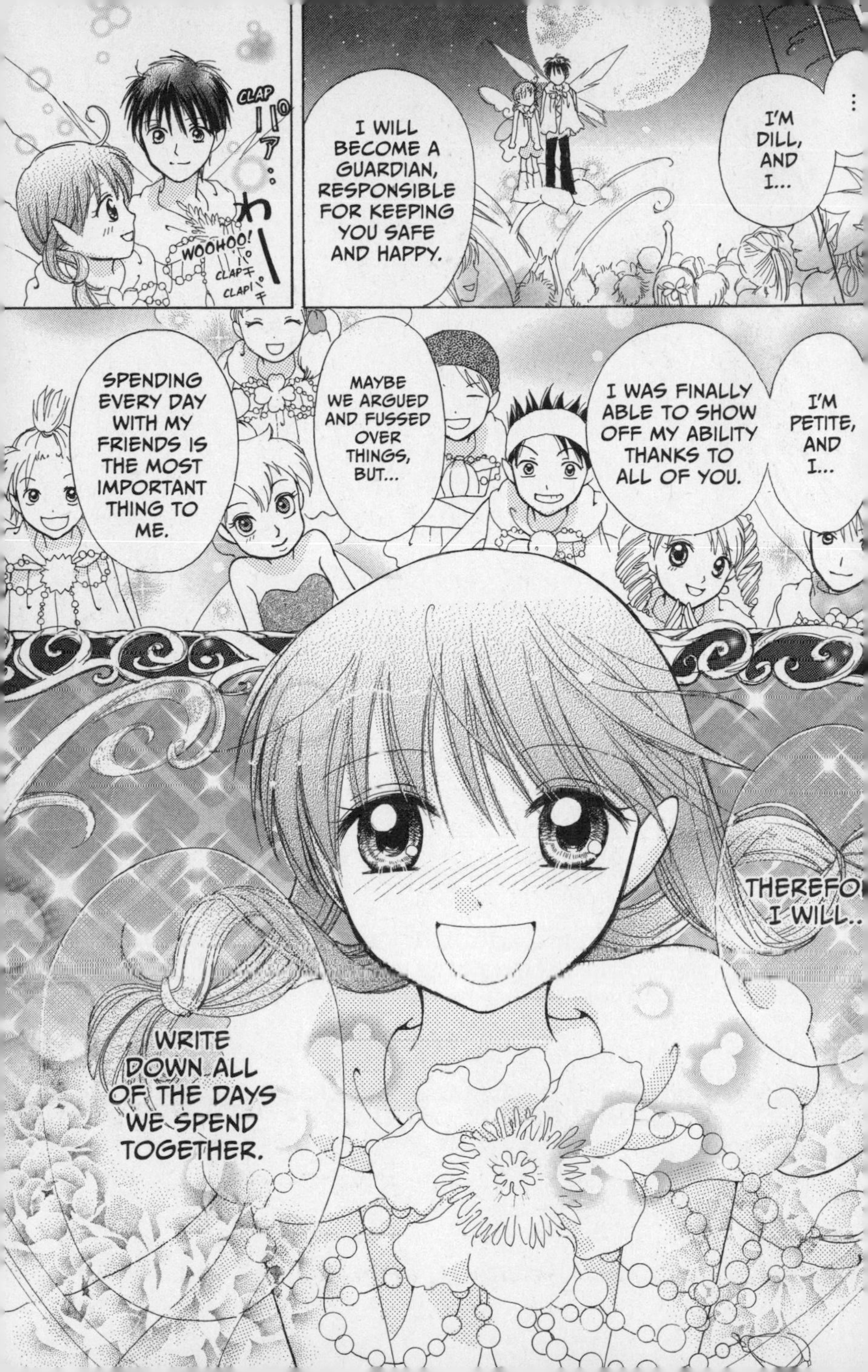

I'M DILL, AND I...
I WILL BECOME A GUARDIAN, RESPONSIBLE FOR KEEPING YOU SAFE AND HAPPY.
CLAP
WOOHOO!
CLAP CLAP
I'M PETITE, AND I...
I WAS FINALLY ABLE TO SHOW OFF MY ABILITY THANKS TO ALL OF YOU.
MAYBE WE ARGUED AND FUSSED OVER THINGS, BUT...
SPENDING EVERY DAY WITH MY FRIENDS IS THE MOST IMPORTANT THING TO ME.
THEREFO I WILL..
WRITE DOWN ALL OF THE DAYS WE SPEND TOGETHER.

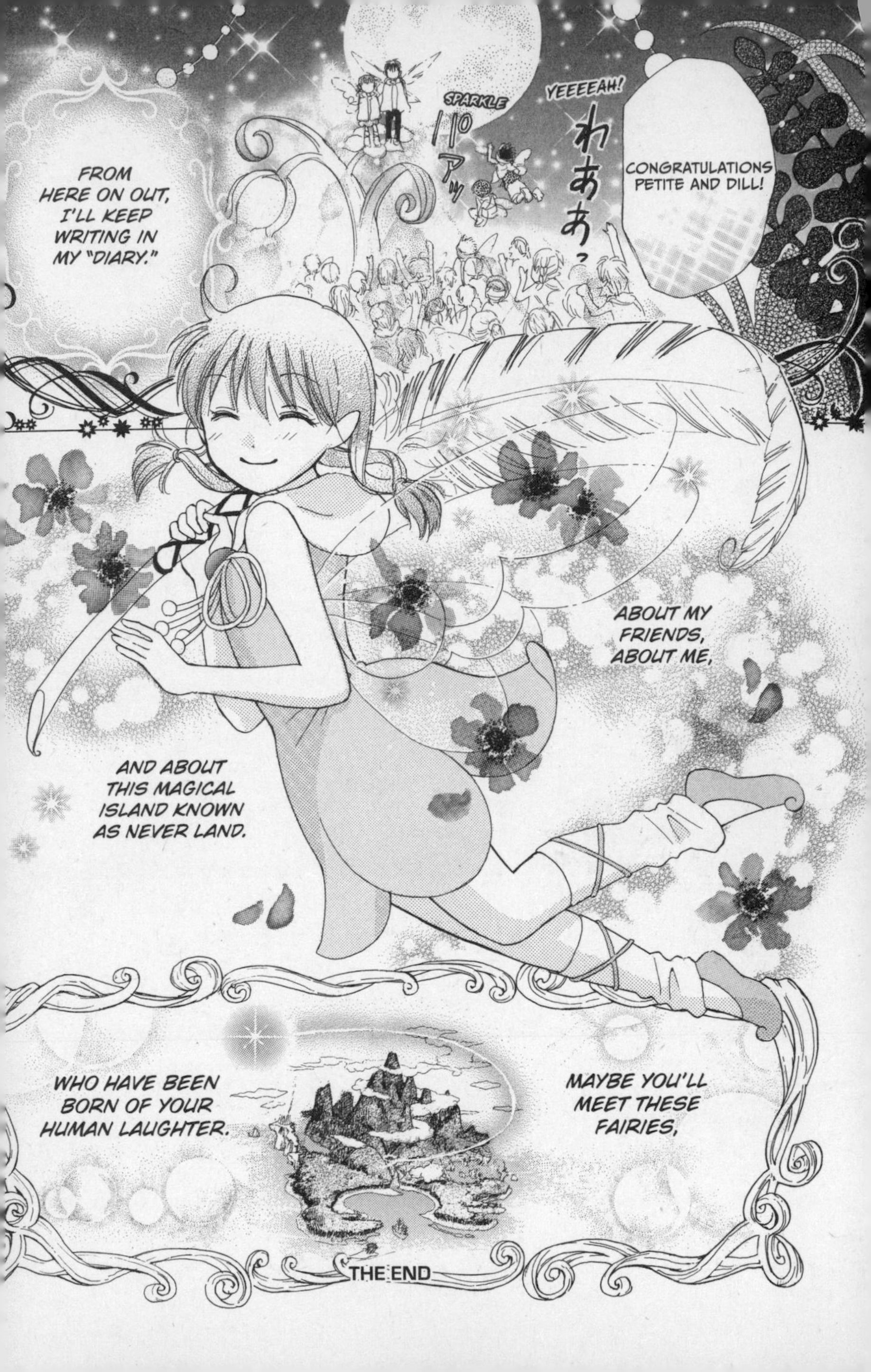
CONGRATULATIONS PETITE AND DILL!
YEEEEAH!
わああっ
SPARKLE
パアッ
FROM HERE ON OUT, I'LL KEEP WRITING IN MY "DIARY."
ABOUT MY FRIENDS, ABOUT ME,
AND ABOUT THIS MAGICAL ISLAND KNOWN AS NEVER LAND.
MAYBE YOU'LL MEET THESE FAIRIES,
WHO HAVE BEEN BORN OF YOUR HUMAN LAUGHTER.
THE END

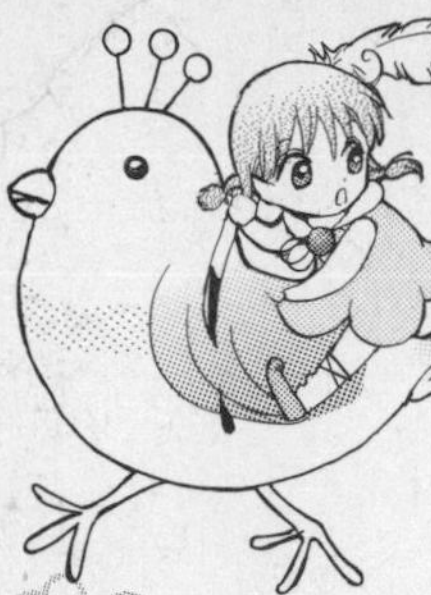

AUTHOR'S NOTES AND CHARACTER INTRODUCTION

HELLO THERE! JUN ASUKA SPEAKING. THANKS FOR PICKING UP THIS MANGA.

PETITE IS THE STORY OF A FAIRY BORN IN THE DISNEY FAIRIES WORLD, FILLED WITH ALL SORTS OF ADVENTURES WITH TINKER BELL AND HER FRIENDS.

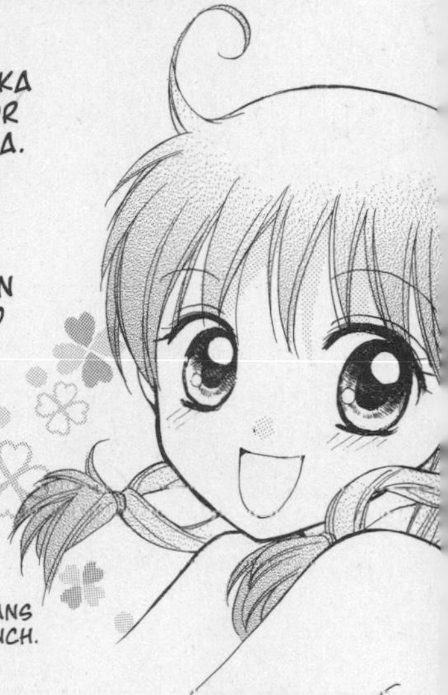

PETITE

HER NAME MEANS "TINY" IN FRENCH.

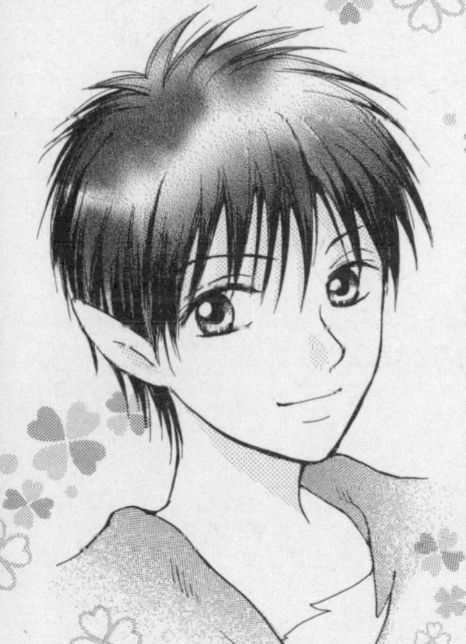

DILL

FROM THE HERB. ORIGINALLY HIS NAME WAS AMBER, BUT THAT'S A GIRL'S NAME IN AMERICA.

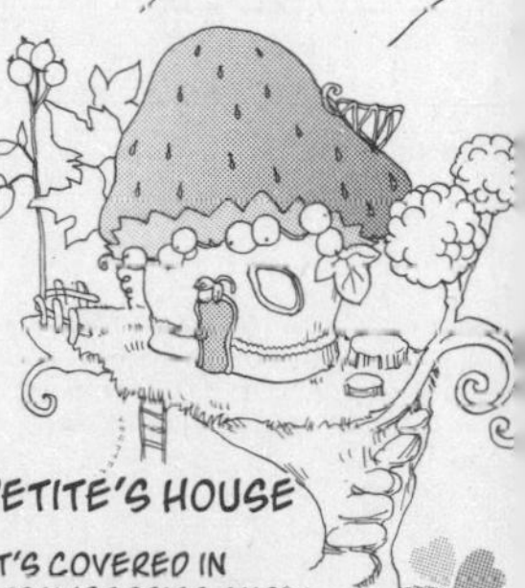

PETITE'S HOUSE

IT'S COVERED IN STRAWBERRIES AND OTHER BERRIES.

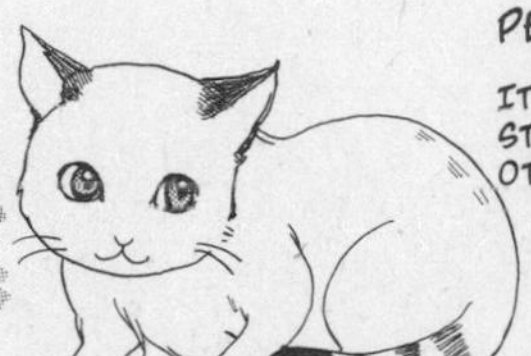

TOMTE

THE NAME OF A TYPE OF FAIRY IN EUROPE. I FEEL KINDA BAD FOR DRAWING HIM TO LOOK SO SCARY.

INTRODUCING THE FAIRY FRIENDS

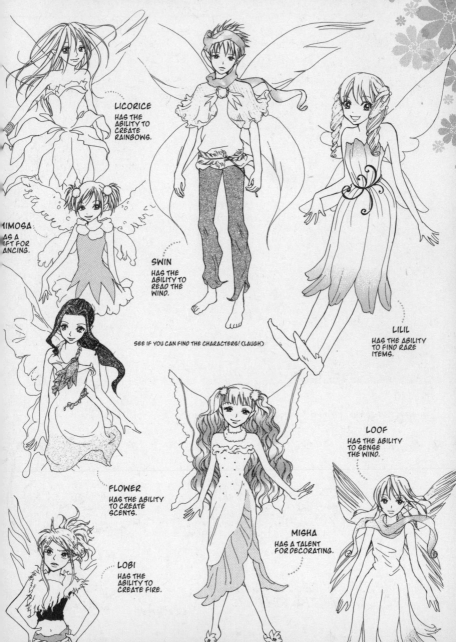

LICORICE
HAS THE ABILITY TO CREATE RAINBOWS.

MIMOSA
AS A GIFT FOR DANCING.

SWIN
HAS THE ABILITY TO READ THE WIND.

SEE IF YOU CAN FIND THE CHARACTERS! (LAUGH)

LILIL
HAS THE ABILITY TO FIND RARE ITEMS.

LOOF
HAS THE ABILITY TO SENSE THE WIND.

FLOWER
HAS THE ABILITY TO CREATE SCENTS.

MISHA
HAS A TALENT FOR DECORATING.

LOBI
HAS THE ABILITY TO CREATE FIRE.

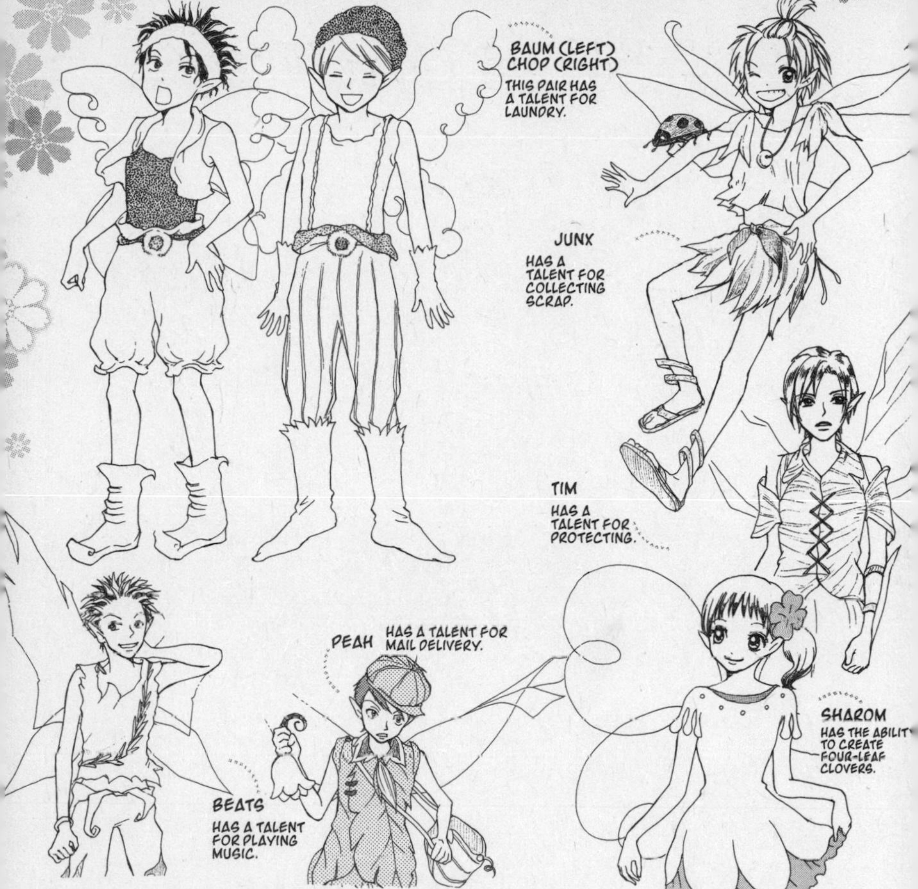
BAUM (LEFT)
CHOP (RIGHT)
THIS PAIR HAS A TALENT FOR LAUNDRY.
JUNX
HAS A TALENT FOR COLLECTING SCRAP.
TIM
HAS A TALENT FOR PROTECTING.
SHAROM
HAS THE ABILIT TO CREATE FOUR-LEAF CLOVERS.
PEAH
HAS A TALENT FOR MAIL DELIVERY.
BEATS
HAS A TALENT FOR PLAYING MUSIC.

I THOUGHT OF AROUND 30 (?) OTHER FAIRIES, ALL WITH DIFFERENT ABILITIES LIKE WEATHER FORECASTING AND WAITING ON TABLES. THEY ALL HAVE STRANGE NAMES...

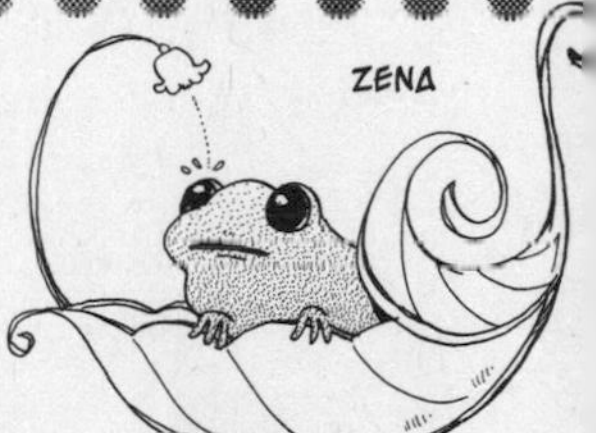
ZENA

SPECIAL THANKS

THANKS TO SHIHO AND YUKI FOR YOUR HELP!

I WAS GREATLY ASSISTED BY MARUYAMA, BY MY EDITOR AT NAKAYOSHI, MY FAMILY, MY FRIENDS, MY CONTACTS AT DISNEY, AND ALL THOSE WORKING AT DISNEY.

AND, OF COURSE, A BIG THANK YOU TO YOU, THE READER!

I'LL DO MY BEST!

JUN ASUKA

Check out the next Disney Fairies Manga!

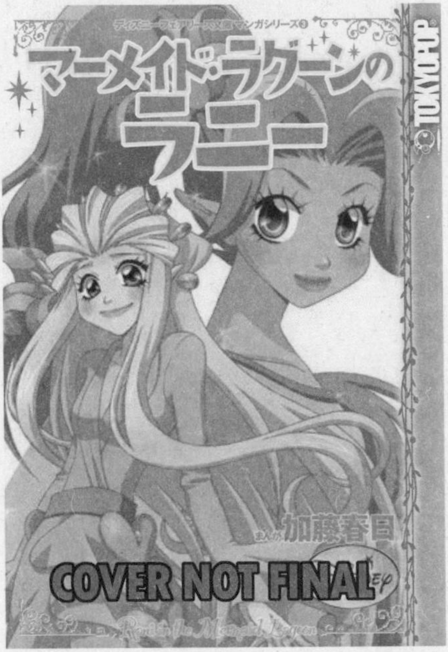
マーメイド・ラグーンのラニー
TOKYOPOP
加藤春日
COVER NOT FINAL

Rani and the Mermaid Lagoon

Rani cut off her wings to save Pixie Hollow and her fairy friends, but a fairy who can't fly is unheard of. After a disastrous accident at the Fairy Dance, she runs away to try and find her own place to belong. Maybe the mermaid lagoon could be her new home. Join Rani and the rest of the Disney fairies — and mermaids! — on this magical adventure.

Discover what awaits Rani when she travels beneath the mermaid lagoon!

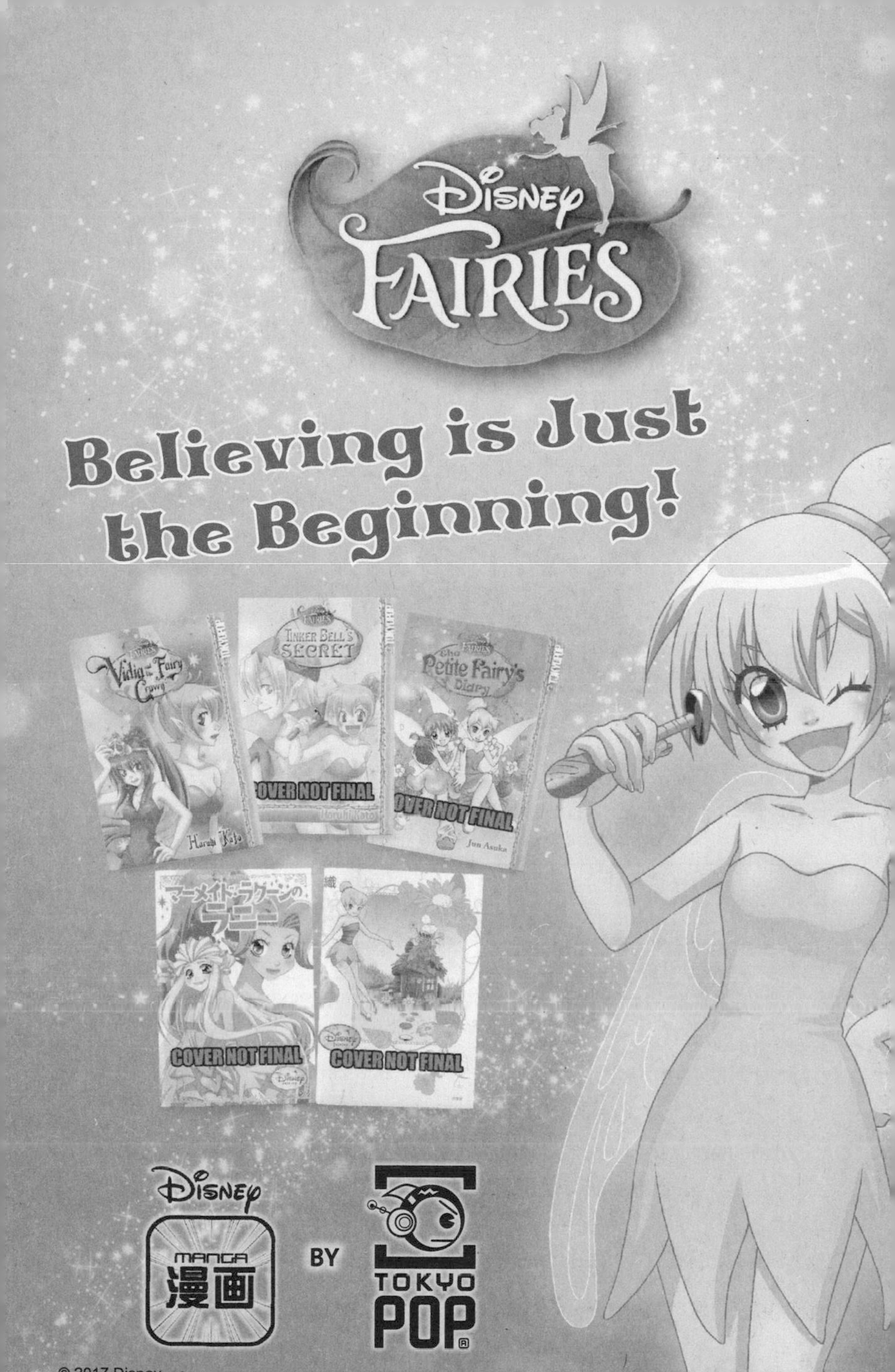
Disney Fairies
Believing is Just the Beginning!
Vidia and the Fairy Crown
Haruhi Kato
Tinker Bell's Secret
COVER NOT FINAL
Haruhi Kato
The Petite Fairy's Diary
COVER NOT FINAL
Jun Asuka
マーメイド・ラグーンのラニー
COVER NOT FINAL
COVER NOT FINAL
Disney
MANGA
漫画
BY
TOKYOPOP

DESCENDANTS

Full color manga trilogy based on the hit Disney Channel original movie

Inspired by the original stories of Disney's classic heroes and villains

Experience this spectacular movie in manga form!

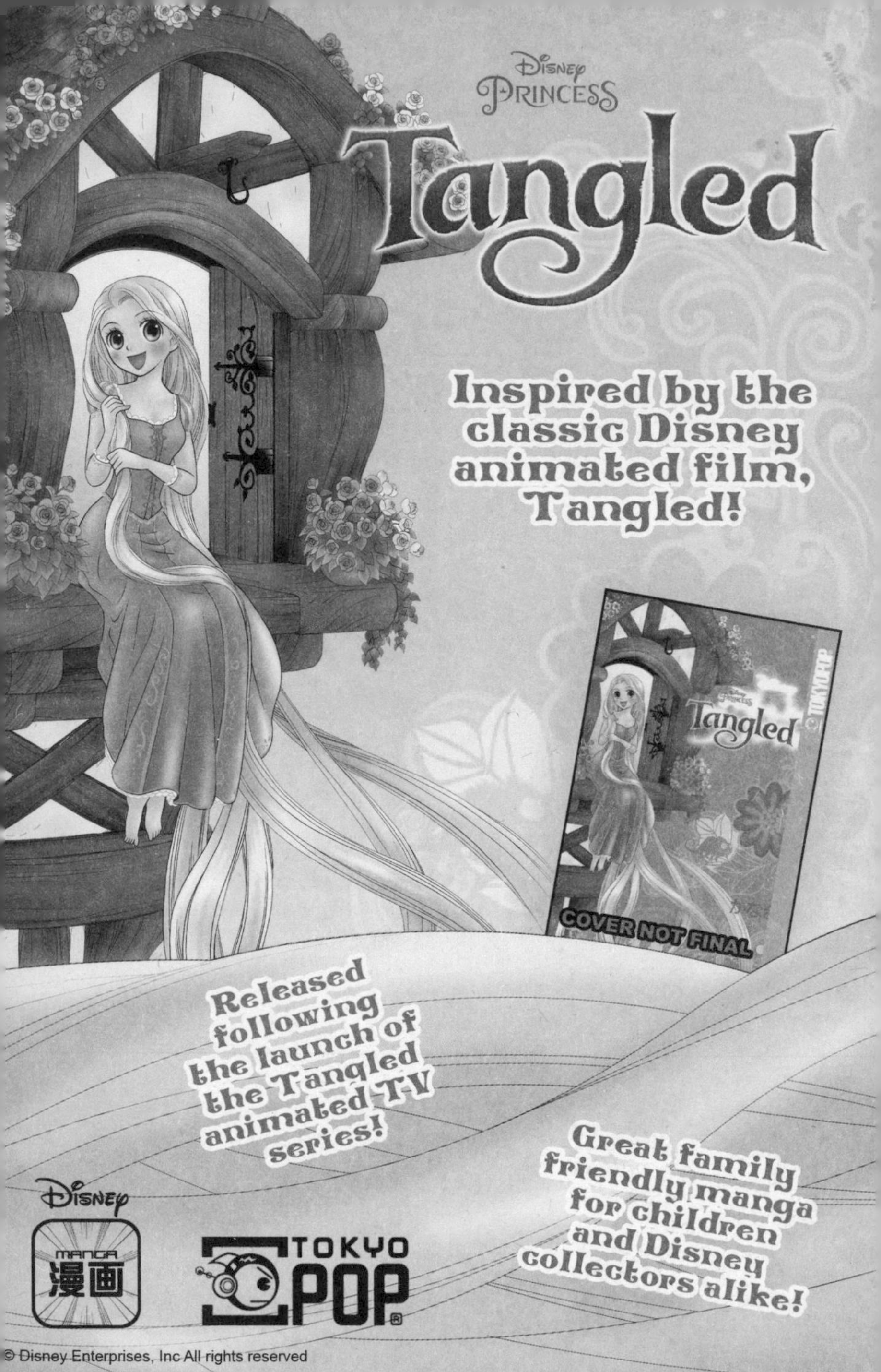
Disney PRINCESS
Tangled
Inspired by the classic Disney animated film, Tangled!
COVER NOT FINAL
Released following the launch of the Tangled the animated TV series!
Great family friendly manga for children and Disney collectors alike!
Disney
MANGA 漫画
TOKYOPOP

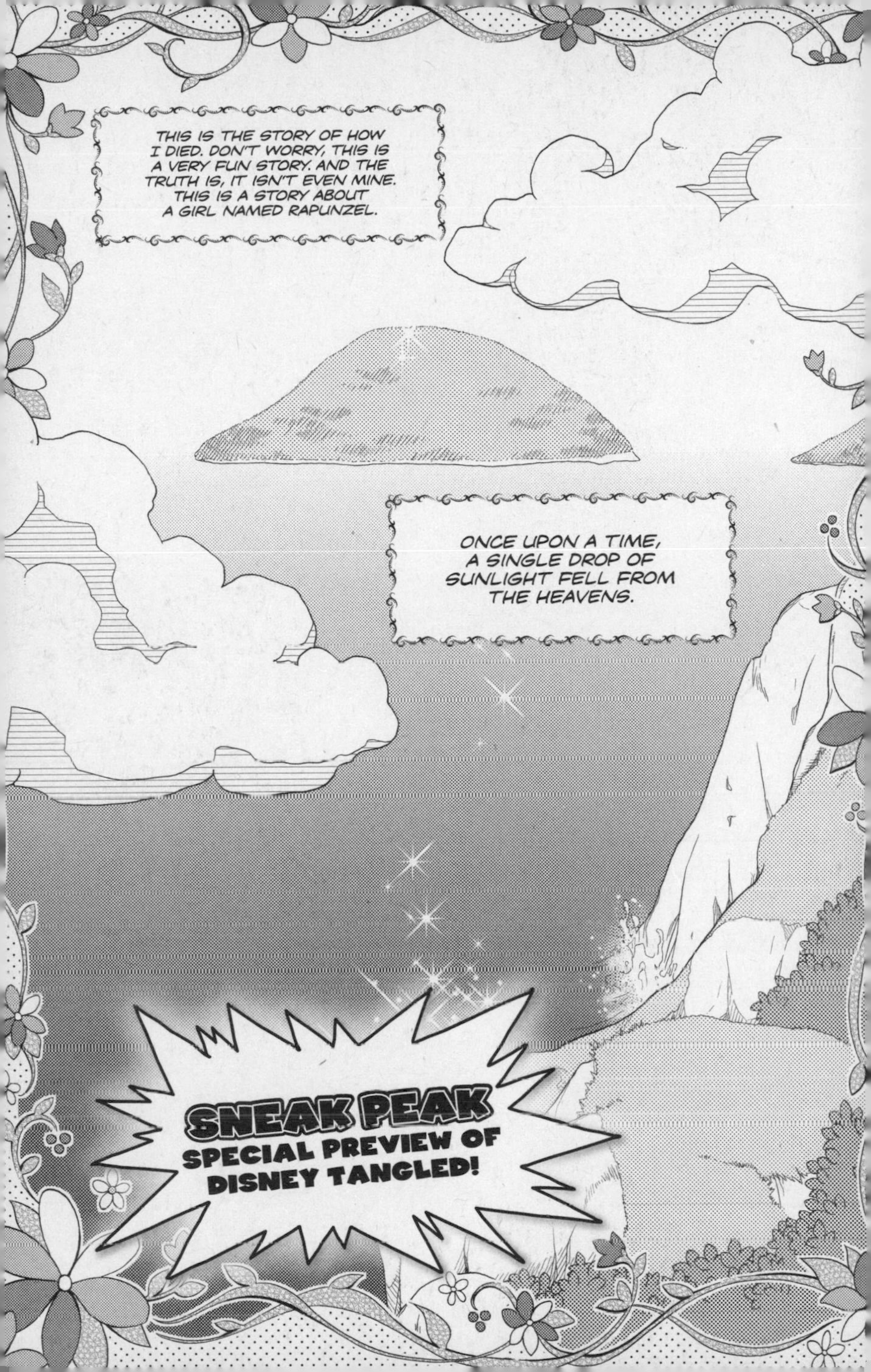
THIS IS THE STORY OF HOW I DIED. DON'T WORRY, THIS IS A VERY FUN STORY. AND THE TRUTH IS, IT ISN'T EVEN MINE. THIS IS A STORY ABOUT A GIRL NAMED RAPUNZEL.
ONCE UPON A TIME, A SINGLE DROP OF SUNLIGHT FELL FROM THE HEAVENS.
SNEAK PEAK
SPECIAL PREVIEW OF DISNEY TANGLED!

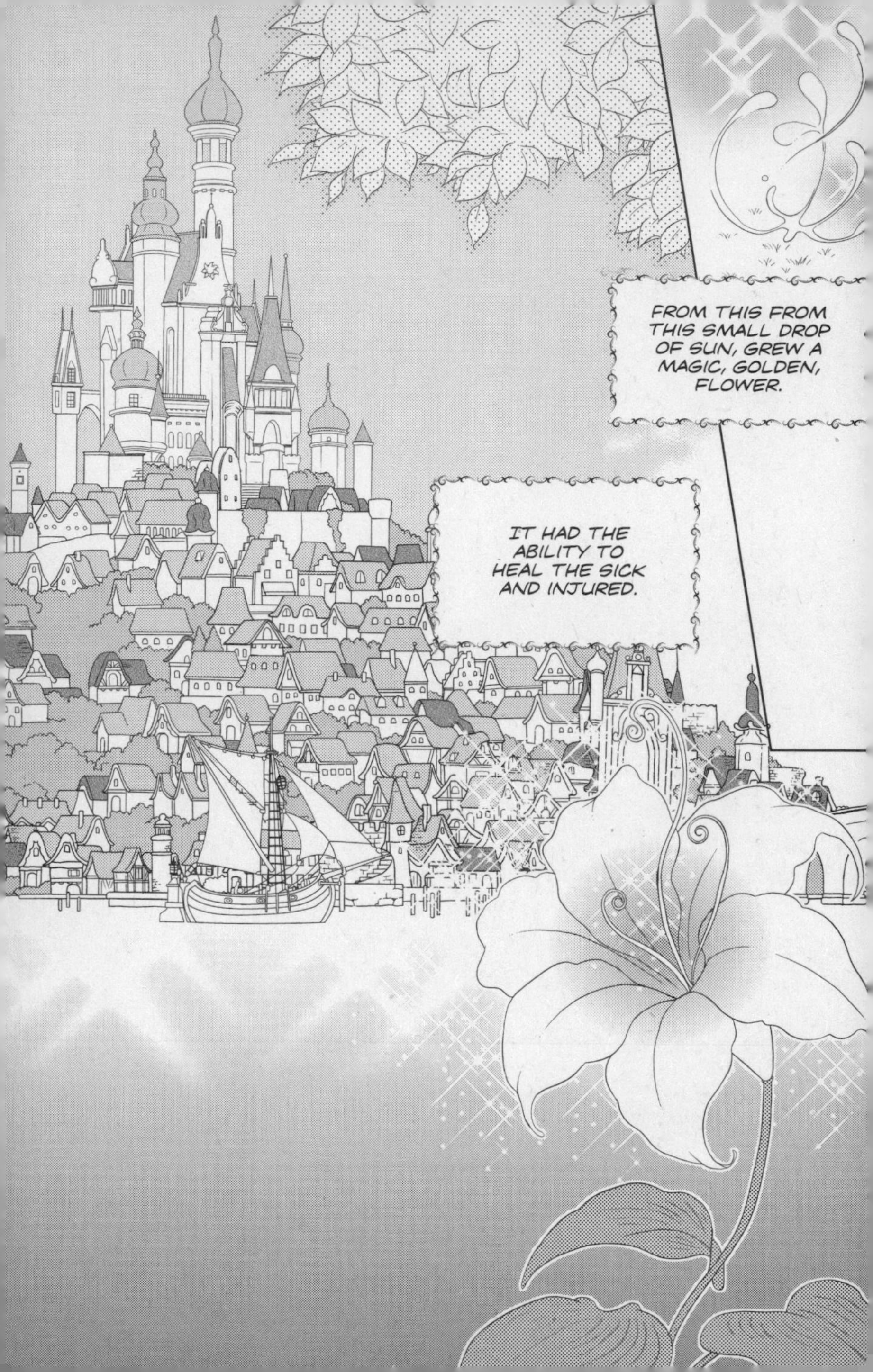
FROM THIS FROM THIS SMALL DROP OF SUN, GREW A MAGIC, GOLDEN, FLOWER.
IT HAD THE ABILITY TO HEAL THE SICK AND INJURED.

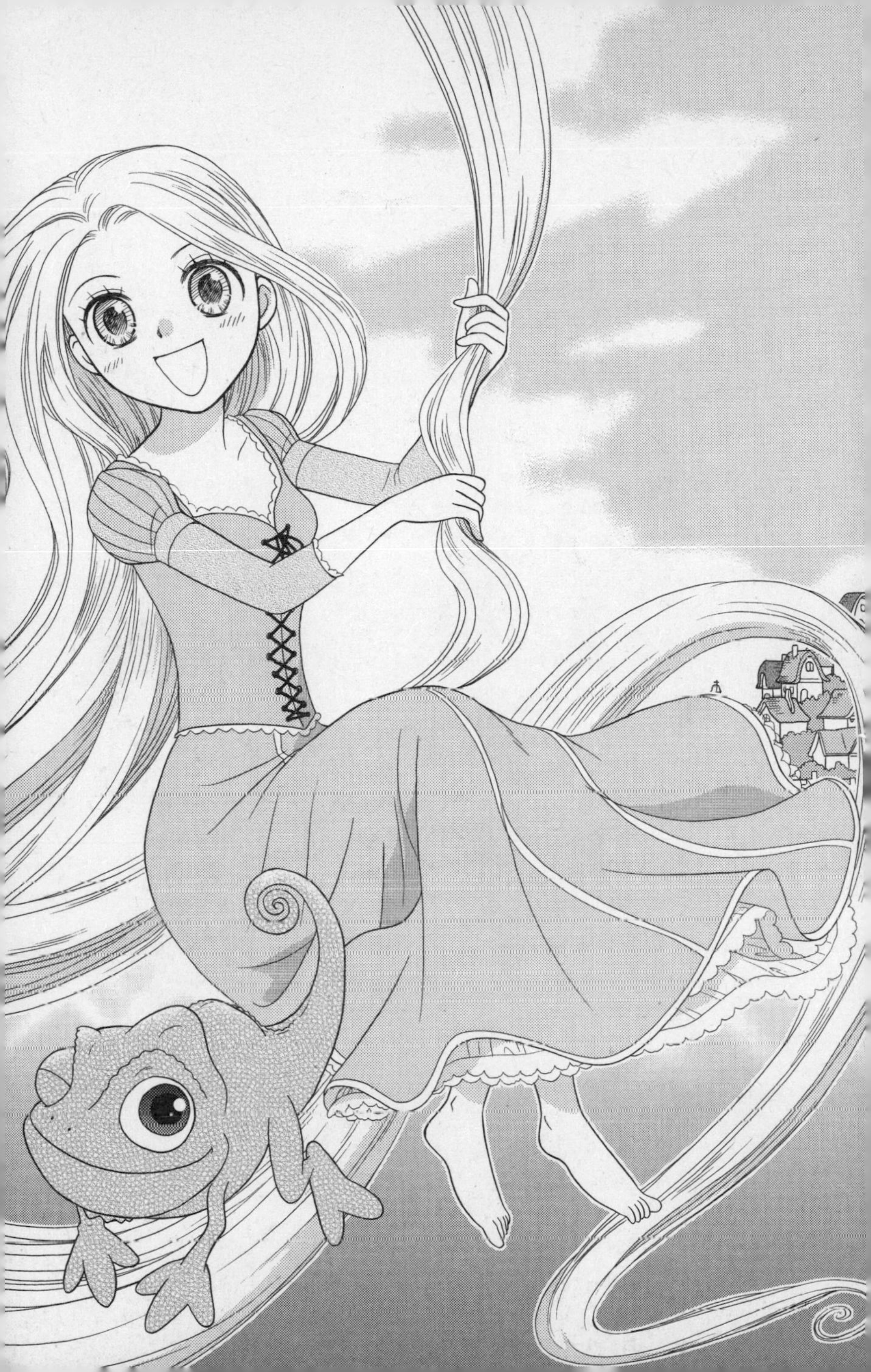

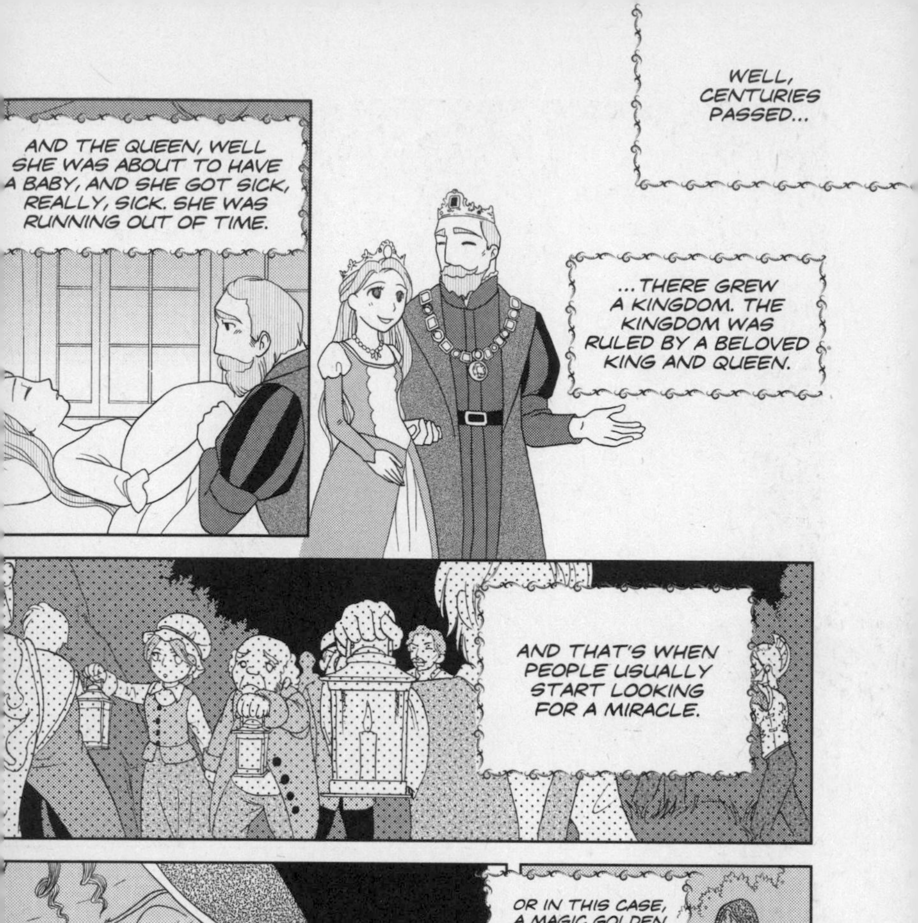
WELL, CENTURIES PASSED...
...THERE GREW A KINGDOM. THE KINGDOM WAS RULED BY A BELOVED KING AND QUEEN.
AND THE QUEEN, WELL SHE WAS ABOUT TO HAVE A BABY, AND SHE GOT SICK, REALLY, SICK. SHE WAS RUNNING OUT OF TIME.
AND THAT'S WHEN PEOPLE USUALLY START LOOKING FOR A MIRACLE.
OR IN THIS CASE, A MAGIC GOLDEN FLOWER.
INSTEAD OF SHARING THE SUN'S GIFT, THIS WOMAN, MOTHER GOTHEL...

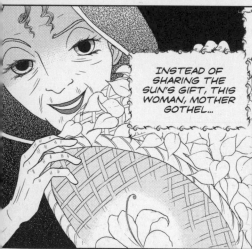

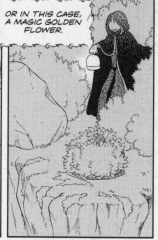

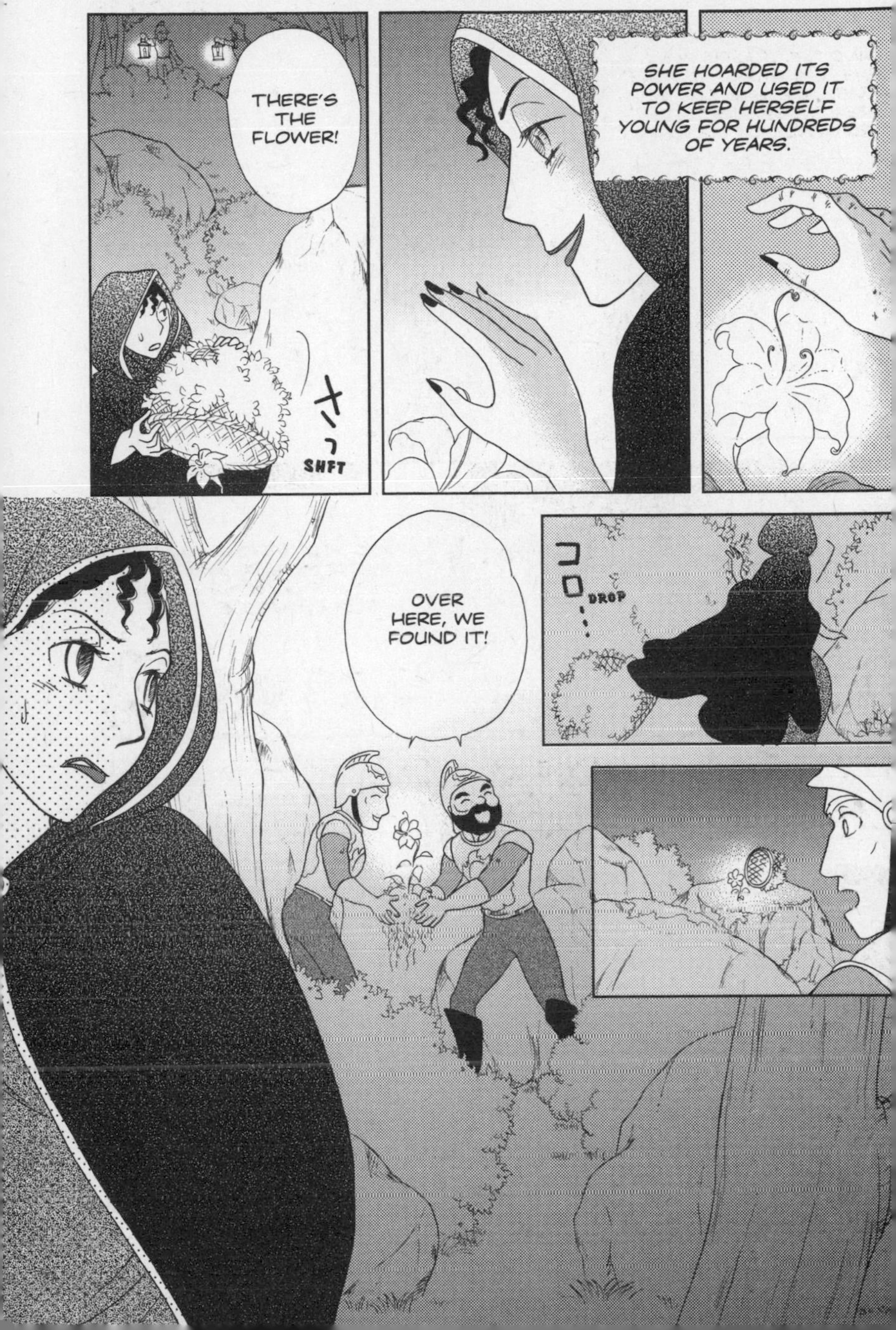
SHE HOARDED ITS POWER AND USED IT TO KEEP HERSELF YOUNG FOR HUNDREDS OF YEARS.
THERE'S THE FLOWER!
さっ
SHFT
コロ…
DROP
OVER HERE, WE FOUND IT!

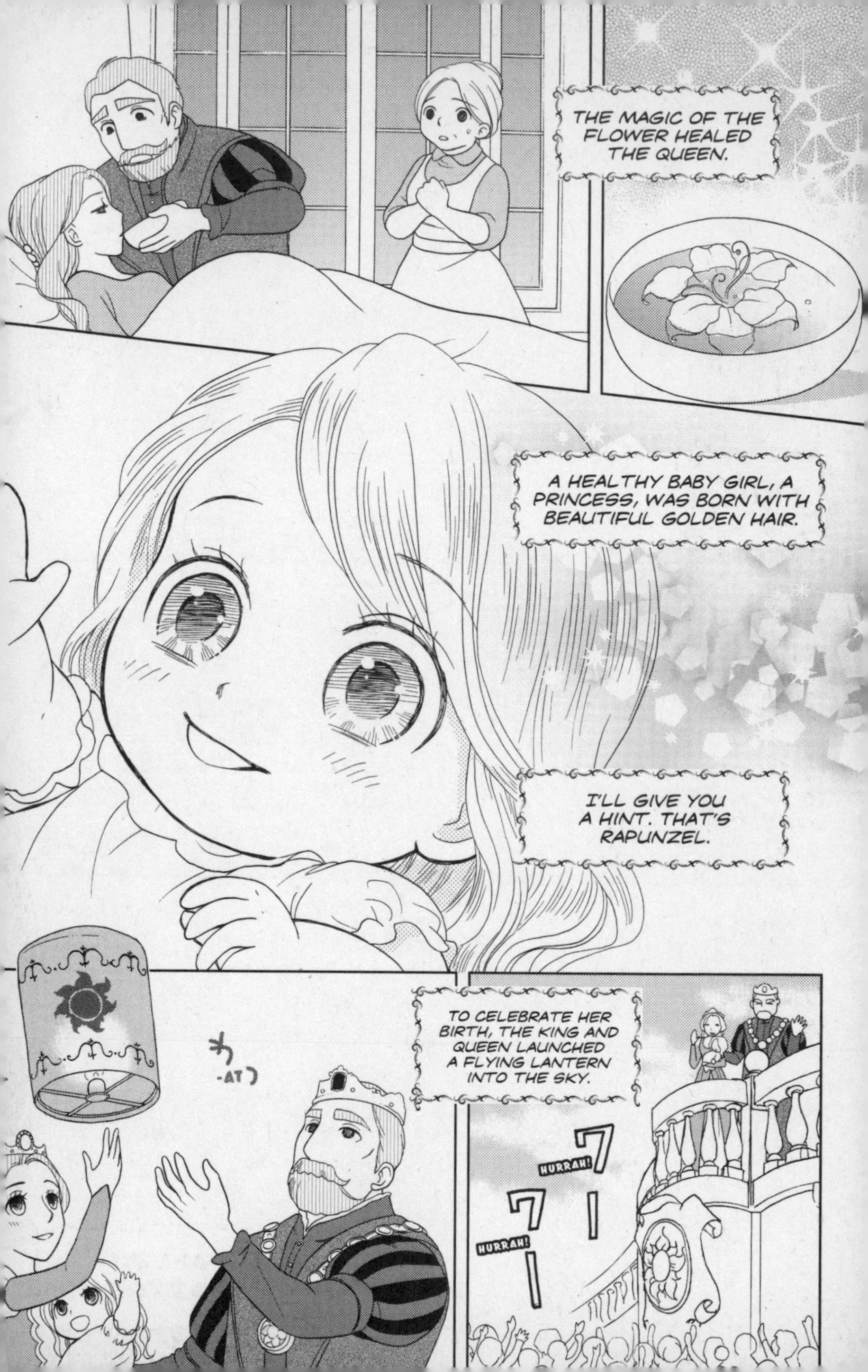
THE MAGIC OF THE FLOWER HEALED THE QUEEN.
A HEALTHY BABY GIRL, A PRINCESS, WAS BORN WITH BEAUTIFUL GOLDEN HAIR.
I'LL GIVE YOU A HINT. THAT'S RAPUNZEL.
TO CELEBRATE HER BIRTH, THE KING AND QUEEN LAUNCHED A FLYING LANTERN INTO THE SKY.
HURRAH!
HURRAH!

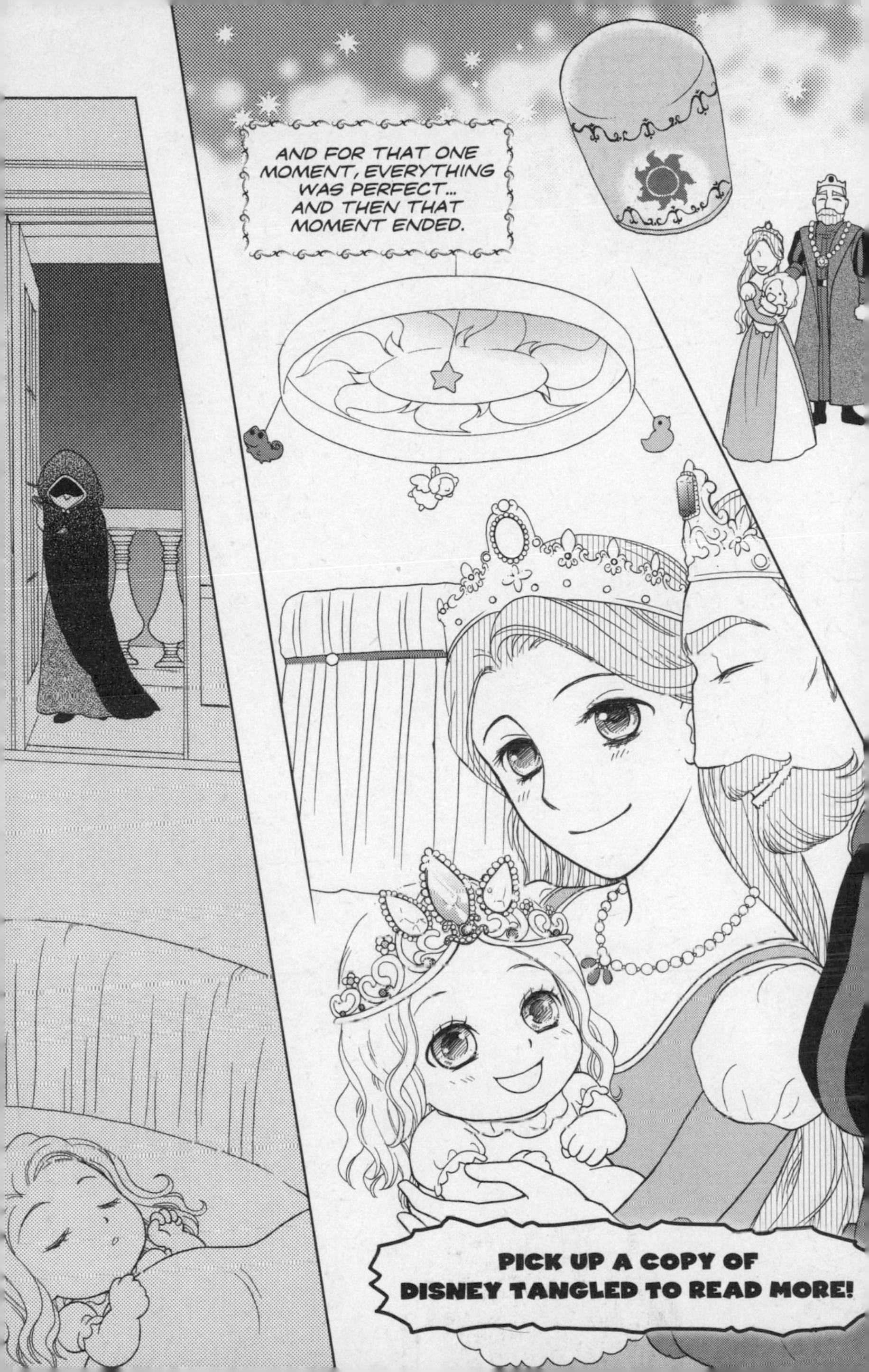

AND FOR THAT ONE MOMENT, EVERYTHING WAS PERFECT... AND THEN THAT MOMENT ENDED.
PICK UP A COPY OF DISNEY TANGLED TO READ MORE!

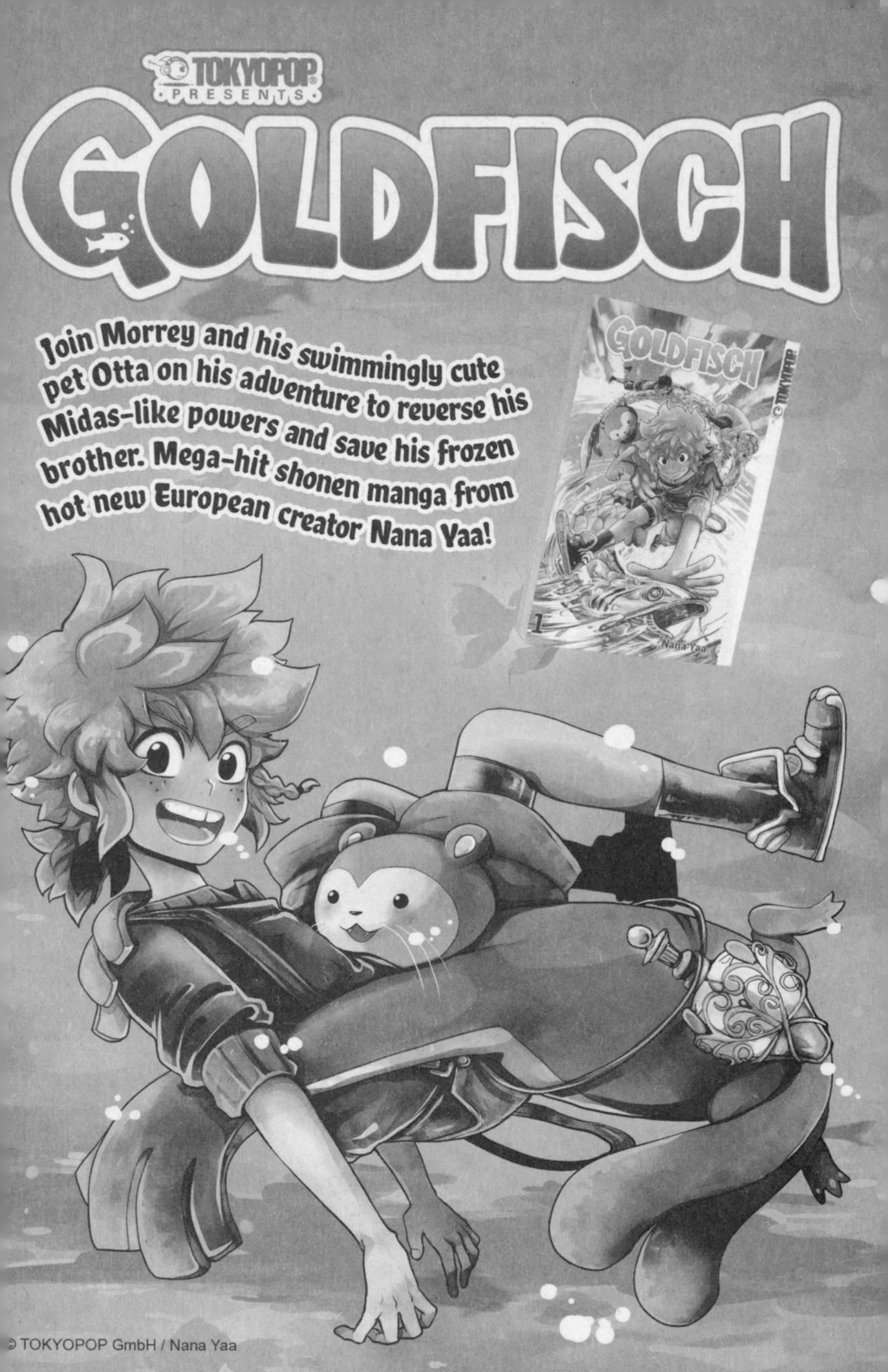
TOKYOPOP PRESENTS
GOLDFISCH
Join Morrey and his swimmingly cute pet Otta on his adventure to reverse his Midas-like powers and save his frozen brother. Mega-hit shonen manga from hot new European creator Nana Yaa!
GOLDFISCH
TOKYOPOP
1
Nana Yaa

GRIMMS manga Tales

The Grimm's Tales reimagined in manga!

Beautiful art by the talented Kei Ishiyama!

Stories from Little Red Riding Hood to Hansel and Gretel!

TOKYOPOP
Ocean of Secrets
OCEAN OF SECRETS

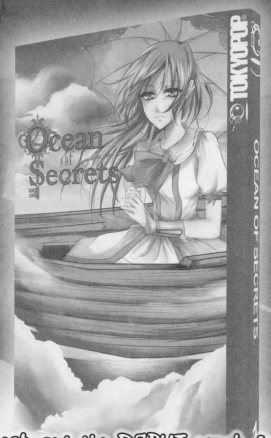

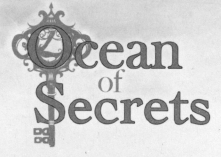

Disney Fairies: The Petite Fairy's Diary
Author/Artist: Jun Asuka

Publishing Assistant	- Janae Young
Marketing Assistant	- Kae Winters
Technology and Digital Media Assistant	- Phillip Hong
Retouching and Lettering	- Vibrraant Publishing Studio
Translations	- Jason Muell
Graphic Designer	- Phillip Hong
Copy Editor	- M. Cara Carper
Editor-in-Chief & Publisher	- Stu Levy

A  Manga

TOKYOPOP inc.
5200 W Century Blvd
Suite 705
Los Angeles, CA 90045 USA

E-mail: info@TOKYOPOP.com
Come visit us online at www.TOKYOPOP.com

f www.facebook.com/TOKYOPOP
y www.twitter.com/TOKYOPOP
▶ www.youtube.com/TOKYOPOPTV
p www.pinterest.com/TOKYOPOP
🄾 www.instagram.com/TOKYOPOP
t. TOKYOPOP.tumblr.com

ISBN: 978-1-4278-5702-6
First TOKYOPOP Printing: October 2017
10 9 8 7 6 5 4 3 2 1
Printed in CANADA

STOP

THIS IS THE BACK OF THE BOOK!

How do you read manga-style? It's simple! To learn, just start in the top right panel and follow the numbers: